Dead Reckoning

Dead Reckoning

Gordan A. Kessler
8/18/03

Gordon A. Kessler

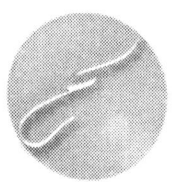

Copyright (c) 2001 by Evergreen Books Ink

Library of Congress Number:		2001118331
ISBN #:	Hardcover	1-4010-2650-8
	Softcover	1-4010-2649-4

All rights reserved. No part of this book may be reproduced or transmitted in any form or by any means, electronic or mechanical, including photocopying, recording, or by any information storage and retrieval system, without permission in writing from the copyright owner.

This is a work of fiction. Names, characters, places and incidents either are the product of the author's imagination or are used fictitiously, and any resemblance to any actual persons, living or dead, events, or locales is entirely coincidental.

This book was printed in the United States of America.

To order additional copies of this book, contact:
Xlibris Corporation
1-888-7-XLIBRIS
www.Xlibris.com
Orders@Xlibris.com
12228

Dedicated to the thousands of American citizens who have lost their lives to terrorism.

Many thanks and much love to Karen, Colleen, Hazel, Orville, Roxy, Suzann, Bonnie, Richard, Brad, Robin and Bob.

Special thanks to the Naval Criminal Investigative Service for their willing help and to Leonard Bishop writer and teacher extraordinaire for "daring me to be a great writer."

Also a special dedication to my grandson Parker and granddaughter Priya.

dead reckoning: an inexact calculation of position considering direction and speed and using allowances for wind, current and compass error. Navigation of a ship underway in a very unstable environment (water) using basic instruments and without the use of electronics, lines of position, or reference to visible objects whose positions are known. dead: those deprived of life. reckoning: a settlement for debts owed.

Prologue

MURDER ON DECK

April 27, 0200
USS Atchison, Mediterranean Sea

SENIOR CHIEF PETTY Officer Gustauve Franken was trying to enjoy a *Cohiba Robusto* cigar when Ensign Nader fell to his death from the signal bridge.

Moments before, Chief Franken had been taking in the rare night's solitude with a satisfied curl on his lips. He enjoyed good Scotch—preferably Chivas—full-figured women, light seas during clear moonless nights and, of course, the hard to come by Cuban cigars. Over the years, he'd experienced his share of all of these things, and tonight, with the help of God and a Russian sailor in the last port, at least he was able to enjoy two of them.

Darken ship was the order on the *USS Atchison*. With only starlight to outline the features of the small frigate and the churning water's white phosphorescence off the fantail, the world was simple and black and gray. Celestial reflections winking from the ebony water on both sides of the ship gave the sea the illusion of subdued life. But the chief knew first hand from countless onslaughts the anger the unconquerable Mother Ocean could unleash. He'd seen the sleeping water that was life to so many awaken from a nurturing calmness into massive swells—and take life as she had given it; without warning, reason or conscience. Tonight, under the glitter of a million stars, she slept peacefully leaving man to do his own killing.

This was the best place to absorb the serene night, twenty feet above and behind the signal bridge, with nothing to block the view of the entire superstructure of the small ship. It was also the best place to sneak a smoke. During a *darken ship* exercise, smoking wasn't allowed topside, but since the skipper had banned all smoking below, the chief had no choice. After all, it was just an exercise. This night had been too beautiful to savor without a flavorful smoke to help bring out its full-bodied effect.

A metallic screech interrupted the calm. Chief Franken turned forward and frowned down at the signal deck. The hatch to the Combat Information Center swung open and seemed to hurl out an intruder into the charmed night.

It was that new *ring*, the Annapolis man. The chief recognized the young, black ensign in the explosion of light from the hatchway, but he could see little else from his now nearly disabled eyes even after the complaining hatch closed. He wondered why the hatch curtain hadn't captured the light as it should have. In times of *darken ship* the curtain was supposed to prevent inside light from being seen by other ships or planes when a hatch was opened. He decided that it must have either caught on something or someone had held it.

Ensign Charles Nader secured the steel door and then stood shirtless, jerking his head around warily.

Hidden in the shadowy grid work of the mast, the

chief squinted at the dark figure, forcing his eyes to adjust. The young ensign seemed to be looking for someone—or was being looked for.

Franken ducked and considered smashing out the prized cigar's fire against the back of a steel support. Instead, he turned away from the disturbance and faced aft. He placed one foot on the first crossbar of the radar mast and crossed his arms over his bony knee. The hull of the small ship was barely longer than a football field, making it pitch even in the lightest seas, but tonight the old salt hardly noticed its mild rocking. He paid no attention to the continuous vibration of the steel deck from the *Atchison's* two steam-turbine engines spinning her twin screws. He ignored their rhythmic pulsing—and the young ensign below—hearing only the sibilant water rushing from stem to stern along the vessel's flanks.

Glancing up with hooded, gray eyes at the great star-speckled void above, Franken quickly picked out his old companions, Orion and Taurus, fighting their eternal battle in the heavens. He gave a big smile and drew hard on the fat cigar then looked down at the seven hash marks covering his left sleeve and considered his long, eventful career. Those marks symbolized more than twenty-eight years of faithful service to the US Navy. He gazed back out to sea thinking that even though he'd spent ten thousand nights on the water, he could recall few when he'd felt this kind of peace. Extraordinary nights like these made life worthwhile.

He released the smoke slowly from below his trim mustache as the ship began a turn to starboard as part of an evasive maneuver. It would make several course changes over the next few minutes in a mock attempt to avoid a nonexistent enemy submarine. The Navy loved its drills. It was what it did best.

The chief adjusted his stance to compensate for the

slightly rougher seas caused by the ship's slow turn. He had another pull from his cigar, feeling little guilt at taking advantage of his Rusky counterpart back in the last port-of-call. A man could buy or barter for about *anything* in Marseilles, France. A pack of American Camel cigarettes in trade for half a dozen of Cuba's finest cigars seemed too much of a bargain to pass up. He blew the smoke out in a small stream and watched as the gray plume floated aft, to the starboard side. The fifteen knots of ship's speed and the five knot *leste* wind, bringing warm, dry air from the north of Africa, carried it away in a protracted curve.

A soft thumping came from below like rapid footsteps on the signal-deck ladder. Franken grimaced at the disturbance. Ensign Nader, the ship's new weapon's officer, was spoiling his evening. But perhaps Nader was leaving. More likely, there was another intruder coming up to join the young man.

The chief placed his cigar on the joint between one of the radar-mast crossbars and a vertical support where he thought it would be secure and not show its glow. He would wait until Nader left before continuing his peaceful diversion. If the young officer caught him smoking during *darken ship* with the *smoking lamp* out, there'd be a hassle, but not a big one, since Franken was the senior enlisted man. He could talk his way out of most any reprimand. But still, there'd be a hassle, and on this fine night the chief wished to avoid it.

With the obtrusive light from the hatchway hidden behind the steel door for a couple of minutes now, the chief's eyes had again become acclimated to the night's dark depth. When he looked below, he was shocked at what he could *now* see. The Ensign clutched what appeared to be a Beretta pistol in his right hand. *What the hell is that boy doing with a gun? Gawd, this is nuts!*

Nader took a step back. He patted his pants pockets with his left hand, then turned the semiautomatic pistol upside down and raised it, grip first, to his face. He appeared to be inspecting its magazine port. After a pause, he flipped it over, then clutched its slide and pulled it back to reveal the chamber.

"Shit!" he said and let the slide snap into place. He stepped cautiously to the signal light pedestal used for Morse code communications during radio silence.

Again, hasty footfalls clanked from one of the ladders on the side of the deck.

Chief Franken's pulse accelerated as he hunkered lower.

Young Nader raised the pistol. He backed away. A shadowy figure emerged, his back angled to Franken.

Then a second dark shape appeared—a much larger man—his back also angled to the chief. Nader stepped back to the waist-high safety bulwarks that bordered the signal bridge, forty feet above the main deck.

The young man was cut off. He wouldn't have time to open the secured hatch back into the CIC before being intercepted by the two aggressive shadows. The only other way to leave the signal bridge was from one of the two ladders that were now blocked by the new intruders.

"Don't come any closer," Nader said to the smaller shadow edging up from the left.

The unrecognizable shape heeded.

The chief's eyes widened. He couldn't understand what was happening. It didn't make sense. *This is a US Navy warship, for Christ's sake!*

A low voice came from one of the shadows, both now moving closer from each end of the small deck. The chief couldn't tell from which the voice came and he had to strain to hear, "Don't do anything stupid, kid."

Both pursuers leaned anxiously, predator-like, getting closer.

"I mean it!" Nader blurted.

"Keep your voice down!" the bigger shape said still speaking just above a whisper but a notch louder than before. He advanced another step but the smaller one held his ground.

Enough of this foolishness. Franken picked up the cigar and cupped his hand over the smoldering end. He rose, thinking that he'd call out and put a stop to this nonsense, but then paused, and considered what was being said.

"Get a hold of yourself," the smaller guy said. "We're not going to hurt you. Relax. All you've got to do is hang on for another two weeks and this'll all be over. Come on. We both wear the *ring*. We're brothers. Let's go to my stateroom where we can talk."

The chief was stunned as he realized that this might have something to do with the strange goings-on on the ship lately. Now, he thought better of disturbing them. Something was happening on the *Atchison*—an accidental death and two AWOLs all in the last week. He might get to the bottom of it if he didn't interrupt them and listened carefully. If only the moon were out so he could get a better look at them—see their faces. One thing he knew regardless of the lack of light was that if the smaller guy had a stateroom and wore the Annapolis *ring*, he was an officer.

"No way, you treasonous son of-a-bitch," Nader said. "That ring must not mean a thing to you."

"Okay, you want out? You're out."

"I was never in."

"Have it your way, but give us the gun," the larger man said and drew nearer, now within eight feet.

Chief Franken strained to hear anything familiar in the voices, but the whispering disguised them. It still didn't jell. He wondered if it could be some kind of racial confrontation. So far, it didn't seem so.

"I'm going to report you, by God," Nader said. "They'll put you away."

"Our word against yours, kid," said the smaller one. He seemed to be calmer than the other man, a cooler head. "What can you prove? Who do you think they're going to believe? You point the finger at us and you can be damn sure we'll take you along for the ride."

Ensign Nader raised the gun to his own temple.

"I'll kill myself—I will. Then they'll get you."

Franken was sure the young ensign was bluffing. From the way Nader acted when he cocked the weapon earlier, he doubted if the gun was even loaded.

The big man said, "That won't do shit, you dumb snitch. They'll just call it a suicide."

The smoother talking, calmer one chimed in, "Drug related. High on coke."

Franken raised his eyebrows and began rolling the cigar between his fingers. *Drugs! A dope deal gone bad, maybe.*

"Bullshit!" Nader said. "I've never touched that crap. They'll get you. They'll find out before you have a chance to go through with it. You lied to me. There's more to it than just the drugs—a lot more. They'll find out."

"They'll find out that you were just another mixed up junkie, kid," the calmer one said. "Won't that be a shame for your folks—for your girlfriend back home. They'll think their sweet little Annapolis boy was a dope head—and a traitor."

Nader spat his words, "Bastards, murdering bastards!"

Laughter broke out from the main deck far below as two sailors came outside for fresh air. One was jokingly accusing the other of cheating at spades.

Franken watched as the three on the signal bridge froze in place. After a few seconds, the young ensign moved first. He brought the gun down from his temple and hefted one leg over the short safety wall.

"I'll jump," he said, then nodded toward the new voices below. "They'll get to me first. You won't have time to do anything. They'll find the gun and think I was pushed. There'll be an investigation, and they'll have your asses!"

Franken gaped at the young man. He wondered what could cause a bright young *gung ho* officer like Nader to threaten suicide. What could be so important? *This is insane.* Maybe he *should* say something now. If he'd just ask what's going on, maybe they'd leave Nader alone and this could be sorted out.

But a gut feeling told Franken that it wouldn't be that easy. He didn't know who the other two men were, and they also could have guns—loaded ones. If he stopped them now, maybe they'd come after *him*. After all, Nader did call them *murdering bastards*. Maybe they'd wait until he least expected and then slip a shiv between his ribs while he slept.

This drug stuff bothered Franken. This suicide stuff knotted his stomach. This treason stuff scared him shitless. And this whole confusing mess caused his skin to break out in cold sweat. *Surely, these bastards will give the boy some room.*

"Just give me the damn gun, Nader!" The larger man approached to within arm's reach.

The calmer man got excited. "Don't crowd him!"

"Screw you. Rot in Hell!" the young ensign said as he brought his other leg over the elbow-high wall, forty feet of air between him and the hard steel, main deck below.

The big figure bolted. He grabbed for the gun. They wrestled briefly.

Nader yanked the pistol away. His momentum brought his body too far over the side. Nader's left hand groped, searching empty air for a hold as he began to slip.

The larger enemy slapped at Nader's arm, trying to grab it. He snagged Nader's wrist.

Nader worked his open hand and stared at the man gripping his forearm.

The big man held for a moment—then let go.

Nader expelled the air from his lungs in a sort of shocked whimper. He fell.

The other guy stepped up quickly, arms reaching. Too late.

The world seemed to pause, silenced by the implications of what had just happened.

A sound like a sack of potatoes striking the deck made Franken cringe and his cigar rolled from his fingers. Then excited voices came from the two noisy sailors below on the main deck.

"What the hell?"

"Good God, it's Mister Nader!"

On the signal deck, the calmer man pulled the big guy back from the side.

"You big asshole!" he said. "Why'd you let him go? We could have taken care of him and thrown him overboard like the others."

"Dumb shit was going to do it anyway. He was just playing us. He wasn't in the deal—he was a fuckin' snitch."

"Forget it. I figured that cokehead Ingrassias would come in handy someday. Get your ass down to his berth and back up to Nader before Doc gets to the body. I'll get those two away from him."

Both men turned to leave. But the larger man paused and seemed to be looking directly at the chief. Franken couldn't make out his face or his features, not even his rank, but he could recall only two men near this guy's size on the ship. Both came on board at the last port. One a Marine Captain and one a cook. But the ship had taken on so many new crewmembers and officers in the last month, there could be others he hadn't seen yet.

The big man surely couldn't see Franken. It was too dark. Franken was mostly hidden by the mast. But the guy lifted his face and sniffed the air. The course changes hadn't been helpful in keeping Franken unnoticed.

He smells the cigar!

The evasive maneuvers the ship had been going through had brought the cigar smoke to the big man's nose.

Franken turned and ran aft to the edge of the small, steel platform he'd been tending, not attempting to be the least bit stealthy. Whatever kind of game these two were playing was a deadly one and he wanted no part of it. If it was drugs, it wasn't small change. It must be a major operation. For now, he'd save his own skin and avoid any confrontation. But he had to get away without being recognized. He could report what happened to the captain or the executive officer later.

The chief jumped down eight feet to a catwalk leading to the fantail, ducked into a hatch and hurled himself down four flights of steps to the noncommissioned officers' berthing area. Within thirty seconds, he was inside his quarters with the hatch dogged.

Leaning against the steel door, chest heaving, Senior Chief Petty Officer Gustauve Franken suddenly caught his breath and wondered. It'd been too dark for them to recognize him. But then realization gave him a stinging slap to the face. He rolled his eyes and let out a ragged sigh. He'd left something they could identify him by. They'd be coming for him next.

He'd boasted to half the crew about scoring the hard

to come by *Cohiba Robustos*. He was so proud of them that he'd leave the cigar bands on while he smoked them for the sole purpose of gloating to himself. And sometime during the excitement—he'd lost the cigar.

Chapter 1

NAUGHTY AND NICE

April 30, 0655
Naval Criminal Investigative Service
US Navy Shipyards, Washington DC

IT WAS THE last thing on her short list, but time was running out. Special Agent Janelle "Spurs" Sperling bit her lip as she went back over the six items.

1. Pack uniforms—she put a check beside it, hoping a full year and five pounds wouldn't make a noticeable difference in their fit.

2. Water the plants—check. She'd managed that on the way out the door of her apartment at 0500 this morning. Mrs. Walton, her neighbor from down the hall, would take care of them twice a week while she was away.

3. Call *the Admiral*—bad idea. As in the past, she wouldn't know what to say to her father. She lined it out.

4. Get tampons—check. Surely they had such provisions on a modern naval vessel, but to make sure, she'd picked some up at the Gas'n Go on the way to the shipyards.

She took a sip of tepid convenience-store coffee and

glanced around the side of the fabric-covered partition of her workspace. The other fifteen cubicles were eerily silent. In another hour, the large room would fill with a clamor of voices and the beeps, whirs, and zips of printers, fax machines and photocopiers that could drive you nuts.

Numbness came over her. She'd been too busy getting ready before, but now it was finally starting to sink in. Not only was she embarking on her first undercover assignment, but it was a seagoing job to boot. Somehow, her minimal training as a weapons officer while in the Navy Reserve had been a more important factor in her being assigned to the case than her lack of experience as an undercover agent.

She set the Styrofoam cup on her white-veneered desktop and pushed back from it. Her gaze rested on a thirteen-year-old photo pinned to the wall behind her computer monitor. It had been taken at a time that seemed so distant that sometimes she questioned if it actually had ever been. A time when her mother was alive. She smiled at the picture of a twelve-year-old girl holding the reins of a beautiful white stallion. The horse seemed huge in comparison to the small girl. As she gazed at the photo, her mind journeyed back to the red hills of Oklahoma.

* * *

She rode like a Rough Rider up a steep hill, around outhouse-size boulders, and into the darkness. The night called her in, as it had so many times before, its cool caress against her flushed cheeks. She rode into it, deeper and deeper, feeling as if she were gliding through a passageway into another dimension where the effort of thought was unnecessary and the world around her was uncomplicated and made sense. Just a slight thing, even for a twelve-year-old, someone who didn't know better would have thought she wasn't near big enough to even mount the horse she managed bareback. Her strawberry-blonde hair streamed behind her as her tears flowed, and lightning played across the heavens. She coaxed the horse on with her heels and tugged at the two-year-old's mane in rhythm with her bony legs slapping against his flanks.

"Take me away, Rocket," she pleaded, bleary-eyed into the big white stallion's ear. "Take me far away from here."

It was *only* a rabbit she'd killed, not a person. But still, it was a harmless little bunny, and she'd done it showing off to her schoolmates. She swore she'd never show off again. Never in her whole, entire, forever life, would she ever show her vanity again—she'd vowed to God—or he could *strike her as dead as Grandpa Dover's ass*. That was what her mother always said when she made a promise—and Spurs was sure the Lord would hold her to this one.

She'd been showing off her calf-roping abilities to her school chums by lassoing a tree stump, when out popped a little gray bunny. She couldn't pass up the opportunity to demonstrate her roping prowess on a live subject and quickly threw the lariat around it, pinning it to the tree.

But then, when she jerked back on the rope, as she would to tighten it around a calf's throat, it slipped from the stump and yanked the rabbit off its feet by the neck. The faux bovine was suddenly lying lifeless at her feet. The other children laughed, and she laughed too, not because it was funny, but because she was so surprised and confused, then suddenly embarrassed and ashamed.

She always laughed when confronted with uncomfortable situations; it was the way she had dealt with confusion and pain as far back as she could remember. Everyone thought it was a sign of strength—her mother said she was tough. She could recall her mother tucking her into bed one night, leaning over her, her mama's eyes intense and glazed with tears. "You're damn tough, Janelle," she'd said. "Tough as Oklahoma red mud. You can't get it out of your clothes. It sticks to everything so damned tenaciously you can hardly ever get it all scraped from your shoes. Tough like Janelle. I wish I could be that tough, girl." Her mother looked away. Her voice began to tremble. "But I can't. I give in too easy. But you just go ahead and stick to it, Janelle." Her mother turned back to her, this time her eyes flooding over. She took Spurs by the arms and gently shook her, then finished what she had to say in a sobbing, sort of urgent whisper. "Stick to anything you start, any commitment you make and see it out. You keep laughing when they tell you that you can't do it, and you just stick to it like that old Oklahoma red clay. Don't you be like your mama. You start to do something, you see it through. You make a promise, you stick to it." Her mother then ran from the room.

Spurs never really understood what her mother meant—what commitments or promises her mother hadn't kept. She supposed it didn't really matter.

* * *

The annoying buzz of the clock radio alarm Spurs had set for seven a.m. snatched her back to the large empty room and away from the smell of Rocket's lathered body and the chilly breeze on that Oklahoma night. She'd taken this memory trip before, countless times. She never knew why. It was such an insignificant memory of a time that seemed too distant to have been real. But this was the first time she remembered why she had ridden off in tears on that particular night. Of course, it had been the *rabbit*.

She should now be heading for the door to make an 8:30 flight to Madrid, Spain via New York. A slap on the top of the radio silenced its insistent reminder and she went back to her notepad and the last two items on her list.

5. Interview the dead man's parents—check. Her visit with the Naders the night before had provided little information to help the investigation. But she'd carried away a deep sadness for their loss and a determination to find out the truth about Charles Nader's death.

And last;

6. Question Henry Dubain.

She lifted the telephone receiver, pushed her strawberry-blonde hair behind her left ear and dialed the number beside the name. Twice before, there had been no answer. Normally she'd be more considerate than to call someone so early, but in this case, it was the last chance she'd have to talk to the man. Besides, a Navy man—even an *ex*-sailor, should have been up and done with morning chow by now.

This time, after the fourth ring, it picked up. Spurs leaned forward.

"Yeah?" The voice was groggy.

"Mr. Dubain?" Spurs asked, checking off the last item on her list.

"Who wants to know? It's seven a.m. Somebody'd better be dead."

Spurs had to assume a name, now, incase Dubain would rat on her to his buddies on the *USS Atchison*, the ship on which she was to conduct the undercover investigation. Her boss seemed to think her being known to be Admiral Sperling's daughter aboard the ship could be an asset. Spurs wasn't pleased with the idea, but she figured Director Burgess knew what he was doing. She'd come up with a name using her own initials and had decided—ignoring what she was sure Sigmund Freud or any of his psycho-analytical cronies would have said—to use her former fiancée's last name.

"Mr. Dubain, my name is Jill Smith. I'm with. . . ."

"Did you hear me? I don't wanna buy anything. Shove off!"

"But, Mr. Dubain, someone *is* dead."

Spurs heard nothing from the other end and wondered briefly if Dubain had hung up. Her eyes caught Ensign Nader's Annapolis graduation photo pinned to the gray fabric in front of her. She said, "Ensign Charles Nader."

More silence.

"Mr. Dubain, are you still there?"

"Damn. I knew it. I just fuckin' knew it!"

"Knew what? That Ensign Nader would die?"

Once again silence. He was choosing his words. "Hey, what is this anyway? I'm out. I got off the *Bounty* and rotated back over three weeks ago. I've been out of the Navy for—thirty-nine hours now. Who the hell are you?"

"My name is Jill Smith. I'm a special agent with NCIS."

"Jeez, leave me alone. I haven't done anything wrong. I've got nothing to say to you."

She'd hoped for a more cooperative lead to gain insight into the recent past of the *Atchison*. "Please, give me a minute of your time, Mr. Dubain. We—I need your help."

He paused again, then said, "How'd it happen? How'd Nader get it?"

"He fell from the signal bridge. It's officially being called a suicide. Tell me, Mr. Dubain, why did you just call the *Atchison* the *Bounty*?"

"Why do you think? Everybody's gone crazy on that scow."

"How do you mean?"

"I've said enough. It ain't my business anymore. Leave me alone."

"Mr. Dubain, I need your help. Just a few more questions."

More silence. His tone mellowed. "You've got kind of a sexy voice. What do you look like?"

She'd been afraid of that. According to Dubain's military records, he hadn't exactly been an angel during his four years of enlistment. He'd been called on the carpet a number of times for minor infractions—those things happen, but it was the second of two serious charges he'd been acquitted of that bothered her the most. The first was a marijuana possession that had been dropped because the evidence turned up missing.

Then, the biggie. He'd been acquitted of attempted rape after the victim changed her story. Notes from the investigating agent indicated the young yeoman had decided that Scumbag-Third-Class Dubain had been three sheets to the wind and it was due to the alcohol that he'd molested her. *Just a poor, misunderstood, drunken sailor. He didn't mean any harm. Poor boy. Out there at sea for such a long time. He just needed a friend—some affection.* Stereotypical. Expected. BULLSHIT!

"Mr. Dubain, please."

"All right. But not over the phone. And not at my place either."

"According to the address I have for you, you're not far away, a fifteen minute drive." Spurs tapped her pencil on the desk as she considered taking a later flight. She didn't want to. It would mean a longer layover in Madrid. But this interview was important. "Would you be able to come to the shipyards?"

"Hell, no. Someplace neutral, real neutral. The Sleepy Eye, down on East Franklin."

"A motel?"

"That's right. Come by yourself—and dress like a hooker."

The Navy released hundreds of nice guys from active service every week. *She* had to get a sleaze ball. "Mr. Dubain, I see no reason. . . ."

"I do! Otherwise, it's no deal."

Even if Dubain had very little of importance to tell her, just finding out why he thought the secrecy was so necessary could be an important insight into what was happening on the *Atchison*.

Spurs checked her watch. She might have just enough time. Between the drive to the motel, maybe fifteen minutes interviewing Dubain and then the drive to Dulles Airport, she'd have only the next ten minutes to appear as a prostitute—but that was if the traffic was good. She glanced at her sea bag and remembered the three-foot-square, silk scarf she used to bundle up what little valuables she kept. Her father had brought it home from Singapore and gave it to her mother the week before her mother drowned.

Dubain was impatient. "Too long," he said. "No deal."

"No, wait. I'll meet you there in thirty minutes."

"All right then." He sounded too pleased. "But I might not have time to take a shower. If you don't mind, I don't."

His flirtations told her she'd be in for more than she was interested in, but she figured she could handle former Petty Officer Third Class Henry Dubain.

"How will I know what room?"

"You'll know," he said and hung up.

Chapter 2

DOWN AND DIRTY

0735
Sleepy-Eye Motel
Washington, DC

THIRTY-FIVE MINUTES later, Spurs stepped onto the curb a block down from the Sleepy-Eye Motel. The size seven and a half, lime-green pumps she'd borrowed from Miss Barnes the receptionist were a size and a half too big, but matched the green and red scarf she wore as a dress much better than any of the military issue footwear she'd packed. A couple of Kleenexes in the toe of each shoe helped the fit.

The street was deserted except for a wino polishing off his brown-bag breakfast on the steps of a large house next to the motel. Most likely a halfway house, it had torn window screens and flaking white paint. Another man lay prostrate on the porch. Under her breath, Spurs gave thanks that their meeting was during daylight.

"Turn the car around and wait across the street, will you?" she told the young, civilian-dressed petty officer driving the unmarked, dark blue Chevy sedan.

"What happens if you need help?" the driver asked with true concern in his voice.

Spurs opened her purse and took out a six-inch fingernail file she'd sharpened to a razor's edge. She pulled the scarf away from her chest and carefully slipped the homemade knife under her bra, then tossed the purse back into the front seat of the car.

"I won't," she said and turned toward the motel.

After breathing in a good sample of the cool morning air, she took two steps and her right heel went sideways causing her to stumble. A hundred feet away, the wino frowned at her as if he were an astrophysicist disturbed while in deep contemplation of the origin of the universe. The drunkard, who was probably between thirty and fifty years of age—hard to tell on an alcoholic, especially such a dirty one—pulled his paper bag to his chest. After a moment of consideration, he wiped his nose on the sleeve of his olive drab, Marine Corps issue overcoat and hung his head with eyes closed.

As she approached, Spurs could make out what used to be a bright-red patch with three green stripes and crossed rifles through the filth on his sleeve. She wondered if he'd found the coat after it had been discarded, had been given the coat by some benevolent, former-Marine sergeant, or had actually earned those three chevrons himself. She began to feel sorry for the man, wondering what kind of life he'd had—what atrocities he'd witnessed that could have driven him to such despair, until, as she passed, the man yelled out, "incoming!" and tossed his empty wine bottle in front of her. She stopped in time to avoid the green bottle itself, but emerald shards and a mist of warm wine covered her feet. Her left foot went sideways again and the derelict chortled.

"Another confirmed kill!" he said, snorting back mucous as he laughed.

The man deserved a good slap upside his stocking-capped head, and if it weren't for concern of a bacterial infection, she would have given it to him. She paused only long enough to shake the glass fragments off and then continued at a somewhat swifter pace toward the nearby motel, feeling the prick of at least one sliver of glass that had slipped down the front of her right shoe.

Upon reaching the Sleepy Eye courtyard, she wondered how Henry Dubain could expect her to know which room he would be in. Checking the front desk was an option, but she preferred not to appear as a whore to anyone more than necessary. With the secrecy Dubain seemed to deem important, he might not have used his real name to register anyway. She stood on one foot and leaned against the large post supporting the Sleepy Eye's marquis. After slipping off her shoe, she turned it upside down and shook it out while glimpsing over the red doors of the old, two-story motel. The well-weathered roof was rippled and the white walls chipping. All of the doors looked the same.

She quickly brushed her bare foot with her hand, dropped the shoe and slipped it on, then took care of the other one as well. Stepping closer, she scanned from left to right, then saw markings on one of the doors toward the middle on the second floor.

Below the room number 223, drawn in what appeared to be white toothpaste, was a semicircle resting on a horizontal line with a dot in the center. The drawing might remind someone of the sun setting on the horizon, but seafarers knew it as the symbol for the naval term, *dead reckoning*—an inexact calculation of a ship's position using speed, time traveled, and direction, but only estimated values of wind and current.

She went to the wrought iron stairway, climbed it and approached the door. After three raps on the hard wood, the chain lock rattled and the dead bolt clicked. With the opening of the door came a pungent mix of body odor and a men's cologne she thought might be Brut. A small but muscular man in his early twenties greeted her wearing only a towel around his waist. He stroked a short, adolescent beard while looking her up and down, eyes wide and grinning, then stepped back.

Spurs asked, "Mr. Dubain?"

"Come in," he said, again in the flirting tone.

As soon as she complied, he wiped the toothpaste from the door with his hand and quickly closed it. After cleaning his palm on the towel, he hooked the chain and flipped the deadbolt lock back into place, then turned to her and leaned against the door, still smiling.

"You're better than I'd hoped for!"

Chapter 3

IF THE SHOE FITS

SPURS CASUALLY TOUCHED her chest, ensuring that the fingernail file was still there and smiled back. Henry Dubain couldn't have been more than five foot five, dark hair with a narrow face and slim build. In her three-inch heels, they were eye to eye.

It was a move she hadn't expected. He came at her like a rattler. Spurs instinctively grabbed his right wrist with her right hand before he'd made contact. She directed his force to the queen-size bed. He fell into it, face first. She raised her eyebrows pleased at the hand-to-hand she'd been taught in Officer's Candidate School.

He rolled off the bed angrily, stood and glared back at her from six feet away.

"Hey, what is this?" he said. "I thought we had a deal."

"You've been too long at sea, Dubain. *This* was our 'deal'; I need information. You were going to give it to me. *That* was our 'deal.'"

"It's *no* deal then," he snarled back. "No play, no pay!"

Dubain was too much like so many of the rest. The

schoolyard bully that used to wrestle her down in fifth grade and spit in her face. The boys in high school that tricked her into a barn at a party and then got handsy with her. Dubain would not be one to trick her; he would not spit in her face. She had been determined ever since, that no boy—no man—would do that again.

"Listen, Dubain. There've been people dying on the *Atchison*. You might be able to help before more lives are lost. You sailed with them. They were your friends."

"I sailed with them, but they weren't my friends. I learned quick. You can't trust any of 'em. Not one from the Captain on down. Now, get naked or get out!"

"Why couldn't you trust them?"

"I said, get naked," he said and lunged at her.

This time he snagged the top of her scarf dress above her right breast and pulled down.

Spurs brought her left arm up, blocking his hand away, then grabbed his wrist again. She forced his back to her by this time circling his forearm around and between his shoulder blades where she held it high and as firmly as possible. She pulled the fingernail file from her bosom and pushed the point against his right jugular.

"I've had about enough of you, Mr. Stud Duckling. I don't know what kind of hormonal disease you're suffering from, but I assure you, I'm not going to be your cure. Unless, of course, you leave me no other choice but to bleed you like a pig in a slaughterhouse. Now, would you like to face charges on assaulting a federal officer or would you like to be nice and talk to me?"

He struggled for a moment, trying to jerk away, but Spurs kept the pressure, thankful that she had the advantage and didn't have to go against him face to face.

"All right, all right. We'll talk."

She released his arm hoping it would make him more

cooperative.

He pulled away and turned to her, rubbing his wrist, but he wouldn't make eye contact.

"Look, if they know I've talked to you, I'm dead. They'll kill me like they did the others."

"Who're they?" she asked, tucking the file back in place.

"That's the problem. I don't know. It could be anybody on that ship—it could be anybody anywhere—even you."

"Then *why* would they kill you?"

"Because I know about the drugs."

Spurs frowned. It was like pulling teeth from a Brahma bull. "How? What drugs?"

"The supply officer, Ensign Ingrassias, told me. I was assigned to him. He said the ship was being used to smuggle some kind of a new synthetic cocaine back to the states."

"Is he involved?"

"I couldn't tell. It was like he wanted to be, like they'd approached him, but he wasn't sure if it was worth the risk. I think he was afraid of the guys doin' it."

"Why did he tell you?"

"We were kind of buds, ya know? We burned a few together, snorted a little."

"This was on board ship?"

"Yeah, I know what you're thinking. That kind of thing doesn't happen anymore on navy ships. But you don't understand. You don't know the *Atchison*. It's one fucked up boat. Everybody's weirded out. It's like a hand-picked crew of misfits."

"What about the officers?"

"It's the same. The XO, Lieutenant Commander Reeves, might be all right. I can't really tell. But the rest of 'em, including the Captain, Commander Naugle, I wouldn't trust as far as I could heave 'em. I think the skipper's been tryin' out too much of the stash he's runnin'. And the ship's lieutenant, Lieutenant North, he's like always watching you, like if you make a move you're not supposed to, he'll keelhaul you or something."

"What about Ensign Nader?"

"Yeah, Ensign Nader." Dubain sat down on the bed and stared at the floor, shaking his head. "Nader was one of those *gung ho* Annapolis types. Straight as a cannon barrel, but he was a good guy. When he found out we were homies—you know, both of us born and raised in South DC—he kind of cut me some slack. I don't think he was in on the drugs, but knowin' him, he probably tried to do something about it. He was a fool. I stayed out of it and finally got the hell out of there."

Spurs stepped in front of him and stood five feet away. "How long had the smuggling been going on?"

Dubain cocked his head and looked toward the door. He didn't answer.

"Please, Mr.—please, Henry."

He lowered his head and stared down at her feet. His eyes rose slowly, taking in her calves, knees, thighs, crotch, waist, then stopped at her breasts.

Spurs felt a shiver and shifted her weight. She folded her arms across her chest.

"Henry?"

He licked his lips, his gaze still below her neck, and finally said, "Everyone acted strange since we left Charleston four months ago. I'd say there were drugs put aboard by the time we dropped anchor in our second foreign port, Marseilles, France. We had liberty there three more times while I was aboard, but I don't think that was the only place we picked the stuff up. I wouldn't doubt if it was everywhere we cast lines."

"Did you ever see any of it?"

He finally looked higher and stared hard into her eyes. "No, and I'm glad I didn't. I think that and the fact that I got the hell out of there is why I'm still alive." He shifted on the bed and once again looked at the door. "The dope would be pretty hard to spot anyway. It's supposed to be really unheard of stuff, like a pinch will get a dozen guys as high as a pelican."

Spurs glanced at her watch. She'd have to run through the airport, as it was, to catch her flight.

"Is there anything else you can tell me?"

He seemed to think for a moment.

"Yeah, two things. The first, keep me the fuck out of this."

Spurs frowned at him. "I see no reason to get you involved at this point. And the second thing?"

"You got a nice ass," he said and sprang forward, bringing one hand up under the scarf.

A rattler with tentacles.

He pushed her against the wall, slamming her head hard and knocking over a lamp on the nearby dresser. He pinned her there with his legs in between hers and groped under her panties. Spurs shook off the stars as Dubain pressed his mouth to hers. She felt the towel he'd had around his waist fall to her feet and she jerked her head away.

This time, he had her good. She tried to talk tough, but her words came out in a feeble pant. "You're a persistent little bastard." But she couldn't show her fear.

"Come on, bitch," he breathed, "you won't regret it."

She struggled for a moment but testosterone and more time in the weight room won out. Maybe going along with him briefly would reward her with the opportunity to get away. "Okay, Henry. You've got me."

Nose to nose, he kept his full weight against her.

He reminded her of the schoolyard toughies who picked on her as a child. Dubain would not be another bully to spit in her face.

She said softly, "You want a little piece of me? Huh, Henry? You want some?"

He grinned showing green-edged teeth.

She took a long breath then cringed at the Jack Daniels saturating his. Raising her eyebrows she forced a smile back. "You really want it, don't you, Henry? You know, I might even like it."

His smile grew into childlike glee as she kicked his discarded towel out of the way then placed the three-inch heel of her right shoe against the top of his bare foot for good aim. She brought her foot up.

His eager anticipation cleared from his face, his expression going dumb as realization came, but not soon enough.

She stomped her heel into his foot as hard as she could.

With an agonizing cry, he let her go and tumbled to the floor wearing nothing but a grimace and a hard on.

"Henry, you really know how to please a girl," Spurs said as she went for the door.

Writhing on the bright red carpet, he did not try to stop her. She was outside before realizing she'd lost Miss Barnes' right shoe and wondered if it might still be buried in Dubain's foot.

Chapter 4

FLIGHT OF THE INVESTIGATOR

April 30, 1330, American Airlines Flight 634
One Hour Out Over Atlantic Ocean

"LADIES AND GENTLEMEN, this is your captain speaking. Due to some unexpected storms in the North Atlantic, I'm afraid we'll have to deviate our course a little. We'll be flying into London's Heathrow Airport for a short layover before flying on to our destination, Madrid. I'm sure it will delay us only a couple of hours. Madrid is aware of our change of flight plan and will post the delay to insure that any parties meeting you at the airport won't worry and will be able to make other arrangements. Again, we're sorry for the inconvenience."

"Oh, wonderful," the elderly lady sitting next to the aisle said, clutching her purse as she had been for the past sixty minutes. She wore her salt and pepper hair in a bun on the top of her head and a large floral-print dress that fit like a sack on her squat little body.

Spurs had quickly dressed in the airport into her summer-white uniform to start "feeling the part," like an actor or an undercover investigator should. She reasoned that the two jobs weren't all that different except, as an actor, if you didn't perform convincingly, the audience probably wouldn't kill you. She smiled at the woman as she finished stitching up a small rip in the sleeve of one of her uniform blouses.

"Don't worry," Spurs said reaching over the empty seat between them and patting the old woman's hand, "I'm sure it'll be only a short delay as the captain said."

"Oh, I'm not worried, but I'll bet my son will be. He always worries about his old mother." She looked at Spurs with wide smiling eyes. "He's in oil, ya know."

"Ooh, that sounds slippery," Spurs said.

The old woman just looked at her, puzzled.

"I'm sorry, it was supposed to be a joke. Not a very good one, I suppose."

The woman gave a slight curve of the lips and nodded.

Spurs said, "I tend to joke when things get tense or worrisome. Sometimes, it's a curse."

"Are you worried?"

Spurs sat back. "Just a little anxious. I'm going to Spain to meet my ship. It's got a lot of problems that I'm supposed to fix."

"You're a mechanic?"

"No, ma'am, just a problem solver."

The old woman nodded again and laid her head back on the headrest. After a moment, she closed her eyes, and Spurs gazed out the small, round window next to her. Between wisps of clouds were the ocean waves—tiny white lines on the blue-green mat 30,000 feet below. The butterflies still played in her stomach as they had when she'd boarded the plane, and she felt a slight case of the shakes. It reminded her of the first time she'd calf-roped in the rodeo at age eleven. There was so much to remember, so much to do, so much to be responsible for. But finally, the months of training would soon be put to practice.

* * *

Spurs thought back to when she'd been given her assignment the previous morning. NCIS Director Harley Burgess had called her at her cubicle and requested her immediate presence in his office. His voice was blank of emotions. As she gathered up a notepad and pen and walked down the long echoing hall to meet him, she wondered what she'd done to deserve a reprimand from the boss.

She'd never *really* met Director Burgess before, just shook his hand at the brief graduation ceremony after she completed the NCIS Basic Agent Course at the Federal Law Enforcement Training Center in Glynco, Georgia. But he seemed to be a pleasant man, bald and chubby, not what someone might think an ex-CIA spook would look like.

Burgess was on the phone when his secretary ushered her in. He leaned back in his leather swivel chair behind a highly polished, cherry-wood desk, his waxed crown reflecting the sunlight flooding through the large picture window behind him. It was like a beacon, and she had to squint and suppress a laugh—although a nervous one—as she approached his desk.

"Yes, Mr. Secretary," he said into the phone, "I have one of my best people on it."

She was reminded of the man's position, and it made it easy to forget his lighthouse forehead. Was it the Secretary of the Navy or the Secretary of Defense he was speaking to?

She glanced around the room while waiting for permission to sit. It was like a photo gallery. Lining three walls, above the many bookcases, were dozens of framed pictures of Burgess shaking hands and rubbing shoulders with various foreign and US dignitaries. Burgess shaking hands with the Shah of Iran, with Golda Meir, Margaret Thatcher, with Presidents Ford, Carter, Reagan, Clinton, and both the senior and junior Bushes. Pictures with people she didn't recognize, all regally dressed. On the far wall hung a mounted, seven-foot-long swordfish, its tail curled out and mouth open as if still fighting its fate.

Burgess' desk was clear of pictures, cluttered with stacks of folders and the usual desk paraphernalia. But on each side of his desk were two small stands, each dedicated solely to a single 8X10 sitting on top. On the right was a photo of Burgess and a lady who was probably his wife, both of them in evening attire.

The photo on the left was different than all of the rest. It was taken in front of a boat with Burgess and another man, probably thirty years his junior and a good six inches taller, in casual clothes instead of the formal ties and tuxedos that the subjects in the other photos wore. She wondered if the younger man might be Burgess' son. They stood next to what was probably the same seven-foot swordfish that now lived on the wall, only it was hoisted up on a pole. Both men wore sunglasses, big smiles, and shirts you'd buy at a tourist's trap in the Bahamas, their arms on each other's shoulders. The name of the boat in the background was blocked partially by the huge fish; *Cham_ _ _ on*. Probably *Champion*, she thought.

"And what about our golf game on Saturday. Okay, no mulligan's this time. See you then, Mr. Secretary."

He hung up and said, "Have a seat, Agent Sperling. That one." He pointed to a high-back, leather chair to the left of his desk. He smiled pleasantly as he watched her step over and sit down.

"Thank you, sir." She glanced at the swordfish again as she sat. "Nice fish."

Burgess kept his smile as he turned and gazed at his trophy catch. "Yes. Yes, it is, isn't it?" He looked at the photo Spurs now sat beside, and she could see something distant and affectionate in his eyes. "It was our last catch on our little boat before Fran got it."

She didn't understand. "Your ex-wife, sir?"

He chuckled and glanced over his shoulder to the other picture. "No, I've been married to the same girl for over forty-two years. Her name is Susan. The hurricane's name was Fran."

Spurs felt her face flush. "Of course," she said and nodded.

He paused before saying any more, still watching her with the smile that made her think of a father admiring his child on the kid's first bicycle solo.

"I'm sorry that this is the first chance we've had to talk, Janelle—oh, uh, I see you have a nickname," he said, glancing back at an open file on his desk. "Spurs, I believe."

"Yes, sir," she said, smiling, "some of my friends call me that."

"Does that include me?"

She grinned at him. He was good at breaking the ice. "Of course, sir."

"Good. And you've been out of training for what, a month now?"

"Three weeks, sir."

"How do you like it so far?"

"Just fine, sir—well, can I be frank?"

"But of course, by all means," he said, his face showing a practiced concern.

"I'm getting a little bored with the paperwork, you know the filing and things. I was hoping I'd be assigned a case by now."

Burgess pulled a file folder from a stack on the corner of his desk and opened it. He leafed through it briefly. "Funny you should mention that, Spurs," he said. "I just might have one for you, but I'm concerned that you may not be ready."

Spurs' eyes grew big. "Sir, I'd do anything to prove that I am. I was second in my training class at the center—top of my class in forensic psychology in college."

"Yes, I see that. But those aren't the reasons I'm considering you for this case. Normally, for what I have in mind, we'd use a more experienced field agent."

Spurs sat on the edge of the chair. "What I lack in experience, I'm sure I can make up in enthusiasm, sir. I have a bachelor's in criminology."

"From Oklahoma University, yes, I know, but that isn't it either, Spurs, and too much enthusiasm can get you killed in this business."

She sat back and tried to calm herself, realizing she was looking like a rookie—the kiss of death for an investigator, rookie or not.

"Then what is it, sir?"

Burgess' eyes met hers over his reading glasses. "You're in the Navy Reserve?"

"Yes, sir, joined in my college freshman year. Six years now."

He looked back to her file. "Trained as a weapons officer?"

"That's right, sir."

"You've spent some time at sea. How did you like shipboard life?" He seemed to ensure good eye contact on this question as if how she'd dealt with being out to sea would be a major factor in determining whether or not she was suitable for the assignment.

Spurs was only half truthful. On board ship, she was fine, as long as she didn't have to get into the water herself. "I enjoyed it, sir."

"I guess it figures, your father's Admiral Oliver T. Sperling. He's retired now isn't he?"

"Yes, sir."

"I've met your father. He's a good man—tough, but good. And your mother drowned. I'm sorry."

"That was a long time ago, sir, when I was twelve." Concerned that he might be searching for a reason to disqualify her from her first chance at an assignment as an investigator, she changed the subject. "What kind of case are you considering me for?"

"It would be in line with your fields of interest: criminal investigations and counterintelligence. Undercover, aboard a ship."

Spurs swallowed hard. "Contraband, theft?"

"Murder."

Spurs blinked. "Please give me a try, sir."

Burgess looked back at her file. "I'll catch hell from Paul Royse. I understand my assistant director is your father's stepbrother—your step uncle, so to speak. I'm sure that had nothing to do with you getting a job here."

"Uncle, sir. I don't think about the 'step' part. But, even so, there's no nepotism I'm aware of, sir. I passed all of the tests in the upper ten percent of the class."

"Uh-huh. But you're very close to your uncle?"

"Yes, sir. I pretty much grew up on his ranch in Oklahoma. And, after my mother died, Uncle Paul and Aunt Katherine took care of me—raised me. That was when he was FBI. I guess he's why I wanted to be here. He said it would be a rewarding career and I could still be near the Navy."

Burgess nodded. "And your father will want a piece of my hide, too. There's too much at stake right now to worry about that, though. You fit the profile, except for lack of experience. However, as I tell any of my undercover operatives, if I give you this assignment and you find you're in over your head, you will abort and seek safety immediately."

Spurs smiled. "Yes, sir."

"You're sure? There's considerable danger. Your life could be at risk at any time without you knowing it."

"I'm sure, sir."

"All right, Special Agent Sperling, but if you feel that this assignment is not for you at any time during my briefing, you'll stop me and not breathe a word of it to anyone, understand?"

"Of course, sir."

Burgess unlocked a desk drawer on his left and pulled out a two-inch-thick folder.

"Again, I must warn, the security of the United States Navy might depend on you. Our own security at NCIS might already have been compromised—penetrated."

"A spy, sir?"

"A traitor."

Spurs frowned as Burgess went on. "You'll be stationed on the *USS Atchison*, a frigate." He handed the thick file to her. "We've had two AWOLs and two suspicious deaths on board the ship—all in the last ten days. We've interviewed the relatives of all but the latest dead man and we've conducted an on-ship investigation. There appears to be nothing out of the ordinary—except an inordinate number of misfits aboard the *Atchison*. Your assignment will start with interviewing the family of the latest man killed—an Ensign Charles Nader. They live here in DC. You'll put the pieces together while aboard the *Atchison*. You'll be undercover, assigned as their weapons officer in place of Nader."

Spurs leafed through the folder as she listened. "Where's the *Atchison* now, sir?"

"Rota, Spain."

Spurs lifted her eyebrows. "How will I proceed, what will I be looking for?"

"Here's the risky part. We think that this problem may have something to do with a drug-smuggling ring funded by Arab terrorists. *Allah's Gihad*, to be exact. Also, it may be beneficial for you to operate as yourself instead of with an assumed name. Being Admiral Sperling's daughter might be an asset. Most of the salts know or know *of* him. Might give you some weight. We'll alter your PR file—take out any NCIS training recorded and maybe add a little black mark or two—say a minor drug bust that you were acquitted of due to lack of evidence. That'll help you fit in *well* with this crew."

"Will I be alone, sir?"

"We recruited a crewmember onboard some months ago when we were tipped of the drug ring. Due to security reasons, I can't give you his name, but he'll make himself known to you when the time is right."

"Security reasons, sir?"

"In the event that you should back out. Trust is a precious commodity in this case."

"Who tipped us of the drug ring?"

"I'm sorry, that's one of those need to know things, and you don't need to know."

Spurs looked back at the file. "There seems to be an urgency, even above these disappearances and deaths, sir. May I ask about that?"

"You may ask, but I can't tell you. And not because I don't want to. All we know is that our man aboard feels things are festering, getting ready to pop." He pushed away from his desk and leaned toward her with his elbows on his knees. "You'll be in danger from the moment you step on that ship to the time this case is solved. But don't forget, we have two agents assigned overtly to the fleet on the flagship, the *Enterprise*. If you need more help than your contact can give you, go to them. But until then, you must report through that contact aboard the *Atchison*, understand?"

Spurs found herself daydreaming briefly. Her ex-fiancée, Doug Smith, was an F-18 pilot assigned to the *Enterprise*. She realized Burgess was staring at her, his question finally soaking in. "Oh, yes, sir."

"You should find transcripts from all of the interviews the two fleet agents conducted with the *Atchison's* crew. The two AWOLs' families and one of the dead crewmember's families were also questioned. You'll find those reports in the file, too, along with a print-out summary on each member of the crew. Senior Special Agent Taylor will have your airline tickets and orders ready for you by 1300. He'll give you a final briefing. Also, before you go, you'll need to interview Ensign Charles Nader's family."

Spurs paged through some of the reports. "How many women are aboard the *Atchison*, sir?"

"None."

She frowned, but Burgess continued. "But the good news is," he said as he found a note placed by his phone, "before the *Atchison* shoves off, day after tomorrow, there'll be twenty-three reporting for duty. It'll be the first detail of women to serve on that ship."

Spurs nodded and glanced at the file folder, then back at Burgess, feeling dazed by it all. She had been eager to become an investigator, to be assigned a case, but undercover and aboard ship were more than she could have ever hoped for.

* * *

The airliner buffeted as it changed its heading, trying to skirt the foul weather ahead. Spurs smiled down at the white Navy uniform blouse on her lap.

It was the opportunity of a lifetime.

Chapter 5

COMING ABOARD

May 1, 1530,
US Naval Station, Rota, Spain.

THE FOUL WEATHER that had forced Janelle Sperling's flight from Dulles to layover in London delayed her arrival in Madrid an additional eight hours. She was forced to take a later connecting flight to Rota. Sleep had come in nods and her once spotless and crisp polyester, summer-white uniform was smudged and wrinkled. She was pleased, however that even after nearly a year *and* five pounds, the blouse and skirt still fit nicely.

Spurs stepped out of the taxi, grimacing at the bright day. The morning's menacing storm clouds had made way for a neon blue afternoon sky. She handed the Spanish taxicab driver an American twenty-dollar bill for a ten-dollar fare as he laid her bags in front of her. "Keep it," she said.

She turned away and plodded past the last freight building on Pier Six with her sea bag in one hand and a handbag in the other. The *USS Enterprise* suddenly loomed before her causing a flutter inside her chest. She dropped her bags then gaped up at the *Big E*.

The massive warship was moored a stone's throw out. Its nearly two hundred million pounds of steel and aluminum enclosed over a million pounds of human flesh as it floated high and proud. It was even more of an awesome sight than she'd expected, but as she looked at the tall, gray lady, she couldn't help thinking about her ex-fiancée.

She scanned the enormous, gray superstructure from the water, up its tremendous hull to its flight deck, then to the top of its island in the ship's middle, some twenty stories above the sea. Somewhere aboard the mass of metal was the Marine aviator she'd promised to marry more than five months ago. She shaded her eyes with one hand and squinted at several groups of men leaning on the lifelines along the nearly quarter mile long ship. They were only tiny blue and white specs lining the side. It had been six weeks since she'd seen Lieutenant Doug Smith. While eyeing the huge flattop, she wondered if it had been another woman—or this ship's sex appeal that had stolen him away.

Sighing, she turned to the *USS Atchison* tied off at the adjacent dock. Soon she'd become one of the first female members of the small, ancient frigate's 217-*man* crew. The tiny ship's purpose was to provide support and protection to the *Enterprise*, but from Spurs' understanding, the vessel was so old and slow that its mission seemed almost in sympathy. She wondered if the *Atchison* wouldn't serve her country better scrapped and made into something more useful like a trillion coat hangers or maybe a hundred train cars full of beer bottle caps.

She took a deep breath of musky sea air and narrowed her eyes. The next few weeks were sure to prove interesting. Something strange was happening aboard this ship. *Two men dead and two missing in the last ten days.* There are accidents and people die and disappear in the Navy; it's the nature of the beast. With what she had learned from Henry Dubain, and the fact that there had been so many accidents and disappearances over such a short period of time—from the same ship, this new problem seemed all too obviously related. Drug trafficking and missing crewmembers.

Even though she'd inherited a cocky confidence from her old sea-dog father, thinking of her very first undercover assignment brought back her queasy stomach and the shakes she'd felt when boarding the plane the morning before at Dulles. "He's out of the chute," she said aloud, thinking of her childhood calf-roping days. "Time to tie him up."

Being a military brat, she'd been all over the world but never by herself—never *really* by her self. Of course, in college at Oklahoma University, in Officer's Candidate School, and at NCIS training, she'd been alone—in a way. Then, at least, she'd shared the experience with her peers. This time would be much different. As she gazed up and down the last bustling dock on Pier Six in Rota, Spain, amid the clanking of steel, the fizzing of acetylene torches, the popping of arc welders and the whine of forklifts, she definitely felt alone.

She lifted her bags then staggered from their weight toward the ship. Looking over the *Atchison* and not paying much attention to the goings-on around her, she was startled by the warning honks of a swerving high loader. The big yellow forklift careened away at the last second and she stumbled back, falling to her butt spread-eagled over her sea bag.

"Idiot!" she said, frowning at the young heavy-equipment operator who drove away wearing a wide smirk while giving her a mock salute over his shoulder.

As an officer, it was important for her to maintain her composure, but her first urge was to show the smart-ass her middle finger, which she did shortly. Still grinning, the young seaman in blue fatigues gave her a nod before turning back to his business. She quickly stood up and brushed off her uniform while scanning the area to ensure that no one else had viewed her newborn-colt-like clumsiness. Then, grabbing up her bags, she headed once again across the pier to the *Atchison's* berth, taking care to be more watchful.

She gave a brief visual inspection of what was to be her home for the next few weeks and wondered how the small ship would ride the waves and if her sensitive gut would hold up. There were sure to be storms, and the smaller the ship the more tossing it would do. The vessel she approached now was one of the smallest in the US Navy and barely large enough to be considered a *ship*. Orange rust streaked her hull, and much of the gray paint that wasn't discolored had risen in cancerous bubbles with oxidizing steel underneath.

Spurs paused briefly at the foot of the gangway, leaned forward, hefting her sixty-pound sea bag over the right shoulder of her petite frame and then stomped up, squinting from the bright May Day sun.

Halfway up the thirty-foot incline, she glanced across the dock once again to the *Big E*, wishing somehow her assignment could be aboard that giant Cadillac of the sea. She would rather be chipping paint and swabbing decks on the huge, nuclear-powered aircraft carrier than be the new weapons officer of the bucket she now boarded. But the *Atchison* would have to do. As in that first time in the rodeo, all eyes would be on her. She would have to prove herself again. Prove herself not only as an undercover Naval Criminal Investigative Service agent, but as a Naval officer, and also as one of the Navy's new battle-ready, seagoing WINS (Women in Naval Service). When she proved herself to the US Navy, then maybe she could finally prove herself to her father, Rear Admiral Oliver T. Sperling, USN, Retired. The last would be the toughest.

The Admiral was of the old Navy. He stood firm against allowing gays into the military, blacks to achieve command rank, and women to serve aboard ships, especially warships. Not being a white, heterosexual male made her substandard, incapable, inept.

Spurs reached the upper platform and set her duffel bag and handbag on the gangway. She quickly straightened her blouse and skirt, stuffed a few unruly strands of her strawberry-blonde hair under her cap and stiffened to attention.

Turning to the US flag posted aft, she brought her right hand up knifelike and snapped a guidebook salute to the colors of her country.

The Officer of the Deck (OOD), a tall, slim lieutenant standing next to her, answered the salute then looked her up and down as she dropped her hand and turned to him. Once again, she cocked her arm and raised her fingertips to her temple.

"Request permission to come aboard, sir," she sounded boldly, holding her hand steady above her brow as she waited for the OOD to return the greeting and allow her to step across to the *Atchison's* quarterdeck.

The young lieutenant looked at her with a blinking frown and asked, "May I see your orders please, Ensign?"

The strong smell of fresh enamel paint made her small, freckle-splattered nose twitch as she pulled her orders from her left skirt pocket. While holding the salute, she shoved the papers to the OOD's waiting hand. The three-page document mentioned nothing of her undercover duty. Not even the captain of the ship would be informed of the true assignment. Only her contact would know.

The lieutenant scanned her orders, then studied her.

She noticed his blue eyes and long lashes. She'd learned in criminal psych class that eyes could be very revealing to an experienced investigator. They could tell many things about the person behind them; his honesty, integrity, humor, intentions. This man's eyes were honest and bright. He could be a needed ally in the future. But while mentally critiquing the first member of the crew she'd met, she remembered something her mother had told her about eyes.

Sometimes they lie.

The officer's questioning expression faded and his blue eyes seemed to smile even though his lips didn't. She took note of his square jaw, sharp nose and high cheekbones and saw something familiar. Maybe she'd seen him when she was in the reserves or perhaps at her father's retirement party six years earlier—probably someone who looked like him—it didn't matter. She noticed his summer-white uniform was impeccably clean, pressed and attended to without even the smallest *Irish pennant* or loose thread. Above a handful of ribbons over his left breast pocket gleamed a set of gold jump wings indicating that at some point during his time in, he'd been a parachutist, possibly in special ops. But he didn't wear the special warfare insignia of a SEAL. Over that strong odor of paint, came just a hint of his Old Spice aftershave.

He saluted and returned her orders.

"Very well, Ensign Sperling. I'm Lieutenant Darren North."

She remembered what Henry Dubain had said.

This was the Lieutenant North that was "always watching you, like if you make a move you're not supposed to, he'll keelhaul you."

Yes, it'll be an interesting cruise, she thought, bringing her hand down smartly.

The young lieutenant continued, "The XO, Lieutenant Commander Reeves, wants all new personnel to report in to him. He's topside in the Conn—on the bridge. It's the same thing on this little ship," North said, then his lips did actually curve into a smile as he gazed at her. He added, "Welcome aboard, Janelle."

He offered his hand.

Surprised by his sudden cordiality, she took his hand warily.

"Thank you, sir," she said and forced a courteous smile back.

He pointed to a clipboard lying on a small table. "Sign in, please."

She stepped aboard, lifting her bags for the short distance and placed them by the table, then picked up the pen taped to a string attached to the clipboard and signed. Grimacing, she boosted her duffel bag up to her chest and swung it to her back and then grabbed up the handbag. Pausing, she thought of Dubain's comment about Lieutenant Commander Reeves— "might be all right."

Ignoring her complaining arms and shoulders, she stepped across the deck. It wouldn't be long before she would be afforded the opportunity to rest. With that in mind, she puffed determinedly and trudged toward the ladder to the bridge. After a day and a half in the air and in crowded airports, she looked forward to reporting in and being assigned her quarters. Somewhere aboard this ship, a soothing, warm shower waited just for her.

Walking to the metal stairway, she could still feel the weight of the young lieutenant's gaze and she wondered if he still smiled.

Chapter 6

CONDUCT UNBECOMING

SPURS LOCATED THE ship's executive officer, Lieutenant Commander Reeves, leaning over a nautical chart table on the ship's bridge. He was accompanied by a young boatswain's mate wearing a radio headset, and, next to the far bulkhead, a black Marine Corporal stood with a duty belt slung around his waist and on it a holstered Beretta. She found the extra security interesting. She reminded herself of the need to be careful about asking too many questions and arousing suspicion of her.

The XO studied the map with his back turned, and neither of the other men had noticed her.

"The fleet's leaving port early to try and skirt that squall that's blowing in from the Azores. Looks like we'll be doing a little tossin' by about 2400 tonight," the XO said tapping his compass on the portion of chart he studied. "If we're lucky, we'll just get into the tail end of 'er. But if she changes course—well then—it'll be a good drill for the *legs*."

The term *legs* passed by Spurs hardly noticed. It wasn't long after enlisting that she'd gotten used to the terms and slang used in the male oriented Navy. She knew well that in this case, legs meant the inexperienced. That definition had been derived from its use meaning women and in most cases could be substituted for *pussy*, *chicken*, *gutless*, or *female*.

Spurs noted a trace of a Southern accent in the officer's voice that gave her a relaxed, sort of homey feeling, making her think of lazy, wind-teased cotton fields, rambling estates and spacious mansions. But that feeling didn't last long.

The boatswain's mate looked at his XO. "That isn't going to be just a little gale, sir. It looks like it could build into a major storm. NAVEUR says she might be pushing hurricane winds by sundown."

"What's wrong with you, Botts?" the officer asked, emphasizing disappointment in his voice. He glared. "You talk like a virgin. I broke you in six months ago, boy. You're no leg. Don't act like one."

Botts bowed his head and stared through the map.

Spurs dropped her bags outside the open hatch and stepped in, coming to attention. An anxious tingle rushed through her body and she felt herself shaking once again. The officer before her was her new boss and second in command to the captain. He could make her assignment a pleasure or pure hell. She wanted to give a good impression but wondered if she could, as tired and disheveled as she felt. She cleared her throat and hoped that the nervousness, fatigue and apprehension wouldn't quaver her voice.

"Ensign Janelle Sperling reporting as ordered, sir!"

Lieutenant Commander Reeves twisted his neck to look at her and frowned. He inspected her—every square inch, she felt, until at last his stern look softened and a lopsided grin took over. He straightened and stepped over to a clipboard hanging near the helm. The man carried himself like her father, *the Admiral:* boldly, almost painfully erect and with sure, marching-like steps. Unlike many other officers Spurs had been around, his self-assured manner demanded respect based solely on appearance. After checking the board quickly he looked up.

Spurs wondered if it was the heat, the season, or the length of time since she was last intimate with an attractive man, but the XO was as striking as the young OOD who'd greeted her. He had intense, coffee-brown eyes, a razor-sharp profile and strong features. His voice, although hinting of Mississippi, rang deep—words clear and crisp.

"Ensign J. B. Sperling?"

"That's correct, sir."

"Lieutenant Commander Nick Reeves, Sperling," he said, tipping a salute. "Welcome aboard. We weren't expecting our new weapons officer to be a Wave."

Spurs kept her composure with a blank stare. Wave or WAVES (*Women Appointed Volunteer Emergency Service*) was an obsolete term still unofficially used. WINS (*Women In Naval Service*) was the politically correct, Navy authorized term.

He continued, "I must be honest, miss, I am both surprised and disappointed. A weapons officer aboard this ship must be strong, intelligent and dedicated in order to take the rigors of the billet."

Spurs cheeks burned as if she'd just been slapped. "Excuse me, sir, I am a fully qualified surface warfare officer," she said pointing to the gold "bow waves" insignia on her chest. "What makes you think that I'm not strong, intelligent and dedicated?"

The XO gave a contempt-seething smile. "Darlin', you can't weigh much more than a hundred pounds sopping wet. Hell, you're not foolin' anybody. I know what you women want. You're not out to do a job and serve your country. You just want to prove that you can measure up to men—and you can't."

Spurs tried to contain the pressure building in her temples. "Today's Navy doesn't need to be 90% brawn and 10% brain anymore, sir. As a matter of fact, it's exactly the opposite." She felt her emotional grip loosen as her words came out quicker and a notch louder. "I'm part of today's Navy, sir, and if anybody doesn't understand or like it, I'd suggest they get used to it or get out of the way because I'm here to stay—sir."

She glared, wishing for a stare down. She'd always done well against others in the childish but meaningful game, but her eyes got that dry, wanting-to-blink feeling quicker than ever before. She was thankful when Reeves' lazy gaze turned back to the clipboard, but it made her wonder if he couldn't outstare even her—if he couldn't have burned a hole through the back of her head if he'd wanted to, but for some reason decided against it.

Voices came from the hatchway behind her as a couple of sailors passed by on the catwalk."

" . . . and North says she's taking Nader's place." "No fuckin' way!" "I'm telling you, our new weapons officer is a split-tail." "There goes the ship!"

Spurs twisted toward the hatch. The two sailors paused in front of the hatchway and gaped back like kittens in a tiger's pen until one shoved the other past and their footfalls slapped on the metal deck as they scampered away.

She looked back at Reeves. He either hadn't heard what the two had said, or hadn't cared to hear. His tone was cooler than expected as he hooked the clipboard back in its place. "My, my, Ensign Sperling, you are full of piss and vinegar. Imagine that, an ensign lecturing about the present course of the US Navy to her own XO whom, I might add, has served nearly twenty years at sea. Some folks might consider that poor judgment for a career officer."

Spurs thought about her little run off at the mouth. Sometimes she had trouble containing her enthusiasm and opinions. Her father hadn't been able to muzzle her when she was a child, no matter how many times he'd spanked a blood-red handprint into her bottom.

Reeves stepped back to the chart table and after a pause asked, "Tell me, Ensign, *you're* not a virgin, are you?"

Spurs couldn't help frowning this time. This lieutenant commander was a definite chauvinist. She knew his kind; the good-looking, try-to-impress-women-by-talking-down-to-them, domineering type. Times were changing, but in this man's navy it was obviously at a snail's pace.

He added, "Of the sea, I mean."

Her face cleared. Pride of not being a leg caused a crooked smile. "No sir. I spent two weeks on the *Spartanburg County* sailing from Little Creek to Nassau."

"That's all? Hell, that's about as close to a leg as you can get. I'm talking about high seas. You know what I mean. . . ." His voice lowered and he smirked, " . . . rough stuff."

This time his eyes locked on cold and hard. His eyelids weren't lazy like before.

What a jerk, she thought. So much for making a good impression. Giving this asshole more debate would be a losing game—he was a superior officer. She set her jaw, but lowered her eyes.

"It's been a long day, sir. May I be assigned my quarters?"

Reeves leaned back and rested his right thigh across the corner of the chart table. He picked up his compass and toyed with it as he spoke.

"Certainly."

He glanced to the black Marine corporal standing at parade rest near the hatch on the other side of the bridge.

"All of Nader's gear's been sent back to his next of kin, hasn't it, Sanders?" the lieutenant commander asked the Marine.

"Yes, sir!" the corporal snapped, coming to attention, staring directly ahead. Then his eyes shifted questioningly.

"All right then, show our new weapons mistress to her quarters."

"Aye-aye, sir!" the Marine said and saluted. He stepped across the bridge toward Spurs.

Reeves looked back to her.

"I hope you understand," he said. "We're in a highly unusual situation here, Ensign. Normally Navy Europe tells us when to squat, when to wipe, and what to wipe with. But NAVEUR didn't inform us of your gender—highly irregular. You'll have to make some concessions."

"I understand, sir. But may I ask—what concessions? Why does my being a woman make me any different than the other twenty-three female crew members coming aboard?"

Reeves watched his compass as he toyed with it. "To start with, they kind of surprised us with this WINS detail thing. We were told about it only five days ago. I don't know what the Navy could be thinking dropping this in our laps on top of all of this trouble we've been having. Anyway, we'd been trying to get those orders postponed, and thought we had until you go and show up on our poop deck. For the time being, you'll be assigned our ship's lieutenant's stateroom. You should've already met your bunky. He's on OOD duty."

Spurs' eyes widened as she wondered what kind of insanity had a hold of Reeves. Co-habiting with a male officer wasn't part of her assignment. The Navy would not put up with this. *What's he trying to do, get court-martialed?* It was no less comforting that her roommate was the attractive lieutenant that brought her aboard.

"Sir!" she argued, then realizing she'd raised her voice again she stopped. Maybe this had something to do with Nader's death. Maybe the ship was being run by a psycho XO. In order to find out, she should play along. She continued as calmly as possible, "I don't understand."

He looked at her. "That makes two of us, Ensign. Let me make it as clear as possible. There *are* no other female crewmembers currently serving on this vessel. *You* are the only new crewmember coming aboard at this port. In other words, Ensign Janelle B. Sperling, you're it."

Reeves seemed to enjoy the shock on Spurs face. Director Burgess had assured her that there was a detail of women assigned TAD (*T*emporary *A*dditional *D*uty) with her. She wondered about Burgess' competence, then convinced herself that this couldn't be his fault. After all, he'd been appointed the job because of his excellent work as assistant director of the CIA. There could be no better qualifications than that. Still, she was sure that Assistant Director Paul Royse, being the stickler for detail that he was, wouldn't have allowed this to happen. Too bad he'd been away when she'd received her assignment. She would be sure to discuss this SNAFU with Royse later.

"What about the rest of the female detail, sir?" she asked. "Will they be coming aboard soon?"

"You probably haven't heard about the trouble we've been having—a couple of AWOLs and some accidents and such. We convinced Personnel that now was not the time to try one of their little coed experiments on us. They've given us an additional month to prepare. Your orders must have somehow slipped through a crack. Not a whole lot we can do now. We'll try to get you transferred to a more accommodating ship at the next port. Reeves smiled briefly. "Don't worry none, Ensign. Your bunky until then, Mister North—he's gay."

Spurs looked in disbelief. Not only disbelief for her absurd situation and the unbecoming comments from her new XO, but also in his last statement about Lieutenant North. What a shame that those beautiful eyes had been wasted on a gay man.

Reeves seemed to read her mind and said, "Yep, queerer than a three-winged sea bat." He paused until a smirk took over his face. He chuckled. "Lighten up, Ensign Sperling. You'll have to find a sense of humor if you're going to make it for even an *hour* on this ship. You don't really think I'd bunk you with a gay man, do you? I'll have the lieutenant put in with a couple of the other officers. They won't like it, but it appears we've no other choice." He glanced back to the Marine who'd paused respectfully beside her. "Now go on, Corporal Sanders, take Miss Sperling to her quarters. Then have Mister North join me on the bridge."

"Aye-aye, sir!" the black Marine answered again.

He marched past Spurs and out the hatch, snatched up her bags and turned to her.

Reeves still eyed the corporal and said, "We'll be getting underway earlier than scheduled in order to beat a little storm. We'll shove off around 1700—that's five PM." His eyes shifted to her.

"I do *know* military time, sir," she shot back. "It *is* still required in training and as the daughter of an Admiral.

"Uh-huh—sure you do," he said, his patronizing tone now causing the tiny hairs on the back of her neck to rise. He continued, "I won't expect you to be on duty as weapons officer until 0800 tomorrow, so get some rest. "Evening meal is at 1730, and it's customary for all officers not on duty to join our captain, Commander Naugle, in the wardroom for the first meal at sea. Uniform will be dress whites." He smiled again, pre-telegraphing another inappropriate remark. "We can talk more then, my cute little, freckled ensign."

Spurs cocked her head at Reeves. She wasn't sure what to make of this obnoxious man or the situation. It was hard to believe a US Navy officer of command rank, or any rank for that matter, would conduct himself in this manner in this litigious day and age. The first thing she was to do as an undercover investigator was to watch out for anyone who acted unusual or suspicious and not arouse suspicion herself. The XO had just become her first suspect in the case, but for what she wasn't sure.

"Please follow me, ma'am," the corporal said, breaking the brief spell.

Spurs nodded, looking over her shoulder, then turned back to Reeves, still astonished.

"May I be excused, sir?"

Reeves continued to toy with the compass, then checked his wristwatch. He brought his eyes up to meet Spur's and raised his eyebrows.

"Muster the crew, Botts," he said, still watching Spurs.

The young seaman went to the funnel-shaped boatswain's pipe atop the helm and took down a whistle hanging beside it. He raised it to his lips and sounded an extended, three-toned call and then announced, "Now here this. Muster the crew!"

The XO delayed his answer just long enough to create a bit more tension.

"Carry-on, miss," he said, his hand making more of a wave than a salute. "And you might avoid this part of the ship for the next hour and a half or so. It'll get mighty busy up here, and a little girl like you is liable to get hurt."

Spurs spun half around and followed the Marine onto the catwalk.

Sexual harassment, she thought, a definite case. *How could he possibly expect to get away with such behavior?* She wondered if he might not have been on the entertainment committee for the infamous "Tail Hook" convention.

If it weren't for the mission, she wouldn't put up with being in such a predicament or her new XO's conduct. She wished she could report him to Assistant Director Royse now, and make sure Reeves knew that Ensign Janelle B. Sperling did not take favorably to his chauvinistic remarks. In the least, he'd get a harsh reprimand, and possibly a little heat from the Judge Advocate General (JAG), but then, that would make her appear as a whiny leg and that she would not be. It would be better to tough it out until after the investigation. Finding out why the *Atchison's* crew had been disappearing one by one was the paramount issue now and she didn't have much time to do it in.

Again, as she walked away, she felt the watching, now even probing, eyes.

Chapter 7

NADER SLEPT HERE

SPURS OPENED THE simple wooden door to her new quarters and stepped in from the corridor. Her Marine escort reached through the doorway, dropped her sea bag inside and set her handbag next to it gently.

She took the doorknob, preparing to thank the Marine and close the door. She noticed there was no lock on the knob. *This is bullshit,* she thought. *Bullshit, bullshit, bullshit!*

Not only was the thought of being the only woman among 216 men on a small ship uncomfortable, as her father the Admiral would say, it made her "stick out like a turd in the punch bowl." Not something an undercover NCIS special agent should do.

Spurs wondered if she actually had a contact aboard as Director Burgess had said. Maybe that was incorrect, also. She prayed it wasn't. It may be several hours, even days before her fellow undercover operative made himself known to her. Until then, she couldn't be sure.

"I'll bring your linen, ma'am," the Marine said and

rendered a salute. Without waiting for a reply he did an about face and left.

The cabin was small as she expected but neat and with only the necessities in view. A curtained hatchway and a small interior door were on the opposite bulkhead, nothing pinned or taped on the door or wall. She'd expected the room to be like her ex-fiancée's bachelor apartment back in the world. *Playboy* pinups lining the bulkheads, dirty skivvies hanging from the door knob and saltine crackers jammed into an open peanut butter jar on the small, gray-metal desk across the room.

The young lieutenant's stateroom was clean and uncluttered because he was an officer aboard a United States Navy vessel—and, of course, he was gay. That explained it, she thought, never really knowing a homosexual before. She had nothing to base the assumption on except her father's unswaying opinion. According to the Admiral, gays were out-of-place in this world, freaks of nature. Their lifestyle threatened straights. They were known to coerce younger people into their sick world and were tenacious in forcing their unnatural sexuality on those who didn't care to participate. They'd be especially out of place in the US Navy. Homosexuals were to be avoided, and the only thing they could possibly be good for was decorating, hairdressing, fashion designing, and of course, be the *butt* of sick jokes.

Spurs saw that hers would be the top bunk. The bottom was tightly made as if waiting for a dime-bounce inspection. The thin top mattress was rolled up to one end exposing the webbing that supported it.

She gazed at the bedroll. That's where she was expected to sleep. She was thankful that Lieutenant Commander Reeves hadn't been serious about her bunking with a man. Thankful that she didn't have to sleep on top, a man on the bunk below—snoring, belching, passing gas. No, she thought, correcting herself again, he probably wouldn't do those things. He'd be more feminine and mannerly. He was gay.

She unrolled the mattress, remembering that this was now her bed, but it used to be someone else's.

Her hands trembled as they glided over it.

Not long ago it belonged to Ensign Charles Nader, 23, a young black man just beginning his exciting life at sea. Proud parents back home. Spurs had interviewed them only forty-eight hours ago. They'd been a loving mother and father that boasted of their boy-turned-Naval-officer as they shoved his Annapolis graduation picture under friends' and relatives' noses, forcing them to look at their young, handsome, full-of-life son. Now they were devastated.

Spurs shook her head.

Such a waste. He'd slept here. Dreamed here. Lived here.

Now he was dead, possibly murdered. The investigation conducted by the two NCIS agents overtly assigned to the fleet determined that it was a probable suicide. That was the official story, but there were still some unanswered questions. Why had he been out at two in the morning when he was to be on watch four hours later, at 0600? Why had he gone to the signal bridge, one of the highest points of the ship, and why without his uniform shirt? Why was cocaine found in his nostrils, but none absorbed into his blood system? Why was he found clutching an empty Beretta pistol?

Then, of course, there were the missing sailors— Petty Officer James McCracken, who fell overboard during rough seas, his body lost, Warrant Officer William Holt and Gunner's Mate Joel Tippin, who were officially considered absent without leave, never returning from all-night liberty at two different Mediterranean ports.

After investigating carefully, the two NCIS agents assigned to the fleet had reported back to Director Burgess that they found no good reason for them to be AWOL, only good ones for them to have returned as expected.

These could be terrible coincidences, but with all of the incidents occurring in the last ten days it looked very suspicious.

"Linen," a voice blurted from the doorway.

Lieutenant Darren North stepped in with what seemed to be a forced grin. His eyes still smiled, but now, with her knowing his sexual preference, they'd lost some of their luster.

"Corporal Sanders told me about the mix-up," North said. "I'm sorry about this, but it'll be straightened out soon. We'll be making some temporary accommodations for you until you're transferred. Just have to make do. I'll bunk with some of the other officers."

She gave a half grin. She could think of nothing to say to this man.

"Somebody really screwed up your orders. We'll be getting to the bottom of that, in double time," he said.

Spurs snorted a laugh. "I'll bet you will, sir."

North frowned as he laid her bedding on the bunk.

"Thank you, sir," she said, then covered her mouth and turned away. She felt like a giddy schoolgirl. She should control herself, but she felt stressed and humor was her preferred method of dealing with tense and awkward situations. It was normally better than anger, always better than tears.

"There's the head," North said, pointing to the interior door. "And there's the shower." He pointed to the small hatchway covered with a white plastic curtain. "I just got off duty, but you'd probably like to freshen up, so I'll wait to get my things. I'll just go see what the XO wants then catch up on the news in the wardroom."

Spurs glanced over her shoulder occasionally to North, still pressing her hand to her mouth.

"There's new soap in that drawer if you need some," North said, now pointing to the right side of the desk.

Spurs chuckled again. Remembering an old locker-room quip the boys made in high school, she wondered if it was soap-on-a-rope, so she wouldn't have to bend over if she dropped it.

North raised one eyebrow. "I'll give you thirty minutes." He left the compartment not bothering to close the door.

Spurs leaned on a metal wall locker next to the bunks and laughed to herself. Sexual harassment was a problem in nearly every work environment anymore, but at least she didn't have to worry about that man.

Her humor weakened—left. She stared at the louvers on the locker.

Yes, she did have to worry about him. He'd bunked with one of the dead men, Ensign Nader. He seemed suspicious to Henry Dubain. She might not have to worry about sexual harassment from this man, but Mister North could well be a murderer.

As she considered this new revelation, an uncomfortable sensation flushed through her. Her skin crawled. It was that watched feeling again.

She snapped her head toward the door and caught a glimpse of the spit-shined heels and the back of the tan uniform of a Marine. It wasn't the young corporal's. This man was much larger. She hesitated too long before hurrying to the doorway and looking out. The passageway was empty. She closed the door and rested against it.

Chapter 8

THE NOTE

BY 1630, SPURS had showered, changed, and, for the most part, was refreshed and ready to leave her quarters. She'd taken the time to put her things up neatly and felt fairly squared away. Mister North hadn't returned and she was glad. North seemed nice, but what little she knew about him caused her to question his sincerity, gay or not.

She thought of how awkward she felt and how little privacy she would enjoy on the ship. One thing was certain. Without locks on the doors she would be too leery of who might be lurking outside to take a long, leisurely shower. Every shower would be only the essential, get-it-wet-and-get-out-type Navy showers.

Spurs stood in front of the half-length mirror mounted on the door to the head and straightened her fresh white jacket and skirt. She reached to the bottom bunk to get her cap where she'd left it before her shower. After lifting it into place she fussed with her hair, angling her face from side to side at the mirror. She smiled, thinking how well the Navy's dress-white uniform complimented her appearance. Still, but unjustly so according to friends and family, she wished she'd inherited her mother's ample bosom and her father's flat hinder, instead of her Mom's ample rear and the Admiral's flat chest. It was a curse to be a perfectionist. She sighed. But then, giving herself a wink, she did a snappy about-face and started toward the door to the passageway.

As she passed by, something caught her attention on the bunk where she'd recovered her cap. A folded piece of paper. It must have been placed underneath the cap while she showered. A chill tickled her spine as she considered it.

She leaned down, pausing as she gazed at the paper. Then, reaching for it, she glimpsed back to the closed door and around the stateroom before actually seizing it.

Carefully unfolding the paper as she stood up, she wondered who could've placed it there. It could've been any number of people; Lieutenant Commander Reeves, Mister North, the mysterious Marine, or even someone she was yet to meet.

She turned toward the door watchfully and discovered that what she'd found was a hand-written note. Could it be from her contact, a witness to the "suicide" or someone who knew about the disappearances?

It simply read; "I Saw What Happened. Tonight—01:00, Signal Bridge. Tell No One."

Chapter 9

PAYBACK

May 1, 1200 EDT
Naval Criminal Investigative Service,
US Navy Shipyards, Washington, DC

NCIS DIRECTOR HARLEY Burgess leaned back in his leather swivel chair and rubbed his burning eyes as the intercom buzzed on his desk. Already, it had been a long morning.

He pressed the speak button. "What is it, Barbara?"

"Assistant Director Paul Royse is here to see you, sir," the Director's secretary said from the outer office.

He rolled his eyes and touched the speak button again, hesitantly. He knew why Royse was there. Special Agent Janelle Sperling was not only one of his subordinates, she was his niece. Royse and his paraplegic wife had just returned from two weeks vacation touring the Middle East. It had taken Royse less than four hours back on the job to discover his young investigator niece, whom, naturally, he'd put under his wing, had been assigned her first undercover operation while he'd been away.

Burgess cleared his throat.

"Send him in, Barbara," he said. He swung his chair around and looked out the window with his back to the room.

After a few seconds, he heard the door open and Royse walk in. He thought about Royse—an ex-Navy jet jock, washed out because of an inner ear problem. Royse had spent the next seventeen years of his life in the FBI before coming to NCIS four years ago.

In a way Burgess felt sorry for him, his wife being a paraplegic and all. Except for an occasional moment of weakness at a local pub, Royse spent every waking hour that he was away from work by her side. Over the past couple of years he'd been visiting with doctors at Bethesda and a number of other major hospitals over the country and he'd been saving his pennies. He'd mortgaged his house, sold his ranch in Oklahoma and was looking into loans, trying to come up with enough money to pay for a new experimental surgery to make his wife whole again. Being experimental, the surgery wouldn't be paid for by the Navy and the estimated three to four million dollar price tag was much too high for even a career Senior Executive Service appointee. The trip to the holy, Christian shrines of the Middle East had been extravagant, but maybe Royse had been hoping for some sort of divine healing for her.

Burgess thought of Royse's weakness. It may be a tool to this Janelle Sperling thing. He'd allow the Deputy Assistant Director to speak first but maintain control. He'd counter any objections Royse would voice.

"Director Burgess, what in the hell is going on?" Royse blurted, his voice quavering with anger.

"Welcome back, Paul," Burgess said, unfazed, still not turning to him. "How was Jerusalem?"

"Burgess, I asked what the. . . ."

The Director's voice came calm but firm. "You'd better sit down and relax, Paul. Unless you want some more time off. A lot of time off."

A few seconds passed before Burgess heard the leather upholstery scrunch in the chair to the left of his desk. He swiveled around and looked at the lanky, graying redheaded man, remembering that Royse seldom looked anyone in the eyes.

"I'm not real sure of what you're so excited about," he said. "But if you explain it to me respectfully, I'll listen and try to answer any questions you might have." He grinned.

Royse glared back, then dropped his eyes to the front of the desk and stared blankly as he spoke. "Why did you assign Janelle Sperling to the Chameleon case? Shit sir, we're talking international terrorism, possibly treason."

"I didn't."

Royse's eyes snapped up to meet Burgess'. "She's on the *Atchison*, isn't she?"

"Yes, I believe she is," Burgess said and pulled a pair of reading glasses from their sheath on the desk and put them on. He reached for a stack of folders on his right.

"Good lord, sir, this is her first mission. Hell, she's only been out of training for three weeks."

"I realize that, Paul," he said thumbing the edge of the stack as if searching for a copy of Sperling's orders. He then lifted the top stapled sheets from the pile, placed them in front of him and pretended to scan them. "She isn't involved in the Chameleon investigation. Remember, I recruited a crewmember on board to handle that case. It's something completely unrelated. A young crewman committed suicide and his parents are raising a stink. She's just there for looks. It's a pure gravy assignment. Nothing dangerous."

"If that's all true, why does personnel say her records have been altered to show that Ensign J. B. Sperling is a male? She's using her real name instead of an assumed one. It looks like a set up. She couldn't have been assigned to the *Atchison* alone as a female—there aren't any other women on board. Now, she's an obvious target. Anyone with any sense is going to be leery of her, that she's NCIS, coming on board right after two deaths and two AWOLs. . . ." Paul Royse paused, appearing deep in thought. He frowned as though having a revelation. "Jesus, she's a decoy, isn't she?"

Burgess fought to hold his composure. "Good God, no, she's not a decoy. If you think that I would intentionally put one of our people in jeopardy to solve a case, you are very sadly mistaken. I don't think I like your implications and as you know, I am not one to take a personal attack well. I assigned her on this case because of her qualifications. She seemed to fit perfectly. She's a Navy Reservist trained as a weapons officer and that was the position that the *Atchison* needed. We can't pussyfoot around with her just because she's your niece, you know that."

Royse seemed to ignore Burgess, and verbalized his own thoughts, "I've got to send her a message, let her know the danger."

"You'll do no such thing, Royse," Burgess said. "You know better than that. You would be risking her life along with the other investigator's. Besides, our other agent will inform her of the situation. Probably already has. Now, you'd better relax." Burgess changed the subject. He hated what he was about to do but felt he had no choice. "How's Katherine?" he asked.

Royse glared at the Director.

Surprised by Royse's unusual, intense eye contact, Burgess didn't wait for a reply. "Must be tough on the poor woman, being a paraplegic but still having all her mental faculties. Wondering how her husband can remain faithful. Wondering if he has. Hoping he has." He stared back at Royse's glaring eyes. "It must be even harder on you, Paul. Having to help her with her bedpan. Watch her wither away. All the while trying to keep your hands out of the cookie jar."

Royse's eyes narrowed as he listened. Burgess drove the point home.

"I hear there's a new bar maid over at the Globe and Anchor, Paul. I hear you've got cookie crumbs on your fingers. It'd be a shame if Katherine found out."

The intercom buzzed again breaking the stare down between the two men, and Burgess' secretary spoke, "I'm sorry to disturb you, sir, but there's an Admiral Sperling on the phone. He says it's urgent."

Burgess raised his eyebrows then glared at Royse. "You called Sperling?"

Royse turned away, his jaw set, ruddy face reddening even more, ready to explode.

Burgess looked to the intercom speaker. Retired Admiral Oliver T. Sperling was Royse's stepbrother. Sperling's father had married Royse's mother when Paul Royse was five.

"Thanks, Barbara," he said, holding his anger at bay, then punched the *line one* button on the speakerphone. "Oliver. Long time. How's Oklahoma?"

"Don't give me any of your bullshit. You know why I'm calling!" Admiral Sperling's voice boomed, loud and raspy.

"I think maybe I do. Paul Royse is in my office now and we were just discussing the misunderstanding."

"Misunderstanding my ass! I don't care to hear your excuses or explanations. You just get my daughter off of this Chameleon investigation. You know better than to pull this kind of shit. If you don't have her mainside in forty-eight hours, you'll wish you'd retired while you still had some dignity."

His threat was enough to light Burgess' fuse. He fired back. "Now you listen here, you pompous bastard. You're not going to tell me what to do. You may still have some influence, but you're retired, remember. Cool your engines. First of all, your daughter is not assigned to the Chameleon investigation. Hers is a simple suicide, only for show, just to get her feet wet. It's only coincidence she's on the same ship. The other investigation is wrapping up and she is in no danger."

"Don't try to whitewash this, Burgess. How then do you explain her being the only woman assigned to the ship? You're setting her up."

Burgess regained his composure. He'd expected both confrontations but not at the same time. "It was a simple mistake. Someone in personnel shuffled the orders and the other twenty-three women were put aboard the *Ticonderoga*. She should have her work done and be off the ship in their next port."

Burgess noticed Royse roll his eyes.

The Admiral said, "You'd better be right Burgess. I'm not beyond coming up there and ringing your neck, personally."

"I'll pretend you didn't threaten me, Admiral Sperling. Now, is there anything else I can do for you today?"

"Don't screw up, Burgess. If my daughter gets so much as a broken nail from this I'll hunt you down and rip your fuckin' head off!"

"Goodbye, Admiral."

Burgess disconnected. He smiled at Royse and it seemed to shove him out of his seat. Burgess watched the tall, lean man's back as he walked to the door and opened it.

"Give my regards to Katherine," Burgess said like scooping saccharine.

Royse looked over his right shoulder as he passed through the doorway. He narrowed his eyes and clenched his jaw.

"I'll be second in line if anything happens to Janelle Sperling," he said and closed the door behind him.

So far, so good, Burgess thought. But he wished he hadn't been forced to such extreme measures. Agent Sperling was an unwitting game piece in a very deadly game.

Chapter 10

GANGWAY!

1635
USS *Atchison*

SPURS WAS AN obvious surprise to the crew. As she made her way through the maze of passageways to the mailroom, every face she met seemed astonished, then insincerely polite after they snapped to. At this point she wished the XO could have piped over a preparatory, "Now hear this; there is a woman aboard. I repeat, we have a female on this ship. Zip your flies and pick up your dirty socks!"

Since writing one of those having-a-good-time-wish-you-were-here-type notes on the back of a post card in Rota, she figured she'd better mail it. There didn't seem to be a whole lot else to say to her father, the Admiral. They didn't talk that much anymore. Not knowing exactly why, she suspected the Admiral's part in the silence had something to do with her being a woman wishing to do a *man's job*.

She recalled the time she'd called him from her baccalaureate, all happy and smiles, excited about graduating from OU with honors, eager to tell him of her plans to join the Navy and be an officer aboard an aircraft carrier or destroyer. He'd reduced her to tears with one word. *Ludicrous*. He'd told her it was "ludicrous" to even *think* there could be a good reason for women to serve aboard military ships, let alone warships. He and his beliefs were *so* "old Navy." But she had respected his opinions and had adopted most of them when she was younger and more impressionable. Now at twenty-five, she had discovered a few views of her own. But for the most part she *was* her father's daughter. She did not go along, however, with such an archaic attitude toward women. The Admiral resented that and she resented his resentment. Someday, maybe they could be friends again.

According to the first gaping mouth she'd run into after leaving her stateroom, the mailroom was one deck below and six compartments forward. At least she thought that was what the young seaman vacuuming the carpeted halls of officer's country had said. He'd just kind of mumbled and stood to the side leaving her enough room to steer a landing craft through.

She went down one ladder and then forward, stepping through two of the small, oval hatchways.

The cold gray belly of this unfamiliar ship was a lonely, hard place. She could easily become claustrophobic. She felt abandoned and betrayed as she proceeded, and the loneliness ached in her heart.

A detail of five sailors met her as they moved briskly in the opposite direction. A petty officer first class was in the lead. They had brought with them a rush of air smelling of floor cleaning disinfectant. The old warship, although rusting and obsolete on the outside, was kept spotless inside.

The detail stepped to the side courteously, the petty officer in the lead saying, "Good afternoon, ma'am."

"Good afternoon, sailors," she answered as they hurried past.

Then she heard their whispered remarks.

"What's she doing aboard?" "Oh God, not us, too!" "They're like a cancer. What the hell do they want?"

The last comments came from the petty officer and it was louder than the others. "Get used to it boys," he said. "There're more coming aboard next month and there's nothing we can do to stop it. We're stuck with them until they prove to the brass that they can't hack it."

Soon three more sailors passed carrying mops, buckets and other cleaning supplies. Only the last man that scooted by had taken the time to recover from his surprise and ask respectfully to pass with, "By your leave, ma'am?" They all seemed to be in a very big rush. She sensed Commander Naugle ran a very tight ship.

A commotion and voices came from the forward compartments. Spurs frowned as she paused in the third hatchway, trying to make out what was happening. She heard running. More voices. Some close, sounding frantic. These weren't the sounds of men stepping quickly to get a job done like the others. These men were escaping like gazelle from a pride of lions. A gaggle erupted several compartments ahead, words unclear. What was it? It was hard to make out over the din of footsteps and blurted exclamations.

"Gangway!"

This time she heard the call as the noise came closer. Suddenly, bodies appeared shoving through the small hatch two at a time from the next compartment. Half a dozen young enlisted Marines stampeded toward her, their faces fearful, showing some surprise as they saw Spurs but seeming to care much less than the previous sailors had. These young men were running from something they obviously felt threatened them. The six fled in a pack from the hatch and slowed little as they approached her.

"He's right behind us!" one said. "God, I don't want any more PT," said another. "Hell, I don't want to get stomped!" said a third. "You see the shiner on Peterson?"

"By your leave, ma'am?" they asked in unison to pass. But not waiting even for an instant for her answer, they forced their way past.

Spurs had to step aside or be trampled. But she said nothing, more curious than annoyed by their lack of manners and military courtesy.

More frightened voices came from forward compartments, nearing her.

"Gangway! Make a hole! Gangway!" they called out.

Spurs proceeded through the passage, taking guarded steps. The chaos of scattering men seemed unending.

Another group of three jarheads met her at the fourth hatch, and she had to swing back to avoid harm as this bunch sprinted past.

These young Marines seemed frightened half to death by someone—or something.

Spurs' shuddered with a sudden chill as she also considered retreat. Whoever—whatever was making its way toward her must be a terrible thing. But what kind of incredible occurrence was this? She hadn't seen anything in comparison since the morning her detail had gotten their Marine drill instructors in Officer's Candidate School.

"Make a hole! Move it! Look out! Gangway!" came the frantic shouts now only a couple of compartments away.

Spurs stopped at the sixth hatch in view of the mail room service window. The passageway had become still, like the eye of a hurricane. Nothing moved. The corridor seemed empty, lifeless.

As she grabbed the right side of the hatchway with her right hand, the postcard slipped from between her fingers and fell back to her side of the opening.

She bent to pick it up and suddenly found herself staring at what had to be at least a size fifteen, spit-shined shoe inches from her face.

The sight jarred her. She rose slowly, not knowing what to expect, her face coming up cautiously, nearly touching the leg in front of her.

This was the terrible thing from which the crew had just fled. Huge calves behind perfectly pressed, tan slacks. Enormous thighs. Clenched fists. Trim, but still remarkably large waist, angling up to a massive chest. Thick, bulging biceps.

Spurs stood erect, eyes level and looked at the giant's sternum. Inches away from her nose was a pair of gold jump wings and a silver SCUBA badge. Her sight inched to a name tag reading Capt. R. D. Chardoff. Below the short, wide neck hung a pair of silver Marine-captain's bars, then a square, jutting jaw. His glaring eyes, gray and unflinching, seemed to burn into hers. His chiseled face, pocked with acne scars, was topped with the short stubble of a leatherneck's high and tight haircut.

He stood, one leg on each side of the hatchway, head bent forward, his predator eyes inspecting the prey before him.

Spurs gaped, looking into the huge man's menacing, hypnotic, gray eyes. Her lips tried to form words.

The mammoth Marine's mouth spread into a huge toothy smile. His harsh breath seeped out smelling like hot crankcase oil, making her eyes water.

"Buh . . . ," she swallowed, blinked her eyes, tried again, the request finally coming out. "By—your leave, sir?"

She waited for him to speak to prove he was human,

but then found herself hoping he wouldn't for fear of wetting herself.

He scrutinized her like the big bad wolf examining Little Red Riding Hood. He leaned back against the side of the small hatch, moving no more than an inch, but indicating she was to pass. His enormous body still blocked free and unmolested passage.

Spurs felt no choice. She stepped right leg first through the hatchway, brought her body to his, her breasts rubbing against the Marine captain's steel plate belly. She felt his lungs taking in and expelling air and even the pulse from the pump under his tremendous chest that must also have been huge to deliver nourishment over such a colossal area. The iron ridge around the hatch opening scraped painfully against her spine, but she forced her way past, still looking up into the man's intense, gray eyes.

Finally, she popped through and stumbled forward, then looked over her shoulder to see the monster still staring malevolently, unmoved. A wave of fear finally hit Spurs' body and she trembled, staggering to the mailroom window. Reaching the small counter extending from the opening, she leaned against it and felt a vibration come over the ship as if it were trembling also, and a resonating hum filled the passageway. The ship's engines had come to life. They would shove off soon.

She looked back to the hatchway. It was empty.

Chapter 11

SURPRISE PUNCH

IT TOOK SPURS several minutes to stop shaking. The meeting with Captain Chardoff had left her feeling like a rabbit face-licked by a coyote. He was so huge. She easily understood why his men were running if the discipline he dished out was half as malevolent as his looks. But why should she fear him? After all he was a fellow officer. Although a superior one, he still lived by the same code of honor and integrity as she did. Even though they belonged to different branches under the Department of the Navy, they were on the same side.

She had forgotten all of that while squeezing past him in the hatchway.

Spurs dropped the post card to her father through the mail slot in the door instead of bothering the busy yeoman sorting mail with his back to her. She didn't wish to surprise any more crewmembers than necessary. It'd be nice when the scuttlebutt got around and everyone on the ship knew she was aboard. Maybe then she'd feel more comfortable, more a member of the team instead of an outsider—instead of a turd in the punch bowl. After that her next task would be to convince the crew that she was as much of an asset as any male crew member and being female did not make her a liability.

With twenty minutes left before shoving off, Spurs decided to take a brief tour of the Combat Information Center, which was to be her duty station. After the climb of five stairways, she introduced herself to the four astonished sailors manning the radar and weapons systems. They were busy readying the units to get underway. Petty Officer Second Class Manny Jabrowski was in charge as he had been since Ensign Nader's death.

Spurs took the time to look over each of the fire controls. The enormous destructive capabilities of even this, one of the smallest active ships in the US Navy, still amazed her.

She gazed over the sailors' shoulders at the one red sonar screen and five green radar and target designator screens. Several small, green computer screens lined the wall. Numerous keyboards, some with lighted green and red buttons, were within easy reach of the four men on watch at their stations. In seconds, with the flick of a few switches, they could arm and fire eight ASROC antisub rockets, launch six 12.75-inch torpedoes or shoot a pair of three-inch antiaircraft guns. She hoped she could remember her weapons training well enough to bluff an adequate job while conducting the investigation. She was sure she'd have to rely on Jabrowski's hands-on experience.

As she walked to the hatchway to go to chow, she noticed an unmanned station, covered with a white drop cloth. She paused in front of it. "What's this?" she asked Jabrowski.

He glanced at her, looking almost cross-eyed over his large nose and answered, "The new weapons system, ma'am."

She raised the cloth and immediately recognized the state of the art technology underneath. "This is a cruise missile fire control center. This ship doesn't have cruise missiles."

Jabrowski looked back at his computer screen. "Evidently the ensign hasn't had time to see what's covered up just forward of the fantail. Tomahawks, ma'am. Four of those bad babies. We've had the system installed for a couple of months, but we haven't tested it yet. We're supposed to have a team of specialists coming aboard soon to get us on line so we can fire them."

"But why? I mean, why aboard the *Atchison* instead of one of the guided missile frigates."

"The skipper talked them into it—Commander Reeves helped with his weapons background," he said proudly. "And it took a lot of talking, too."

"I still don't understand?"

"Well, the way I got it figured, the captain kind of got the Secretary of the Navy in a sort of Catch-22. See, they were planning on scuttling this old girl after this cruise. She ain't much good to the new high-tech Navy. Everything's faster, has more firepower. The Navy wants to build all these new ships that can carry new weapons, Tomahawks and such. But they don't have the money like they used to. Anyway, the old man told his plan to a congressman friend of his who serves on the Armed Forces Sub Committee. With all the military spending cuts Congress wants to make, it didn't take long for the Secretary of the Navy to order Admiral Pierce, our fleet admiral, to try us out with cruise missiles. If we can handle it, they won't scuttle her. Instead they'll retrofit her with new, faster engines and new equipment, modify her hull a bit, and not have to build an entirely new ship. Then if it works for us, there's a whole slug of small frigates and escort ships that can be converted, too. It'll save the Navy a ton of money. The old man's pretty aware, don't you think ma'am?"

Spurs listened, still digesting her discovery. "Yeah, pretty aware," she repeated.

"It's funny though, Ensign Sperling, how one hand doesn't know what the other's doing."

"How's that?"

"Well, I mean, with you coming aboard and all. I'm sure that it wasn't in the plans to initiate a new weapons system the same time that we're receiving twenty-four inexperienced WINS. That's a perfect example of how things get *SNAFUed*. Personnel not knowing what Operations is doing. Then I heard about the mix up with your orders, saying you were a male officer and all and putting you aboard by yourself at a port of call ahead of the rest. And now, I hear the other women aren't coming aboard and they're talking about dumping you at the next port. It's typical. And besides that, we have these crewmembers disappearing and getting killed, you know. I'm surprised NCIS dropped their investigation so soon—I mean, without putting someone aboard undercover."

Spurs curled one corner of her mouth weakly. "Yeah."

Jabrowski frowned, his lips parted. He looked around at the other three crewmen at their stations and they glanced back, then all looked to Spurs.

Oh, great! she thought. If these guys already suspected she was undercover, how long would it take for the murderer?

Not wishing the conversation to go further, she stepped through the hatchway as nonchalantly as possible and found the *Atchison's* topside alive. The bridge piped orders, loud and tinny, from the speaker overhead, "Single up all lines." Crewmembers fore and aft stepped briskly as they pulled huge ropes from four giant steel turnbuckles along the port side of the ship.

She descended the staircase-like ladder from the signal deck and saw Commander Reeves in his traditional white dress uniform standing forward, his back to her, on the catwalk next to the bridge's port hatchway. He surveyed the commotion, his eyes scanning continuously from the dock to a small tug. The tiny boat blasted steam-powered warnings, while spewing thick, oil-black smoke from its wide stack. It trudged further out into the harbor, chugging, pushing through the water as if it were all it could do to shove forward another five meters. Immediately, the pungent diesel's exhaust overwhelmed the fresh salt air as the world around Spurs seemed to be put into motion. It was as if the ship were being released from the arms of its *au pair*, reaching for its mother as they broke away from the pier and headed out toward a wide expanse of ocean.

Spurs remembered Commander Reeves' warning and heeded it, not wishing to get in the way. She turned aft and walked toward the fantail, but stopped and leaned on the lifeline facing the stern when she saw a large canvas covered cube amidships near the helo flight deck. Some of the most frightening weapons the world had known waited underneath like sleeping cobras. Tomahawk cruise missiles.

She stared at it for a moment, wondering if it could possibly have anything to do with Ensign Nader's death. To this point, she'd thought it was more likely drug related, that maybe he'd stumbled into the middle of a drug deal and was snuffed to keep him from talking. This was a new angle that needed to be investigated. And there was still the possibility of his death being suicide.

She thought about what Jabrowski had said—about crewmembers disappearing and getting killed. He'd said "getting killed" not committing suicide, or dying. It could be that he perceived a different meaning of "getting killed" than she did. Or, it could be that he knew more than he was saying. Leave no stone unturned, that's what Deputy Assistant Director Paul Royse had taught her. There seemed to be a number of boulder-sized stones.

Chapter 12

COLD NORTH

SPURS FELT THE lifeline she leaned against swing slightly as though someone else had pushed against it. She looked to her right and saw Lieutenant Darren North.

"Tomahawks," he said looking at the covered cube. Even in his khakis, North looked like he'd just stepped out of a recruiting poster; handsome, clean, perfectly pressed.

"Yessir," she said, turning away to face aft. "I've been told."

"You can call me Darren when we're not on watch and the enlisted men aren't around."

"No thank you, sir."

"It's no special treatment, Spurs. You're out of training. You're in the real Navy now."

She knew this wasn't some kind of move the lieutenant was making on her. It was customary for the officers of a ship, excluding the captain, to call each other by their first names. Besides, he couldn't be coming on to her—with his sexual preference there could be no other motive.

"I'd still rather not, sir."

"You don't like me, do you Ensign?" North said, still gazing to the stern.

He'd taken her by surprise. She didn't know how to respond. Shifting her eyes around the ship, she looked for an answer. The huge dock they'd just embarked from now appeared as only a thin line that separated the water from the shipyard structures along Rota's seafront. Still the feeling of motion had not come over her, as if the rest of the world were moving, leaving her, abandoning her. North's words rang true. She was in the *real* Navy now.

Not finding the appropriate answers around her, she began looking for an escape. It may not be good to tell the ship's lieutenant her true feelings. She'd never really known a gay before. She relied on her father's brash opinion of them.

"Ensign Sperling, we can be friends or we can be enemies," he said. "But I asked you a question, and I expect an answer."

The ship seemed to bolt and she gripped the lifeline. Water off the fantail turned into a turbulent foaming stream. The little tug fell back on the starboard side and started a turn back to the shipyards, making its way past other moorings.

Sea spray misted the back of Spurs' neck and for the first time she heard the calling of the gulls that saturated the sky as the noisy tug departed. Drawing in a deep breath, she considered her answer. The sea air was even thicker now, more humid than along the pier. Laced within it was the briny scent of life, as if it were the breath of something enormous and living.

She heard a hatch *clank* closed and saw the black

Marine corporal she'd met earlier coming up from the ladder one deck below. She was thankful for the distraction.

As he stepped up he smiled and saluted. "Sir, ma'am."

Spurs and the lieutenant saluted back.

"Afternoon, Corporal Sanders," North answered.

Sanders walked past, going forward toward the bridge.

They were alone again. Spurs felt cornered against the lifeline, nothing around her but cold steel. How'd she get into this? She knew of only one way to deal with it. Honesty.

"I'm sorry, sir. It's just that I've never been around a gay man before. I don't understand or approve of the lifestyle and I don't feel comfortable around you."

North's face tightened. He watched over his shoulder as Sanders stepped into a hatchway. The ship rocked lightly as the world full of moored ships drifted away and became gradually smaller.

"Who told you that I was gay?"

"Commander Reeves, sir," Spurs answered. She felt a sudden urge to expound and quote the commander. "He said that you were queerer than a three-winged sea bat."

North puffed. The side of his mouth curled. "Lieutenant Commander Reeves and I don't exactly see eye to eye, Ensign. I think you'll discover that soon enough."

He turned to her and she felt inclined to look to him. He continued, "Besides, if you can't understand, how can you approve or disapprove?"

Spurs straightened and looked away without an answer.

"You will ensure that your personal opinions of me and gays will not impede your performance or effectiveness to do your duty on this ship."

"Aye-aye, sir."

"Off the subject, you should feel a little more comfortable. I moved into the stateroom across the passageway. You have your own private quarters now."

She glanced over her shoulder at him.

He turned away but then looked back and said, "By the way, you'd better hold onto your bunk tonight. Looks like we'll be steaming into one hell of a storm."

Lieutenant North paused and seemed to study her. Over his shoulder she could see a wall of dark clouds hugging the horizon. An occasional flash of lightning muted by the distance highlighted them.

North smiled for a moment then shook his head before heading toward the bridge.

It suddenly occurred to her—when he'd greeted her, he'd called her Spurs.

Chapter 13

THE LAST SUPPER

SPURS LEANED FORWARD on the lifeline, looking toward the hinder of the ship and thought of the possible suspects she had for any wrongdoing—murder. She'd gleaned little information from the summarizing print-outs of each of the crew's personal records given to her by Director Burgess. She'd studied them well on the long trip from DC to Rota.

North was on her suspect list, even without good reason. His PR file was clean. She tried to convince herself that her suspicion of him wasn't because he was gay. For now, the smart-ass XO was second for being such an asshole to her. His record was also clean. The huge Marine, Captain Chardoff, was third because of his size and malevolent looks—and he had a few blemishes besides the ones pockmarking his face, including assault on a fellow officer for which he had been busted down from the rank of Major.

That was everybody. Just about every officer she'd actually met, so far. Three suspects in who knows what for being gay, chauvinistic or ugly. It sounded like an old spaghetti western—*The Gay, the Chauvinistic and the Ugly*. But to suspect an officer—they were the guys in the white hats—the good guys. The *usual suspects* should come from the enlisted men. It would be rare that US Navy officers would take part in any kind of conspiracy, illicit drugs, murder.

It'll just take time, she thought. She had to be patient. The puzzle pieces were sure to fall into place after she'd been on the ship a few days. This investigation could even take weeks. It would be three months before this float would be over and the fleet was due back stateside. And they were set to transfer her off of the ship at the next port, a couple of days away. She'd have to somehow convince them to keep her aboard to be sure she'd have time. Surely she could crack this case within a week or two. If she lived that long.

She thought of her contact aboard ship. Had she met him already? Director Burgess said that her undercover companion would make himself known to her as soon as he could do so safely and without causing suspicion that might jeopardize the investigation. She hoped he would do so soon.

The loneliness she'd felt earlier now gave way to the feeling of being outnumbered, causing her to study everyone she passed in the corridors and on the catwalks, wondering not only if they might be involved in Nader's death and the disappearances but also which one might be her contact.

At 1740 Spurs sat at the large table in the wardroom along with six of the other eight officers on board. They waited for Commander Miles Naugle, the ship's skipper. By the talk at the table in the room that doubled for the officer's mess, this was not unusual—"past practice," one of them called it.

The *Atchison's* rocking had been expected, but expecting it did little to ward off the twinge of nausea in her stomach. The sea hadn't been rough—far from it, but still she rocked. Spurs found herself watching the clear water glass in front of her, the liquid inside tipping an inch from one side to the other about every five seconds. Soon she realized that visualizing the rocking magnified the affect to her gut and she looked away.

She'd been introduced to all of the other officers except the remaining absentee, who was now serving a watch as Officer of the Day. That man she had not cared to see again and was glad that he was not in the wardroom. It was the Marine, Captain Chardoff.

The officer's reactions were as expected. Insecure thoughts behind insincere greetings and smiles. Bright, cheery eyes that questioned her face then seemed to become unbearably heavy and drop to her chest, occasionally bobbing back up, but mostly attending to her breasts. The officers were not admiring her military medals. This was especially true of the younger men. She wondered what they would do if she had a large bosom—probably drool uncontrollably down their uniforms. It was some sort of syndrome experienced mostly by men at sea and in bars. She was glad the syndrome hadn't come over her yet. What would these jerks think if suddenly her eyes became transfixed on their crotches?

Other than their wandering gazes, all of the officers seemed to give the young ensign every bit of the courtesy and respect that a fellow officer should receive, but there was an awkwardness at the table. Spurs couldn't put her finger on it for sure but it seemed the feeling was a cross between "mind your manners around mother," *Guess Who's Coming to Dinner*, and "who brought the bitch to the stag party?"

But she was nicely surprised that Lieutenant Commander Reeves had lightened up some. He sat to the left of the empty chair at the far end of the table waiting for Commander Naugle. He glanced to her occasionally with a pleasant smile and spoke a kind word or two like, "how's your quarters?" and "if there's anything you need, just ask." His concern seemed somehow genuine, so she answered him, "Fine" and "Okay." Maybe she should try to get along with him since he was apparently trying to get along with her. It certainly wouldn't hurt the investigation. But it hadn't changed her opinion of the man. He was still an asshole. Just that now, he was a two-faced asshole.

Next to Reeves sat Lieutenant Mike Daniels, the African-American operations officer, a tall, muscular man. From his PR file, Spurs remembered he'd done poorly on his last two years of fitness reports seemingly contributed to some domestic problems at home. Right of him was her old "bunky," Darren North. Lieutenant Junior Grade Brad Goodman, the chubby faced engineer wearing an Annapolis ring, sat across from her. He'd been AWOL twice, keeping him from promotion to full Lieutenant.

On Spurs' side of the table was the empty seat of Captain Chardoff next to Commander Naugle's. Then, Lieutenant Tell Jolly, with skin the color of fresh licorice. The small, sinewy ship's medical officer seemed to wear an eternal smile. He had been charged with dereliction of duty because one of his patients, having stepped on a nail, had to eventually have his leg amputated due to a rapidly spreading infection. The charges didn't stick. Next to Spurs was quiet, droopy eyed, Ensign Benjamin Ingrassias, the *Atchison's* supply officer. On his record was a drug bust that nearly got him discharged.

The chatter at the table grew to an incomprehensible clamor between the men as they grew impatient. Spurs said little, and only when asked a question.

After more than ten minutes of waiting, one of the orderlies that had served them water and tea returned and stepped to Lieutenant Commander Reeves' side, leaned to the officer's ear, and then said something in a whisper that cleared a smile from the commander's face. Reeves rose from his seat and followed the attendant out of the room.

"Oh God, not again," said Lieutenant Junior Grade Goodman from across the table.

Beside Spurs, Ensign Ingrassias said, "What's this make, five?"

"Six," said Lieutenant Daniels.

Spurs turned to the ensign on her right and asked, "What's going on?"

"It's the skipper," Goodman said before Ingrassias could speak. "He's drunk again. This is it. If no one else has the balls to report him, I will."

Lieutenant North had been quiet since sitting at the table. Spurs could tell that he felt as much of an outcast as she. He said, "You'd better not let Reeves hear you say that."

"Too late," came a loud voice from the hatchway. Reeves stepped in.

All heads bowed. He hadn't had much time to do anything but turn around in the passageway, perhaps at most, peek in on the captain.

Reeves paused a moment then said, "Gentlemen—and Miss Sperling, the captain has a migraine and regrets that he will be unable to join us for the evening meal." He walked toward his seat. "He has asked that we forgive him and enjoy our supper." He looked to Doc Jolly as he pulled his chair from the table, motioning the attendants to begin serving. "Doc, please attend to the skipper after our meal." He sat and scooted to the table. "Mister Goodman, you'll relieve the watch."

Goodman looked up from his plate as a large rib eye was served.

"Now!" said Reeves, watching his own plate being filled.

"But sir," Goodman said, "I have the midnight watch."

"And the present watch, Mister Goodman. And if you say another word, you'll be watching sunrise."

Spurs expected a tantrum, a fit of some kind. But there was none. Mister Goodman obviously knew better. He stood from his seat, pulling his eyes away from the anxiously awaited meal, laid his cloth napkin beside it and left the table quietly.

The meal passed uneventful and somber. Spurs tasted her steak, had a spoon of green beans, half a glass of Seven Up, and two dinner rolls without butter, hoping the bread would give her the necessary sustenance without irritating her churning stomach. She was relieved when the officers were excused, and she was able to slip away. Half expecting her strict new XO to make her finish her plate, she covered it with her napkin and left through the hatchway before any of the others.

Chapter 14

LOOSE LIPS

AT SUNSET, SPURS stood alone on the signal deck and watched as a tinny, prerecorded version of taps sounded *colors* and the sun dipped into the darkening sea. The sway of the ship was more than she had experienced before, even on the short trip aboard the *Spartanburg County* steaming to Nassau. She had felt queasy then and was told to just deal with it. She now held tight to the bulwarks from where it was said that Ensign Nader had jumped—and dealt with it, the motion shifting her weight from one leg to the other. The event she now experienced seemed to help her forget the twinge of seasickness in her abdomen.

She watched as the *Atchison's* stem dipped into the turquoise sea before her and cut through, laying it open in white slices that curled away from the bow and sizzled past the hull. The frigate's screws churned in a rhythmic hum as she gazed past the bow to the last quenching gold and white rays of sunlight. She smiled, the sea-freshened air in her hair, light ocean spray on her face. This was the ecstasy her father had spoken about—the solitude, the wonderful emptiness that filled the soul, stretching it to the point of bursting with an awe-inspiring realization of insignificance in the enormity of the world.

On the horizon off the starboard side, the blackening silhouette of the *Enterprise* was pinned against a dimming, sapphire mantle. It was the only other ship within sight. Even more than a mile and a half away, she posed magnificently.

Spurs noted the ship had begun a slow turn to port and then heard footfalls on the left side ladder disrupting her peace. She turned to see Commander Reeves step up, seeming surprised to run into her.

"Well," he said, "good evening, Ensign."

"Good evening, sir," she returned and began walking—staggering toward the starboard steps. The ship's course change had caused the vessel to rock more, making movement increasingly difficult. The angling deck would not cooperate, not take her determined steps seriously. It was as close to feeling drunk as she had felt without drinking.

"No," he insisted, "Please stay. Don't let me run you off. Besides, we need to talk."

Spurs didn't wish to talk. She couldn't imagine what he would have to say that might be of interest to her. She wished he wasn't such a jerk. He'd been very polite to her at chow. But what could he possibly say to excuse himself of such blatant chauvinism earlier? She stopped halfway to the ladder and waited. Reeves walked to where she'd been standing and motioned for her to come back.

"Come on," he said, "I won't bite."

Reluctantly, she returned, but within two steps the playful deck tipped; then pitched up after the ship made a slapping stab at the sea and she found herself off balance and groping for a handhold on the short safety wall. Reeves reached and took her by the forearm to steady her, but before regaining control, the side of her head struck the commander square in the mouth. She pulled away, getting a good hold on the bulwarks and saw him reel back from the stinging pain he must have been feeling. Still frowning as he looked to her, he raked his top teeth over his bottom lip and then shook his head with a grin while holding his jaw.

Again the deck dipped low, then it pitched up playfully, tipping them too far for their feet to stay planted to the painted on non-skid surface on the steel deck. This time Spurs held firm to the bulwarks, but Commander Reeves seemed to have been unprepared. He staggered back, then stumbled to her. Spurs held up one hand to brace against him, still holding on with the other as he fell into her.

His weight jarred her and before she realized, she had clung onto him. He clutched the rail of the short wall with his right hand, his left arm around her middle. Looking up into his face, she saw a gleam in his eyes. He smiled. Chuckled. Relieved that he was not angered, she laughed also. Somehow, he looked different now, almost human.

A spot of blood appeared from the corner of his mouth as he grinned. She snatched a handkerchief from her pocket and dabbed it against his lip. As she pulled it away she felt entranced, and he seemed to be also, their eyes locking like infrared sights on their targets.

The ship had adjusted its course and stabilized somewhat, and there was no reason to cling to each other. If one of the crew should see them, there could be a misunderstanding. The two eased away from each other.

"Pardon me, sir," Spurs said, straightening her uniform.

"The pleasure was mine, I assure you," Reeves said,

his grin slowly fading as he leaned on the bulwarks and looked out to sea.

Spurs joined him, leaning against the rail.

"I wanted to apologize to you, Ensign—can I call you Janelle, or Jan?"

She surprised herself when she answered without considering the XO's chauvinist attitude when they met. "Friends call me Spurs." But perhaps she should give him a second chance. It would be better for the investigation if she were able to speak with him openly and without them harboring any hostilities toward one another.

"Spurs—yeah, I like that. It fits. I'll bet you're a cowgirl."

"Sort of, sir. I've done some riding and a little roping. I was Junior Girls Champion in calf roping."

"I'll be damned," he said then looked toward the *Enterprise*—the *Big E*. "A real cowgirl. So, what in the hell did you join the Navy for? What were you trying to prove?"

Spurs felt the hair on the back of her neck raise. "Prove, sir?"

Reeves looked back to her, seeming to realize that he'd stepped on her toes.

"Easy Spurs, I just meant, why would a beautiful young woman, intelligent enough to make Honors at Oklahoma University, join the Navy? There's a lot better money in civilian life."

Spurs frowned.

"Yeah," he said, "I took a good look at your records. You were also an honor graduate at Officer's Candidate School."

She smiled. "I didn't join to prove anything, sir. There are a lot of opportunities for women in the service nowadays. It's an equal-opportunity employer and the pay might not be great, but the scale is the same for men and women. You don't see that too often out in the real world. Besides, I had to see what my father thought was so great about the sea."

"Admiral Oliver T. Sperling? Seems to me that you could have afforded a more prestigious school with an admiral for a father. Hell, maybe even made a go for Annapolis."

"I would have liked to, but the Admiral wouldn't allow it. I liked OU."

"He's retired now, your father?"

"Yeah, six years ago, after forty-five years. All that time he was at sea and I never got a ride on anything bigger than a commuter shuttle in San Francisco. The first ten years of my life I spent bouncing around with my mother from Honolulu to Manila to London to Washington, DC. We'd stayed with relatives on their ranch in Oklahoma for a couple of years. Then, when mom died when we went to visit my father in Okinawa, I went back to Oklahoma to live. The Admiral—my father, retired the summer I graduated from high school. He wanted me to go to one of those all-girl schools back east. I guess that's when we really started drifting apart. Then, when I joined the Navy, he really went ballistic. He wanted me to go to school and get cultured and learn the arts and marry a career naval officer like my mother did. Instead I became a cowgirl and then got a *man's job* at sea."

"How'd your mother die?"

"She drowned."

"I'm sorry."

"That was a long time ago. Like I said, we were visiting the Admiral in Okinawa. Mother and I went out on a local beach to get some sun. She told me that she was going for a little swim. She trotted out into the water and never came back. They said the undertow got her—pulled her out to sea." She paused and stared out blankly. "It was really strange. I just sat there on my towel, waiting for her to come splashing out of the water and take me home. But she never did." She looked at her hands folded across the bulwarks in front of her. "Some Marines found me the next morning and took me to the Admiral. We'd been staying with Aunt Katherine and Uncle Paul on their ranch. He sent me back there to live. They always treated me like a daughter."

"You were what, only twelve?"

She nodded.

He looked back to the *Enterprise*. "It must have been terrible."

She also looked. "Hell of a ship, don't you think, sir?"

Reeves grinned still staring at it. His Southern twang came alive as he spoke. "Yes, she is. Ninety-one-thousand tons, 1,101 feet long, 133 foot beam, 39 foot draft. Powered by four steam turbines hooked up to eight big, beautiful A2W nuclear reactors." He took a deep breath still gazing at the aircraft carrier. "You know, those reactors use over 90 percent pure Uranium-235. The standard commercial nuclear-power plant uses only two to five percent."

Spurs watched the commander's intense stare as he narrated more. His words were spoken as if he were reciting poetry from a tech manual.

"Three 20mm Phalanx guns, two Sea Sparrow launchers, two Mk 91 fire control systems. She carries on her decks; F-14s, A-7s, A-6s, and occasionally F-18s along with various other fixed wing and rotor-type aircraft. A crew of over 6,000 sailors including a small compliment of Marines call her home."

He turned to Spurs, his face becoming solemn. "I should have been on her," he said.

"Maybe someday?"

"No, Spurs. Not this sailor."

"Why's that, sir?"

He looked back at the ocean. "The Navy's chosen a different path for me."

It seemed a good time to change the subject again. "What did you want to apologize for, sir?"

"For the hard time I gave you earlier. I know you probably thought I was a real asshole."

Spurs grinned. It seemed enough of an answer. "You shocked me, sir," she said. "I'd hoped that such chauvinistic attitudes had died with the *old Navy*. There are nearly 11,000 women serving at sea now. We've proven ourselves in most every job the Navy has to offer from deck hand to jet-fighter pilot to ship's captain—women have been killed and even captured in combat. It's time we got an honest and sincere break. And I'm not saying to give us anything that we don't deserve. Make the standards—both physical and mental, the same for men and women. Those who can hack it, no matter who they are, no matter what gender, should be allowed to perform whatever tasks they're qualified to do."

Reeves smiled. "I'm well aware of the accomplishments and contributions of women in the Navy, Spurs. There have been some drawbacks and things that can't be adjusted overnight. I appreciate your impatience, but don't push too hard. It causes friction when you rub two tough old sticks together fast. Rub them slow and you won't start a fire. Most men believe in equality nowadays. Don't set fire to the cat, then throw it in our laps. Let us get used to it first. We have to pet it a couple of times before we can find out it's not that bad."

Spurs looked down as the commander continued.

"There are many hurdles; Navy wives don't care much about their husbands serving extended times with women aboard ships, accommodations must be made for women's special needs—pregnant women aboard ships create a whole new set of challenges. I know we'll be better off once the transition is over and we have men and women serving alongside each other as equals. I'll remind you that a man, Admiral Zumwalt, was responsible for changing the Navy's policies to make better use of women's talents, to try to do away with legal and attitudinal restrictions."

Spurs frowned and looked at him. "Then why did you give me such a bad time?"

Reeves lowered his voice. "I was testing you."

"Testing?"

He kept his whisper. "I've got to tell you that from first appearances, I had my doubts about you being able to handle your assignment. I thought I'd test you, you know, give you a poke and see if you'd squeal. You did squeal—but not *too* loud."

Spurs eyes widened. A relieved smile came over her lips.

"You're my contact?" she said.

Now it was Reeves' eyes growing big. He frowned and scanned around them. "Loose lips *do* sink ships, Ensign, or haven't you heard?"

She realized her blunder and put her hand to her mouth.

"I'm sorry. I got carried away. It's just that I was beginning to wonder."

"Well, quit wondering and keep your voice down," he said with a slight smirk on his face. "There's another reason I tried to scare you off."

"What's that?"

He turned to her. "You're a very beautiful young woman. A simple mistake and you could end up dead."

She wondered if she were older and ugly would he

think it would be less of a loss. "I understood the risks when I hired on with NCIS."

"Yes, I suppose you did."

"Tell me what's going on. Does it have anything to do with the Tomahawks? What have you found out?"

"Slow down there, Annie Oakley. We've got plenty of time. And by the way, I hope you'll understand when I treat you like alligator crap around the crew. The one thing we can't have is suspicion."

"I'll understand."

"Good. Now, as far as the investigation goes, according to my sources the Tomahawks aren't concerned. Their deployment on this ship is routine and not involved. No one knew about them outside of the top Navy brass except the captain, Lieutenant North and myself until we put them on board three months ago."

"But if North is somehow involved. . . ."

"You're getting ahead of me. Like I said, according to my sources, the cruise missiles aren't."

"What sources are those, sir?"

Reeves took a quick glance around ensuring their privacy. "I have an informant in Barcelona."

"NCIS?"

"No, a civilian—a woman."

"Are you sure she can be trusted? I mean, she didn't just walk up and tell you? You checked her out?"

Reeves frowned. He paused before saying, "Miss Sperling, may I remind you that this is not *my* first rodeo.

Spurs bowed her head. "Sorry, sir."

"It also coincides with what I've been able to piece together. As near as I can tell, Ensign Nader was in the middle of a drug smuggling ring working on US Navy ships. He'd started getting second thoughts and wanted out, but they wouldn't let him. He either couldn't take the pressure and jumped to his death or had endangered the drug operation and was given a little help by his cohorts. The crewman that went overboard the week before was in the same fix. The two AWOLs are probably dealing with the druggies on shore somewhere, maybe helping to convince other sailors to join them."

"But Nader's parents were so sure he wasn't involved in drugs. They said he was a clean kid. He was an Annapolis grad."

"You know that doesn't matter. Even the most squeaky clean can get muddied up with drugs. It just happens." Reeves looked at the aircraft carrier. "There seems to be a new synthetic cocaine out on the market called Japanese Rapture, or Jap Rap. It was developed by some Japanese scientists and they sold the formula and processing equipment to a group of Muslim terrorists that call themselves *Allah's Gihad*. Unknown to our simple-minded American GIs, the terrorists are selling this new high at cut rate prices to flood the market with a cocaine-like substance that is one hundred times as potent, twice as addictive, and ten times deadlier.

"We think that they've given samples out to some stateside drug kingpins and those sons-of-bitches ordered a whole shit-load. They've devised a plan to transport the stuff back to the US aboard Navy ships. They're paying off a number of young sailors with some big bucks and getting them to smuggle it aboard several ships of the Sixth Fleet. This stuff's so potent, a soda straw-full could keep most of Hollywood high for a month—or kill them in a second."

Spurs felt a rush. She'd wanted to get involved. To do her part in something big. This was big. She hoped she could handle it.

Commander Reeves continued, "The going price for this rat poison is twenty-five thousand a pound. And it's nearly undetectable, even by dogs. They're carrying it aboard in their shoes, their skivvies, swallowing it in balloons and stashing it on the ships by the sea bag full. I'm guessing that by the time we steam back to the states, between all of the ships in the fleet, we'll be carrying over ten tons of the shit."

"Good lord, what can we do? How do we stop them? Can we suspend all shore leave in the ports that we suspect it's coming from?"

"That's no good. These guys have a free reign in Europe. They can distribute from anywhere."

"I don't get it. It'd seem easier for them to use another method—civilian flights maybe, or merchant ships since it's so hard to detect."

"Evidently, using the US's own military is part of *Allah's Gihad's* plan. They corrupt our own people. Screw up some of our young officers. Cause scandals. Basically embarrass us. That's worth a lot to these bastards."

"What can we do?"

"For now, just wait. We have to look for a break. Something to tip us to their leader. If we can get to their boss, we can stop an epidemic of death worse than the plague of the middle ages."

Spurs stared at Reeves.

"I need you to stay sharp," he said. "Do exactly as I tell you. *Allah's Gihad* are bloodthirsty killers. They wouldn't hesitate to slit your throat."

Spurs nodded.

"Now for the bad news," Reeves continued. "I believe the man in charge of the American's part in the operation is an officer aboard this ship. His code name to them is Chameleon. And he has at least two other people on board."

It would be someone with connections and influence. Spurs asked, "Not the captain?"

"No, Captain Naugle has problems, but illicit drugs is not one of them. He's retiring after this cruise. He'd been planning on it since we left the states. That's all he'd talked about. His trouble came when his wife of thirty years sent him a *Dear John* letter two months ago. I don't care—drug dealers, terrorists, or *tsunami*, I'm going to see to it that the man makes it through this cruise without incident and gets the retirement he deserves. If Admiral Pierce suspects he's been drinking while captaining this ship, he'll lose everything. That's not going to happen. And, by the way, the skipper wants to see you sometime this evening."

Spurs acknowledged with another nod. "Do you have any suspects? What about this Marine captain—Chardoff?"

"He's a definite maybe. If he is in cahoots with the terrorists, he'll be one dangerous mother."

Spurs nodded again. "What're he and his men on board for, anyway?"

"They're attached to us officially for training purposes. They'll disembark from the *Atchison* to go on their training missions as if from a troop ship or carrier like they'd normally be attached to. Unofficially they're here to help us with security for the Tomahawks. I have three other suspects; Ensign Ingrassias, Lieutenant Junior Grade Goodman and Lieutenant North. Be careful around any of these men. I suspect either North or Chardoff is the Chameleon. Whatever you do, don't trust North for anything. If he's who we're after, he'll kill you just as easy as lie to you. He'll probably pretend to be an ally if it's to his advantage."

Spurs shuddered. She didn't know for sure if it was the cool of the evening or the danger she sensed. The suspects were almost half of the other officers on the ship.

Reeves looked at her. "You're not to contact anyone

concerning this investigation or speak to anyone about it except me. Do you understand?" His face was stern. This was an order.

"Yes, sir."

"I'll relay anything we dig up to our agents on the *Enterprise*. Any radio communication is out. We have no idea who all is involved. It could be anyone from ship's captains to radiomen." He paused. "Scared?"

She shook her head too meekly to be convincing.

"You'd be a fool if you weren't."

"There's something I'd better tell you," she said.

Reeves raised his eyebrows in the diminishing light.

"There was a note left in my stateroom earlier. I didn't see who left it, but it said. . . ." She stared at the sunset. " . . . 'I saw what happened—Signal bridge—0100 tonight—Tell no one.' It was unsigned," she said and turned, frowning at Reeves. "How should I handle it?"

"Meet him."

Chapter 15

CAPTAIN CONFUSSION

LIEUTENANT COMMANDER REEVES stopped at Commander Naugle's stateroom after Doc Jolly left the skipper with some ibuprofen for the pain. Reeves left something that magnified Naugle's suffering—the name of his ship's new weapons officer.

The captain was trying to compose a letter to Ensign Nader's parents offering his condolences, but his throbbing brain wouldn't allow him to think of the appropriate things to say. He would be glad when the mess was over.

After Reeves left, Naugle soaked a washcloth with cool water and placed it on his forehead. He glanced around his stateroom where his many awards, medals and trophies were displayed. His eyes rested on a 10"x13" portrait standing on the desk. The fifty-nine-year-old sailor gave a deep sigh, gazing at the picture of his son wearing an Annapolis football uniform. Kelly Naugle had been one of the all-time best quarterbacks to wear the Navy blue. He'd graduated in the top ten percent of his class.

It was his destiny to receive more—many, many more accolades.

But one man spoiled all of that. Admiral Oliver T. Sperling.

Captain Naugle reached slowly toward his son's two-dimensional face. His eyes welled with tears and he clenched his teeth before making contact with the picture glass. He remembered the tragic day. The impersonal phone call he'd received from a young Naval personnel officer. Not from the boy's commander, then *Captain* Sperling. That bastard hadn't had the guts.

Lieutenant Junior Grade Kelly Naugle had flown his A-6 attack fighter into the frigid waters of the Norwegian Sea near Greenland with an empty fuel tank. It took the *USS Constellation* six hours to find the downed airman and recover his frozen body. It should not have happened. Naugle's son should not have died as he did. Sure, there was a fuel leak, a sudden storm, a Swedish tanker in distress and an ocean full of icebergs, but still, something could have been done. It had been then *Captain* Oliver T. Sperling's decision to assist the swamped tanker instead of holding course in the squall to wait for Kelly to return. Captain Sperling didn't know the A-6's fuel pump would fracture and leak like a fountain. But damn it, Sperling could have—should have done something. That was nearly fifteen years ago.

Naugle's cheeks streamed with tears. His breath caught. Two fingers of his right hand glanced off the glass as an involuntary whine came from his soul. He slapped his palms against his crew-cut skull, fingers spread wide. The whine grew louder, gradually erupting into a tormented wail. He pulled his hands down the sides of his face, the washcloth falling to the desk, his fingers furrowing his fleshy cheeks. Then, balling his fists, he slammed them on the desk conceding to a blubbering, grief-ridden fit.

The Navy wanted him to retire. The admiral of the Sixth Fleet had told him that he'd served his country with honor and the highest commitment to duty for the past forty-five years and now it was time to serve himself.

But Naugle knew there was more to it than that. He knew of the rumors that had been spreading over the last several weeks. His people were talking. "Naugle is losing his grip," they said, "He's not in control"—making errors, forgetting which port they were heading for, forgetting orders he'd just made and making them a second and even a third time.

The last incident seemed to have been the kicker. He'd called the Sixth Fleet commander, claiming he had an emergency, interrupting an important call Admiral Pierce had been having with the Secretary of the Navy. Pierce had put the secretary on hold to answer Naugle's call, but Naugle forgot what he'd wanted to discuss with him.

Pressure, pressure, there was always so much pressure. But he couldn't retire. The Navy was his life. The memory of his son was his life. A man in his position could not be found out to be a human marshmallow. He must control himself. But he couldn't. The grief he felt for the loss of his son was back in full force, as if it had just happened and it grew stronger everyday. The worry of being forced to retire nagged everyday.

He *was* losing his grip. But before he did, maybe he could get even. Maybe he could make Sperling pay. With his daughter on board, revenge was his if he wanted it. Then he could concentrate. Then he would be in command again. Revenge.

Moments passed. A soft knock came on Captain

Naugle's door, startling him as he sobbed softly in the wake of his tantrum.

He pushed his face up from his crossed arms on the desk and wiped his cheeks.

The soft tap came again. He got up from the desk and went to his bunk and lay down before answering.

Chapter 16

MEETING THE CAPTAIN

AFTER LEAVING THE XO, Spurs went to Commander Naugle's stateroom and tapped on the door.

There was no response and she tapped again.

"Enter," came the low reply.

She stepped in the door and found the skipper, fully dressed, lying on his bunk, holding a wet washcloth across his forehead. In his late-fifties, he was of medium build, had thick Popeye forearms, chipmunk cheeks and a head full of short, sandy stubble.

"Ensign Janelle Sperling, reporting as ordered, sir," she said, standing at attention.

"Relax, Miss Sperling," he said, glimpsing from the corner of his eye. His voice came out raspy like from a mouthful of pebbles. He gave three phlegmy coughs. "Have a seat." He motioned to a chair next to his desk.

Spurs obeyed and sat, waiting for his next words.

"Sorry I haven't been able to greet you more formally," he said. "These damn migraines. Anyway, Nick, uh, Commander Reeves, told me all about you. You sure surprised us."

"I was surprised, too, sir."

"Yes, I guess you probably were," he said, still holding his head, his eyes only slits. "I don't believe in beating around the bush—are you NCIS?"

Spurs hoped the captain didn't notice her cringe.

"NCIS, sir?"

"I know you can't answer. I just thought I'd try. I hope you're not here to investigate me—my alleged alcoholism."

Spurs sat quiet. She was sure her silence and feigned ignorance were giving her away. Nervously looking around the stateroom, she wished to tell the man that he was not under investigation. That, as far as she was concerned, he could ride out this last voyage and retire without incident. Still, as she scanned the room, she found herself looking for a bottle or a flask. There was a picture of an attractive, middle-aged lady on the skipper's desk. Next to it was a picture of a young man in a football uniform. She saw no container and smelled no liquor. But he knew she was coming and had plenty of time to hide his hooch.

"Sir, even if I were with NCIS, I don't believe they investigate alcohol problems. Don't they just deal with criminal investigations?"

"A drunken skipper wouldn't be criminal?" He grunted. "If it's about Nader, I don't think you'll find any wrong doing aboard this ship. We had a formal investigation and we've been cleared. His death and the other problems we've been having are all coincidental. No less terrible, of course. Nader was a fine young officer. His death was a tragedy. But then, my entire crew is a group of outstanding individuals. I'm a lucky captain." His jaw clench as if he was in pain. "Speaking of such, my son was lucky enough to serve with your father on his first cruise on the *Constellation*. Kelly was a lowly ensign like yourself."

She was about to ask him where his son was now, but Naugle spoke first.

"Anyway, I hope you'll be comfortable aboard this vessel. We're pleased to have you." He held out a hand, still not looking.

Spurs took it as her cue to be dismissed. She stood and took a couple of steps to him and shook his hand. He winced and squeezed his forehead. The headache seemed relentless. He coughed twice more.

"Pleased to be on this fine ship, sir. And, sir, I'd like to stay on for the extent of my orders."

"If that's what you wish, then I see no reason not to allow you. I'll make it so. But you'll let me know if there're any problems or anything I can do for you, won't you, Miss Sperling?"

"Yes, sir," she said, releasing his hand. "Thank you, sir."

Chapter 17

A BRIEF TOUR

AFTER LEAVING THE captain's stateroom, Spurs decided to have a look about the ship. She descended five decks to check out the engine room, taking a quick look at the two steam turbines that propelled the vessel. They appeared smaller than she'd expected, even for the *Atchison*, possibly even inadequate. It gave her an insecure feeling looking at them. She was impressed by their spotless appearance, however. The only grease she saw in the compartment was on the four leering sailors manning their stations. She wanted to take them aside and tell them why she was able to handle her job, why she could do it as well as anyone else. She felt the need to convince them, but telling wouldn't help. She would have to show this crew. Somehow, she would show the whole damn crew that she was not an anchor to this Navy but as much of a propellant as both of the engines before her.

Three decks above on the way back up, she noticed a sailor on a four-foot stepladder painting something above a hatchway with stencils, a brush and a can of paint.

She stepped up to the little oriental seaman and saw that he was painting *WOMEN'S HEAD* in large black letters.

She smiled, finally feeling like there was something actually being done to acknowledge she was on board. The hatch stood open about a foot, but she couldn't see inside and the curiosity finally overcame her. She reached up and tapped the seaman on the arm.

"Sailor," she said.

Startled, the sailor gasped, the ladder tipped and the paint and man fell.

"Stupid son-of-a-bitch!" he said, falling back.

She grabbed him from behind, under his arms, preventing injury, but the paint spilled and now oozed out into a widening puddle.

The sailor's dark blue cap ended up sideways, covering his left eye.

"Dammit!" he said trying to stand as he looked at the mess of black enamel, "Stupid son-of-a-bitch!" He turned to Spurs with his teeth clenched. "You are one. . . ." He paused as he straightened his cap and gaped wide. "Woman—lady." He looked at her uniform. "WINS, officer . . . and I'm a stupid son-of-a-bitch. Sorry, sir—ma'am."

"Nothing to be sorry for. I'm most of those things," she said, then looked at the paint. "I'm the one that should be sorry. Here, let me help you clean that up."

She reached for some rags beside the ladder.

"No!" he said. He snatched up all of the rags. His English was perfect as he said, "That wouldn't do, ma'am. It was my fault. I'm just kind of goosy. We weren't expecting any female crew members for a couple weeks."

"I'm here early, kind of an advanced party." She smiled. "May I go inside?"

The young sailor looked at the hatch to the head then back to Spurs. "Oh, uh, sure."

"Just for a look," she said, feeling the need to qualify her request.

He nodded and smiled and she did the same.

She was disappointed when she stepped through the hatchway. Along one bulkhead were eight urinals. On the adjacent wall to her right were two toilets without stalls sitting out in the middle of nowhere, next to a double, curtainless shower stall. On the opposite wall were two sinks with a small mirror above each.

She turned back to see the sailor watching her then looked back at the urinals.

"What's your name, sailor?" she asked.

"Hwa, ma'am. Seaman first class. The guys call me Jitterbug, cause I'm so jumpy."

"Well—*Jitterbug*. I'm Ensign Sperling. Tell me," she asked still staring at the pissers, "where are the other women's heads going to be?"

"This will be the only one, as far as I know, ma'am."

"How about mirrors, stalls, more toilets and sinks?"

"Don't know anything about toilet stalls or more sinks, ma'am. But as far as I know the mirrors stay," he said.

"But when are those coming out?" she asked, pointing at the urinals.

"No plans for that, ma'am. My understanding was that the, uh, *necessary adjustments* would be temporary."

Spurs twisted around to see if he was for real.

He smiled back sincerely. He was serious.

She stepped out of the head and grinned back. She held out her hand.

"Thanks for the tour, Jitterbug."

He looked surprised and wiped his right hand on his blue shirt making long black streaks.

"It was a pleasure, ma'am."

Chapter 18

PROUD PARENTS

2230

 SPURS SAT UP in the bottom bunk as the rocking of the world around her worsened. She'd moved her linen to that lower bunk, not wishing to be any further away from the ship's center than necessary. She had lain down at 2130 but couldn't sleep. Two things kept her from dozing: anticipation for the meeting she was to have at 0100 with the mysterious note writer and the increasingly rough seas.

 Clinging to the top bunk above her, she swallowed several times trying to keep down the mostly bread supper she'd eaten. She wasn't able to suppress it very long. The urge to vomit soon became overpowering and she staggered to the head, making it to the porcelain thrown just in time to expel the two diner rolls, a small chew of meat and the spoonful of green beans she'd had for the evening meal. Tomorrow she would only have crackers, she thought. Now her stomach was empty, but she was not hungry. A sip from a water glass was all she could consume. At first light, she'd ask Doc Jolly for some Dramamine patches.

There was no use trying to sleep any longer. Soon, it would be time to go to the signal bridge for the meeting.

She glanced at a Tupperware container in her locker. Inside it was a bundle of letters. Her thoughts drifted to the visit she had with Ensign Charles Nader's parents back in DC, two short days ago.

* * *

The tall, elegantly dressed black woman stood in the doorway fingering a large, gold shamrock broach as she stared at Janelle Sperling.

"Mrs. Nader?" Spurs asked.

"Yes. Are you one of Charlie's friends?"

"No, ma'am. I'm an investigator for the Naval Criminal Investigative Service." She pulled out an ID card that had been made up with her assumed name on it and showed it to her. "My name is Jill Smith."

"Please come in," Mrs. Nader said, pulling the door wide and stepping back.

Spurs walked in and followed her into a sitting room of the large, ornate, turn-of-the-century vintage, Victorian home. On a small tapestry upholstered sofa with Queen Ann legs was a graying, black gentleman and a pretty young black woman holding hands.

"This is my husband, Mike, and Charlie's girl friend, Sheryl," she said, looking to them. "Honey, Sheryl, this is Miss Smith."

"Good afternoon," Spurs said.

After being invited to sit, offered tea or coffee, and some pleasantries about the weather, Spurs got down to business.

"We're not sure of the cause of your son's death,"

she said, setting a large tumbler of iced tea on a doily on the hand rubbed walnut coffee table in front of her. But officially, we're calling it a suicide. . . ."

"Suicide!" Mike Nader leaped from his seat and rubbed his thick hair. He turned away. "My son would not—could not commit suicide."

"We don't think he did, either," she said calmly.

He spun around to her seeming bewildered. "What do you mean?"

"He had cocaine in his nostrils. . . ."

"My son did not use drugs!" Mr. Nader blurted.

"Oh, not Charlie," Mrs. Nader said.

Spurs sighed and nodded slowly, then continued what she'd started to say, " . . . but none of the cocaine had been absorbed into his system."

"Meaning?" Mr. Nader said. His tone was still harsh and defensive.

"Mike," Mrs. Nader softly scolded, patting her husband's hand.

Spurs said, "There should have been at least traces of cocaine found in his blood if he'd snorted it while he was alive. In other words, we are relatively sure that someone wanted it to look like he'd been on drugs. That someone put it in his nostrils after he fell to his death."

The Naders and their son's girl friend glanced at one another.

"This still doesn't rule out suicide, but it makes it a lot less likely."

Mr. Nader looked puzzled. "So why are you calling it a suicide without finding out for sure?"

"We're not, sir—that is unofficially. We feel that if we officially call it suicide, we can put an agent undercover and no one will suspect that we're still investigating. It may give us a better chance to find out exactly what happened."

"You don't mean you're going undercover?" Mrs. Nader asked.

"I can't say, ma'am. Did Charlie have any enemies, or did he ever talk about being in danger, threatened or anything unusual happening?"

The couple looked at each other and then back to Spurs.

"No," Mr. Nader said.

Mrs. Nader put her hand on his forearm. "What about the letters?" she asked.

Charlie's father raised his eyebrows then walked over to a small roll top desk. He took out one of several bundles of letters. He brought them to Spurs and placed them in her lap.

"Whatever he told us since he'd been on that ship is in these," he said. "He didn't like to use the phone. Said it was a waste of money. You might find something of interest in one of them. The last one, maybe."

Spurs smiled up at him. "Thanks."

"It's just a loan," he said. "Charlie's letters are all that's left of him besides some pictures and memories."

"I'll be sure to take care of them. I'll bring them back to you as soon as I can."

He nodded.

Spurs spent the next twenty minutes talking to the Naders and looking at old photos of their son. Charles Nader's fiancée seemed shy, not speaking unless coaxed, and, even then, her voice was quiet and shaky. It took very little for her eyes to tear up. When the young woman broke into sobs after coming across a photo of her and Charles on senior prom night, Spurs decided she'd imposed upon them enough. She stood up and they accompanied her to the door.

"Be careful, Miss Smith," Mike Nader told her. He shook her hand. "But see what you can do to clear our son's good name. It's very important to us, as you can see."

Spurs felt a warmth deep in her chest for this grieving family. "I'll do my best."

"Yes, do be careful," Mrs. Nader said. "Charlie wouldn't want someone getting hurt because of him."

Spurs smiled back. She noticed Mrs. Nader rubbing the gold shamrock again. A small diamond glistened in the center. "That's a beautiful broach, ma'am."

Mrs. Nader looked down at it. "Thank you. Charlie gave it to me when he was in training in San Diego. It's called *Mother's Medal of Honor*. He gave his father a tie tack just like it."

Spurs looked to Mr. Nader's dark brown tie. A miniature version of the broach pinned it.

"Charlie was special, Jill," Mrs. Nader said.

Then, for the first time without being spoken to first, Charles Nader's fiancée spoke up. "He loved his country. He was a hero to us. Please don't let him be remembered as some kind of a dope addict."

Spurs patted the younger woman's hand, then hugged Mrs. Nader. "I won't." She nodded to Mr. Nader. "You can count on that."

* * *

Spurs closed her locker and sat back on her bunk, thinking about Charles Nader's dad. He must have been a very good father. She briefly compared him to her own father, the Admiral, and realized she'd never even shaken *his* hand. When she was a child, the few times the Admiral was around much, she couldn't recall him ever kissing her, hugging her—or even touching her except to pick her up and place her in her mother's arms when he was leaving.

Chapter 19

MEETING THE STORM

00:50

THE WIND UP Baby Ben clock read ten minutes till one. Spurs sat on the edge of her bunk, swaying from side to side and slipped on her shoes. The signal bridge was only a three-minute walk, but Spurs wanted to be early. She stood, but paused, waiting for the floor to tip toward her cap hanging on the latrine door, then she quick-stepped to it. After spinning around as the deck tipped toward the doorway, she leaned back and took short, halting steps in that direction.

Outside her door, she made her way, zigzagging, pushing off from the bulkheads on either side of the corridor. When she reached Lieutenant Commander Reeves' stateroom, she hesitated. Reeves was to be waiting in the shadows near the bridge as a witness and as protection, just in case. Mr. Note Writer could be a murderer just as easily as an informant. He could want to get rid of her instead of giving her information as the note implied.

Spurs listened at the door to see if Nick Reeves was

stirring, but heard nothing. She tapped softly, not wishing to disturb the captain or any of the other officers in their surrounding staterooms.

With no answer, she tapped again and whispered, "Commander? Lieutenant Commander Reeves, are you awake?"

Still no hint of a reply, she touched the doorknob. Perhaps he was sleeping. He'd better not oversleep. She didn't wish to do this alone. Looking up and down the empty, dimly lit passageway, she began turning the doorknob.

"Commander?" she whispered a bit louder, "Commander Reeves?"

She opened the door slowly. There was a light on in the room.

"Sir, are you awake?" Gradually, she pushed the door wider.

Now half open, she peeked her head inside and looked around. A lamp beside his bunk was on, but there was no sign of Reeves. She stepped inside, thinking he could be in the head, not wishing to disturb him, but also not wishing to go topside alone.

She shut the door in case someone might happen by and stepped toward the closed toilet door.

The ship pitched suddenly and Spurs staggered back. The small lamp beside the bunk flickered and went out, throwing the room into complete darkness as the head door began to open. The door banged against the bulkhead and Spurs felt something strike her foot.

The light blinked again and came on. The toilet was empty. The rough seas had caused the simple, hollow-core door to loosen from its jam and swing wide.

On the floor lay a pen, the thing that had struck her foot. She picked it up to set it in a pencil holder on the nearby desk and saw a notepad that Reeves had been writing on. He had made a list of women's names, all but the last two crossed out; Bridgett, Gina, Carla, Yvonne, Delores, Nikki, Sasha, Kabran, Maria and *Janelle*. She decided it must be a list of first names of the officers in the WINS detail—her name included—for some kind of nametags, perhaps.

Spurs hoped Reeves was already on the signal bridge or at least on his way. She felt comforted knowing he would be there watching, then uneasy that he might not.

The ship's rocking increased with every step she took toward the signal deck. Traveling to a higher part of the ship magnified the effects of the growing storm outside exponentially. She remembered how Commander Reeves had spoken about the "squall" just before they met. "It'll be a good drill for the *legs*," he'd said.

Spurs stepped into the Combat Information Center, where three sailors manned the fire-control consoles.

"Anyone been through here lately?" she asked.

Petty Officer Jabrowski was at the controls. He looked to her. "Good evening, miss," he said. "No, no one's been through either hatch for the last hour except the Officer of the Deck."

"Who is that?"

"Lieutenant North, miss," he said. "Anything I can do?"

Spurs shivered. Could it be North she was to meet and if so, was he a murderer or an informer? If it was North, he might try to do her in. Otherwise, if he just had information to give her, he'd had plenty of opportunities to do so before this.

"No thank you, Jabrowski."

"Ski, miss," he said, smiling. "Everyone just calls me plain old Ski."

She forced a grin and staggered through the room to the hatch leading out onto the signal bridge.

As she placed her hand on the grab handle, Jabrowski rose and walked toward her. He said, "Be careful out there, miss. We're in a *force eight* storm." He took a black slicker swaying from a coat hook near the hatch and held it out. "Only essential personnel are allowed topside."

"Thanks, Ski."

As she reached her arms into the raincoat, she wondered about Ensign Nader on the night of his death. He'd been just outside of the CIC on the signal deck when he fell. He may have gone out through the very hatch she prepared to exit. Maybe Jabrowski knew something. He already seemed to suspect that she was an undercover investigator. She needed to know more. This was no time to be shy.

She turned to him. "Ski, were you on duty the night that Ensign Nader died?"

Ski lowered his eyes. "Yes, ma'am."

"Did you talk to him?"

"Yes, ma'am."

"Tell me about it, Ski."

"Pardon me, ma'am," he said and took her by the arm and pulled her as far away from the others as he could. They stumbled to the bulkhead from the rocking and clung onto a horizontal I-beam support along the middle of the wall.

He whispered, "It was about 0130. The Ensign came in all excited. He seemed scared, worried maybe. He said someone was after him. He had a loaded gun. He kind of scared me, too. I'd never seen him like that before. He was normally real calm, pleasant in a serious sort of way."

"What happened?"

"He was tired. Said he needed to hide out and get some sleep. That they would get him if he went back to his stateroom. He said he trusted me, but nobody else. He couldn't be sure of any of the others, not even the captain. I told him to get between those two lockers over there," he said pointing to a couple of gray wall lockers, "and I'd cover him up with a blanket. He didn't say a word, he just crashed and I did as I said I would."

Spurs noticed a kind of guilty look on Jabrowski's face. "Tell me Ski, what happened?"

"You've got to understand me, ma'am, I was scared. There'd been a lot of bad things happening on the ship. It was just too weird." He looked her eye to eye and swallowed.

"Go on, Ski," she said.

"I called the captain. I didn't want to bother him but I thought I'd better go to the top instead of through the OOD. Anyway, the captain didn't answer. I figured he was probably sick again, so I buzzed Commander Reeves. He told me to try and disarm Ensign Nader when I was sure he was asleep. He said to buzz him back after I did. Nader was out like a light. I guess he hadn't been sleeping much. I took the ammo clip out of his sidearm and I noticed he had another loaded magazine sticking halfway out of one of his pockets, so I took that out too." Jabrowski's eyes teared. "I'm sorry ma'am. I hope what I did didn't cause Ensign Nader to get killed. He trusted me."

"I don't know, Ski," she said, "but you're doing the right thing now. What happened next?"

"Well, when I put the blanket back over Ensign Nader, he woke up. He seemed startled like he'd had a bad dream or something and he started babbling."

"What was he babbling?"

"He said, 'The *Enterprise*, it's going to be the *Enterprise*!' He said he had to warn them. That *they* would overhear the radio. He looked up and said something about the signal light and then jumped to his feet and ran to this hatch and left. I started to follow him, but decided I'd better call Commander Reeves back and tell him first."

"Keep going," she whispered, noticing the other sailors taking curious glances at them."

"Well, Commander Reeves told me to sit tight and within a couple of minutes, he came in and asked where Nader was. I told him and so we both went outside and that's when we heard a bunch of people down below and saw Ensign Nader lying there, dead."

"Who was down there?"

"Let's see, there was Doc Jolly, Seaman Wright, Big Track and Stemps, Lieutenant Goodman, Captain Chardoff and . . . ," he paused, trying to remember, "Lieutenant North."

"Why didn't you tell the investigators this before?"

"Commander Reeves told me not to."

She turned toward the hatch, then curious about one more thing she looked back. "Who was the OOD that night?"

"Same as tonight, ma'am. Lieutenant North."

Spurs felt that chill again. She turned back to the steel door and opened it to a fire hose-like deluge of water. She stammered back one step with the rising deck, then flung herself out into the howling squall.

Nothing she had ever seen compared.

The *Atchison* fought the sea's onslaught fiercely, listing to one side, then the other, pitching up like a rearing bronco, then slamming down in a shuddering crash, sending white foam spraying. The steel lady finally submitted to a huge, vengeful wall of water pounding her topside and the torturous cycle repeated. The charcoal gray sky was indistinguishable from the sea except when brilliant flashes of lightning scribbled overhead and gave the turbulent sea the look of a giant, boiling caldron of black oil. This was not a good time or place to meet anyone but your maker. She had no choice, almost hoping the mystery crewmember would not show.

After nearly losing her footing on the deck and her hold on the hatch, she welcomed Jabrowski's arms reaching out and steadying the hatch by the grab handle.

Spurs stepped around and shoved against the hatch—Ski, finally taking the hint, moved back in and closed and secured it.

She pushed herself away from the bulkhead, trying to time her movements, her steps, with the motion of the ship. Impossible. She stumbled to the middle of the bulwarks where she had spoken with Commander Reeves earlier, where Ensign Nader was said to have last stood.

Grabbing the rounded top, she held tight with her right arm, and then looked back at the ladders on each side of the deck. Sea spray splashed her face as she checked the time. The luminous dial of her watch read 0100.

A shadow ducked out of sight on the left ladder. Could it be Reeves or was it the informer? She was surprised to see movement on the right ladder, also. At least she thought she had seen something, possibly the top of a head as it ducked.

She waited, trading glances from one now empty ladder to the other. One must be Reeves, one the informer. *Why doesn't he show himself?* She caught a glimpse of movement from the other side while watching the left stairway. Looking right, she thought she had picked up on it. The hatch. Had it moved, begun to open? No. She raised her eyes, then her face.

Thunder cracked. Lightning lit up the gray mass of steel. A man stood looking down at her from the radar mast, twenty feet above the hatch. He stared down with studying eyes, as stiff as a gargoyle, the lightning making his face glow. She hadn't seen this man before.

Spurs waited for him to move, but he wouldn't. She glimpsed to the ladders and thought she'd seen movement on the left again. The place was getting too damned crowded.

The man hanging onto the radar mast finally swung around one of the poles and leapt toward her on the mast deck above. She was amazed by his agility. He was no lubber—definitely a salt. He moved as if on stable land. Nearly to the end of the deck above her, he seemed to fall. No, he'd flung himself into a prone position above the hatch to the Combat Information Center and was now peering at her from the edge.

Spurs watched, clinging to the safety wall.

The man reached out with one hand, motioning her to come.

She looked to each ladder, not seeing anyone, hoping who she had thought she had seen before was Reeves or merely shadows and not people. The man that beckoned her didn't seem to be a threat. He'd have to drop ten feet to the signal deck in order to reach her. It didn't appear to be his intention.

Spurs released the wall as more sea spray assaulted her and burned her eyes. She took one step, stumbled, fell to her hands and knees, picked herself up nearly to her feet, fell again, staggered up, took short swift steps toward the hatch and finally fell into it. She held tight to the outside grab handle and straightened herself, then lifted her face. The man was directly above, his head, arm and shoulder hanging over the side. His face was frantic.

"NCIS?" he yelled over the wailing storm.

Spurs nodded, blinking the salt water from her eyes. "Who are you?"

"Gus Franken, Senior Chief Petty Officer."

"Why the secrecy?"

"They'll kill me if they know I'm talking to you."

"Why?"

"I know what happened to Nader."

"Tell me!"

"Two men, one real big son-of-a-bitch. Couldn't see their faces, but I think I know who they were."

Spurs frowned thinking of Chardoff. The ship pitched and hammered the sea with a terrific jolt, the water slapping the hull. She staggered, still gripping the handhold.

"Sounded like they were trying to talk the kid outa snitching. They talked about drugs, but I don't think that was it. It was like they were using drugs to cover something up. They accused one another of treason."

"Did they push him?"

"They were fighting over Nader's gun. He slipped. The big guy grabbed him, but then let him go."

The wind howled through the radar mast, an eerie prolonged breath.

"Who do you think it was?" she asked, but before the chief had a chance to answer, he suddenly disappeared, apparently pulled away from view.

Some kind of a struggle ensued. Seconds later his body came back, slamming down halfway over the wall. His head bounced against the top of the steel hatch and Spurs had to duck. Momentarily, he looked back at her, upside down, arms hanging limp, eyes wide with fright, blood leaking from his mouth and forehead.

He was yanked back out of sight like a toy.

Spurs thought of Reeves. He could help.

She stepped back, still holding the grab handle, trying to see what was happening above.

Arms flailed. There was a fight. More arms reaching, heading toward the side. She wouldn't be able to hear a splash due to the mean sea, but it looked like someone went overboard.

"Help!" she screamed, "Somebody help!"

She'd have to go inside and get Jabrowski, not wishing to confront whoever may be on the side ladders.

Just as she began to pull up on the grab handle to undog the door, a pain exploded from the back of her head. She lost balance. Fell. The deck tossed. She felt as though she was being dragged. Couldn't see by whom. A stinging pain came from her ribs as she was slammed against the short safety wall on the side of the signal deck and she saw stars.

Someone was trying to throw her overboard. She struggled, weakly, her arms not cooperating, the pain from her head shooting through her body, burning now. She hit. Grabbed. Kicked.

The assailant lifted her over the safety wall. Sixty feet from the water. She was going in. Spurs saw flashes of memory. Of her mother trotting out into the water, never to return. Fear locked her body, but then, as she felt herself slipping, she grabbed, caught an arm with one hand, reached and held on with the other. She would take him with her.

Chapter 20

THE PLUNGE

SPURS DIDN'T SEE the ocean coming, only felt the icy Atlantic water as she slammed under while still clutching the arm of her assailant.

With her nearly overwhelming fear of deep water and her being only an adequate enough swimmer to make it through Officers' Candidate School, she was sure she would drown. The waves were too violent—rolling, tumbling, cresting to more than twenty feet.

But this asshole would drown with her.

Finally coming to the surface, she tossed her head and gasped in as much air as she could hold and the waves came down on her. As she went under again, a light showed from the ship while it sped away. They could not save her. The sea was too strong. It would be next to impossible to even sight her.

Again she came up, this time nearly thrown out of the water by the forceful sea, and she felt the man's arm around her midsection. *He* now had *her*. She fought, struggling, kicking to get away. The sea could kill her but not this bastard.

He held her from behind now. She jerked her head back into his face and felt his nose pop against her skull.

That was good. He released her. She almost smiled. Then someone new bumped in front of her, his head rising from the water, nudging into her chest. The dimming light from the ship showed across his face. Chief Franken, eyes wide and dead.

The man who had held her suddenly went berserk. He obviously hadn't appreciated getting his nose broken. He pulled her around to face him in the malevolent water. It was North. His backhand came across her face stunning her and they went under again. This time she had not taken a breath and a crashing wave drove her deep. The water churned.

She felt North's hands again and was sure that he would hold her down, choke or strike her again—but he didn't.

His arm came under hers and pulled until she saw a white light, running, bleeding through the water. Now air again and she gasped, spitting out salty ocean. The ship was a hundred yards out now and still moving. The sea pushed them away. Searching lights shot from the *Atchison*'s starboard side, occasionally flashing in her eyes, but never finding her.

She heard North's voice. "Kick, tread water! Fight the ocean, damn it. Not me!"

Chapter 21

ABOVE AND BEYOND

USS Enterprise

    LIEUTENANT JORDAN WYCOFF and his crew of three were warming up the engines of their SH-3 Sea King helicopter when the man overboard call came in. Within fifteen seconds they had lifted from the *Enterprise*'s deck and dipped their rotor into the wind. One hundred feet out, Jordy banked the aircraft left and raced toward the *Atchison*.

    The Sikorsky model S-61 helicopter they flew was put into service by the Navy in 1961 and designated the SH-3. As an amphibious, all-weather craft, it had served the country well in every conflict from Vietnam to the Persian Gulf and in a number of different roles including antisubmarine warfare (ASW). Until recently, it had been used to transport the President of the United States. In Jordy Wycoff's hands and in many others like him it served as one of the Sixth Fleet's search and rescue helicopters.

    Jordy gritted his teeth as the wind buffeted the helo, pushing them down, closer than safe from the chopping ocean. He pulled his craft up another ten feet, but kept it as low as possible.

Only thirty seconds earlier, he had aborted a foul weather rescue exercise because of the rough sea. No reason to risk lives for an exercise. But now, it was for real.

He turned on his directional searchlights even before the small frigate came into view. The report was two men overboard.

"Jesus, you copy?" Jordy asked into his microphone.

"Loud and clear, boss," the crew chief, Jesus Montana answered, standing tethered in the right side door.

"Mac?"

"Roger," Kyle MacNulty confirmed, peering out of the left side.

Jordy glanced at his copilot. He saw the sweat beading on his partner's cheeks.

"Gonna be a tough one, Timmy."

"Just hope it's worth it—hope we're not too late," Ensign Gilbert Timmons said.

Their rotorcraft shuddered. They gripped the controls tighter.

"There's the *Atchison*, eleven o'clock," MacNulty's report crackled in Jordy's ear.

"We'll start searching two clicks back."

A blinding flash pulsed, thunder exploded.

The lighted instruments went dark and the Sea King's big rotor stuttered. The helicopter hesitated briefly, seeming suspended in mid-air, then dropped fifteen feet.

"Holy Christ!" Timmons yelled.

"Restart sequence!" Jordy ordered, grimacing as he wrestled the control stick to go into auto rotation. Timmons reached for the switches on the console, flipped one on and off quickly, then jabbed a black button labeled engine start.

The engines sputtered—came alive. The instruments lit.

Jordy pulled the Sea King up. He looked to Timmons' relieved eyes.

"Everyone all right back there?" Jordy asked into his mike.

"Still holding on, boss," Jesus said.

"Damn, Jordy," MacNulty said, "this is no good! We've gotta go back. We're gonna buy it in this shit."

"All right," Jordy said, "everyone calm down. We've got a job to do. We'll be back on *old 65* before you know it."

For the first time in ten years of flying choppers, Jordy truly wondered if they would return. The controls seemed stiff, vibrating. He gripped them firmer still then looked to Timmons and saw him now gaping back—Timmy was wondering, too.

As they banked right and Jordy brought their craft several feet closer to the raging ocean, Jesus called out, "There! Swimmers in the water!"

Chapter 22

THE BRAVE AND THE DEAD

The Atlantic Ocean

IT'D BEEN AN exhausting seven minutes battling the relentless waves that seemed like a full fifteen rounds with Mike Tyson.

Spurs found it necessary to grab North's arms about every five seconds when the sea would engulf them. She didn't understand why he hadn't finished the job he'd started on the ship. The same kind of job that his cohort had done on Franken. She didn't want to depend on North's arm, but obviously being the weaker swimmer, she had no other choice.

Though North's arm had helped, it seemed less helpful with each onslaught. He was tiring, barely able to keep himself afloat now. Without his strength, she would soon drown.

A bright light suddenly danced around them, then held straight into their faces. A chopper.

Within seconds, the helicopter was hovering above them, at one moment fifteen feet away, the next forty, as they rode the ocean swells. A harness attached to a thin tether fell into the sea nearby. Spurs expected North to pass it to her, then assist her in putting it on. He didn't. She watched him reach into it himself instead. The bastard was saving himself first. This was the way he'd kill her.

"Come here!" he yelled over the roar of the chopper and the raging storm.

Another wave slammed her under. Her body was too weak to fight. His arm wasn't within reach. She struggled to come to the surface, but couldn't. She went under, further, deeper into the maelstrom.

Surface sounds muted—the helicopter, the raging storm. It became silent. Peaceful. And she thought of death. Her exhausted and aching body considered it. Hope seemed distant, leaving her like the lights flashing on the surface. Life above the water drifted away—unreachable, pulling away from her with each second. Her lungs needed air, aching for breath. Maybe sucking in the cold water would be better than fighting it. Maybe it wasn't as bad as she thought it would be—the end of her life. This *was* the way her mother died. This was the way she would die also.

Neptune's icy fingers caressed her spent body. She finally welcomed it with relief and the sea seeped into her throat.

But then, hands found her—real, human hands—and pulled her head and shoulders up, out of death's clutches.

"Damn it, hold on," North yelled as the crashing waves and helicopter's roar filled her ears once again.

She coughed out water.

"Can't," she said, upset at herself for having to admit it, her arms limp like unfeeling rubber hoses.

"You have no choice!" North hugged her tightly. He motioned for the crew chief on the helo to take them up.

Spurs felt herself being lifted. It gave her new strength and she clung like a declawed cat as they were pulled from of the water. Now, she could hear only the urgent, beating rhythm of the helo's big rotor as its tremendous backwash chilled her already cold, soaked body.

A giant fist of ocean suddenly struck them and Spurs slipped down to Lieutenant North's middle.

How she could find the strength to hold on another second, she didn't know. Hooking both arms into the safety harness North wore, she prayed to God that they would hurry.

A strange feeling came over her as they inched toward the chopper. The hair on her arms and head, although wet, tingled. She realized it was a build up of static electricity. A charge that would soon be unleashed.

The open side door of the Sea King was finally within arm's reach. They were eye-level with a man holding his arms out to them. His helmet said *Jesus* on the front. Spurs' prayers seemed to be answered, until the lightning struck.

The flash was blinding, the shock stunning, the thunderclap deafening.

For an instant, Spurs didn't know if she'd been knocked loose and was falling or was still gripping North. Her sight blacked out, then came back with pulsing flashes. She looked at Jesus to see his face strained, eyes bugging abnormally. His safety harness sizzled. As Jesus tumbled from the open doorway, Spurs realized the helicopter was pitching to its side, and about to go into the sea.

She felt her stomach float as the rescue cable spent out quickly. Everything played in slow motion. As they dropped toward the deadly ocean, the cable hoist smoked. Spurs was amazed to see North's right hand spring out and snatch the lipped edge along the bottom of the doorway as his left arm still held her.

Somehow, the pilot regained control and pulled up. The hoist came to the end of its line which looped from the chopper, down into the water and back up to North's harness. She looked just below them to see Jesus' limp body dangling from the end of his much shorter safety tether.

They hung only a few feet from the rolling water and once again the angry ocean lashed out. The attack loosened Spurs' grip. She slipped, but didn't fall in as she expected. North had caught the hood of her slicker. She dangled, arms treading air, trying to get a hold. She was surprised by his strong hands. Flailing wildly, she finally caught onto his forearm with her right hand and he released her hood. Her hand slipped down to his wrist and she could feel what little strength that she had left waning.

The helo cut an urgent path through the turbulence, swinging them from underneath. She cursed the pilot in her mind for going so fast, then knowing she could only hold on for a few seconds longer, cursed him for being so slow.

Spurs looked at the boiling water below. She looked up to North seeing his somehow calm yet determined eyes, and became ashamed by what must be a scared, weak-kitten expression that she gave back.

Then came the lights. The *Atchison* rocked in the storm only a couple hundred yards out. The chopper sped toward her. The thunder crackled and lightning ripped the sky and Spurs winced, hoping the old saying that lightning would not strike twice in the same place applied to moving objects, also.

As they approached, the flight seemed irregular,

jerky. The previous lightning attack must have affected the aircraft.

Now the flight deck came into view. Spurs saw a group of four or five men standing to the side, holding onto safety lines. Lieutenant Commander Reeves was one. She saw Doc Jolly and Corporal Sanders, another seaman she did not know—and Captain Chardoff.

Chardoff turned and hustled off as they approached.

The ship tossed wildly. Landing would be perilous. Dropping onto it at its nearest point, she might get by without injury, maybe just a sprained ankle. At its furthest point—when it dove deep with the sea—she could easily break her neck. As they came over the bobbing flight deck, averaging twenty feet away, she felt North release her.

"Let go!" he yelled.

Chapter 23

HARD STARBOARD

BOATSWAIN'S MATE BOTTS was at the helm when Captain Chardoff rushed in. He looked over his shoulder to see the big Marine captain dripping ocean from his black raincoat as he said something to Lieutenant JG Goodman who was standing duty as Junior Officer of the Deck. Botts didn't hear what he said. The fierce storm was too loud. He guessed it was something about the helo attempting to land on the fantail.

Goodman had ordered Botts to hold course. It had been a challenging job for the past forty-five minutes. In a force eight storm it was important to head into the wind. Turning away could be dangerous. It would make the ride even rougher for the crew, risking injury. It would cause undue stress on the ship, perhaps causing fractures in the hull that could swamp, even sink the ship. It could even put them in danger of capsizing.

It was especially critical with a helicopter attempting to return two crewmembers. Botts did not envy the chopper crew.

Suddenly, Chardoff yelled, "Look out!"

Botts looked back to him then ahead to the direction the Marine's finger pointed. He squinted to see.

"Small boat, dead ahead!" Goodman cried out.

Botts searched the rolling ocean in front of him as the stem dove deep then lifted high. He could see nothing but the ash gray sea. Petty Officer Carter, manning the surface radar, alternated glances from his green screen to the outside.

"Nothing on radar, sir!" he said.

"I don't see it, sir!" Botts said.

"Good God, man!" Chardoff said, running to the center of the windows in front of them. "It's there. A small boat. Twelve o'clock!"

"Collision course. Come hard starboard!" Goodman said.

"But, sir," Botts said, "the helo!"

"Damn it, Botts," Goodman yelled, "that's an order! We're going to ram her. We're going to kill people if you don't. Hard starboard. Now!"

Botts didn't understand. It was difficult to see out into the storm. The radar didn't pick up a small craft, but in weather like this it was certainly possible. They must see something he didn't.

"Hard starboard, aye-aye, sir!" he answered and spun the ship's wheel clockwise.

The already tossing frigate became as wild and unmanageable as a rodeo bull.

Chapter 24

DEATH LINE

THE STRAIN WAS taking its toll on North. He grimaced. Below her, Jesus' body hung limp—below that the *Atchison's* deck rocked. She needed to time her fall just right to ensure as little injury as possible, but that would be like a crapshoot. Then, it seemed the ship was turning. That'd be the wrong thing to do in a storm like this. Turning away from the storm was dangerous for the ship and for them. It would cause the vessel to rock and list even more.

Commander Reeves rushed onto the deck below. He fell to one hand to steady himself and lifted the other beckoning her to drop.

"Now!" North shouted.

She didn't have a choice. After she dropped, North could either release himself from the harness and drop also, or he might even be able to pull himself into the helo and ride back to the more stable *Enterprise*.

Spurs let go as the deck rose dramatically more than before. She brushed by Jesus then braced herself, eyes forced shut, muscles tightened, fists clenched, waiting for what seemed like seconds for the impact. When she slammed onto Reeves, the air expelled from her lungs like a burst balloon. They both lay flattened on the flight deck. In an instant, the other three men nearby rushed out to assist them.

As they lifted her away, she looked back at the helicopter. The deck went crazy. She was sure now that the ship actually had turned away from the storm.

The aircraft seemed to drop from the sky as the *Atchison*'s deck came up just shy of meeting it. North fell, sprawled out onto the middle of the landing platform. Jesus' dangling, lifeless body hit the deck like a bag of pipe wrenches, then was snatched back as the ship dipped away.

The helo and ship separated far enough to cause North's safety harness's tether to become taught and nearly lifted him from the deck. He tried to sit up. He reached out with weakened arms, barely able to bring them up from the deck, but no one would or could assist him.

The helo fluttered in the sky like a wounded dove. It passed over them within a few yards, then cut back. The pilot seemed to be trying to regain control—realizing he had a man in the harness, trying to keep from swinging him into the ocean or into the ship. When it swooped past, North's safety tether looped around a post-like lifeline stanchion on one side of the fantail.

The *Atchison* rode a huge swell rising to collide with the helo and Jesus' rag doll-like body smacked onto the steel. This time the ship swatted the chopper. Sparks flew from inside the Sea King. Fire erupted from the engine housing below the big rotor, rolled across the ceiling inside and belched from the side doorways.

The helo bounced up, hesitated, and then came back down, crossing overhead. One of the helicopter's crewmen had released his safety line or was broken free from it and either leaped or fell from the other side door, his body in flames. He flopped onto the ship, thirty feet in front of them as North was pulled along the deck in the opposite direction away from the helicopter because of his looped tether. He hit the lifeline at the stanchion it was wrapped around.

Spurs glanced at the others with her and could see that they weren't about to attempt a rescue of either man. The torching crewman was past hope. She bolted toward North, reminded as soon as she did of her drained strength. She tumbled, got up, then ran to him using her hands on the deck to keep from falling.

She reached North as Jesus' limp body hooked the lifeline on the opposite side of the ship. The young, dead crew chief acted as the chopper's anchor, as the *Atchison's* fantail pitched high, then dove deep, waves washing over the entire topside and everyone on it aft of the superstructure. The forceful water shoved down on Spurs, almost taking her with it, but she managed to hold onto North's harness.

The tangled helo was yanked back like a yo-yo. It engulfed in flames. The rotored fireball struck the edge of the fantail, teetered momentarily, then flipped into the ocean, popping, crackling and sizzling.

North sat dazed, tangled in the lifeline and safety tether. He looked up at Spurs hopelessly, his arms limp, then at the rapidly disappearing safety cable he was attached to as it snaked across the deck following the helicopter into the deep.

Within seconds the steel tether would drag North under with the helo. Spurs tugged on the harness, attempting to lift it over North's head but his dead weight didn't cooperate. She fumbled with it, but it seemed stuck, finally yanking it with all of the strength she could gather.

No good.

"A knife!" North said feebly, "Something sharp!"

Spurs thought of the fingernail file she always carried. She'd sharpened it to a nice sharp edge in case of an emergency—you never know when something like that might come in handy to a girl. It certainly had less than two days ago with Henry Dubain. She fished into her drenched pocket and was surprised to find it still there as the slack in the line pulled tight. She took the file out.

North's eyes bugged and his body jolted. Spurs' hand came up with her homemade knife. She slashed at the nylon harness. It frayed but didn't come in two. The cable suddenly yanked him around the stanchion and he skidded across the deck. He followed the chopper, which had now completely submerged, lighting the abyss with metal burning fire. Halfway across the landing platform, the harness broke loose and disappeared over the side.

Chapter 25

TIT FOR TAT

SPURS RAN TO North, but not to comfort or save him. She drew her fist back, glaring. He was the man who had just saved her life, but now they were even. He was her prime suspect involved in Nader's death. He was also the bastard whose arm she'd grabbed when she was thrown overboard. He'd tried to kill her and why he had saved her later didn't matter. She was upset at herself for needing saving, for showing her weakness, especially to North.

Lieutenant North's face showed pure surprise. She caught him in the mouth with her first weary strike and raised her fist for another when she lost balance and rolled backwards. Two men grabbed her arms and another two made their way to North as the ship turned back into the storm.

* * *

Within ten minutes Spurs and North sat wrapped in blankets in front of Reeves inside the lieutenant commander's stateroom. Doc Jolly had just left after attending to them. Corporal Sanders stood by the hatchway, trying to maintain parade rest against the rocking ship. The two soaked sailors glared at each other, North feeling his chin. His nose was already beginning to swell from the head butt she'd given him.

"What in the hell happened out there?" Reeves asked.

Spurs was exasperated. She raised her voice. "I told you, the son-of-a-bitch tried to kill me."

North rolled his eyes.

"Calm down," Reeves said. "Let's not jump to conclusions here, Ensign. What you're accusing Mr. North of is a very serious matter. If you insist on this claim, there'll be a very extensive investigation. This ship could be in port for weeks, possibly leave the fleet."

Spurs caught what Reeves was saying. If she raised a stink about what happened, the Jap Rap investigation could be compromised. That was a much bigger matter, affecting many more lives.

"Just tell me what happened, Ensign Sperling," Reeves said.

Spurs cleared her throat. She glanced at North. North looked away, shaking his head.

"I was on the signal bridge, and. . . ."

"What in the hell were you doing on the signal bridge during a force eight storm?" North asked, his voice weak, speech slurred.

"Getting fresh air, okay . . . ," Spurs nipped, then remembered his rank, as her head became light and she leaned back against the bulkhead, ". . . sir?"

"Mr. North," Reeves said, "I'll ask you to hold your questions and comments until the Ensign is finished. I'll listen to your side of the story then. Go ahead, Ensign Sperling."

"I saw Chief Franken. . . ."

Now, it was Reeves doing the interrupting. "What?

You mean Senior Chief Petty Officer Gus Franken?"

"Yes, sir," Spurs said. "He went overboard, too. He's dead."

"I don't know if Chief Franken is dead or not, but you couldn't have seen him on this ship tonight."

"Sure I did, sir. I talked to him. Somebody . . . ," she began, then thought about what Reeves had said of the investigation. If what had happened appeared purely accidental, there was sure to be a simple inquiry, but a full-fledged felony investigation that would surely spoil their mission, wouldn't be necessary, " . . . that is, he slipped and fell over."

"I don't know who you saw and talked to, but it wasn't Franken. Our chief didn't report back from liberty in Rota yesterday. He's AWOL."

Spurs glanced at North, then back to Reeves.

"But, sir," she began, "he. . . ."

"Okay, so you thought it was Franken. Had you met him before? How did you know it was him?"

"No, sir, he said that was his name."

"I see." He turned to the corporal and said, "Sanders, have Mr. Goodman muster the crew and account for all hands." He turned back to Spurs as the corporal acknowledged and left the room. "We'll see who, if anyone, is missing. Go on with your story. How did you end up overboard?"

Spurs took time to consider. "It felt like someone threw me."

"Threw you?"

"Yes, sir."

"And you think that someone was Mr. North?"

"Yes, sir." She frowned at North, then looked back to Reeves and said, "May I ask where you might have been when all of this took place?"

He looked straight faced at her and said, "Although

I hardly see how that's relevant, I was in my stateroom in the middle of trying to figure out what to do with you and the rest of the WINS when one of Lieutenant Chardoff's men, Sergeant Krebs, reported an emergency on the fantail. Said the tarp had come off of the Tomahawk missile station and he was afraid someone might have tampered with the missiles. The man overboard sounded while I was aft."

"And did something happen to the missiles?"

"No. By the time I got there, the Marines had them covered back up and they said nothing had been damaged."

Spurs glared at him and his lame but possible excuse. She wanted to ask him why the hell he hadn't been watching the signal deck as he was supposed to. He paid no attention and turned to North."

All right Lieutenant North, what's your story?"

North wiped away the droplets of water trickling down his face. "I stepped onto the quarterdeck to check the storm, and I heard a commotion overhead. When I went up the port side ladder, I saw Miss Sperling about to fall over the bulwarks. I reached for her and she grabbed me and pulled me over with her."

"Did you see anyone else on the signal bridge with the Ensign?"

North paused. Spurs couldn't tell if he was trying to make up a story to cover up something or that he too was choosing his words carefully to avoid a nasty investigation.

"No, sir, I did not."

Chapter 26

AFTER THE STORM

May 3, 2200

FOR THE NEXT day and a half after the squall, the sea was calm. Spurs and North were flown to the *Enterprise* to meet with the Sixth Fleet Commander, Admiral Pierce, to give a complete account of the incident that had taken four lives—five according to Spurs. The Fleet Operations Officer, Captain Novacek and the Fleet Legal Officer, Captain Chang sat in. The two NCIS agents stationed on the flagship did not. If the assumption were that there had been no criminal activity involved, NCIS would not be responsible to investigate. Even if this incident had involved a murder and an attempt on her life, the NCIS investigators would not want to let the cat from the bag yet. She didn't bring Chief Franken up. Reeves had instructed her not to, concerned that it could jeopardize the Jap Rap investigation. She had to bite her lip. After three hours of grueling questioning in separate rooms, they were heloed back to the *Atchison*.

The fleet passed through the seven-mile wide Strait of Gibraltar at sunset. Evening chow had stuck in a lump in Spurs' gut. She was glad that the ocean had settled, hoping it would ease her stomach, but even the mild rocking kept her nauseated.

She spent the rest of the evening in her stateroom analyzing what little clues she had. She laid them out in front of her on the small metal desk; a photo of Ensign Nader on the Bridge with Commanders Naugle and Reeves, eight letters to his parents and girl friend, notes taken at the Nader's, and the message left by SCPO Franken.

Nader was a happy young man, a wonderful life ahead of him. His parents attested to that. So did his girl friend. They'd spoken of marriage. He'd looked forward to a long exciting career in the Navy. His letters said nothing to indicate that he was depressed or had problems. He had always spoken out against drugs.

The last letter to his parents postmarked five days before his death hinted at some kind of danger. It was what he said in the last couple of sentences that was troublesome:

I'm anxious to try out the new weapon's system. It'll be exciting to get them on line and snapped in. I've only seen them fired in training films, but this time, I'll get to push the button.

There is something strange about the Tomahawks that I can't put my finger on, though. It'd be better if I didn't speculate about something that's probably just my imagination. But in the event that something should happen, I'd like you to always remember I was fully aware that honor sometimes demands a high price.

Spurs rubbed her finger across the young man's picture. An intelligent looking guy. He would have gone far.

"'Honor sometimes demands a high price,'" she said aloud.

The Tomahawks. He said there was something strange about the Tomahawks. What could he have meant? The mission of the cruise missiles set by the Navy—the ship—Commanders Naugle and Reeves?

She placed the letters back into their plastic container and picked up the note from Franken and looked it over again. She remembered the description he'd given of the men who had confronted Nader that night. He couldn't be one hundred percent sure who they were, but he had a good idea. He'd never told her. All he'd had time to say was that one was very large. Chardoff's size. She'd noticed only one other man nearly as big on the ship. It was one of the cooks. She figured that by now she'd seen about every crewmember. If she could rule the cook out, she could be relatively sure that Chardoff was her man. Not positive enough to arrest him, but sure enough to watch his every move. Maybe it was time to pay the cook a little visit.

She stood up from the desk and slipped the rest of her slim clues into the shallow Tupperware container while considering the possible motives for Murder. Reeves was sure it was an international drug ring headed up by Arab terrorists to introduce a new, deadly drug into the United States on US Navy vessels. Franken seemed to think that the drugs were used as a cover up. Spurs tucked the container under her mattress and went out the door. As she walked the passageway from officers' country to the crew's quarters below, she heard what sounded like a muffled moan.

She staggered slightly, still not completely in control of her equilibrium. Using her right hand to steady herself against the wall, she pushed away from it lightly when the stateroom door ahead of her popped open.

The door stood ajar about six inches, then creaked lightly as it closed with the next rock. Once again a low moan came from inside the stateroom as she stepped closer.

The nameplate on the door read *Captain R. D. Chardoff*. A light shone from inside. The ship rocked the door open once again. This time she could see in.

She stepped further down the hallway, watching the door while she passed. It closed quietly as the ship tilted back. She stopped in front of it, knowing well that her curiosity was overruling good judgment.

The hatch opened again and she could see a lit television screen. Her first thought was that Captain Chardoff was watching some sort of training films on his VCR, but as she leaned closer she saw that it was something much different. On the screen was a nude woman gagged and tied to a pole. He was watching some sort of sick bondage film. She heard another deep moan and put her face to the doorway's four inch opening. Chardoff stood with his back to her in front of the TV, naked, his massive thighs driving fervently into what Spurs could only guess was his own hand. She frowned in revulsion. He was in the midst of feverish, passionate sex—with himself. Henry Dubain was right, the entire ship was nuts.

The door rocked closed and she had to pull her head back. When it opened, the hinges mewed louder. She didn't need or wish to see more and she began to leave, but this time she wondered if what Chardoff was watching was just a "B" movie or even XXX porno.

A man came into the picture on the TV wearing nothing but a black silk hood. He carried a huge, serrated hunting knife. The woman's face contorted in fear as she cringed against her bindings. If this was acting, it was deserving of an Academy Award. Chardoff's muscular backside worked wildly, glistening with sweat. The hooded man on the TV screen raised the weapon. The bonded woman's eyes widened and she struggled against the cord that tied her.

At the same time that the sharp blade sliced, Chardoff's body went into spasms and he groaned like a rutting bull.

The woman's throat gushed red and Spurs winced and jerked her head back, glancing her cheek against the door. It swung wide, creaking loudly. She turned and bumped into a fire extinguisher hanging nearby and knocked it to the floor, then ran for the steps down to the next deck without looking back.

As she descended in leaps, Chardoff's voice boomed through the passageway, "Little bitch!"

She heard the door slam as she cleared the landing.

Chapter 27

WHAT'S COOKING

SPURS FOUND PETTY Officer Second Class Johnny Big Track in the galley, butchering chicken. When she entered the hatchway, he looked up from his work, standing with his left side to her, his left arm raised, a large meat cleaver in his hand.

The huge man stared at her lethargically with sad, dark eyes. His large body was remarkably similar in size to Chardoff's, except the Native American had a little bit of a paunch. His hair was short but thick and black and he had a broad face. He brought the cleaver down with a sharp *whack* without looking at the fowl.

Spurs stood eyeing him back. Big Track turned away.

"Something I can do for you, miss?" His voice was low, slow and gruff.

"Yeah," she said, stepping closer. "I was wanting to check next week's menu. I'm allergic to apricots. I was going to ask if the choice hadn't been made, to not have apricots. Maybe pears or apples instead."

The big Native American raised the knife again. He

slammed it down, focused on his work. She moved around to his front.

"Don't have apricots anyway," he said, sounding irritated. "You want pears, it'll be pears."

She saw the big man's right arm bandaged and in a sling.

"What happened to your arm?"

"Grease fire."

"When?"

"Five days ago. Just before evening chow."

"Was it bad?"

"Bad enough to take me to sick bay on the *Enterprise*. Spent two days there on my back. Went nuts. Had to get back to work."

Spurs considered what he was saying. His grease fire would have been the evening before Nader fell.

Big Track seemed to be having trouble positioning a fryer on the cutting board in order to cut off its drumstick. She reached over and pulled back on the chicken leg for him.

"You a good cook?" she asked, still analyzing. He could be lying about the timing.

He raised the cleaver and she noticed a heart-shaped tattoo on his arm with *MOM* printed in big, red letters.

"Yeah, I'm good."

Spurs had a frightening thought. "You are left handed, aren't you?"

"Nope," he said, staring into her eyes as he slammed the cleaver down.

The huge kitchen knife struck, chopping the chicken leg off two inches from her fingers.

Cook Big Track replied, "Terrible with my left hand."

Spurs gaped. She looked at her fingers, the cleaver buried in the cutting board. She raised her undamaged member and looked up at Big Track. He stared back then gave her a hand towel and grinned. It took effort but she grinned back.

Her little interview was inconclusive. Chardoff was definitely top on her bad guy list, but she wasn't sure on what list to place Petty Officer Second Class Johnny Big Track.

Chapter 28

HEAD START

AFTER LEAVING BIG Track in the galley, Spurs took the time to check out the new women's restroom. She went one deck below, saw the hatch she thought was the correct one and entered without looking.

Undoing her belt as she stepped in, she looked up to see two sailors standing with their backs to her at the urinals.

Her face reddened, first with embarrassment, then with anger.

"What in the hell are you men doing in here!"

The sailors turned their heads looking surprised. One glanced at the other and began smiling. The other smiled back.

"I asked what you're doing in here, sailors. This is the women's head!"

Still no answer, but the man that had smiled first turned to her without zipping up. The other crewman did the same, both of them snickering.

"Attention, men," the smiley one said.

There were more giggles as they stood with their flies open, hands on their members.

Spurs suddenly realized that she hadn't looked before entering. Maybe she had gotten the wrong head. On a ship they all look the same. She wasn't used to the vessel yet and all of the decks and hatchways were similar.

"At ease!" she said and turned, stepping back out as the two seaman burst into laughter.

She hurried away but then stopped and turned back around to examine the stenciled letters above the head entrance.

WOMEN'S HEAD it said in big, black letters.

"Dirty bastards!"

Chapter 29

ALONE IN A CROWD

THEY DROPPED ANCHOR in Barcelona harbor early in the afternoon. Spurs was given all night liberty and took the time to sightsee by herself. She opted to wear her summer whites instead of her civilian attire or *civvies* thinking she wouldn't spend more than a couple of hours ashore.

The bullfights didn't appeal to her, and she didn't know much Spanish. She spent the afternoon and early evening browsing in the markets and shops.

Darkness found her at a window table in a small cafe, sipping on a tiny cup of thick Spanish coffee. She decided it was one of those acquired taste sort of things, but topped with whipped cream, it wasn't bad.

She looked out onto the small street lined with quaint cafes, bars and small shops. A number of Spaniards walked along the sidewalks, but few Americans that she could tell for sure. Some sailors wore their uniforms. Occasionally, she recognized a couple of sailors from the ship wearing their street clothes.

She sipped on her coffee as the twilight's purple shadows grew along the narrow brown brick street until a familiar figure caught her attention. He walked in her direction but across the street and wore civvies, sunglasses and a Kansas City Royals ball cap. It was Lieutenant North. She ducked behind the window edge and peeked out just far enough to see.

A small, white Volvo coming from the same direction passed him and slowed, then parked at the curb. He glanced up and down the street, then stepped into a doorway. A dark-haired woman wearing a beige overcoat, black scarf and sunglasses got out of the car, scanned around her, then hurried to the same entrance.

A tryst with a lover or hooker? With what she knew about North's sexual preference, probably not, but perhaps he was bisexual. Spurs bit her lip. A meeting with a foreign agent?

Spurs stared at the doorway for a full fifteen minutes before North came out, stood briefly, then walked back the direction he'd came. About fifty feet down the sidewalk, he paused by a streetlight and looked back. The woman soon emerged and trotted to her car. After she was safely inside, North continued on and the Volvo sped away.

"Suspect number two," Spurs said, then licked the cream from her third coffee off her lips.

She watched North until he was out of sight but stared blankly at where he'd disappeared around the corner of a building.

Now she had at least two prime suspects. North and Chardoff. Like Reeves had said, one was probably the Chameleon. They were either involved in some sort of illicit drug operation or selling cruise missile secrets, possibly even Tomahawk parts to God knows who. *Allah's Gihad*? Drugs—maybe? Weapons? Both? And what about Commander Reeves? Was he really to be trusted? A phone call to her NCIS boss—and uncle—Deputy Assistant Director Paul Royse would do no harm.

Chapter 30

PHONE HOME

THE SCANT LIGHTS along the narrow Barcelona road made dim circles on the bricks and the shadows took over the streets.

Spurs stood from her small table, tossed a wad of paper *pesetas* next to her empty coffee cup and went for the door.

At the *Centre de Telefono* on a nearby corner, she called the Naval Criminal Investigative Service in Washington, D. C., gave the receptionist her name and asked for Paul Royse. She looked around the empty, glass enclosed room as she waited. Over a dozen pay phones covered two walls.

Ten seconds later, Royse picked up.

"Spurs, are you all right?"

Warmth spread over her body. It was so good to hear a familiar voice. A voice of someone she trusted. Deputy Assistant Director (DAD) Royse. The acronym seemed to fit. He treated her more like what she thought a father should than her own father, the Admiral.

"So far. You guys really dropped me in the cow pasture blindfolded."

"I know. It wasn't my idea. This might sound incredible but I believe Director Burgess set you up. He knew this mission was too involved and dangerous for a green agent. He's using you for a decoy to throw off *Allah's Gihad.*"

Spurs didn't like the implication that she was green, even from Royse.

"I can handle it. There's a heap of strange things happening here, but I'm going to break the case soon."

"No way. I heard about your little swimming incident and the helo crash. Drop everything and go to the airport. I'll arrange for your ticket back."

"No, I'm okay. I'm getting close. I'll have the Chameleon hog-tied and on your doorstep within the week."

"The Chameleon?—No, Spurs. Leave that to. . . ."

A huge hand swung down on the phone and she was bumped to the side. She stumbled and looked up. Chardoff towered over her, grinning. He'd disconnected the line.

Chapter 31

LOVERS AND FRIENDS

"EXCUSE ME, ENSIGN," Chardoff said. "Guess *I'd* better watch where *I'm* going or *I'm* liable to get hurt."

He pulled the receiver from Spurs' hand and looked at the phone buttons.

"Glad there's a free phone—I've gotta call Mom," he said, dropping a coin in the slot, then he looked to her. "It's a personal call. Do you mind?"

Spurs glanced around the room at the other thirteen phones. No one stood in front of any of them. No *Out of Order* signs. The room was empty except for her and the Marine.

"Asshole," was all Spurs could think of to say.

"Sweetheart, is that the best you can do? Now, be a good little cunt and go away."

She backed off, seeing the large K-bar knife in its scabbard on his belt. This was not a good time or place for a confrontation with this big ape. She'd have to call Royse back later.

Her thoughts were interrupted by yet another familiar figure—her ex-fiancée, Doug *Bird Dog* Smith.

He walked by the windows, arms around the shoulders of two companions. All wore civvies and big smiles as they talked. It appeared that they'd started drinking early.

Spurs missed him. She had to at least say hello. Maybe they could have a drink together.

Without looking back at Chardoff, she trotted out the door to see that the three were walking toward what appeared to be a popular bar as several other military sorts preceded them in. Suppressing an excited yell—trying to avoid appearing like an infatuated teenager missing an old lover, she jogged to catch him before he went through the door. But her emotions were so taken aback by the sight of a friendly face that she couldn't contain herself.

"Doug!"

He hadn't heard. She trotted up behind and got in on the middle of their conversation.

" . . . at least my pickle button doesn't stick, Cards," Doug said to his black companion on the right. "Between that and your loose cannon plugs, we ought to change your handle to *Ol' No Shot*."

Spurs knew that the pickle button was the button on the stick of a fighter plane used to fire a particular weapon after it had been selected. The cannon plug he referred to was probably the electrical connector on a fighter plane's wing pylon that couples a missile to the fire control wiring harness.

The smaller man on his left patted Doug on the back in an odd sort of soft and feminine way and said, "Nothing's wrong with your pickle."

Doug turned to him and smiled amorously. The man leaned his head on his shoulder.

Spurs was sure that this was some kind of a male play-gay-so-everyone-knows-you're-not sort of game.

Cards pulled away from Bird Dog's arm and said, "Hey, I told you two, no funny business while I'm around. I'm straight, remember?"

He turned back to see Spurs looking at the three bewildered.

"Well, hi there, pretty ensign," Cards said. "I like girls, really."

The three men stopped in front of the bar and the other two turned to her smiling.

Bird Dog's smile turned to shock.

"Spurs?"

"Hi Doug," she said stepping up to him, somewhat surprised at his reaction. His face became red as if he'd been caught doing something he wasn't supposed to.

"What are you doing here?" he asked.

"I'm on the *Atchison*."

"What? I thought you were going into NCIS."

She frowned at him. *Good move, Doug. Let the world know.*

He seemed to realize his mistake. "My big mouth. But these guys are okay."

The tall, broad-shouldered black guy on the right asked, "Hey, Bird Dog, where have you been hiding this cute little quail, or should I say secret agent?" He reached his hand out. "The name's Robert Stedman, Spurs. But you can call me Cards."

She shook his hand as the shorter, boyish faced man on the left said, "Well isn't this just too cozy. Everyone has a nickname except me." His voice was soft. He turned to her and offered his hand. "I'm Victor Bowser," he said, "I guess you can call me Vic." They shook. "So you're Spurs. Doug has told me a lot of nice things about you."

"Oh?" she said, looking to Doug.

"Yes," Vic continued. "I'm sorry things didn't work out for you two."

Cards punched Doug in the arm. "Kind of got your tit in the wringer, huh boy?"

The *Bird Dog* Doug Smith appeared dumbfounded, seeming to have lost his speech.

"I think we'd better go inside, sit down and talk," Vic said looking to Doug. "Let's get this over with and behind us, Doug."

Chapter 32

GAY BARCELONA

"YOU GO IN," Spurs told the others in the doorway of the bar. "I've seen and heard enough."

Several eager patrons squeezed by them and went through the door of the tavern.

"Spurs wait," Doug said. "You don't understand." He looked down. "I don't even understand."

Spurs stared at him as he continued.

"I really cared for you—I still do, it's just that all my life I've had this kind of funny feeling. It's like the whole world thinks a guy has to be macho and want to be with women. I went along with it because I thought I had to. I thought there was something wrong with me. I really cared for you, Spurs. You're a wonderful girl, but I was so confused about my own sexuality. Then I met Vic back in Virginia and everything changed. He made me realize that I wasn't sick. I was just different than most guys. He made me feel special."

Spurs' cheeks burned. She turned and walked away, briskly. The street was filling with the evening crowd of sailors, tourists and locals going to the bars and restaurants.

"Wait, please," Bird Dog said.

She heard running from behind. Someone pulled her shoulder and turned her around. She expected to see Doug. Instead, it was the tall black man, Cards.

"There's something you really don't understand about this," he said. "You know, I was kind of like you when I found out about it. Of course Bird Dog and I were never lovers or engaged or anything. I'm as straight as a guy can get. When he told me that he was gay, I nearly shit. At first I was pissed, I mean we were best friends."

Spurs looked up at him. "I'm listening. Tell me what I don't understand. How am I supposed to react to this?"

Several people passed, a couple of them bumping into the two. A young sailor holding hands with a pretty young girl went by.

Cards took Spurs by the arms and she looked up at his pleading eyes.

"You've got to understand that Doug isn't any different than he used to be. He's still a great guy. He's bright and funny and intelligent. That hasn't changed. He doesn't want to hurt anyone. Especially you. He fought with this for quite a while. He didn't ask to be gay. He was born that way. He's been imprisoned by other people's prejudices for a long time. Now he's finally free. But he still has to deal with the prejudice." Cards paused. "I know exactly what that's like. Maybe you do too. I didn't ask to be black, but I'm proud I am, and I'm going to make the best of my life and not worry about ignorant people. You didn't ask to be a woman. I'll bet it's been hard for you to be doing a *man's job*, hasn't it. But you're going to live your life, do the best you can with what God gave you to work with, and the hell with everyone else, right?"

Spurs bowed her head and looked away. The few

words Cards had spoken were worth a lifetime of bigotry preached to her by her father. It didn't matter how much she told herself that the Admiral was always right, she'd known deep down inside since she was old enough to tie her shoes and think for herself that he had been disgustingly wrong about gays, blacks and women, besides every other race and religion that wasn't his own.

"Tell him I'm sorry," she said. "I'll try to understand."

"It'd be better if you told him."

"I can't. Let's leave it like this. It's the best I can do, right now."

She looked up to him and he smiled and patted her arm. She turned away confused and angry. She wasn't watching where she was going and bumped into someone on the street. Someone in a red dress and high heels. Someone with walnut brown skin and bright red lipstick. A blonde wig, jarred to the side. Short, curly black hair underneath. Another person stood to the side with milk-white skin and a tight pink dress.

"*Que pasa, hermana?*"

Spurs looked up at the woman. She quickly recognized the masculine nose and jaw veiled in thick makeup. A transvestite. Another queer! The world seemed loaded with gays.

She bolted, hustling toward a taxi a block away.

"*Loca puta,*" she heard one of them say. She stepped quickly. It was too much—sickening. She felt about to vomit.

Nearly in a run as she sought escape, she glanced off of several people on the crowded street. A pair of hands seemed to come from nowhere. She was suddenly grabbed and held by her forearms. Oh God, she thought, it's probably another one. She wrenched away and looked up.

"Hey, easy, Ensign Sperling!" Lieutenant Commander

Reeves said, his white uniform brightened by the colorful lights from the bars and dance clubs surrounding them. "You all right?"

Spurs immediately relaxed. It was someone straight—someone down to earth—someone on her side.

"Oh God," she said, eyes rolling. "I'm glad to see you."

"Well, thank you Ensign. I'm glad to see you, too."

"I'm sorry, sir," she said. "It just seems like everyone around me is a homo."

He raised his eyebrows.

"How about a drink?" he asked.

She glanced about. "Okay, but not here."

"Have you ever seen a live Flamenco show?"

Spurs smiled. "No, I'd love to, sir."

Reeves smiled back then raised his hand to a cab a half a block away.

"Taxi!" he yelled.

The cab pulled up immediately and he opened the door for her.

She seated herself and scooted over to the opposite side and he slipped in beside her. "Thank you, sir."

He grinned. "Call me Nick."

Chapter 33

FLAMENCO FEVER

AFTER A FIFTEEN minute drive away from the seaport's bars and red-light district, through a dark, forsaken industrial area filled with dilapidated buildings, abandoned warehouses and empty textile plants, and down several deserted narrow alleyways, the cab stopped in front of *El Club Del Flamenco*. Reeves assisted Spurs out of the car and tossed in several *pesetas* to the driver. Along the dimly lit cobblestone street were late-model Mercedes, Saabs, and Volvos. Spurs wondered if the black car parked closest to the door was not a Rolls Royce. Around many of the vehicles were finely dressed men, standing patiently, some leaning against the ancient mortar walls of Barcelona's oldest sector.

The vigorous strumming of guitars pulsated from the doorway of the club. Reeves took her by the arm and escorted her eagerly to the door. The smile on his face was endearing, like that of a child on his way to the circus. A colorfully dressed doorman with a top hat and ruffled shirt opened the thick wooden double doors. They entered to find a heavy-set balding maitre d' who ushered them to a table, second row from the dance floor in the rapidly filling room. Three guitarists sat on stools to the back of the spotlighted wall in between two closed, red curtains. Around them were couples in their nicest evening attire: dark suits and tuxes and brightly colored and sequined evening gowns.

The vibrating strings rattled Spurs' lungs as she glanced over the audience. The lights dimmed. She could feel the anticipation of the crowd, building up like the electrical charge she'd experienced before the lightning had struck the helo.

The other patrons appeared to be locals, no other military or obvious Americans. Nearly glowing in their white uniforms, she and Reeves stuck out from the rest of the audience like ice cream vendors at a funeral.

Reeves ordered drinks in the leaning waiter's ear. Spurs couldn't hear what. The waiter quickly returned with two glasses of what he called in English "a nice, native *Rosa Barcelona*," and they sipped from them casually for the next few minutes as she took in the crowd. Spanish citizens, smiling, joking—laughing out loud. They only occasionally glanced back at her and Reeves. Some of the men were smoking large cigars. But this was not a back-street dive. She examined their attire once again. The men's tuxes were silk, their ruffled shirts, also. The women's gowns were long, low-cut and formal. They were all dressed as if they were attending a presidential inauguration or the Academy Awards.

Soon, castanets began clacking rapidly. The guitars silenced. The crowd hushed. The lights rose. The castanets stopped. Silence.

The audience watched the curtains, excitement in their faces.

As the waiter returned with two glasses of red wine and placed them on the table the castanets started again, slowly. A man's thick-heeled shoe appeared from behind the right curtain. A woman's high-heeled shoe came out from the one on the left. Their heels tapped on the tile floor. The castanets clicked along like drumming fingers. The guitars accompanied, strumming softly.

The sound built, some of the crowd joining in, clapping along. The man and woman came out from behind the curtains striking their heels and twisting their bodies. The woman's red dress was tight at the thighs, and when she spun it flew out from just above her knees exposing trim, shapely legs. The man's tight black pants showed every curve, every bulge of his athletic body. Dressed as a matador, he wore a short, black jacket and a flat, wide-brimmed, black hat.

They crossed the floor, their backs arched, stepping boldly. They paused to spin around each other in the middle, her castanets clicking, his hands clapping sharply. Then they headed for the audience, looking momentarily into the eyes of each of the patrons sitting in the front row.

Without even a glance to each other to pick a target, the matador's eyes found Reeves. The woman's found Spurs. They advanced to them, stamping their feet, clicking castanets and clapping hands to the rhythm of the strumming guitars.

Spurs checked Reeves, his expression dead pan, watching the *matador* approach. She looked at her counterpart, stomping closer, castanets in one hand, a colorful fan fluttering in the other. They drew nearer, staring at the two.

The crowded room witnessed the show intently, wordlessly, their clapping hands now silent.

Spurs watched Reeves and the young, delicately featured *matador*. The man brought his face to within inches of the commander, Reeves looking back still unfazed, without blinking.

The woman was now in Spurs' face and she turned to her. She saw that the young woman also had delicate features. Auburn hair. Full, wet, cherry-like lips. Beautiful, sensuous, brown eyes. Her low cut dress left no guess that she had full, firm breasts. Thin waist, shapely hips.

Her face neared to within inches of Spurs'. She ran her tongue across her sexy mouth and stared deep into Spurs' eyes, drawing uncomfortably nearer. Spurs felt a warmth rush through her body. It raised. Burned. She pulled her head back but the woman moved closer. Her eyes asked Spurs to kiss her. Her lips parted showing the tips of straight white teeth. Her mouth begged for a long, passionate, wet kiss. Her eyes, lazy, staring, longingly inviting. Spurs' own eyes could not wander. They were drawn in to the woman's.

Something deep within told Spurs to go ahead, kiss this lovely young woman, experience her exotic beauty, taste her sensuous juices. The enticing Spanish woman was a beautiful art form. Something that should be appreciated. She told herself that these were not gay thoughts; she didn't like other women sexually—had never experienced a gay relationship of any kind—even the thought of it was repulsive to her, yet. . . .

She didn't know where the forbidden notion had come from and once she had time to analyze it with her society-taught morality, she jerked her face away, dashing the temptation.

The woman also moved away and Spurs looked at Reeves. The two men seemed to be in a stare-down. She wondered what went on inside Reeves' head. Could he also be tempted to kiss the young man? Did he also have these strange, suppressed feelings that should never be explored or let out, but be held down, covered up, strangled, ashamed of. No, not him. He was just being his cool self. Able to handle any situation. In control, even as he sat there, the crowd watching, the young man glaring.

The two flamenco dancers crossed behind them, changing partners. Now the young *matador* drew closer to Spurs, the young woman closer to Reeves.

The young man's lips parted. His eyes did not ask for, they demanded a kiss. He brought his face to hers and once again, she pulled back, but he pursued quickly. She felt the heat of his body, heard his heavy breath, took in his scent. It was not an offensive or pungent odor, but a mild musky smell with its own clean sweetness. She felt her nostrils flare, her face flush, a burning from within warmed her breasts. She didn't turn away and when his kiss met hers, it was welcomed. But it was only a light touch, brief, disappointing. His lips glanced off of hers, in the same instant, the matador rose and glared at the young woman.

The female dancer's lips lingered on Reeves', and as she finished the prolonged embrace, she turned to the male dancer, her head bowed, eyes glimpsing up guiltily. He scowled back and began to move calculatingly around the table like a barnyard rooster about to run off one of his hen's new suitors. The woman slinked behind Reeves, looking as though she was using him as a shield. The man stopped five feet in front of the commander, glaring first at the young woman, then at Reeves. He reached under his short jacket.

Then the gun appeared.

The crowd gasped. He pointed the revolver at Reeves, the commander still looked back unflinchingly. Calmly.

Spurs knew this was part of the act. It had to be.

The *matador* pulled the hammer back. His eyes squinted.

Spurs had doubts. Was this real? The gun certainly was. Had the two dancers been in a jealous fight moments before taking the floor? Did the woman go too far with the act? Had he told her that he would kill the next man she kissed? Was he about to actually shoot Reeves?

Spurs rose from the table.

Reeves still sat, staring back at the gunman.

She started toward the pistol.

Suddenly; *POP, POP, POP!*

Chapter 34

GUN PLAY

THE AUDIENCE BROKE into screams. Many rose from their seats. The club filled with gasps. Spurs' hand was nearly on the pistol before she realized it didn't smoke. Reeves didn't slump in his chair. He sat, still in his deadpan stare.

Spurs stopped. She gaped at the man, then at Reeves. Now she realized the crowd's staring eyes. The room was quiet.

The Spaniard tossed the handgun to Spurs and she caught it clumsily. Now he pointed his finger at her, looking serious, determined, dangerous, and slammed his heels on the floor three more times. *Pop, pop, pop.* Then his stern face brightened into a wide smile.

The room erupted in laughter.

Spurs knew her cheeks flushed deep red, already burning from the passion of the two dancers, now intensified by the embarrassment. She flipped the gun back to the young man and quickly found her seat as the two dancers went to the middle of the floor, dancing around each other gaily like courting pigeons.

Reeves raised his eyebrows, then lifted his voice above the still roaring, now applauding audience.

"Having fun?"

Spurs blinked slowly and curled the corner of her mouth. "You knew, didn't you?"

Reeves shrugged, smiling, then turned to the dancers. The crowd clapped with the rhythm of the guitars and Reeves clapped along. Everyone seemed into the beat.

The young woman now floundered around the man's extended leg. He watched her arrogantly as she slipped to the floor, her arms reaching pleadingly. He turned away and walked boldly toward the curtain on the left. She collapsed to the floor as if crying. As soon as her eyes left him, he turned, came back to her quickly, then gracefully, nearly effortlessly, lifted her from the floor and swung her around him, both of them now showing big smiles. They twirled, their outside arms reaching. Faces beaming.

The guitars stopped with the loudest of strums.

The dancers hustled from the floor behind the curtain on the left.

The crowd exploded. They stood, clapping wildly. The two dancers whipped out from behind the curtain, now out of character, grinning meekly.

Reeves stood, beating his palms then nodded at Spurs seeming to want her to stand. The audience not only watched the dancers on the floor but most were alternating glances from them to her.

She smiled then, also. She stood up and clapped.

"Bravo!" Reeves said, then turned to the dancers. "Bravo!"

The crowd joined in with their praises. Their applause built even louder.

The flamenco dancers bowed now with broad smiles.

Their outstretched arms offered Spurs and Reeves to the crowd and the applause became deafening.

"Bravo," Spurs said, "Bravo!" as the waiter presented them with two more tall glasses of red wine.

Chapter 35

A BIG LETDOWN

SPURS LOOKED ABOUT the room and nodded with a faint smile. What else could she do but go along with the gag in which she had been the target.

When she turned back to Reeves, she found he was already seated. He shoved the fresh glass of wine toward her and she sat down.

"Funny," she said, her voice elevated so that Reeves could hear her easily over the crowd. She gave him a lopsided grin. "Very, very funny. But just you remember, paybacks are hell—superior officer or not."

He smiled and raised his glass briefly as if toasting her.

After only a couple of sips of the second glass of wine, Spurs felt a fire smoldering from within. In the whirlwind of the evening, she couldn't tell if it was a physical burning or if it might have been psychological. As she leaned toward Reeves to ask him how many times before had he brought women to this place to humiliate them, she knocked over her wine glass. The white tablecloth grew crimson from the red *Barcelona*.

Now, embarrassing herself with her own clumsiness, she said, "Let's get out of her."

Reeves stood up without a word and threw down a small stack of *pesetas* for the waiter.

When they left *El Club Del Flamenco* in the cab, Spurs thought they would be heading back to the ship. Reeves had just told the cabbie, *Parador de Barcelona*. Spurs thought it might be Spanish for the shipyards of Barcelona.

It had been a tiring but exciting evening. She tried to deny to herself that she hadn't been turned on by the flamenco dancers, especially by the sensuous beauty that nearly kissed her. Her attraction to Commander Reeves, or Nick as he had asked for her to call him, was hard to deny also. He was like what she pictured her father might have been when he was younger. She wondered if the Admiral hadn't looked—even acted like Reeves did now, thirty years ago. If she couldn't get her father's approval, should she try to get Reeves'?

The taxi driver glanced over his shoulder at her as he drove.

He spoke in broken English. "*Señorita*, be careful. The murderer is out *anoché. Es muy mal*—very bad."

She frowned at him curiously, then at Reeves. He nodded.

She asked the driver, "Murderer?"

"*Si, Señorita*, he killed nine Mediterranean women. This evening, here in Barcelona, a woman I know, Maria Sevilla, makes ten. But no be scared much, he kills mostly whores. Still, be careful, *por favor*."

She asked Reeves, "You've heard about this?"

"Maria was my informant." Reeves eyes went blank and his face grim. "Interpol won't put out the MO to the public. They're afraid it'll jeopardize their investigation. But we have reliable information it was a knife. That seems to be the weapon of choice around here." He stared out the side window.

Spurs thought about Captain Chardoff's knife. She reached across the back seat of the taxi to Reeves and placed a consoling hand on his. He gazed at her. She turned away.

"Have a boyfriend?" Reeves asked.

Spurs looked to see him still staring. She smiled and turned away again, pretending to study the ancient back streets of Barcelona.

"I was engaged up until a couple of months ago," she said. "There's no one now, nor am I looking."

She glanced at him coyly without intending to. Realizing it, she dropped her eyes. Her head began spinning, like she'd had too much to drink. Maybe she had. It had been months since she'd drunk more than a few sips of alcohol. Still, she wouldn't have thought that less than a glass and a half of wine would make her intoxicated.

He moved closer and put his right arm around her. "You're a beautiful woman," he said. "I can't help but feel attracted to you." He drew his face nearer.

She looked up into his brown, paternal eyes.

His left hand came up and gently caressed her cheek, then he kissed her teasingly, pulling away after only a brief touch.

She brought her lips to his.

His large but gentle hand moved from her face to her throat. She could feel its light grasp most of the way around her neck. He caressed her softly while kissing her face passionately, then took his hand away and nibbled down to her collarbone. Now the roving hand unbuttoned her blouse and quickly groped in and seized her right breast.

Spurs tried to push him away, her hand shoving

against his shoulder, but he was too strong.

"No," she pleaded softly.

Reeves didn't pay attention.

"Please, Nick. No!"

He continued.

She put the heel of her right hand under his nose and gave it a solid shove.

This time he reeled back.

They passed the street she'd been on earlier when she had the thick Spanish coffee. They were going the wrong way to go to the ship.

"Where's he taking us?"

Reeves frowned at her.

"I'm sorry, I thought . . . ," he began, then turned toward the cabbie.

Spurs looked at the attractive Naval officer. She was rejecting him. Tonight he'd been a friend. He'd cheered her up. They'd had an exciting time. She felt safe and secure with him in the middle of a chaotic world. She had failed with Doug. She had failed with her father. She shouldn't fail again.

"*Amigo, por favor . . . ,*" he said to the cabbie.

He was going to ask the driver to take them back to the ship. Tonight was her chance to prove to herself that she was worthy of someone's affection. But to make love with Reeves—to have sex—would be far too much too soon. Maybe they could drive around some more—talk.

"No," she said and leaned to him. She didn't know what had come over her. The dizziness increased.

They gazed at one another momentarily. She smiled.

He wrapped his arms around her, kissing her feverishly.

* * *

As they pulled up to the *Parador de Barcelona*, an ancient castle turned into a spacious hotel by the Spanish government, the cabbie repeated his warning. "Remember, *señorita*, the murderer," he said. "Be careful."

They checked into the hotel and were in their room so quickly that there had been little time to think. Her head was still spinning from the wine. Was she doing the right thing—no, she thought at first. But then, how could this be wrong? He was an attractive man. He was sure of himself, intelligent. He was wise and realized how to deal with her from the start. Testing her at first, then discovering she could handle her assignment, he had trusted her, opened up to her, and done away with the chauvinist act he put on when she first boarded the ship.

Now, forgiving that he got a little carried away in the cab, to her, he seemed kind, gentle, caring and considerate. His passion for her seemed to overflow, and it had been so long since she'd been on the receiving end of such ardor. Even with her fiancée, Doug, what seemed at first a mutual fervor of love seemed to wane during the months following their engagement. Then, tonight, she finally found out why. He was gay. How could he have been gay when they first met? The first time they made love? The times they shared the weekends together, locked in passion, only finding a few spare moments to break apart to eat and sleep. Was it something she'd done? Had she driven him to homosexuality?

After they'd entered the hotel room, Spurs went directly to the restroom and vomited. When she staggered out, she was about to tell Reeves of her dizziness. Tell, him that they were moving much too fast, anyway. Apologize to him—it was the wine. Wine had never affected her like this before, but that's what it had to have been. Perhaps, he'd understand and not be too disappointed.

But he was waiting naked in the bed, the sheet up to his middle.

Reeves smiled at her and she came to him. She gave him a half smile and sat on the edge of the bed.

"I'm sorry . . . ," she began.

He sat up before she could finish and pressed his lips to hers.

He kneaded her breasts then moved his hands down her body to her butt and gripped firmly.

Again the dizziness took over but this time, she seemed to lose complete control of her senses, unable to push him away, unable to say anything to stop him. Surely he would stop. Her breath, after all, she thought—she'd just thrown up. He would—should understand.

He released her lips and forced her underneath him, then began pulling off her clothes. The room spun. She was sure she'd be unconscious soon. Her thoughts were deadening, arms unable to move. Now, she felt in a daze and wasn't sure, but she thought she was completely nude. His lips were exploring her body from her forehead down to her nose, mouth, neck and breasts. He began suckling on her left nipple. She could feel his penis chafing against her as he writhed. But it wasn't hard. There was no erection. She had no doubt, though, that his feverish passion would soon give it life. Maybe he'd had too much to drink, also, although he didn't seem impaired otherwise. Maybe he'd find it useless and give up.

She watched his thick, dark brown hair as his tongue flicked around her chest playfully. Still, movement of her arms was drudgery, nearly impossible. Finally, she brought them up, trying to grab his hair, his ears, anything to get a hold of to pull him back, but her energy ran dry and her arms collapsed on his back.

What's wrong with me? she wondered. Had she been drugged? Was it the last glass of wine? What would have happened if she'd drunk it all and not spilled most of it? No, surely it was only the alcohol she was feeling. She was just not used to it, that's all. But, less than two drinks?

He licked at each breast, pulling them together so that he could mouth both nipples at the same time.

He moved lower, licking, kissing slowly down her stomach, below her navel and lower.

God, how was she going to get him off of her?

He came back up and pressed his lips to hers, again. On her thigh, she could feel that he still didn't have an erection. Finally, she found the strength to move her right hand down to his middle. She brushed against his testicles and he flinched at first. Her hand was placed awkwardly, almost as if she'd intended to caress his manhood—but that was the furthest from her mind.

He pulled his head back, pausing only briefly to smile amorously as if considering her tender, sexual gesture then pressed his lips back to hers.

The thought of it made her feel sick again. She wished she could throw up once more, this time puke into his mouth as his kissing became even harder, more passionate to the point of frenzy.

Still, she could feel only a limp organ between his legs and thankfully so. At the same time, however, she was becoming more aware by the second of something about to explode in Reeves, but it had nothing to do with anything *below* his waist.

The pressure from his mouth became pain. He jerked up. Both of his hands were suddenly around her throat. He squeezed. She gasped for air but his grip was too tight. She couldn't understand what he was trying to do. Surely, he was only *temporarily* getting carried away—

upset about his informant being killed. He would let up soon.

But he didn't. She mustered the extra strength to bring her left hand up and tried to pull his hands away, her other hand still on his flaccid organ and testicles. He was too strong, she much too weak.

The situation was becoming critical. Soon, she would black out—die. *God, no!* She must find the strength, dig deep for the power to stop him. But, he was so strong, and her weak state made her feel like a rag doll in the jaws of a rottweiler.

He was going nuts. Crazy.

The pain. Stars as her vision blurred, then darkened.

He was a bully—a schoolyard toughie, holding her down and spitting in her face. *No! Never again!*

At long last, her right hand energized and she squeezed the package it encased and then wrenched harder than she thought was possible in her condition.

His eyes bugged. He stared down at her for a second as she kept the pressure. Finally, he grimaced and let go of her neck. His eyes rolled back like a dying calf in a hailstorm and he fell away from her and off the bed.

Spurs' strength was coming back quickly, along with a nearly overwhelming headache. She sat up and began gathering her clothes and dressing as quickly as possible as Reeves got up painstakingly. He sat on the edge of the bed with his back to her, holding his head in his hands.

"I'm sorry," he said. "I hope I didn't hurt you."

He glanced over his shoulder as Spurs gaped back rubbing her throat.

"Since my wife died, fifteen years ago—I haven't been able to. . . ."

And what am I supposed to do? she thought, *Say; oh,*

that's all right. I understand. You're pissed that you can't get it up, so you try to strangle me. Perfectly normal. Choke me some more, please!

Chapter 36

PREPARATION FOR THE DAY OF RECKONING

May 4, 0200
Near Tripoli, Libya

UNDER MOONLIGHT, THE black clad soldiers moved like shadows across the white sand beaches of Libya. This special unit of *Allah's Gihad* had been training together for over nine months in anticipation of the day they would become heroes of the Muslim world. They had trained individually to fight to the death in honor of Allah since they could hold a knife or throw a stone.

"Run Fahmi," Tijani Hewidi yelled, waiving his arm to his old companion. "Catch up with the rest!"

Fahmi Amin staggered, tired legs dragging, chasing the group of fifty-three armed terrorists wearing black dungarees and watch caps. Their AK-47s held at port arms in front of them, they stabbed the sand with chopping steps, raising their knees high as they raced to the edge of the water. Black and green painted faces, streaked from perspiration, showed the strain of a four-hour workout.

Fahmi fell in the moist, almost fluorescent sand, raised to his feet, then stumbled falling face first again, this time scooping up a mouthful of beach.

The rest of the group had reached the water's edge and then turned to circle back toward the palm trees lining the shore.

Tijani Hewidi and Saddam Al-Hodeibi stepped up to Fahmi. Hewidi bent down and took his childhood friend's face by the jaw and raised his head from the sand. Fahmi's large brown eyes were out of proportion to his face. The long, jagged scar that ran from Fahmi's left temple to his chin reminded Hewidi how his friend had saved his life—pushed him away from harm—when an Israeli soldier's jeep had gone out of control and ran Fahmi down when they were both ten.

Fahmi's body lay heaving, his mouth wide, gasping for oxygen.

"Fahmi, get up," Hewidi said. "You must get up. You must be strong for the fight against the infidels. Do not disgrace us Fahmi. Do not disgrace me."

Fahmi Amin lifted his upper body, shoving against his rifle in the sand. As Hewidi stepped back, Fahmi brought his knees up, planted one foot and then the other and staggered to stand. He leaned forward, making Hewidi think he would fall again. Tijani Hewidi took a step toward him, his hands out, then paused.

"Fahmi, for Allah. We live for Allah. We fight for Allah. We die for Allah—now, run for Allah."

Fahmi Amin stomped forward without looking at Hewidi, his mouth still agape, drawing deep vital breaths. He staggered more, then trotted off tagging behind the rest of the group.

"Fahmi will not make it," Saddam Al-Hodeibi said, shaking his head and rubbing his goatee. "He will be the cause of our failure."

Hewidi didn't look to Al-Hodeibi, but watched his childhood companion.

"He will make it," he said, knowing he most likely would not. Fahmi was a devout Muslim besides the best friend Hewidi had ever had. Their fathers had been best friends and had fought against the Jews in the Seven Day War.

"But he is so weak!"

"The strength his body has not is made up for by the spirit in his soul."

"But what if the spirit is not enough? What happens if he becomes a burden?"

"If that happens, we will deal with it as we have dealt with it in the past," Hewidi said, then turned to Al-Hodeibi. "We will kill him."

Hewidi turned away, seeing a messenger running down from the village.

"Master Hewidi, Ma'amoun Al-Tayib orders you to come now," the young boy said puffing. "He has news."

Hewidi and Al-Hodeibi smiled at one another then sprinted toward the village, the young runner racing behind.

Ma'amoun Al-Tayib sat behind the large table in the three-room stucco home that their brother to the cause, Mohamar Kadafi, had provided. Around the aging and thin holy man, a dozen cases of weapons and ammo were stacked near the walls. He looked up as Hewidi and Al-Hodeibi rushed in.

They caught themselves in the doorway and bowed to their leader, their faces glowing anxiously.

"Master," Hewidi asked as he bowed, "is it time? May we now have revenge for our dead brothers against the great Satan?"

"Nazir Aziz and his men are prepared to attack the American embassy in Mauritania. He will begin in two days. The American warships now in the Mediterranean are sure to go to their rescue within hours of his attack. You will go now to the ambush site near Oujda and be ready when Aziz seizes the Embassy. The *Chameleon* is soon to change colors."

"And what if our brother Nazir fails to gain control?"

"That does not matter," the holy man replied. "The Americans will be drawn into our plan. They will not disappoint us."

"Praise Allah," Hewidi said.

Al-Tayib looked to the side and pointed at three aqua, beach-ball-size objects sitting on the floor.

"These have come from our Russian friends, acquired at great risk from their Navy. Take them with you. Your American traitors will know what to do with them when the time comes."

He reached beside his chair and pulled up an aluminum briefcase, then laid it on the table in front of him. He snapped it open and turned it to show the other two men. It was jammed with bundles of US hundred dollar bills.

"Here is Saddam Hussein's gift to the American's helping our cause. You will take it with you. The other half of the ten million dollars will be provided after the deed is done."

Al-Tayib stretched his arms out and looked at the weapons' crates. "Share these arms with my children. Train them quickly, make them comfortable with the guns."

Al-Hodeibi stepped to one of the open crates and looked in, touching a rifle. "But master, these are American M-16s. We have already trained with the AK-47s Iran furnished us."

"Do as I ask. These are what the Americans use. This is what we will have to use for our task."

"Yes master," Al-Hodeibi said, raising one of the weapons out of the crate.

Ma'amoun Al-Tayib stood from the table. He smiled, showing black decaying teeth.

"Soon, my children," he said, "very soon, we will have vengeance and make the great Satan cry like a baby. Mohammed's warrior from Iraq has helped to buy many useful things. Soon all of Islam will reap a long overdue reward. And we, *Allah's Gihad*, will be heroes among our people!"

Chapter 37

Q AND A

AFTER A QUIET taxi ride with Reeves back to the ship, Spurs went to her stateroom, showered and hit the rack. Too much had happened too fast to digest. Her fellow investigator was some kind of an S&M psycho. Even if he hadn't intended to hurt her, somehow got carried away because of the wine, she wasn't about to get into the choking bit. That was for perverts, and she would not play. Perhaps something was in his drink, as it might have been in hers. Maybe those ritzy-titzy Spaniards thought it was funny to drug up Americans. But then, it could have been Reeves that put something in her drink. She couldn't remember when he'd had the opportunity—she hadn't left to go to the powder room—but the night had become a blur. She wouldn't rule out that he'd been in some sort of drug-induced rage, but she certainly wasn't going to consider it an excuse.

Still, she needed the lieutenant commander for the case. It would be difficult without him, even though she would like to bring him up on assault charges. Attempted rape would be out—she doubted if Reeves could even get it up to choke *his own* chicken.

Reeves had told her about Ensign Ingrassias' possible drug use. Since Nader was found with cocaine in his nostrils and Ingrassias was the only crewmember suspected of using dope, he would be the one she would question next. She would do so first thing in the morning.

She fell asleep and dreamed about Rocket, the horse her Aunt Katherine and Uncle Paul had given her when she was ten. Spurs and her mother lived with them while the Admiral was at sea. It was the day of her tenth birthday when the long awaited colt stumbled into the world. Uncle Paul promised she could have the colt for a birthday present as soon as it was born, and its arrival seemed perfectly planned. He wasn't anything special, just a spindly, gaunt little white colt with a black mark in the shape of a rocket above his right eye. But when he grew into a beautiful white stallion, he gave validity to his name, and Spurs rode him through the countryside around Guthrie, Oklahoma. She loved the feel of wind in her hair, the movement of Rocket's muscular body under hers and the feeling of freedom as the two roamed the red dirt hills at a gallop.

In her dreams, Spurs felt that wind, smelled Rocket's lathered hide, and remembered that freedom.

* * *

At 1115 the next morning, Spurs was finally ready to catch up with Ensign Ingrassias. A punishing early-morning headache—she guessed from the red wine the night before—had slowed her down, but it had finally subsided and she felt clear headed and eager to get back on track.

Once again, they were preparing to get underway, this time heading for Bizerta, Tunisia. She looked forward to Livorno, Italy, where the rest of her group of twenty-four were to come aboard. But that was some time away, yet. She hoped she'd have things tidied up by then and be back stateside. Many arrangements were to be made, specialty supplies to be ordered such as tampons and other toiletry items the ship hadn't seen in its forty-five years of service.

Spurs walked in on Ingrassias unexpectedly in the supply room. As she stepped through the hatchway, she saw him setting at a desk, smoking while looking over a list on a clipboard. She smelled incense and noticed the ventilation fan above his desk was on high.

When he looked up to see her, he smashed out the end of his smoke, threw it to the deck and put his right foot over it.

He looked to her with a guilt-flushed face.

"Something I can do for you, Sperling?"

Spurs stepped over to his desk and rested her right hip on it.

"I was hoping that I might be able to help *you*."

"Help me? Help me how?"

"I thought you might like some ideas on what to order for the female crew members coming aboard."

He smiled. "Yeah, sure, that'd be great, uh, but not right now. I've got a shit load to do. Maybe you could make me a list or something."

"Be glad to," she said and lifted from the desk.

She turned to leave but then paused, knowing that Ingrassias still watched her nervously.

"Isn't incense considered contraband on board ship?" she asked with her back still turned.

"Yeah, its just that there was some gun oil that leaked

out and stunk up the place. I was trying to get rid of the smell.

"Gun oil?"

"Yeah."

"It must be doing a pretty good job, I don't smell *any* gun oil."

"That's why I used it."

She turned to him and noticed him try to kick the joint on the floor under his desk.

"How about smoking below decks? The captain's banned that too, hasn't he?"

"Yeah, I guess you're right. I forgot."

Spurs reached under the desk with the toe of her right foot, scooted the homemade cigarette out and picked it up. She raised it and took a good look, then sniffed.

"Funny looking cigarettes you smoke, Ingrassias."

"I roll my own. What of it?"

"You're just begging to get caught, aren't you?"

"Leave me alone," he said turning away. "Either bust me or leave me the hell alone."

"Now, how would I bust you?"

"You're NCIS aren't you?"

God, she thought, *I really do stick out.* "Why do you think that?"

"Come on, the whole ship knows. Everybody's been wondering why they'd send a woman on board undercover. Shit, man, you might as well be wearing a sandwich sign that says *I'm the heat.*"

"All right then, smart ass, tell me why I shouldn't bust you."

"There's no good reason. Go ahead and do it. Get me the hell off this ship."

"Why are you so eager to leave?"

"Either arrest me or leave me the hell alone. You

nosing around asking questions is gonna get someone killed."

"I bust you, and you're going to spend ten years in a federal prison. Is that what you want?"

Ingrassias was silent. He didn't look at her.

"What happened the night that Nader died? You know, don't you?"

"I don't know shit."

"You're lying."

"I told you...."

"Ten years, Ingrassias. Don't you know what'll happen to a little doper like you in a federal pen? Answer me and you won't have to find out—personally."

Ingrassias looked at the hatch then back to Spurs.

"I'll tell you all I know, if you get the hell away from me as soon as I do."

"Go ahead."

"I was sleeping in my bunk," he said, nodding to a bunk near the far bulkhead. "Captain Chardoff busted in and started slapping me around. He punched me a couple of times to make sure he got my attention." He rubbed his mouth. "Then he told me that he knew I had some cocaine and he wanted some of it. I gave him a bag, but he just took a pinch and put it on some cigarette paper and stuffed it into his shirt pocket. I told him to keep the whole thing, but he threw it back at me. Then he told me that I'd been dreaming and fell out of my rack. He said he'd kill me if I told anybody any different."

"What else?"

"That's all I know, honest."

"What about any of the others that are missing—Chief Franken?"

"Franken came down and leaned on me the day after Nader died, too. I told him what I just told you. I don't know anything else."

"What about *Jap Rap?*"

"I don't know what you're talking about."

"Jap Rap. It's a new drug—a synthetic cocaine, many times more powerful. Haven't you heard of it?"

"No. You got any?"

Spurs flipped the joint onto Ingrassias' desk and turned away. She went to the hatchway.

"Remember," Ingrassias said. "Don't tell anybody I talked. Especially that bastard Marine. You keep my secret, I'll keep yours."

Chapter 38

STEAMING TO AFRICA

May 8, 1400
USS Atchison

IT WOULD BE more than three and a half days before they dropped anchor in Bizerta, Tunisia. Spurs spent most of that time becoming familiar with the Command and Control Center. The rest of the time, she nosed around questioning crewmembers. By now, she figured most of the crew either was sure she was NCIS like Ingrassias said or at least suspected it. She wouldn't become lax in covering it up, regardless. She continued to observe the ship and all the crewmembers as clandestinely as possible. No one volunteered any information. If something didn't break soon, she felt she'd have to be taken off of the case, thinking she might have lost the effectiveness of being undercover.

A question gnawed at her ever since being pulled out of the ocean after being thrown overboard; who was it if it wasn't Franken that she'd met that night of the squall on the signal deck?

She stayed clear of Reeves, bumping into him only

twice, each time just long enough to exchange a few token words. The last time she did, she let him in on what Ingrassias had told her. She questioned if NCIS had used good judgment in recruiting Reeves. It didn't appear he was doing much investigating. Of course, he had to keep a low profile, and running the ship in place of the migraine-hampered captain did require a lot of time.

On the bridge, she decided to speak with Lieutenant Commander Reeves semi-privately while he was away from the helmsman and the rest of the crew were busy at their jobs.

"Commander, may I see the ship's liberty log?" she asked.

He glanced around to ensure no one was watching or listening in.

"What for?"

"I'd like to prove to myself that it wasn't Chief Franken I saw the night of the helo crash."

"Suit yourself," he said, and walked to a cabinet, opened it and brought out a three-ringed binder. "This is it. We use a clipboard to sign in on, then the sheets are punched and put in here." He handed it to her.

She opened it and leafed back to the first of May. She saw where the OOD at the time, Lieutenant North, had her sign in when she reported on board.

There were many signatures from 0010 up until two hours before they shoved off at 1500. She turned the page to look at the next sheet. It was dated three days later and said "Liberty—Barcelona" at the top. From the indentations, it was apparent that page had been under the previous one on the clipboard when the crew signed aboard in Rota. She could even read several of the harder pressed signatures on the Barcelona page from the Rota one.

Then she noticed something strange about the first

line on the Barcelona page. The signature was that of Corporal Sanders. Nothing strange about that. Botts had signed in back in Rota on the first line and the indentation of his signature superimposed onto Sanders'. But the indentation seemed to be too long.

She flipped the page back and saw where Botts had signed in, then went back to Sanders' signature. She took a pencil from her pocket and tried the old detective trick of lightly shading over the indentions to read what had been written on the previous page. It worked. Botts had signed in, but superimposed in that same space was SCPO Gus Franken's signature at 1440, only minutes after she had. The OOD must have had him sign on a new page when he came back from liberty, then thrown it away and started yet another page for the rest of the crew. Franken had been aboard ship that night.

She looked to see what officer had signed the sheet as the OOD for that time, remembering that North had been in their stateroom about then. It was signed *Capt. R. D. Chardoff.*

Spurs stepped over to Reeves who was studying a nautical chart. She shoved the clipboard to him.

"I did see Franken," she said.

He looked at it as she turned and walked off of the bridge.

She heard him following. He caught up to her as she descended the steps of the port bridge ladder.

"I'm sorry I didn't believe you."

"I'm getting used to it, sir."

"I'd like to make it up to you. I'd like to make Barcelona up to you, too."

Spurs paused on the steps and shrugged, still not looking to him. "Haven't we got more important things to concern ourselves with, sir? I mean *besides* you attempting to murder me?"

"God, Spurs, no! I'm telling you, I don't know what got into me. It was crazy. I've never felt so strange— never done anything like that. Maybe it was something in the drink. A Mickey. Please, please forgive me. Come on. This is important, too. Meet me at the Tunis Hotel in Bizerta the first night on liberty. We'll have a couple of drinks and talk things out."

Chapter 39

DESERT SANDS

May 9
Bizerta, Tunisia

SPURS WAITED FOR Lieutenant Commander Reeves in the bar at the Tunis Hotel just outside of Bizerta. He was late, it was already 1945, and he'd said he would meet her there by 1900 for drinks. She had pulled out all the stops this time and didn't really know why.

She remembered the last time they shared drinks and later a room. It had been nothing but a terrifying experience. As she recalled that night, she slipped the black, high-heel pumps back on that she'd picked up in London while awaiting her connecting flight to Rota the week before. She'd had too much to drink that evening in Barcelona—or had she? She remembered the brutal headache she had afterwards. Such a hangover after less than a glass and a half of wine? And to come on so soon. Maybe someone *did* slip her a Mickey—drugged her, as Reeves had said—for who knows what purpose. Perhaps to kill her—get her out of the way. Perhaps to seduce her. Maybe it'd been Reeves. But maybe Reeves *had* been drugged, also. Now she was thankful for her clumsiness—glad she'd spilled the second drink after only a couple of sips.

Spurs looked to the bald bartender polishing shot glasses behind the bar, and he glanced across the empty room to her. She raised her glass and swirled the last inch of her second whiskey sour and shrunken ice chips.

"Slow night, huh?" she asked.

He lifted his bushy eyebrows and wiggled his brush-like, black mustache as if he was nibbling on something, but he didn't speak. She knew he wouldn't answer. It had taken her two minutes of hand and arm signals just to tell the man what she wanted to drink.

She knocked the drink back, catching the ice with her teeth, sucked it dry and then sat the glass on the small table in front of her. What in the hell was she trying to do? Meeting Reeves would just be leading him on. Besides, what if he hadn't been drugged and *was* trying to kill her. She needed Reeves as an ally in the investigation, but she certainly didn't need another man, for God's sake. She needed to get this case solved, then get back stateside. Maybe she wasn't cut out for this Navy bullshit. Maybe she should try the FBI or some form of local law enforcement. Never totally understanding her father, she didn't know if that would piss the Admiral off or make him happy.

Spurs scooted her chair back from the table and stood up, grabbed her small clutch purse and began walking toward the door. She pulled out ten paper *dinars* and slapped them on the bar in front of the wide-eyed proprietor as she passed.

With a broad smile she said, "Thanks for a shitty evening Akmed. The drinks tasted like goat pee, the bar smells like camel pucky and you look like a dick with ears."

The man smiled back, muttering in Arabic gibberish.

Through the door, she noticed the telephones in the lobby and thought of calling her uncle, Deputy Assistant Director Paul Royse. But for what purpose? She had very little new information that she hadn't given Reeves and he was sure to be contacting her uncle Paul in this port if he hadn't already. The most calling him now would do is piss Reeves off for her going around him unnecessarily. It could get her yanked from the case like her uncle Paul had tried to do in Barcelona.

Outside, Spurs stood on the steps and leaned against one of the large stone columns in front of the hotel. On the way out, she'd asked the desk attendant to call a cab. It was hot and dry, but an occasional cool sea breeze meandered in from ten miles across the desolate sand in front of her. It rustled the palm fronds on the sparse trees around the front of the building. Five miles to the north, the lights from Bizerta made a glowing dome along the horizon. A beautiful evening. One that would not be shared.

Taking in a deep breath of desert air, she looked down at her slick black dress, cut just below the knees with a slit up the right side. She hung her head and smoothed the black fabric on her thigh with her hand. A tear seeped down her cheek as she slumped down to sit on the step. Her hand balled to a fist and she struck her leg. She felt so confused. Confused about men, about the Navy, about the investigation, about life.

When she looked up, she saw a small headlight through her tears. It came vibrating up the road. Too soon for a cab. She wiped her eyes and sat down on the cool steps. A plump moon was rising over the snow-like sand to the east. It made her think of Christmas in Quantico last winter. The snow covered evening when

Doug had proposed. She shook her head and looked back at the approaching light. It was something small. A motorcycle. No, one of those Mopeds.

"God, I hope that's not the only taxi this time of night," she quipped aloud.

Watching the little cycle, she tried to take her mind off of the rest of the world. She wondered what kind of person would drive such a vehicle up to a luxurious hotel this late in the evening. Perhaps a messenger. Resting her chin on her hand, she gazed out as the motorized bike pulled up. It was a man wearing an oversized, dark blue T-shirt, sneakers and blue jeans. It was a *Go Navy* T-shirt. A nice looking man.

"Oh God," Spurs said aloud and hid her eyes with her left hand when she realized who it was.

Too late.

North trotted up the steps, grinning. "Hey, sad lady, your camel die?"

Spurs twisted away as North stopped beside her. "Why me? I don't need this right now."

"How're the drinks?" he asked, motioning toward the hotel door.

"I'd suggest a bottled European beer."

"That bad, huh. Oh well, I didn't come here for the alcohol."

Spurs still didn't look to him. "What did you come for then?"

"You."

"Me?" she said frowning to him. "What do you mean, me?"

He smiled back, those beautiful eyes sparkling. Had he gone nuts? Had he changed sexual preference? She saw the light blue bruise across the bridge of his nose from the head butt she'd given him in the water. It had given *her* some satisfaction then, and even some now, noticing it. Then she thought of another reason he might be there—to kill her.

She scooted away a couple feet nervously and said, "Aren't you barking up the wrong tree here, Fido?"

"I don't think you understand," he said.

"I think you think right. Please go away."

"Okay, I'll go away." He glanced around warily, then lowered his voice. "But first listen to what I have to say, Special Agent Janelle B. Sperling."

Spurs looked up gaping. He was telling her he knew. Why would he do that, unless he was going to kill her? Murder her here in front of the desk clerk.

She snapped her head back at the open door of the hotel, pointing to the small man watching from the desk inside.

"Don't try anything," she said glaring at North as she stood. "There's a witness."

"Good God, Spurs, you still think I'm the bad guy. I don't suppose you'll believe me if I tell you I'm your contact."

Believe him? Hell no, she wouldn't believe him. Reeves said he might try this. She wasn't sure that North was really involved in this Jap Rap scheme, and had actually hoped he wasn't, wanting to believe his story about trying to save her when they went overboard. There was something inside this man she liked. Deep inside, past the attractive exterior, deeper than his homosexuality. A passion he controlled that she knew he had, beyond his pretentious neatness, his proper behavior and his sarcastic humor. She'd seen it on the ship. But now, she felt that she'd been fooled. The Chameleon was changing colors.

North frowned and rolled his eyes.

"Okay, what can I do to prove it?"

"Nothing, I believe you," she said, backing up the steps toward the door.

"Your boss, Director Burgess is like a father to me. We go back a long way. We're old fishing buddies."

Spurs stopped on the steps. She remembered the photo on Burgess' desk. The other man in the picture—that's where she'd seen North—it was him.

"All right, how about this; Assistant Director Royse is your uncle."

She knew that anyone involved in treason this deep could have found that out.

"I believe you," she said still backing away.

North stepped up, following her.

"While he was away in the Middle East, Admiral Burgess assigned you on this mission, right?"

"You asking or telling?" she said still backing cautiously.

"Royse's first name is Paul, his wife's name is Katherine and—he *also* calls you Spurs. Remember, I called you by your nickname without you telling me what it was the day you first came aboard?"

She slowed, but still backed away. She remembered. He was right. He was trying to make contact that first day, but she'd ignored the obvious attempt.

He continued, "You called Royse in Barcelona, but were interrupted before he could tell you I was your contact."

Spurs stopped within arm's reach of the door and stared into North's eyes considering what he was saying. If what he said was true, then was Reeves a third agent? Not likely. No, if it was, Reeves was more likely one of the bad guys. But how else could North know unless he'd talked to Royse himself—or maybe intercepted a message intended for Reeves? Maybe Chardoff had told him, but she was sure the Marine captain hadn't been standing next to her during her entire conversation with Royse in Barcelona.

"Okay," he said, "now let's get down to business. We've a lot to talk about. Let's go for a ride." He motioned to the Moped.

"Wait a minute," Spurs said. "What about Commander Reeves?"

"What about Commander Reeves?"

"He was going to meet me here—an hour ago."

"Must have gotten sidetracked," he said curling the side of his mouth.

She stared at him. The curl came out and he frowned back. He said what she was thinking.

"Now wait a minute. You don't think I did something to Reeves, do you? And that's how I know what Royse said to you? I tortured Reeves and got it out of him, right?" He shook his head. "Jeez, Sperling, I don't know where he is. Honest."

She still eyed him skeptically.

"Come on," North said, turning his back. He went down several steps toward the waiting Moped then stopped midway and looked back. "Quit being so suspicious. I know it comes with the job, but this is ridiculous. I'll take you back to the ship. Your precious little boyfriend, Reeves is okay. I'll show you."

"He isn't my boyfriend," she scolded.

There went that sideways grin and roll of the eyes again. God, she hated it when he did that.

"Okay, I'll tell you what. Have you got a weapon, something sharp—that fingernail file you used to cut me free of that harness?"

Spurs watched him. What was he up to now?

"Well, still have it?"

She'd put a nice sharp edge on that fingernail file to make her more comfortable when she walked alone at night, not to cut webbing to save a man who had been trying to kill her. This current situation more suited its purpose. She reached in her purse and pulled it out, holding it at the ready.

"Good, good," he said. "Now, you hold that to my throat while we drive back to town and I'll tell you all about the investigations."

"Maybe I know all I need to know about Jap Rap."

"Jap Rap? That's all bull manure. You don't know that by now?"

"What investigations are you talking about then?"

"The one you were assigned to—Nader. And the one I've been following for the past two months—Chameleon. Jap Rap sounds like some kind of an oriental boy band. It doesn't exist. Just a red herring to throw us off."

Who could she believe? If she went with North now, she would have a better chance of finding out who was telling the truth. Or he might kill her. She'd have the fingernail file—at his throat.

She stepped toward him, bringing the file to her side.

"Proceed, Mister North," she said formally.

"That's more like it," he said grinning again. "Hey, did you know you had coon eyes?"

"What?"

"Raccoon eyes. You know, the smeared mascara. It does that when you cry."

He should know, she thought. He probably wears it in drag. She looked back to the desk clerk to make sure he still watched then let down her guard and took a hanky from her purse and wiped her face.

"Does this meet your approval, sir?" she asked.

North's smile was wide now. He looked into her eyes, then stepped back and scanned her up and down.

"Just what are you looking at?"

"If we hit a bump and you accidentally slit my throat with that homemade pig sticker of yours, I guess it won't be so bad. I always wanted to die in the arms of a beautiful woman. I had wished it'd be in the heat of passion, though."

Spurs wrinkled her nose.

"What are you talking about? You're gay."

He hiked his leg over the Moped.

"No, I'm not."

She pulled her skirt up halfway and slipped onto the seat behind him.

"But you said you were."

"No, I just didn't say I wasn't."

"But the way you acted when I confronted you about it . . ."

"Corporal Sanders was right behind us. He *is* gay. Helluva good guy. Best Marine on the ship. I didn't want him to hear that BS you were spewing."

"You're just full of surprises, aren't you?" she said, bringing the manicure tool to his right jugular, pushing it against his skin.

"You ain't seen nothin' yet, sweetheart!" he said revving up the little cycle and pulling away.

Chapter 40

HIGH HO, MOPED!

"YOU THINK REEVES is involved?" she asked as they sped down the blacktop. They couldn't have been going over 20 mph on the little cycle, but to Spurs it seemed they were flying at Mach speed. The feeling was wonderful on the beautiful, moonlit night. The wind was refreshing against her sweat-dampened cheeks. The two whiskey sours, although as well watered as Grandma Molly's roses, had lightened her head. She wanted to believe North, but was still afraid to. This brain screwing she was being put through was getting old—very old.

They hit a small dip in the road and the point of her file poked North's throat.

"Hey, ease up with that blade, will you, killer?" he asked.

She pulled it back and was relieved to see that it had not drawn blood. Still, she rested her hand on his shoulder, the file pointed to his neck. She kept her left hand loose on his left side. She didn't want to give him the impression that she was getting comfortable.

"I don't know what to think about Reeves. He's slick, though. I know that," he said over his left shoulder.

She leaned close with her face just behind his left ear.

"What do you mean?"

"I got a look at his personnel file. Then I ran an FBI check on him. He was arrested for murdering his wife, three days after they were married. They couldn't prove anything, so he was released. That was fifteen years ago."

What would North come up with next?

"I think that's when he found out."

"Found out what?"

"That he didn't like women," North said and swerved around a rock in the road.

"Don't tell me. You think he's gay, too?"

"No, I mean he *hates* women. Maybe his mother made him wear girl's underwear when he was a kid or something. I don't know why. I just know he really dislikes females."

As much as she hated to think, that made some sense as she thought back on the time with Reeves at the *Parador de Barcelona* and even when she first met him after initially boarding the ship.

"What about Chardoff?" she asked.

"Yeah, he's dirty. He might be the Chameleon. There're several others on board, too."

"So what exactly is this Chameleon thing? Drugs?"

"Not even close. Weapons. But I can't figure out for what purpose. There's a terrorist group called *Allah's Gihad* that's behind it, that much we know. And, whatever is going on is going to come down fast now. I can tell. There's a kind of tenseness I feel whenever I'm around Chardoff. It's like he's ready to pop."

"Why didn't you come to me sooner and tell me who you were?"

"To tell you honestly, I was afraid you'd blow everything."

"What do you mean by that?"

"When you came aboard, you seemed very immature. You showed strong bigotry, and I thought you were a real smart ass. You stuck out like a hard on in boxer shorts, not only being assigned after a suspicious death, but being a woman. Hell, you even *acted* like an NCIS agent."

"Thanks a lot!"

"Just the facts, ma'am. Now that I've had a chance to get to know you a little better, I don't think you're as immature as I thought originally. You're not so much of a smart ass. And, I think you may have even learned a few things to make you less of a bigot. Actually, I kind of like you."

Spurs gave a half grin and shook her head. "So what's the plan, Double-O Seven?"

"We've got to watch Chardoff. Wait for him to make his move. When he does, maybe we'll catch him taking weapons off the ship, or what ever he's planning. He may do it when he goes on maneuvers with his recon team and the SEALs."

"The Tomahawks?"

"I don't see how this could have anything to do with them. They can't carry those big birds off. I wouldn't leave anything out, though."

"What's Chardoff doing now?"

"Don't worry," he said. "I followed him to the local cat house. He paid for an all-nighter. This is just like any other port. You can get anything you want here. All you have to do is have enough money and look hard enough."

Spurs thought of Chardoff's huge knife and the murdered women.

They began to pass houses and businesses of Bizerta

as they drove into the edge of town.

"I'm starved," North said. "Have you eaten?"

"No. Me, too."

"I've been here a few times before. I know a great little eating place," he said as he turned a corner.

"Lead on, Darren," Spurs said.

North smiled.

Chapter 41

LIZARD'S MOON

THE SMALL CAFE was on the corner of a well-lit street, but few people were out as eight o'clock was considered late in this land.

They walked into a quaint, candle-lit courtyard stopping briefly to allow a small green lizard to scamper from a green shrub across the brick walk in front of them. North stopped at a table, second one in from the wrought iron archway. The place was decorated with potted desert plants and with peppers of different sizes, shapes and colors hung in bunches along the walls. Two old men sat at a table near the far end of the long, narrow courtyard.

"The air's fresher out here than inside," North said, pulling a chair out for Spurs to sit.

There were no menus at the table and Spurs knew nothing of Mediterranean food. She was just about to ask North what was good when the chubby restaurateur turned from his other patrons to see them sit down.

"Dare!" he exclaimed as he raked the fingers of one hand through his cropped black hair. He hustled over, wiping his hands on his apron. "It's been so long. So good to see you," he blurted out as if there was never enough time to say everything that was on his mind. He took North's extended hand. "How 'bout we finish that chess game now." He pointed to a chessboard half full of tactically positioned chess pieces behind the bar.

North smiled and looked across the table to Spurs.

"How about next time in port, Ma'hami," he said.

"Oh, I'm so sorry." Ma'hami turned to Spurs. "Of course you are occupied, and by such a beautiful young woman." He took Spurs' hand and kissed it gently. "Please forgive me Miss. . . ."

"Spurs," North said before she could answer.

"Miss Spurs, how interesting. So will you be having Dare's children soon?"

She looked at Ma'hami with wide eyes, too stunned to speak. She didn't know whether to laugh at the joke or be insulted by the presumption.

Ma'hami turned to North.

"I did hope you'd marry my daughter, Dare. But why don't you quit this Navy stuff anyway and come live with us. We still have plenty of room. You and your wife would have your own, private bedroom. But you would have to share our toilet. We are not rich Americans."

"We'll discuss it," North said and glanced at Spurs.

"I'll leave you two lovebirds alone and fix your drinks. The usual, Dare?"

North smiled at Spurs and she nodded back. "Surprise me," she said.

"Make it two," North told Ma'hami. "And while you're at it, give us a couple of heaping plates of your special hash." He glanced at Spurs again. "That okay?"

"Sure," she said, thankful he'd taken charge. "As hungry as I am, even camel jerky would sound good."

"That's tomorrow's special," Ma'hami said. "You'll

like my chicken couscous much better." The big man then half skipped in excitement to the side door into the diner, but paused at the doorway and looked to the sky. The moon still hung low. From the angle, it was in the center of the entrance archway as if it were a Chinese lantern. It cast long shadows across the bricks.

"And a big, beautiful, lover's moon, too," he exclaimed before going inside. "How romantic!"

"All right, *Dare*," Spurs said, "who is this strange man and why do you call him *Mommy*?"

North snorted a laugh. "It's Muh—hau—me," he said. "I don't know how we came to be such good friends. I think he's lonely and needs some excitement in his life. When ever I come here, I tell him sea stories and we play chess."

"Uh-huh," Spurs said. "And what about his daughter and should I be jealous since we are *lovebirds*?"

"That's another one I can't explain. She's six. He promised her to me when she was born. I'm kind of like her godfather."

Spurs laughed and shook her head.

"I can't believe you."

North's face straightened.

"Every word's the truth," he said, his eyes giving that patented sparkle again. He smiled. "I've never lied to you."

He reached over to her side of the table and put his hand on hers.

She believed him. She turned her hand over and held his.

"You have strong hands," she said. "But how were you able to hang on to the helicopter when it rescued us?"

"I have a lot of hobbies; SCUBA diving, sky diving, flying—and rock climbing."

"That brings to mind another question. You saw who threw me overboard, didn't you?"

"Not exactly. He had his back to me. I didn't see his face. I saw someone that was probably six or six one, wearing a black slicker."

"That's it? You're leaving something out. What?"

"I saw an Annapolis ring," North said.

"That means Goodman."

"Or Commander Reeves."

"Commander Reeves?" Spurs asked. "I've never seen his ring."

"Doesn't wear it often. I heard him say one time that it irritates his finger."

Spurs didn't know whether to hope he was telling the truth or not.

Ma'hami came back carrying a tray with two tall pink drinks with umbrellas on them.

"Here we are, Dare," he said. "Two of the usual Shirley Temples."

Spurs and North laughed.

"Oh, did I get it wrong?" he asked innocently, then uncovered a couple of short mixed drinks. "Well then, try these two whiskey sours and I'll take the Shirley Temples to the two gentlemen across the room."

"Unreal," Spurs said, recovering from laughter as Ma'hami walked away. She meant North was unreal. He was as different as night and day from what she had originally thought. He somehow even knew what she liked to drink.

"Yes, he is," North said, watching Ma'hami leave. Then he turned back to Spurs, still holding her hand. "You are, too."

He raised his drink as if to toast.

"To haze-gray ships, warm Tunisian nights and cowgirls," he said, squeezing her hand.

Spurs raised her glass. She'd never told him she was a *cowgirl*. The only one on the ship that knew that was Reeves. But of course, he had talked to her uncle Paul Royce. She smiled wide.

She glanced to the large blue-white moon in the archway and saw the little lizard looking back, casting a much bigger shadow from the lunar brightness. Its skin was now brown like the bricks. Its eyes glowed yellow from candlelight.

"And to lover's moons and lizards," she said gazing at North.

Chapter 42

TAKING LIBERTY

MA'HAMI'S SPECIAL HASH of chicken meat, potatoes and mixed vegetables was good and filling, the night remained beautiful, and Spurs felt drawn into North's spell.

They'd had an assortment of hot peppers, sampled at Ma'hami's pleading and drank another two whiskey sours to cool their tongues. The old men had left the courtyard and Ma'hami had gone inside to close up and leave the two of them alone.

Spurs' cheeks ached from the laughter, more than she could recall in recent years. She wished to be away from this place—no not this place, but away from the rest of the world, the Navy, the investigation that grew more complex by the minute.

North had just finished telling her about his Aunt Jean in South Carolina, who still lived in a dirt floor cabin, chewed tobacco and wore overalls and boots. Her hobbies were macramé and alligator poaching.

When the laughter settled into broad smiles, they

looked into each other's eyes and leaned close across the small table separating them.

"How about taking a couple hours off from this case tomorrow and do some horseback riding?" North asked.

It was a surprise to Spurs. "No, don't tell me. Darren North, a cowboy?"

"Not exactly," he said. "More a *farm boy*."

"That's even more of a shock! A farm? You?"

"Yep. Born and raised on a farm near Wichita, Kansas. Anyway, Ma'hami has some great Arabians. Whadaya say?"

"Hmm," She said with a smirk. She toyed with a plump, heart shaped red pepper, about the size of a quarter. "We'll just have to wait and see."

Holding onto its stem, she brought the pepper up to North's lips and rubbed it against them.

While gazing at Spurs, he licked the pepper sensuously and then took it into his mouth and suckled on it.

She pulled it out but he took it again.

He brought his hand up and took hers, pulling the pepper from his mouth and moving her hand over to her lips.

She took the pepper in and played with it, swirling around it with her tongue.

He pulled on it but she wouldn't let go, nursing on the small spicy fruit. Finally he pulled hard enough and the stem popped off. They chuckled softly.

She tongued the pepper up between her teeth and held it waiting.

Music came from the café and North glanced toward it. When Spurs looked, she saw Ma'hami standing in the doorway next to a phonograph. His hands were on his hips, and a smile broader and with more teeth than she thought was possible on a human being spread across his face.

It was tango music.

North drew his face near hers, their hands holding in a finger lock. He pulled her up from her chair and out into a section of the floor clear of the tables. Before she knew what was happening, they were strutting across the bricks, the side of her face against his chest, his head angled slightly to hers in an attempt to compensate for their difference in height. He was very light on his feet.

At first, Spurs felt her clumsiness. She'd never tangoed before. But somehow, North's obvious adeptness kept her stepping lively and made her feel as if she were gliding, thoughtlessly.

Spurs had forgotten about the pepper, her head swimming in the middle of all this. She only realized the thing was still clenched between her teeth when, after about the fifth turn and second spin, North faced her. He opened his mouth baring his teeth and placed them gently on the pepper, their lips touching. They lingered, finally drawing into a kiss, both biting into the pepper as they closed their eyes. Their kiss was passionate, long, wet, and—*HOT*!

Their eyes snapped open simultaneously. The mean little pepper erupted a hell's fire in Spurs' mouth. She whimpered. They loosened from their embrace and went for their table and the ice left in their drinks, at first complaining in whines then once again succumbing to laughter.

Taking a moment to recover from the pepper while standing at the table, they drew near again, but before their lips touched, the sound of a jeep pulling up came from the archway and two shore patrolmen jogged through.

"We finally found you," said the first large sailor. He wore a grey helmet. It had a horizontal, wide white band interrupted by a large SP on the front.

"What's up?" North asked.

"Liberty's cancelled," the big sailor said. "Everyone's

to report back to their ships. There're only you two and a couple more left out."

"Why?" North asked.

"We're on alert. Something about one of our embassies somewhere in Africa. It's under siege."

The needle on the phonograph scratched loudly across the record.

Chapter 43

SMALL THINGS

CAPTAIN R. D. CHARDOFF was as impatient as he was intolerant at times. Intolerant of weaklings, small things that had no purpose and got in the way.

The small brown lizard attempted to escape from his path in the archway of Ma'hami's patio, but Chardoff's enormous foot hurried to stomp it. He twisted his toe to make sure the job was complete.

The cafe patio was empty. The clatter of dishes being washed and someone singing *If I Were A Rich Man* came from inside.

The shore patrol had said North and Sperling had been here. Said something about them not going directly to the ship. He had to catch them before they reported in. It would be much easier to dispose of them here in Bizerte than on the ship. They were about to cause trouble, to mess up his plans.

The Marine Corps hadn't given him many opportunities. It sure as hell wasn't going to make him a *rich man*. He'd have to do that on his own. He had been busted down from major. He'd never see a promotion again. They said he was too brash, too hard on his men. And there were the three reprimands marring his record for "accidents" in which some of his men had gotten hurt during different training exercises. He'd told his superiors the truth. They had been "punished" for not being able to pull their own weight. They called it "beating up," but officially recorded each incident as "training accidents during which time Captain R. D. Chardoff had been the officer in charge and therefore responsible."

The Corps had become weak. America had become weak. He wanted to be on the winning team—the one that paid the best.

Chardoff stepped to the door of the cafe and drew out his huge K-bar knife. It had five marks etched into the blade near the handle. In a few seconds there would be another.

The man inside the restaurant might know where North and Sperling went. If he knew and told Chardoff, he'd kill the man for being weak. If the man didn't know where they were, he'd kill him for being ignorant.

Chapter 44

DESERT STREETS

NORTH AND SPURS took the Moped back to the bicycle peddler North had rented it from. The shop was only four blocks from the pier and the only shop open so late. The proprietor was probably waiting for the cycle's return before closing.

The call of nature, encouraged by the four Scotch and waters, insisted Spurs ask for the restroom. North waited out front.

Spurs wasn't pleased when she stepped behind the curtain and found a straddle trench.

After finishing her business, she hastily combed her hair with the assistance of her vague reflection on a stainless steel pan hanging on the wall. She hadn't been inside more than four minutes, maybe five at most, and when she came outside, North was gone. The street was empty. The shop owner was not in sight, either. She stepped out further and scanned the empty street.

The lights in the shop behind her went out and she turned to see someone standing in the darkness, a shadowy figure behind him. She recognized the clothes of the bicycle peddler, but his face was in the shadow as well as that of what looked like a female figure behind him, probably the shopkeeper's wife.

"The man left," he said.

"Where? Where did he go?" she asked bewildered.

He paused. The figure behind him grabbed his arm. "Some men from the ship came and got him. Said he had to go right away. Stay in the middle of the street. You will be okay."

"I didn't hear any men come. I would have heard a jeep."

The man and his wife went back into the shop, and closed the door.

Spurs looked back at the lonely, narrow street that she would have to walk alone to the pier. This wasn't right. It was all wrong. Now she felt as though at least a dozen eyes watched her, but could see no one.

Chapter 45

A SHARP SABER

REMEMBERING THAT THE pier was two blocks down and then two more to the right, she set out down the middle of the street as instructed. Not like she would walk next to the shadowy sides anyway.

After the first block the dark sidewalks ahead seemed alive. There was movement, a lot of movement. Two, maybe three men working their way toward her on the left, the same on the right. She stopped in front of an even narrower alley in the center of the block and saw men coming up from behind her on both sides of the street.

"Oh shit!" she whispered, "North, if I live through this, I'm going to stick one of those hot peppers up your ass!"

They closed in. Her eyes darted around them to the alleys. The narrower passages seemed deserted, but which should she take? The right one would lead closer to the ship.

She kicked off her high heel shoes and sprinted all out. They chased her.

The alley smelled of rotten vegetables, urine and feces. Broken crates, boxes and barrels lined the sides. Litter cluttered the asphalt.

Three more men suddenly appeared in her path, silhouetted by the lights from the pier at the end of the alley. The pier was so close, but yet so very, very far.

She stopped, fifty feet from them and noticed the large silhouette in the middle. He stuck out like a giant among dwarfs. She wondered if it might be Chardoff.

From the direction she had come, seven or eight men, dressed like locals raced toward her. No way out.

A door opened on one of the buildings to her left.

"American woman!" a young boy's voice called, "American woman, come with me quickly!"

Spurs took no time to consider. She leaped to the entrance. The thin young Arab boy pulled her in and slammed and locked the door behind her.

"Come, they will soon break through," he said, and as he spoke came the first of many body slams against the other side of the door.

He led her up some stairs and across a large vacant space. It looked to be some kind abandoned warehouse. Up two more flights of stairs, past two additional large rooms, and they heard the door below give way.

The boy of about thirteen went to a twenty foot ladder hung loosely from the ceiling and climbed it.

"Come on, come on!" he said.

Spurs extracted her sharpened file from her purse, slipped it carefully into her bra, then tossed the small handbag to the side and grabbed the ladder.

"Where are you taking me?"

"To safety, American woman," he said.

"What's your name?"

"Saber Abdul Ali. Please, no more questions, now."

At the top, he beat against the roof access and finally

lifted it.

Their enemies came running up the steps from across the large, dark room.

Spurs followed Saber out onto the tar roof and he pulled the long wooden ladder up just as the men reached where it had hung. They jumped for it but the boy was too quick and Spurs helped him pull it out and heave it onto the roof.

She looked around them.

"What now, Saber?"

The boy shoved the large access cover shut, closed the hasp and found a long bolt and slipped it through the hasp ring.

"We jump the roofs."

Spurs looked over the alley. Even though it was narrow for an alley, it was still a good twelve feet.

Chapter 46

AMERICAN WOMAN

"HURRY AMERICAN WOMAN," Saber insisted.

"The name's Spurs," she said, watching the boy hustle to one side of the roof.

"Jump like I do," he said lowering his head and shoulders, then racing like he was going to knock down a linebacker.

He leaped from the edge, legs kicking, arms thrashing.

Spurs held her breath.

His feet hit just shy of the adjacent roof, toes striking the side of the building, but he came down on his knees on the roof's parapet and rolled safely. Chunks of the old clay sided building crumbled and fell clicking as it landed four stories below. He scampered up and glanced back at Spurs, his chest heaving. He eyed the ground below, then smiled at her.

"See," he said, "it is easy." He stood holding his hands on his hips.

"Forget it," she said, waving him off.

Footfalls came from the other side of the building

eighty feet away. Spurs turned to see one of her Arab pursuers climb up onto the roof from an outside ladder. Another one followed and there was no reason to assume there would not be more.

She stepped back and ran, still barefooted, to the edge, without even considering which foot to push off with, how to jump, how to land. She left the roof thrashing her arms as Saber did. She peddled her legs through the air.

Her flight was two feet short.

Her hands caught the short parapet of the roof and she straddled a drainpipe. Her grip was only good enough to break all of her fingernails. She dug her fingers and toes in like a cat on a tree but slipped and grabbed onto the drainpipe. It pulled loose at the top.

Meanwhile, a half dozen of their adversaries assembled on the roof from which they had jumped.

Spurs watched them hopelessly as the pipe slowly parted the wall. They returned eager smiles. She wrapped her arms and legs around the pipe. Now six feet out, nothing would stop her. She would strike the opposite wall and then fall to the ground in a bone-breaking crash.

As the pipe she hugged gained speed away from the wall, Spurs felt something whip around her. Her descent slowed and stopped. Then she realized it was some sort of small rope like a clothesline that had snagged her. Saber had roped her. He was pulling her back.

The cockiness her father had worked for years to suppress surfaced and she released one hand from the pipe just long enough to give them a quick middle finger.

When Saber had pulled her back to the wall he reached over to help her up and she climbed over awkwardly.

"Thank you, Saber," she said, smiling at the boy as

they held each other. "I owe you my life."

The boy appeared distracted by the men on the other side. He released her and she turned quickly. One of them was going to leap over.

The man cleared his side with too much height. He came down where Spurs had just landed but his upper body leaned over the parapet in a little better position than she had.

Saber was quick to kick him in the face, but with little results. The other men jeered at them. The man reached for Saber's leg but Saber kicked again, striking the man just under the nose. He kicked several more times in sharp, quick snaps. Finally the man slipped down, his face even with the funnel-like top to the loose drainpipe, but still he held to the parapet's edge.

Spurs grabbed the top of the unfastened pipe and slammed it into the man's face one, two, three times before he fell.

Saber turned and ran, Spurs following. Again they dashed toward the edge of the roof.

"No," Spurs said, "No Saber, I can't do it again. There's got to be another way."

"Don't worry," he said, "just follow me."

He leaped over the edge, this time dropping straight down as she ran up from behind.

"Oh, God!" She trotted over, not even thinking of attempting what Saber had just done. Carefully peeking down, she was surprised to see him smiling up at her from a small roof only eight feet below.

"You little jerk," she said, "you scared the crap out of me."

"Hurry Am . . . Spoors," he said waving to her.

She eased herself onto the edge then vaulted over, landing on her hands and feet.

Saber ducked into a window and she followed him

in, then down some stairs. On the ground level, they paused at another alley doorway and then crossed to the next building and went to the back. It was some sort of old factory with rusty steel pipes and tanks filling the space. He ushered her to the last large boiler tank, about eight feet in diameter and opened the steel access door in the center that was slightly larger than a porthole.

The boy pulled out a flashlight hidden in a nearby pipe, turned it on and tossed it in. There was no sound when it landed like there should have been with a metal flashlight thrown into a steel tank.

"After you, Spoors," the boy said, motioning her on.

Spurs didn't think she should argue. The boy had done all right by her thus far. She reached up with both hands onto the inside of the tank opening, about five feet from the floor. Saber laced his fingers together and held his hands out for her to use as a foot hold. She stepped up, put her head through the dark hole and he boosted her in.

Chapter 47

NIGHT IN THE TANK

THE FLASHLIGHT MADE a yellow glow inside the boiler tank.

"Why are you helping me?" Spurs asked Saber in a whisper.

"Because you needed help," he answered.

"But you don't even know me."

"You would have helped me, wouldn't you, even if you didn't know me?"

Spurs had to honestly think.

"Yes, I guess so."

"Shouldn't any person help another if they can?"

"Sure they should."

Saber smiled. His eyes were large and black and he had a thick shock of charcoal hair to match. His lips were plump, but his face was thin as was his body. Too thin. He was obviously malnourished. A boy of the street.

Spurs shined the flashlight around the inside of the tank.

It was damp and smelled of urine, probably from the feather mattress they sat on lining the bottom. She guessed that it had been found in the trash or stolen, along with the few other items in the boy's steel home. A kitten stood at the other end, its back arched, a wooden splint tied to its leg. A homemade wire birdcage hung from the top with a sparrow inside, its wing taped.

"Nice place," she said, smiling at the boy.

"Thank you," he said gleaming back. "I like it more better than the alley."

She nodded. "Are these your pets?"

"If you mean, do I own them, no, I do not. They are their own free people, like everyone should be. I only help them and care for them until they are well enough to be on their own—like me. We are friends."

"How'd you learn such good English?"

"Americans come to this port very often. It pays a beggar to know the language of the rich." He paused and looked at his feet as he squatted. "I think that my father was American."

"Don't you know?"

He looked up. "Not for sure. My mother was a whore, like me."

Spurs sat back, staring unbelievingly at the boy. He didn't seem sad about what he had said. It was a part of his life that he lived with and had adjusted to.

"I'm sorry."

"For what?" he asked. "I am alive. And when I die, I will see my mother once again. And someday, my rich father, in heaven."

"How long has your mother been dead?"

"Since I was five."

Spurs grimaced. "What do you do? How do you live?"

Now the boy looked sad, looking back at his feet.

"As I said, I am a whore like my mother."

Spurs tried to analyze, to understand what he was saying.

He looked up to her questioning face and explained.

"I sell myself to the sailors that come here." A smile came to his lips as he pulled some paper from his pocket then put it in front of the light. It was a single *dinar*, worth less than an American dollar. "See," he said, moistening his lips, "tomorrow I will have bread." His eyes became even brighter. "We can share."

"No," Spurs said smiling. "I just need to get back to my ship. There'll be plenty of bread there."

She had tucked ten dollars into her bra for safe keeping before going on liberty so she reached in next to the fingernail file and pulled it out. Kind of crowded in there anyway.

"Here, this is for you," she said, placing it in his hands. "Don't let anyone fool you, that's worth about fifteen *dinars*."

"But what do I do for this," he asked, his face looking perplexed. "I have never had sex with a woman. Although I think it may be nice."

"No, sweetheart. Let's just say it's for saving my life."

"But *that* I did not do for payment. Those men are bad. They were going to hurt you."

"Yes, they were, and my little hero saved the day," she said and leaned to him and kissed his dirty forehead.

Saber looked stunned, but then a smile split his face, and he began rocking back and forth, holding his knees. A giggle erupted in small bursts, then turned into continuous laughter. Spurs laughed along. Remembering they were being hunted, both quieted, smiling at one another and putting their fingers to their lips.

"It is best that we be quiet and sleep now," Saber said. "In an hour or so, we might be able to get you back to your ship."

He leaned back, but seemed uncomfortable, grimacing briefly, then rolled to his side with his back turned to Spurs.

"Good idea," she said, even though she knew that an hour might be all the time she had. Being on alert, the ship could shove off at any time. But the streets were too dangerous, now.

She lay down behind Saber and noticed a dark spot midway down his back. Before, it had blended with the rest of the dirt on the poor boy's red shirt. But now, looking close with the flashlight, she could see that it was moist in the middle. She touched the spot curiously, hoping it wasn't what it seemed.

Saber flinched.

"Saber, what happened?"

"It's nothing Spoors, but there is more I should tell you." He kept his back to her.

"It's not nothing. You're bleeding."

"I was on the roof when I saw you in the street by the bicycle shop. I was hiding from a very bad man. I think he was after you, also. When I saw you were an American woman, I thought I could tell you the terrible thing I had heard. I did not know who else I could trust, but I knew I must tell someone."

"Why were you hiding from him? Did he do this to you?"

"He bought me for the night. I heard him talking with some other men in the room next to mine in the whorehouse. I don't think they knew anyone listened or at least knew English. At first they spoke of the kind of whore they preferred. The big man said he liked young boys so I knew that I would be told to please him. But then they spoke about something else—something that scared me very much."

He rolled over grimacing from the pain coming from the wound on his back.

"What was it?"

His eyes widened and he began to shake.

"Saber, it's okay. Take your time and tell me."

Tremors took over his body and he began to cry. His breath caught and he gasped for air. Spurs wrapped her arms around him gently. She couldn't imagine what could be so terrible to a strong-willed boy like him. He had just been through hell and yet was unfazed. He lived like dirt, but could still smile and laugh about it. What was so frightening that it could break his strong spirit to tears?

"Shh-shh. Calm down, now. Tell me very slowly. First, how did you get this wound?"

He gasped several times more, but calmed enough to speak. Spurs still held him, their cheeks together, lips next to the other's ear.

"The big American man that bought me did it," he said in a loud whisper. "He made me play a game. He made me go *baa-baa* like a sheep, and pushed a big knife into my back. He said that he cut me to make sure I paid attention and that if he stuck the knife in all the way, I would not make a sound when I died and no one would know. He said I'd better be good to him or his knife would kill me and it would get a new notch."

"The bastard!" Spurs cried, breaking into tears, also. "You poor boy."

She stroked his thick black hair and clutched him tight.

"Do not cry for that, Spoors," he said. "It is the way I live. And probably will be the way I die. I will see my mother when I die, and my father someday, too."

That was all the boy had to look forward to in life—death. Spurs choked, she had cried enough tonight, but couldn't shut it off now.

"Please, don't cry, Spoors. I did not mean to make

you cry. What I must tell you is much worse than what happened to me."

Spurs shook her head. She could not imagine anything worse.

Saber pushed back and looked Spurs face to face from only inches away. His lips began trembling again.

"This man and his friends said that they were going to do something very bad. They said they were going to sink a ship and many people would die. And they laughed. I do not like these men. I have never killed anyone unless they were going to hurt someone. These men I would kill if I could, but they are too strong. Do you have friends that can stop them? Maybe it is your ship they are going to sink!"

He began crying again and Spurs hugged him tightly. She wondered if what he had heard was true—if perhaps he'd heard it wrong.

"Don't worry, Saber," she said running her fingers through his thick hair, "I have many friends that will stop them. They won't sink my ship or any other." She hoped what she told him was true.

She turned off the flashlight and rocked him to sleep in her arms.

* * *

Somewhere between conscious memory and dreams, Spurs made a familiar trip into the red hills of Oklahoma. She was twelve, again, crying, riding through the red dirt on Rocket. Crying because she'd killed the rabbit. That poor little bunny. It haunted her, but why? Was it because it was the first time, and she prayed it would be the last time, she'd ever kill a warm-blooded animal. But was that really the reason she cried?

She tried to remember back before she'd mounted

Rocket, to the time right after the bunny lay still at her feet and the seven or eight school children crowded around laughing. She'd laughed, too, but only for a moment, until she'd realized that maybe her friends had thought she'd intended to kill it—that it was funny to kill, that she was so tough that her heart was indifferent to life and cold as that Oklahoma red clay.

She'd taken a life, and no matter how small, it was still a life, just like her own. She'd thrown the lariat to the ground and run away with an uncomfortable chuckle in her throat that grew and mutated into a groan. She had to go to her mother. She would comfort her—know the right things to say. She would make the pain go away. She would understand that she hadn't intended to harm even a flea on the bunny's back. Spurs had run, her arms flailing, to Uncle Paul and Aunt Katherine's ranch house where they'd been staying. She'd leapt onto the porch and shoved through the back door. . . .

Chapter 48

THEY COME

SPURS AWAKENED TO Saber's stirring. She turned on the flashlight and checked her watch. She'd been asleep for half an hour.

"What's wrong?" she whispered.

He had pushed away and was staring at the small round door. He held his finger to his mouth and seemed to be listening intently.

Someone was walking outside. They beat on metal—possibly one of the other boiler tanks. Hinges creaked like those of the small round door they now watched.

The footsteps came closer. The metal banging came again, sounding as if they were at the tank next to theirs.

Saber turned to her.

"When the door opens," Saber said, "I will go out and fight with them. You run."

The hinges on the tank next to theirs creaked open.

"No Saber, we're together in this," Spurs said and pulled out her fingernail file and held it in one hand.

The footsteps came closer.

"Please do what I ask. I know what I am doing. I can

get away. I have a bicycle hidden nearby. You run. Get back to your ship. Stop these men from killing many people. Don't worry about me. I will be all right. I always am."

Spurs thought about Ma'hami. He was a nice man. He would help the boy.

"There's a man named Ma'hami. He has a café not far from here."

"I know this man," Saber said and nodded. "He has given me scraps and goat milk."

"Go to him," she said. "Tell him that you're my friend. He'll help you."

The banging came, three sharp raps.

Saber stood and leaned with his head and shoulders down, ready to do a bull charge.

"I smell rats," said a voice. "I'm gonna kill me some rats. A stupid whore boy rat and a foolish American bitch rat."

Spurs had no time to think.

The door opened.

"Good bye, Spoors!" Saber said and jumped through the opening.

Spurs followed.

By the time she came through, Saber was getting off of the large Arab, who seemed stunned, laying on his back and shaking his head.

Saber climbed over and got behind him as the man sat up.

Spurs flopped onto the concrete floor like a banked fish. The resulting abrasion on her chin would be a small one compared to what would happen to her if she didn't act quickly.

As Spurs stood she realized her fingernail file had been knocked from her hand. She scanned the floor briefly, but it wasn't in sight.

Saber kicked the man in the back. He turned and grabbed at Saber's kicking foot and snagged it, pulling him in.

Spurs tried Saber's kick and caught the sitting man in the side of his goateed jaw. He let go of Saber but sprang to his feet faster than expected and went for Spurs just as someone grabbed her, pinning her arms.

Now the big Arab was mad.

"Hold her, Fahmi," he said in English, apparently to ensure that she also understood.

He took his time stepping up to her. Blood ran from his mouth, nose and from below one eye.

He drew his hand back and brought it hard across her face.

The pain was a lightning bolt.

"Please Saddam," Fahmi said, "don't do this, now. Let us take her."

Saddam spat curses to him in Arabic.

He put his face in front of hers, blood running from the corner of his mouth into his coarse whiskered chin.

"Now I'll have your American pussy," he said, pressing his mouth against hers.

She pulled her face back quickly, then snapped her teeth onto his nose. Even though tasting the bastard's blood and mucous, she was as determined as a snapping turtle and held on, trying to bite it off.

He wrenched it loose and writhed back in pain, and then was reminded of Saber as the boy's foot caught him in the groin.

It worked before. Spurs whipped her head back catching her unseen captor in the mouth. Teeth popped. She pushed her butt into his middle, causing him to double over her and she stepped to the side and grabbed him by both pant legs at the knees.

She found out that what her Marine Corps hand-to-hand combat instructor had taught her in Officer's Candidate School really did work.

After pulling the man off his feet, with his hands still weakly clutching her arms, she slammed her fist into his groin. The Arab let go and fell to the concrete, rolling into a ball.

"Go, Saber!"

Spurs ran for the open door, Saber sprinting after her. Short yards away, two more men stepped in, blocking the doorway. Spurs set anchor, but Saber lowered his head and shoulders once again and barreled past into the enemy. With his head, he struck the first man in the sternum and drove him into the second man. Saber ended up sprawled out on the floor with them.

"Run, Spoors, run!" he said as he wrestled with them to keep the men down.

The other two men's running feet were coming up from behind.

"Tijani!" said one of them, seeing the others sprawled on the floor.

There was no way they could both escape now. Saber's sacrifice could not be for nothing. Spurs ran past and through the door and sprinted down the alley toward the street.

Glancing over her shoulder, she saw two of the men come out after her, but they stopped, seeming to realize that catching her would be hopeless.

She heard voices as she ran down the middle of the alley. Someone was coming in the street in front of her. They were all over the place, like roaches in a dark kitchen.

She ducked in behind some crates next to a trash dumpster.

Three Arabs came around from the street and trotted by.

More voices. Something rattled like a bicycle.

"Get him! Don't let the kid get away, too!" It was an American's voice.

Spurs heard the bicycle rattle away.

"Damn it!" the man yelled.

She smiled, crouching lower.

"Get the car. Get the car you stupid asshole towel-heads!"

Spurs waited until the voices were gone, then peeked out. The alley was empty. She stood up and cautiously moved out of the trash pile, looking both ways. Heading for the street, she knew that the pier was only three blocks away.

Near the street, she pressed up against the wall of a building before looking out. It seemed empty, but she could hear a car's engine race in the distance. There was nothing nearby to hide behind. She had no choice but to spring out and sprint with all she had toward the ship three blocks away.

Saber suddenly popped out of an alley a block ahead. He raced toward her on his old bicycle, it rattling on the stone street as he came.

Spurs smiled and waved, relieved he was all right.

Headlights came from the alley he'd just exited.

He waved her back as a car shot out.

Spurs ducked into a shop doorway as Saber raced past, the car in close pursuit. It flew by, at least three men inside, and its tires squealed as it turned into the alley behind Saber.

Spurs bolted out and ran madly for the ship. She could see its mooring lights now beside the pier. She ran sucking air frantically.

A clattering crash came from the alley giving her soul a crushing blow. It drove the wind out of her. Her pace slowed, strength drained, but still she ran. Surely, little Saber had escaped, leaped from his bike before the crash. The boy was so resourceful, so bright. Surely he made it.

Now the car backed out of the alley, surprising her. She went into the next one, only a block and a half from the ship, and hid in a doorway.

The car drove by. More voices came. More urgent footsteps. Spurs found a fifty-five gallon drum with a loose top and opened it. It smelled of oil but seemed empty. After climbing in, she found about three inches of oil in the bottom. She set the lid back in place and waited.

Chapter 49

THE RECEPTION

May 10, 0600

THE NEXT SEVERAL hours were full of sleep stealing nods and harsh awakenings as Spurs waited out the hunt that was taking place around her. Exhaustion overruled fear and she'd dozed several times, hunkering in the barrel.

Finally, seeing the dim rays of dawn glow through the small crack she'd left for air, she decided to risk a peek and carefully edged the lid open.

A dirty face confronted her, sending her heart into a panic. The beggar gaped into the drum looking as startled as she did.

"*Ca-hoou*!" he hacked as he turned away.

At first, Spurs thought it was some sort of Arabic alert, like, "Here! She's here!" But after the bum coughed twice more then carped a mouthful of mucous and saliva to the alley in front of him, she realized it wasn't. She watched, raising gradually from the barrel as the beggar staggered away.

Once he was around the corner, she climbed out.

She rubbed her neck and looked down at her once sexy dress. Her body was coated with oil, her hose shredded, feet bare, toes sticking out. Her arms were scratched, knuckles bloodied, fingernails broken and she could feel a swelling in her bottom lip and right eye.

She took several steps to the street and leaned out. It was deserted, but with the morning light growing, she knew that soon the streets would be full of vendors, beggars and a whole bunch of Arabs who were out to kill her.

Only a block and a half from the ship, she stepped to the middle of the street.

"The hell with them," she said aloud, marching toward the pier.

Still, there was no one on the street.

Nearing the ship, she saw that it was preparing to get underway as they began lifting the dock brow. Lieutenant Junior Grade Goodman had been watching her for some distance. He only took his eyes off of her to quickly call out to Commander Reeves. Soon numerous heads appeared over the bulwarks as she approached. Several crewmembers came running to stare. They seemed astonished as they gawked over the side of the ship.

Spurs stepped up the gangplank, glaring back at them. She glimpsed their eyes, never looking more than a split second at any of the two-dozen faces.

Lieutenant Commander Reeves now stood beside Goodman and seemed to have a loss for his smooth sounding Southern words, his eyes mooning and lips parted.

"Spurs?"

Looking out of the corners of her eyes, she could see Commander Naugle watching from the portside-bridge walkway, above. Captain Chardoff came out and looked over the skipper's shoulder. He was the only one that didn't appear stupefied. His eyes were narrow, a slight grin on his lips. Spurs glared back, but said nothing, until coming to the top of the brow. It was her word against his. She didn't have any proof of his wrong doing yet, only hearsay. But she'd have proof soon. She hoped it'd be soon enough.

The crew's comments volleyed at her as she walked through the parting crowd.

"Look at her!"

"Told you they were crazy to put a woman aboard."

"She's been nothing but trouble."

"Now they've reason to get rid of her."

"After they find out 'bout her there's no way they'll put the others aboard."

"Hope she's learned her lesson!"

"Gang way!" she said through gritting teeth. "Make a hole!" She shoved Goodman aside. He backed into Reeves, stepping on his toes. "Request permission to come aboard!" she said as she passed by.

Doc Jolly was at the end of the verbal gauntlet. He also watched, wide-eyed. When close enough he took her arm. She pulled it away, but then allowed him to usher her below to sickbay.

* * *

"What's going on, Doc," Spurs asked Lieutenant Tell Jolly as she sat on the examination table in sickbay.

"All I know is that we're on alert," he said, pressing a butterfly bandage to her right eyebrow. "They cancelled liberty last night and brought everyone in, except you. Chardoff, Reeves, Daniels, Goodman and Ingrassias split up and went looking for you under orders from the old man. No one could figure out where you were. Thought maybe you got your fill and jumped ship."

Spurs shook her head. "What about North? Didn't he tell anyone what happened?"

"I don't know about that. Didn't hear. Someone said Lieutenant North was transferred to the *Enterprise*."

"That's impossible, Doc."

"In the Navy nothing's impossible. Haven't you learned that yet?"

"No, Doc, I mean, he couldn't have been transferred, wouldn't have been."

"And why's that?"

Spurs thought for a moment knowing she could jeopardize the mission if she said more. She was on her own now. What could have caused North to transfer? Maybe the investigation had led him to the *Enterprise*. There would be no other reason for him to have gone. Unless it was some kind of Navy juggle, but that would have only been done if he weren't with NCIS—if he'd lied. Or, perhaps someone lied about his transfer and he'd been killed. They could have done him in at the bicycle peddler's shop.

Spurs felt a sharp pain in her left arm and realized that while she sat on the examination table daydreaming, Doc Jolly had rolled up her sleeve, daubed on some alcohol and punched a hypodermic into her arm.

She frowned. "What's that?"

"A sedative. You need to sleep now."

"A mild sedative, right?" she said as the room began to spin, thinking about everything she must do, about the investigation, about Saber, about the plot to sink a ship, about the Arabs that tried to kill her and who might have killed her little hero. "I didn't—hear you—say—*m-i-l-d*. . . ?"

Chapter 50

COMMANDER PSYCHO

May 12, 0850

SPURS WOKE WITH a lot of questions on her mind. At first, she didn't know where she was, then realized it was her own stateroom. Her body ached, feeling every bump, bruise and abrasion.

Sitting up she felt the abused muscles complain, then noticed that her hands were clean. So were her arms. She threw the sheet off and was relieved to see she still wore her bra and panties. Doc had probably given her a quick and hopefully modest sponge bath. A hot shower was the first order of business.

As she stood, she remembered the sedative, head feeling light. She stumbled toward the shower and took a quick look at her watch. It read 0850. It was unbelievable that she had been under for less than two hours. She winced when she considered that it had more likely been a full day. She stumbled more and cussed her head, but then realized the ship's motion had caused her faulty balance. They were at sea.

She made her shower short and dressed painfully but quickly. There was much to do.

After leaving her stateroom, she noticed that the ship seemed deserted. She stepped out topside and saw Chardoff on the quarterdeck. Most of the crew was topside, some milling around the sides, others in groups doing calisthenics. She quickly ducked back in, unseen. Things had gotten out of hand and she wondered what had happened since she had been put under. She must now go to the Captain of the ship.

Spurs tapped frantically on Commander Naugle's door. She didn't want to be heard by any of the crew, just the captain. But the captain must hear, now. At first there was no answer, but after a pause, she heard the captain order her to enter.

Naugle lay in the same position he had when they'd spoken before, in his rack, wet washcloth over his forehead.

"It's Sperling, sir," she said.

Naugle kept his eyes closed.

"Yes, Ensign. Forgive me for not getting up—damn migraines. How are you after your two day nap?"

"Two days?"

"Doc thought you should rest for a couple. He said you were still asleep when I checked this morning."

"It's time I tell you. I *am* with NCIS. I'm investigating Ensign Nader's death. It's turned into an incredible plot of high treason."

"Good Lord," he exclaimed, taking a second to glance her way. "What's happening—please get my pills and a cup of water." He motioned to the head.

Upset by the distraction, but mindful of the man's intense pain, she went to the toilet, took a bottle of pills from the medicine cabinet and filled a paper cup with water. She wanted to be sure of the captain's total attention so she restrained from elaborating until she returned to his bedside.

When she came out of the head, she saw Naugle shove something under his pillow. It looked like a bottle.

She handed him the cup. He pulled the washcloth off and rose to one elbow, winced and took it. She opened the pill bottle.

"Six," he said.

She handed him the pills and he swallowed them as if he were a starving man given M&Ms.

As he did, she reached under the pillow and snatched out the pint bottle of vodka.

He stared at her a second, saying nothing.

"Not wise to mix pain pills and vodka, is it, sir?" she asked.

He turned away and she slipped the bottle back in its place.

The captain slowly lowered to the rack, handing her the cup and she set it aside. She didn't wish to trouble the man any more than necessary now. There were more critical issues.

After he covered his entire face with the wet cloth, she explained.

"Terrorists are planning to sink a US Navy warship."

"What? What are you talking about?—Oh yes, that treason business."

"Sir, it's going to happen soon. I think Nader was killed as well as all of the other missing crewmembers because they knew too much. There are traitors aboard this ship."

"Don't be ridiculous. My crew is the most faithful in this Navy. I'm a lucky man to be their captain."

"Don't you understand, Captain? Don't you understand that we must act now?"

"Miss Sperling, I think you've gotten in a little over

your head and have been involved in some terrible coincidences and maybe you're jumping to conclusions."

"What happened to North, sir?"

"North? Oh, he was transferred to the *Enterprise*. Good boy, sorry to see him leave."

"Did you see his orders? Did he tell you he was leaving?"

"No. Captain Chardoff received North's orders from a courier before we left Tunisia. Must have been very important. Chardoff said he had to leave right away."

"Chardoff is one of the traitors, sir! I think they killed North."

"Oh please, Ensign," he said grimacing, "please don't exaggerate." His words came slower. "Let me rest for half an hour or so. Then I'll go with you and we'll get this all figured out."

"But Commander, they could sink one of our ships at anytime now. It may even be this ship!"

"Uh-huh," he said lethargically. "Let me rest." He waived one hand slowly, then it went limp.

* * *

After Ensign Sperling left his quarters, Commander Naugle forced himself to a sitting position on his bunk.

They'd had a great idea, retrofitting these old hulks with new equipment that made them faster, more battle ready for half the price of building a new ship. He had a wonderful crew. It would have worked if it weren't for the rest of the mess. These men going AWOL, the deaths. Craziness. He could have gone out with dignity. Instead. . . .

He had no choice. He must do it now while he had the courage. It didn't matter that he'd had a couple of drinks too many. It was now or never. This whole mess had gotten way too far out of hand.

He rose from bed and stumbled to the oak desk near the center of the stateroom. After plopping into his swivel chair, he opened the side desk drawer for a legal pad to draft a letter to Fleet Admiral Pierce announcing his resignation.

He found himself focusing on something else he kept in that drawer—in the back. It was blued and hard and cold. He couldn't take his eyes from it as if it were a king cobra mesmerizing, hypnotizing him, its prey. But it was not a snake, it did not breath, it was not alive. It was cold, hard, blued steel, snub nosed, six shot—a .38 Special made by Smith and Wesson. He pulled the compact revolver out of the drawer and placed it on the desk in front of him, then glanced around his stateroom.

He heard the *voices*—again. He'd heard them before. It seemed there was only one way to get rid of them. The booze helped. The pills helped.

This time, the first voice came from his son's picture on his desk.

"Help me, Daddy," it said. "Please help me."

Naugle's eyes widened.

Another voice blurted from the other side. A football trophy with the bronze figure on top preparing to pass the ball, twisted toward him.

"Kill her," it said. "Kill Sperling's daughter. Get even. Make *him* suffer for a change. Kill the little bitch!"

Now more voices chimed in. Naugle snapped his head around the room, sweat beading on his shiny forehead.

The globe in the corner spoke. "It's time," it said in a sibilant whisper. "You must revenge your son's death, *now*!

The wild boar's head mounted on the wall to the

right bent toward him. Its mouth ruminated as it glared at him. He smelled its breath, sour with decay. "You'd better kill her. Kill her, now," it said. "Or I'll kill you. I'll eat you—and your son, too!"

"Kill her," the globe said.

Naugle picked up the gun, his teeth clenched between open lips. He took short, deep breaths, staring at the pistol.

"Kill her," the trophy figure said.

"Kill her, now!" the wild boar insisted.

"Now!" the globe said.

"Now!" the trophy said.

Naugle's son came alive in the picture on his desk. The young man stepped out of the picture frame, still in miniature, and onto Naugle's writing pad. The boy still wore his Annapolis football uniform.

Naugle tucked his chin and pushed back from the desk, the revolver still in his hand. His tears streamed down his face. He smiled at his boy, amazed at what he watched. Kelly was so handsome, even if he were only six inches tall.

"Please, Daddy," his son said. "Please, help me."

Naugle's world spun. He would help his son. He stood from his desk, his eyes fixed on the door. But within three steps, he collapsed to the deck like a puppet whose strings were cut.

Chapter 51

THE ORKIN MAN

SPURS HAD TO find out if North was on the Enterprise. If he was, maybe he had everything under control and the danger wasn't as immediate as she sensed. He surely would have contacted her if something was going to happen soon—that is, if he was still alive.

A Marine guard stood by the hatch to the communications room. The young lance corporal was dressed in black fatigues and held an M-16 at port arms. He wore a small radio headset over his fatigue cap.

When she tried to enter, he stepped in her way.

"Sorry, ma'am," he said. "No one is allowed to enter right now by order of Commander Naugle."

"I just left the skipper."

"And did he give you a written pass, ma'am?"

"No, I don't need one. I am an officer of this ship, Marine."

"Yes, ma'am. But I can't allow you past."

"You can at least tell me what's going on."

"We're receiving top secret messages from CINC-U-S-NAV-EUR."

Commander In Chief, US Navy, Europe was sending this ship a secret message? Was he for real? Was this some kind of excuse to keep unwanteds from being able to send messages, warnings? Or had North broken the case and CINCUSNAVEUR was about to come down on the bad guys?

"I have top secret clearance, lance corporal."

"Sorry, ma'am, not without permission from the Old Man."

The Marine's stare was intense, his jaw set. He meant business. Something was wrong about all of this. She could feel it. Sure, this may be the way the Navy would handle a case like this. Send a coded message to all ship's captains involved so that they could prepare to take on security forces to arrest the traitors, since they seemed to be high in numbers. The captain being out of commission, Lieutenant Commander Reeves must have been in charge. The ship would probably receive a detail of Marines heloed to the flight deck, then head straight to the nearest port. But it just didn't feel right.

She went forward toward the bridge and was met by another guard. She did not ask, but turned away and headed up the port side ladder to the signal bridge. She still remembered her Morse code. A quick message to North on the *Enterprise*, just to get his acknowledgement couldn't do harm. She'd say something simple like, "Lieutenant North, acknowledge, Spurs." That wouldn't give him away if he were still undercover. If he had control of the situation, he would be apprised even if he didn't personally view her message and then he would surely return an acknowledgement quickly. The next thing to do would be to check out the Combat Information Center and see if all was well in there.

Nearing the top, she saw another Marine guard waiting for her. With her head at the signal deck level, she looked across and saw yet another one on the starboard side.

"Sorry, ma'am, no one's allowed up here."

"But I need to go inside the CIC. I'm the weapon's officer, damn it!"

"That's not possible, ma'am. Orders. All vital areas of the ship are secured. No one is allowed in any of these areas, except by order of the Commander, the XO or Captain Chardoff."

This must be it. The ship had been secured against the terrorists. Maybe the nightmare was over. But Chardoff would be under arrest if it were.

"What's going on, have they got the terrorist, the traitors?"

The young Marine looked at her curiously. "Don't know anything about any terrorist or traitors, ma'am. You'll have to leave now."

"But I'm the weapon's officer!"

She moved up one more step.

He took a step toward her, bringing his M-16 down to the *on guard* position, directing the muzzle at her middle.

She backed down, amazed.

Now what? Things were happening quickly. But she doubted if they were the right things. Where was Reeves? Was he involved? Was North truly who he said he was? Who could help? Who could she trust?

Jabrowski was probably either guarded at his position or was in with them. There were Doc Jolly and, perhaps the cook, Big Track. They would probably both be below decks.

As she rushed below, she realized how much sense this scenario was making. Terrorists had taken over the ship and now guarded all vital areas. The Combat Information Center was being guarded. If somehow those

Tomahawks had been put on line, they were ready to deep six any of the fleet, maybe even the *Enterprise*.

She went down, went inside the hatch to officer's country and descended the ladders toward sickbay, one level up from the crew's berthing area, near the bottom of the ship. Jolly wasn't there. The hatch was open. Sickbay was deserted.

Sensing danger she moved quietly along the corridor to the companionway down to the next deck. She stopped at the compartment before it and saw another Marine guard stationed next to the ladder with his back to her. He wore a headset like the others. She tried to sneak past, but halfway there, the guard turned and brought his rifle down.

"Halt!"

She stopped. "What's going on here? I need to go below."

"Please stand back, ma'am. No one is to go below."

Spurs saw the single stripe on the man's fatigue collar. "Listen, Private. You'd better tell me what's going on. I *am* an officer."

"Decontamination, ma'am. The crew's quarters is infested with fleas carrying the pneumonic plague. They're exterminating."

This whole thing was getting wilder by the minute.

"Exterminating—fleas?"

"Yes, ma'am. Please get back."

"Or what? You'll shoot me, because I might get fleas?"

"The pneumonic plague is highly contagious. It's also deadly and so is the chemical they're using to kill the fleas. The decon team assigned to fumigate was wearing suits and oxygen. You'd be endangering yourself and the ship. No one is allowed through, down or up." The young Marine clicked his weapon off safety. "Now please, step back."

Spurs backed away once again. No one was being allowed through, down or up? What about the exterminators? Was there anyone else down there?

She did a quick about face and walked briskly away. Finding the ladder to the decks above, she ascended and went to her stateroom.

She closed her door quietly, went to her wall locker and pulled out her sea bag. She'd left several extra winter uniforms folded neatly in the bottom, along with her 9mm Beretta. She took it out, pulled the slide back and chambered a round, then shoved it under her belt.

After descending several ladders down once again to the level two decks above the crew's quarters, she trotted through eight compartments forward to the other end of the ship and then went down to the next level. There was another companionway to the crew's quarters on that forward end.

The decontamination story was more bullshit, she was sure. Clearly something else was going on below decks while most of the crew was kept topside. People were disappearing and dying as she stumbled through this incredible maze of deceit and treason. North and Saber, besides the many others. A ship would be sunk soon. Something had to be done quickly. But what? She had to find out more.

She was in luck at the other companionway. This guard also had his back to her. She moved, tiptoeing to the ladder behind him, stepped down watchfully and walked back toward the berthing area.

A muffled scream came from the compartments ahead, then frantic footsteps in the opposite direction.

She pulled out the Beretta and proceeded. Through the first two compartments she saw nothing but empty bunks, stacked four high. Stepping into the next compartment, she saw a man lying motionless against the bulkhead to the side of the hatchway. He wore a green rubber, decon suit, used primarily for nuclear, biological and chemical warfare decontamination, along with a mask and an oxygen bottle. She thought about the chemicals they were using. Had he inhaled and was overcome? If so, she had made a serious mistake. Could the pneumonic plague story be true?

She began itching, feeling the fleas crawling on her skin. She looked at her forearms and saw nothing. It was just her mind playing tricks on her. Why not, everything and everyone else seemed to be.

"Bullshit!" she said under her breath.

She hurried toward the man, gun pointed, her eyes searching her surroundings for whoever might have put him down. She could see the man's body was lifeless, holding a pump-type spray bottle and nozzle in his hands, his face turned away. She kneeled and rolled him over to see his relaxed face, eyes open halfway in a death stare. She'd seen this man before but didn't know his name. One of the crew doing an unnoticed but important duty aboard his ship. Then she saw the three, bloody holes in his suit.

At least two more voices came from several compartments away. Pleading voices. "God, no, sir!" "No, I won't talk!"

Several sharp snaps stopped their words, accompanied by a couple of clicks like a tack hammer striking steel. Spurs had heard the sharp snaps before in NCIS training. Someone was using a silenced gun. Those clicks were the bullets either missing or passing through their targets and hitting steel.

Spurs bolted up and raced aft. At the next compartment, she found another body laying a couple of yards from the hatchway. His bloody handprints were on the bulkhead. She stepped over him and looked at the crimson stains. On the hatchway, along with more smeared blood, were several small dents in the gray paint, shiny steel showing underneath. She ran her index finger over them. They were made by bullets.

Looking into the next compartment, she saw four bodies. She eased in cautiously and stepped over the dead men, visually inspecting each one. All had bullet holes in their suits, two with holes in their oxygen masks. Those masks were no longer clear, their dead faces hidden by the reddened lenses. The fourth body had only one apparent wound in the shoulder from a bullet, but his throat was cut, laid open from ear to ear.

Two more silenced shots came from the aft compartments.

She heard new voices.

"That's the last one."

"Let's go back and check the bodies."

Spurs turned to make an escape. She didn't know who or how many were coming.

She bolted, but felt her ankle being grabbed and fell to the deck, face first. Looking back, she saw the frightened face of one of the men she'd thought was dead.

"Help," he said. "Please help me."

It was Jabrowski. She'd never seen so much fear on a man's face before.

She rolled over, tucked her side arm under her belt and pulled him to her by the collar. He had two wounds in his chest that she could see.

"Hold on, Ski."

She dragged him to the hatchway she'd entered from. Now the voices were close.

"I can't believe my luck, Sergeant Krebs," said the deep voice from the opposite hatchway, thirty feet away. "I'm gonna *have* to kill her now!"

Spurs looked up to see an enormous white-suited

body looking through the hatchway, another man standing behind. They didn't wear the oxygen masks, their charade being over. Their team of unwitting prey dead.

It was Chardoff and a Marine sergeant.

He raised his silenced Beretta.

"Time to say bye, Bitch!"

Spurs pulled out her gun before Chardoff had a chance and squeezed off several rounds without aiming. The noise inside the steel compartment pierced her eardrums.

The bullets struck the metal around the two men and they ducked back. She held her pistol and aimed, waiting for them to look again. When Chardoff's face peeked out she fired two more, this time narrowly missing his head.

She yanked Ski through into the next compartment and to the side out of Chardoff's line of sight.

"Get her!" Chardoff yelled.

Spurs realized the sergeant had an M-16 as fully automatic 5.56mm rounds burst in a heavy volley.

She pointed her pistol through the opening and fired two more rounds. It sounded as though she got lucky.

"Damn it, I'm hit. Damn that little bitch!" It was Sergeant Krebs' voice.

This would be the only chance she'd have to escape with Ski. She tucked the pistol behind her belt, squatted and rolled him over to his stomach, lifted him by the shoulders to face her and pulled his right arm behind her neck, then hefted him over her shoulders holding onto his right arm with her right hand. She pulled the Beretta out and stood up. He was a small man of about one hundred and forty pounds, but still nearly half again her weight. The fireman's carry she'd learned in OCS worked, but for how long?

Spurs turned and took short hurried steps to the next

hatchway. A silenced bullet struck the steel overhead as she passed through, another one glancing and ricocheting past. She turned as she stepped and fired three more hastily aimed rounds.

Through another couple of compartments, the silenced snaps came again. This time they did not click as they hit steel. Ski's body buckled, throwing her off balance as she made the last hatch to the companionway up. She tripped through the oval opening and, trying to regain her balance, dropped Ski, falling back and striking her head on the steel-lipped edge.

She saw stars and realized she'd struck her head in the same place that it was hit before when she was thrown overboard. This time she knew she would lose consciousness. She tried uselessly to fight it and as she did, she saw a large body tower over her. It wasn't Chardoff. It was Big Track. He had his meat cleaver. Her vision blurred and became dark.

It must be my imagination.

Chapter 52

UNSWEET DREAMS

SPURS AWOKE SMELLING mincemeat pie. Everything was dark and she wasn't sure that her eyes were even open when her hand pushed against something that clanked like a steel kettle lid. And that's what it was. She felt the smooth sides of the stainless steel pot she was curled up in. It was the huge kettle that the cooks use to make gallons of food for the crew.

Now she remembered Big Track standing over her with the meat cleaver—and checked her arms and legs, making sure that they were still attached. Just her luck to run into a cannibal in the middle of a gunfight.

Confusion was not the word for her thoughts. So much had happened that she couldn't discern reality from dreams. She wondered if she hadn't dreamed all of it up, that she might even be dreaming now. How could she ever explain even half of this to the captain, or to Reeves—if he wasn't one of *them*—or to anyone else. At least five, probably seven or eight men had been killed—*exterminated*—below decks. That shouldn't be hard to prove. But didn't that mean in order for these traitors to get away with it, they must have control of the ship? They could have complete control with several key crewmembers among them and the rest of the fleet—the rest of the world wouldn't know. Who was to be trusted and who would believe?

Spurs pushed the lid up slowly with her fingertips allowing light in. She rose to peek out, then saw Big Track standing close by. He turned and saw her. His eyes bugged and he reached over and shoved the lid back down.

Spurs was just about to complain, when she heard him speak.

"Evening, Captain Chardoff, Sergeant Krebs. Help ya?"

"You alone?" It was Chardoff's voice.

"No, sir. With you two, there are three of us."

"I mean besides us, asshole. What are you doing here?"

"Cleaning up evening mess."

"Have you seen Ensign Sperling?"

"That little girl officer? Guess I saw her a couple of times."

"I mean tonight, damn it!" Chardoff said and slammed his hand down on the vat lid.

Spurs grimaced from a noise that was like having her head slapped between cymbals.

There was a brief silence.

Chardoff spoke again. "What's this big vat out for? You didn't have stew tonight, did you?"

The lid began to lift.

"Pork and beans, sir," Big Track said. "Over two hundred men love my pork and beans. Most of them have two, sometimes three, helpings of it. Suggest you don't go down to the crew's quarters tonight."

The lid dropped with a clank.

She heard footsteps moving away.

Thirty seconds later, the lid lifted off completely. Big Track's huge hands reached for her. She took his arms and he lifted her easily from the vat.

He sat her down and placed his finger to his lips.

She looked around the galley.

"What in the hell happened?" she whispered.

Big Track shrugged while glancing over the dirty pots, pans and trays. "Evening chow?" he said.

"Don't play that dumb Indian game with me. I've got you figured out. What happened?"

"Saw you with the gun earlier. Followed you down to the crew's quarters where they were spraying for bugs. Had to knock the guard out or he woulda seen me. When I got down there, saw you and Jabrowski. He was dead. Took a wild guess and figured something bad was happenin'. Picked you up and ran up here. You've been out a long time. Thought you might not wake up."

"No one saw you?"

"Nope. I was in stealth mode."

"Do you have any idea what's going on? Have you heard anything?"

"Nope. Last I knew, I was drinking tequila in Brownsville. Musta passed out. When I woke up, the Navy said I'd signed enlistment papers and I'm on this luxury cruise ship."

"Damn it, get real. People are dead. I'm NCIS."

Big Track pursed his lips and held his hands to the sides of his face, eyes wide.

"Does anything matter to you?" she asked.

"I like to cook," he said. "Everything else is just more horse shit. Sorry about Jabrowski, though."

The big Native American picked up a covered platter and handed it to her.

"Here, you might need a snack later," he said lifting the top. Underneath was a mincemeat pie with Spurs'

Beretta on top. "Safety's on, round in the chamber, five in the clip."

Spurs shook her head as she took the weapon, pulled her khaki shirt out in the back enough to make it loose and hid the gun under her belt.

"I like you—I think," she said.

"Want a date?"

Spurs frowned. "Stay here," she said. "I'm going to see what's happening topside. If I make it, I'm going to find Commander Naugle or Reeves and either get this all settled or die trying."

"Not going anywheres. Got lots of pots to clean."

She went through the darken-ship curtain to the outside hatch.

"May the great spirit be with you," Big Track said as she opened the hatch and stepped out.

Spurs made her way to the ladder to the bridge without being seen. She did see several men milling around the lifelines on the sides of the ship. She couldn't tell if they were sentries or sailors taking a break on a peaceful night.

A Marine guard saw her as she stepped up the ladder, and she stopped midway. Reeves came out of the bridge and moved in front of him. She wasn't sure if she should be glad.

"Ensign Sperling, come on up," he said waving to her. "We've been worried about you."

Maybe things could be straightened out now. She ran up the steps and followed Reeves into the bridge, then stopped fast when she saw Chardoff. He wore black fatigues. He smiled.

"You're in this together?" she exclaimed placing her hand on the grip of the gun behind her back, but resisted pulling it out. If the shit hit the fan, she knew where two of her remaining five rounds would go.

"What?" Reeves asked as he turned to her. "In what?"

"He's a murderer. He killed Ski and several others."

"What the hell are you talking about?"

"When they went down to exterminate the fleas, Chardoff and his sergeant killed all of them."

"Wait a minute, Ensign," Reeves said. "I think you're having some kind of a nervous breakdown. Relax and sit down."

He pulled a tall stool over to her.

She knocked it away and it fell.

"I don't want your damn *stool*."

"Ensign, your disrespect and insubordination are inexcusable, no matter your mental and physical state."

She calmed down. This was no time to rant and rave. He may not want to discuss this around others. Even if Reeves was her NCIS contact, he still may have trouble believing everything that had happened to her unless she explained carefully, instance by instance. Even then belief was doubtful. All she needed was to be put under arrest and sent to the brig where she could do nothing but let the diabolical terrorist plan succeed.

"Sorry, sir," she said, glaring at Chardoff. "What happened? Where's Jabrowski?"

"I was on the *Enterprise* answering more questions about the helo crash when it happened," Reeves said. "A sailor reported to sick bay with a fever. Doc checked him over, saw a flea, and then found an infestation of what he thinks could be pneumonic-plague-carrying fleas in the sailor's bunk. Chardoff picked a group of men and secured the ship so it wouldn't spread and then went down with a team to decontaminate. The spray they used got to several of them and they had to be medevacked to the *Ticonderoga* where they have a doctor specializing in chemical contamination."

"You weren't here when it happened?"

"No."

Spurs thought for a moment. The blood in the crew's quarters was surely cleaned up by now, but what about the dents from the bullets.

"Sir, will you come with me?"

Reeves frowned at her.

"If you think it's absolutely necessary."

"I do." She turned and ducked out the bridge hatchway, Reeves and Chardoff following. She slipped around the commander and leaned into a shoulder block that stopped Chardoff. She surprised herself.

"We won't need you," she said, glaring up.

He looked down, his lip curling.

"Wait on the bridge, Captain Chardoff," Reeves said. "We'll discuss your training operation in a minute."

When Spurs was sure they were alone and not being followed she turned to Reeves as they walked.

"Where have you been? What the hell's happening on this ship?"

"I told you, I was called to the *Enterprise*. Why are you acting so crazy?"

"Me? It's the rest of this screwed up crew. Everyone's gone nuts on this ship except me."

She leaped down several steps as they made the bottom deck. Reeves hurried behind.

"What are we doing here?"

"I want to show you the bullet holes."

"What bullet holes?"

"The ones from the bullets that missed. The holes

from the bullets that aren't in the bodies of the decontamination team."

"I told you that the decon team was contaminated. They're not dead. They're just a little sick."

"Did you see them?"

"No, they were gone before I got back."

"Did you confirm their arrival or find out their condition on the *Ticonderoga*?"

"No, but Captain Chardoff said he checked not more than an hour ago. They were fine and should be back by tomorrow, first light."

"Did you see North on the *Enterprise*?"

"No, I wasn't looking for him."

"Did you see his orders or talk with him before he left the ship?"

"No, Goodman told me about it, damn it. What is this?"

"Goodman! And you didn't even check. What kind of an incompetent officer are you?"

Reeves reached out and grabbed her by the shoulder and spun her around.

"You listen to me, Ensign Sperling, you will not speak to me that way, no matter what happened between us in Barcelona."

"Don't you remember, *sir*, nothing *did* happen?"

They glared at each other, momentarily.

She said, "So what are you going to do now, choke me?"

Spurs broke free and hurried into the first compartment of the crew's quarters.

"Cover up sailors!" she said stepping through as a number of sailors in only their skivvies looked up from their bunks. Some were playing cards, some writing letters, some just shooting the breeze.

"Jesus, it's her!" "Now she's coming down here."

"What's she want?" "Woman on deck!"

She passed through two more compartments full of surprised sailors, just as Reeves caught up to her. He grabbed her and spun her around again.

"This is enough," he said.

"Yes it is," she said. "Now look at these dents."

She twisted away and inspected the hatchway. There were no dents. She looked behind her, trying to remember if this was the compartment where she had not only seen the bullet marks but also felt of them. She was sure it was. She looked into the next compartment and saw a sailor with a paintbrush, painting around the next hatchway. A tube of filler stuck out of his back pocket.

She looked back at the hatchway she stood in front of, then felt around it.

"There," she said, "See. Wet paint." She brought her gray-paint-smeared fingers up to Reeves' nose. Then placed them on the hatchway again. She gouged out fresh putty from one of the covered bullet holes. "See!" she said bringing the gray filler up to his face.

"That doesn't prove anything, Ensign," he said. "This ship, like all US Navy vessels, is in a constant state of maintenance and repair. That man standing at the hatchway in the next compartment's permanent and continuous job is to do exactly that."

Spurs glared back. She looked around at the staring eyes and gaping mouths of the crewmembers. She went around Reeves and hustled away.

As she rounded the companionway on the deck above, Reeves caught up with her yet again.

"Spurs, wait!" he said and shoved in front of her.

"Wait for what?"

"Don't you understand? I'm trying to believe you,

but we can't discuss this matter in front of the crew. We don't know who we can trust."

"You're just *trying* to believe me?" She thought of what North had said about Reeves sometimes wearing an Annapolis ring—that the man that shoved her overboard wore one. There was only one other officer on the ship that had one, Goodman. She glanced at Reeves right ring finger, then his left. No Annapolis ring. She softened to him, but only slightly.

"Come on," he said, "even you've got to admit with all that's happened to you and the strange way you've been acting, I might have just a bit of trouble believing you when you say several of our crew have been suddenly murdered while I was away for two hours. This is just a drug ring, not a commando raid."

"I think you're wrong, *sir*. I think that's exactly what it is. What kind of training mission is Chardoff going on?"

"A night recon operation. They're preparing for Mauritania."

"Where are they going tonight?"

"They were given permission to go into Algeria. The landscape is the similar. They'll be coordinating with a couple of SEAL teams from the *Enterprise*. It's just training."

She turned and sprinted to the next ladder up.

"Maybe," she said. "Chardoff shouldn't mind an observer then."

"Who?" Reeves asked running behind her.

"Me."

Chapter 53

NORTH WIND

2355

THE HELO WAS landing when Spurs ran out onto the flight deck to join Reeves and Chardoff. She had stopped briefly in her stateroom to put on her green fatigues, jungle boots, field jacket and fatigue hat. Even in May, the North of Africa could be a very chilly place at night.

The group of sixteen Recon Marines were boarding the twin rotor, CH-46 Sea Knight helicopter, via the back loading ramp. They wore black fatigues and carried heavy packs and assault rifles but no helmets, only their soft covers.

"I'm going with you," she yelled over the rotor noise.

Chardoff eyed her like a starving polar bear.

"I told you, no!" Commander Reeves, yelled back, holding his cap.

"Let her," Chardoff said. "She might learn something."

Spurs followed the last man of the squad onto the roaring chopper, not waiting for Reeves' reply.

She found a seat near the tail of the helo and sat down amongst the astonished Marines.

Chardoff leaped on and the helo lifted from the ship quickly, the hydraulic powered ramp raising as they flew. Once the ramp was closed, the roaring of the two big engines above them quieted some but not much.

She looked out the small window behind her and saw Reeves wave. She did not wave back.

Spurs knew right away that the pilot was a *hot dog*. As it lifted, the chopper banked hard left and nearly tipped Spurs off of her bench seat.

Chardoff hung onto the opposite side of the helo and sat down slowly. He looked as if he was waiting to catch her if she fell across. It would be a convenient way to get her neck broken.

She looked around the chopper at the staring warriors. They passed camouflage sticks around, dabbing the green and black grease-paint sticks on their faces as they watched her.

"Lock and load," Chardoff ordered.

The Marines took ammo magazines out of their pouches, inspected them briefly and shoved them into the ports on the underside of their weapons. She glanced at the magazine of the man sitting next to her. The cartridges inside had crimped ends. They were blanks. Then she saw that clamped onto all the M-16s flash suppressors—the ends of the weapons' muzzles—were red metal objects. She remembered from boot camp that the things were called *gas blockers,* devices used to assist an automatic weapon to cycle the next round into the chamber when firing blanks. They were only necessary when using blank rounds to allow enough backpressure for the weapon to operate properly. Not unusual to not be using live ammo since it was a training exercise, however.

Realizing the dangerous situation she had put herself in, she hoped that not all of Chardoff's men were in on whatever scheme he was up to. She doubted that more than a couple of them could be in with him. Otherwise, he'd probably have killed her as soon as they'd left the ship. And, after all, these were supposed to be dedicated and loyal Recon Marines—the *best of the best*. He probably wouldn't try anything while she was with the entire group. Later, while they were in the field, would be a different story.

Spurs' visual inspection of the Marines ended with Chardoff. He stared back at her smiling big. *He's thinking he has me right where he wants me.* She wanted to prove him wrong.

She lowered her eyes slowly from him, down across the floor of the helo and finally to the bulge in the side pocket of her field jacket where her right hand was tucked. She shoved the Beretta against the fabric inside her pocket as far as she could, making the barrel more than obvious.

She brought her eyes back up slowly to his, then grinned back. He looked down to the bulge in her coat and his face cleared of any sign of amusement. His eyes narrowed then shifted back to hers.

For the next few minutes the ride was tense. Chardoff looked to Sergeant Krebs, the man that had been helping him "exterminate" earlier. She saw that his left forearm was wrapped with a camouflaged bandage. She nodded defiantly, realizing that was where she had shot him. He nodded back one of those yeah-you're-safe-now-but-I'll-get-you-later sort of nods.

The helo came over a clearing in the midst of rolling, rocky hills, tall brown grass and sparse trees and sat down abruptly.

Chardoff stood and pointed to the floor at the front

of the helo near where the aviation-helmeted crew chief stood.

"Leave your gear," he said. "Flack jackets, too. Rifles only."

"The men obeyed without question, throwing their cumbersome packs and protective jackets forward in a pile.

The ramp dropped slowly and two more helicopters landed behind them and began deplaning groups of black-uniformed men—the SEAL teams from the *Enterprise*. When the ramp was down completely, Chardoff's men rushed off. Chardoff was last. He hesitated.

"After you," he yelled out and waved his hand.

"Think I'll stay," she said, once again making the Beretta obvious.

"Suit yourself," he said. "We'll get a chance to re-hash some old business before the night's over."

"Look forward to it," she said.

He trotted down the ramp and followed his men through the tall, brown grass toward a group of trees about three hundred yards out.

Spurs stood as the three-man helo crew watched her.

She yelled to them as the big engines shut down, "Just here to observe." She walked over to the crew chief and asked, "So what's the plan now?"

"We wait until 0500—until they're done playing their games."

Spurs went back to the tail and watched for a couple minutes until the last of the men had disappeared into the trees. She stepped off of the ramp and ran ninety degrees to the right of them to higher ground. She didn't know what for sure she was doing or even why, just that something was set to happen tonight, she was sure, and she had to find out what in time to stop it.

At the top of the nearest hill, she fell prone and

watched for movement from the trees that the men had run into, now five hundred yards away. The bright moon gave the tiny emerging figures contrast to the lighter rocks and surroundings. They came out ten yards apart, moving steadily toward what appeared to be an abandoned stone barn, over twice the distance away from her. She wondered what was in that building and if it was germane to Chameleon. Looking to the next hill for a new and closer vantage point, she noticed four tarpaulin covered trucks parked in a line along a small trail.

There were more than just the two US Special Forces groups out there tonight. Each of the trucks could hold as many as twenty men. She may find some answers there.

She ran down the back side of the hill and took a wide angle to the trucks, coming up on the trail behind them. She stayed low, running through stickers and thorn bushes along a ditch that ran parallel to the path.

When she came to within a hundred yards, she saw two sentries, both with what appeared to be M-16s. One stood at the front of the trucks, one at the rear. Both looked ahead. If her luck held out, she could get very close.

Edging up to within twenty yards of the closest sentry and the back of the last truck, she hid behind a boulder as large as a kitchen stove and considered her plan.

These men were not American military. The closest one had a broad, bushy mustache and smoked a cigarette. That mustache would be well trimmed if he was an American GI and, besides, no American serviceman would ever be allowed to smoke while on guard duty. However, he did wear the same sort of fatigues that the others were wearing.

A look inside the trucks might provide information: what they were carrying, who they were, anything that could piece the puzzle together.

Spurs found a rock that filled her palm and hefted it to the other side of the truck. The two men looked to one another from each end of the row of vehicles and then ran to the other side. Spurs leaped up quickly and sprinted to the back of the first covered truck and vaulted in.

She lay silently while listening to the two sentries scampering around the trucks. It sounded like one or both of them jumped into the back of the vehicle in front of the one she was in. They seemed calmed as one said something to the other in what sounded like an Arabic dialect and then it sounded as if the two men had jumped to the ground.

"Bah, bah," said one of the Arabs, like a sheep or goat and they both laughed.

The moonlight coming in from the back of the covered truck did little to illuminate the inside. She felt around, finally coming up with an empty cigarette pack and some spent 7.62mm cartridges that looked old, tarnished in the dim light. The rifles she thought that the Arab sentries were carrying fired 5.56mm ammo. These had been in the back of the truck for months, probably years.

It had been a wasted risk and now she had to figure out how to get away. But then she thought about how the two Arabs had checked the truck in front and none of the others. Thank God, they hadn't looked in the one that she was in. But why didn't they? Something important was in that second truck.

Spurs peeked out the back and didn't see either sentry but did hear their voices. She went to the front of the truck bed and parted the tarp slightly. The sentries were standing together, two trucks up.

She would not have a better chance. She returned to the back and lowered herself to the ground from the tailgate, and then ran around the side, opposite the Arab gunmen. Then, reaching from the side, she raised her foot up to the high rear bumper of the truck and lifted and swung herself up and around and stepped over the closed tailgate.

Sitting in front of her was Lieutenant Darren North.

Chapter 54

DEADLY GAMES

May 13, 0130

 SPURS POINTED HER gun, not recognizing North at first, then aimed at him when she realized that it *was* him. Where had he been? Was he in cahoots with the Arabs? He was sitting against the front of the truck bed on the floor in a patch of moonlight showing from a large tear in the tarp above. She soon realized that he was tied up and badly beaten. She ran to him and knelt by his side. He looked up groggily.

 His hands were tied behind his back, his legs tied together and he was gagged. He had a dark bruise over his right eye, a blackened left eye, a swollen bottom lip and a gash on his chin. She quickly took the gag off and he smiled to her. The eyes weren't nearly as sparkling and charming this time, but they were no less welcome. She kissed him gently on the forehead.

 "Are you able to walk?" she asked frowning over his injuries.

 "Water," he said, nodding to a utility belt with two canteens hung on it, "and I'll race you back to the ship."

She untied his hands and reached over to the belt, taking care to not make noise.

She took one canteen out and unscrewed the lid and he took it eagerly, gulping the first few ounces.

"What happened?" she whispered.

"Tell you later," he said as they both untied his legs. "We've got to get out of here. They were going to kill me when they heard the signal."

"What signal?" she asked.

He took a final gulp of water just as what sounded like fireworks erupted. But Spurs knew it wasn't fireworks. More likely an ambush. An ambush of the Marine Recon squad and the SEAL teams who were only armed with blanks.

"That signal," he said. "Too late."

Chapter 55

NO TIME LEFT

WHEN THE TWO Arab gunmen climbed into the back of the truck, they saw North gagged and tied up as he was supposed to be.

"Time to die, American dog," one said. The other laughed.

Spurs hoped they wouldn't notice too soon that the rope across North's legs had only been laid there and the gag hung loosely from his mouth. She and North had been in too big of a hurry to do a very convincing job. She also hoped that they wouldn't immediately notice that he sat slightly farther away from the front of the truck bed than before, and that he had a little strawberry blonde as a back cushion.

They didn't.

North pulled the Beretta out as they approached. Their eyes grew big as he fired two shots into each of their chests and they fell to the floor.

"Let's go," he said handing the pistol back to her and picking up one of the M-16s.

They leaped from the back.

"Chopper's this way," Spurs said and started across the ditch toward the hill she'd observed from.

"Stay low," North said and followed.

He caught up as they jogged around the hill and slung the rifle over his arm.

They paused, looking into each other's eyes, his arms around her shoulders. He grabbed her up and kissed her. She struggled at first. There were more important matters to attend to. But her body gave in. This was something good, something true in her confused world and she took of it. She kissed him back passionately, her backbone melting, she hung in his strong arms.

He released her and smiled that charming smile.

"They snatched me in Bizerta," he said. "Found out I was CIA, on their trail. Damn glad to see that you made it."

"CIA?"

"Yeah, I guess I'm kind of a double-double—working inside the Navy for the CIA."

"What's going on?"

"They've just ambushed our two Special Forces units; the Marine Recon team from the *Atchison* and a couple of SEAL teams from the *Enterprise*. The terrorists are going to get aboard both ships, without anyone thinking twice, dressed like our people. Especially since some of ours are mingled with them."

"Chardoff."

"Who else. Once aboard, they'll knock out all the weapons on the *Enterprise* and firebomb the flight deck. On the *Atchison*, they'll arm the cruise missiles and fire them at the *Big E* and sink her in the Strait of Gibraltar."

"Impossible!"

"No. Likely if we don't stop them. If they sink her in the middle of the strait the way they're planning, they'll stop all maritime traffic to and from the west end of the Mediterranean. All ships will have to go through the Arab-controlled Suez Canal until they get the strait cleaned up. That could take a very long time with eight of the *Enterprise's* nuclear reactors spilling radioactive uranium all over the shipping lane. The danger will be minimal under seawater, but the fear of radiation and possibility of thousands of tons of ordinance blowing up will keep everyone away. The Arab countries, although innocent of any wrongdoing will make a killing, while Western Europe will suffer. *Allah's Gihad* will become heroes among their Muslim brothers."

"What are we going to do?"

"We'll try to hijack one of the choppers and go back to the *Atchison*. On the way, we'll radio the Fleet Commander on the *Enterprise* and warn him. They'll knock down the other two choppers full of terrorists before they can say, *Marine Barracks, Lebanon*."

They resumed their run back to the helicopters and then slowed when they came into view of them, not knowing if the pilots could be trusted. All three aircraft sat quietly. They moved around to the back, watching the three crew chiefs standing outside talking to one another as they smoked and watched the trees for their cargo to return.

North and Spurs quietly stepped up the ramp of the helo Spurs had arrived in.

By the time they were halfway to the cockpit, they realized the terrorists were only a hundred yards behind.

"Get this bird up!" North ordered the pilot, holding his M-16 out.

"What the hell?" the pilot asked, he and his copilot twisting around to see him.

Outside there were gunshots. The three crew chiefs

collapsed. Then two carefully aimed shots snapped through the helicopter's windshield and into the cockpit from the outside. Both pilots slumped.

Chapter 56

YOU PEEKED

WHEN THE TEAM of terrorists boarded the helicopter, Spurs and North had gone undercover—really undercover.

The impostors stomped on board and four went to the front, stepping over the discarded packs and flack jackets as the first two reached into the cockpit and pulled the two dead American pilots out. They dragged them off the back and fired several rounds into their bodies as two new pilots climbed into the vacant seats.

The engines on the other two helicopters cranked to life.

Chardoff came forward carrying a silver case the size of a medium suitcase. He set it between the pilots.

"Don't screw up!" he said and then returned to the back of the craft.

Spurs was thankful he didn't notice any difference when he stepped on her hand. She wiggled her fingers carefully, also thankful that the heavy son-of-a-bitch hadn't broken her fingers.

The packs smelled of canvas, camouflage grease paint, and gun oil. Not a pleasant odor but easily accepted.

When that last man climbed over her, the pack covering her face slipped down a couple of inches from the one on her head. Now, she could see out into the troop hold easily but hoped the shadows from the packs would conceal her. It would be much too risky to move the lower pack back into place.

The engines started as the last man to board trotted up to the pile of discarded gear and threw himself on top. He lay between North and Spurs and she hoped that North's cover hadn't shifted any more than hers.

Noticing the packs move exaggeratingly with every breath she took, she resigned to take short, quick breaths. She could see the side of the dark-complexioned terrorist's face. He had a broad, bushy mustache similar to the one the sentry at the trucks had, but along with it was a deep scar that ran from his left temple to his chin. She wasn't sure, but he looked a little like one of the Arabs that she and Saber had fought with back in Tunisia—maybe the one that held her from behind that they called Fahmi. She couldn't move without being noticed. If he turned just right, and in the right light, he would surely see her blue eyes staring back at him, mere inches away.

Glancing around the inside of the helo, she saw at least twenty men and figured that there was probably as many on the other two helicopters. There seemed no chance of stopping the terrorists. How could either North or she prevent them from carrying out their plot? But they would try.

The events over the past couple of days had caused an unquenchable resolve to boil over from the depths of her soul. Now, she was prepared to die for her country. She would die for Nader, for Franken, for Jabrowski.

And there were the many others that had been killed along the way from Jesus, the crew chief who'd helped to rescue them from the sea, to poor little Saber. She would willingly die to avenge Saber.

She considered pushing out of the gear and leaning into the cockpit and shooting both pilots. There should be at least two rounds left in her pistol. She might make it before they got her. If she missed, it would do little good. North had probably already thought of it and dismissed the idea. He surely had a plan. She should follow his more experienced lead.

Anxious minutes dragged on. The helo banked and lights from the ship showed through the small windows on the sides of the aircraft like search beacons and panned along the inside. They were coming in to land.

The Arab on top of the gear reached for the rifle he'd laid at his side. His hand went under the pack it was next to and found Spurs' hand. He felt her fingers curiously without looking.

She watched his face as he frowned.

The helo hovered, dropping cautiously to the flight deck as the man turned to her slowly. He looked into her eyes, his eyebrows raising. He stared, much too long.

What could she do? She was caught. As soon as the Arab opened his mouth, they would have her, and North, too.

He still looked to her, frowning, his lips seeming unsure of the words they were to speak.

Chapter 57

NAUGLE'S LAST STAND

USS Atchison
0500

INSIDE COMMANDER NAUGLE'S stateroom, the wild boar head was silent and still. The globe did not speak, nor did the trophy. Young Kelly's picture did not beg for help or vengeance.

Naugle's head did not ache. He'd been sitting in the dark, as he had many nights, not wishing company of any kind. He preferred sitting where he was, dozing occasionally, dreaming of the past, wishing the clock could be turned back to the happier days, when Kelly was at Annapolis.

"My, God," Naugle said. "What have I done?"

He looked around the room that had been animated before, speaking to him, giving him the terrible advice. It remained silent.

Outside the dimly lit passageways of the *Atchison* no one was prepared for what was about to take place.

What *had* he done?

There'd been no one to hear Commander Naugle's

voice. Nor had there been anyone to hear his desk drawer open. No one would hear the gunshot.

Within the next few minutes, all hell would break loose. By then the gun barrel would quit smoking and the blood that would soon leak from Naugle's temple would coagulate into a large, dark red puddle on his desk.

Chapter 58

UNDER SIEGE

Helicopter landing on the *Atchison*
0515

THE ARAB TERRORIST on top of the packs gasped lightly. His eyes bulged as he squeezed Spurs hand hard, but only briefly. It was almost as if he'd had a heart attack or a narcoleptic episode. In the next second, his eyes and his body relaxed and were still.

The helicopter jostled as it touched down and the ramp dropped. The entire group deplaned quickly, except for the pilots and the dead man holding Spurs' hand.

North shoved the man forward as he pushed out of the pile. The terrorist had a bayonet stuck in his back. North must have taken one off of one of the packs.

Gunfire popped outside, erupting all over the ship.

North raised his rifle as the gear tumbled away from Spurs and the pilots turned to him. He fired one shot in each of their faces as Spurs struggled out of the gear.

Looking out, they could see Arab terrorists swarming over the ship. Several unarmed sailors gaped like deer in headlights and were cut down.

"What can we do?" Spurs asked. "What's our plan?"

North reached into the cockpit and picked up the radio mike. He worked it several times, then leaned in again and turned knobs.

"Don't have one yet. A bullet got the radio. If we blow it here—get killed trying to help—we won't be able to save the *Enterprise*."

They watched the melee helplessly.

Chardoff came out of the bridge hatchway dragging something heavy. He pulled it, stepping backwards as if towing two hundred pounds of sandbags. Next to the bulwarks, he hefted his load over his head with a tremendous yank. It was Commander Naugle—a dark red line on his temple. Chardoff heaved the skipper over, Naugle's body falling like a limp doll onto the deck thirty feet below.

"Damn!" North whispered.

"Son-of-a-bitch, son-of-a-bitch!" Spurs added, hitting one of the packs as she gritted her teeth. Saber, Jabrowski, and now Captain Naugle. There was a big score to settle.

Two of the bad guys came out of the aft hatch onto the weather deck, leading nearly a dozen sailors with their hands on their heads. More sailors came out in small groups, their arms above their heads and followed by a couple of the armed men in black. They were herded to the port side lifeline. All but four of the terrorists went back inside for more, and a number of shots were fired, but the shooting came less frequently as the seconds passed.

A group of seventy or eighty sailors were packed against the side and more came out, some holding bloody wounds. One injured seaman stumbled through the hatch and was immediately shot twice in the head.

Now the goateed terrorist who seemed to have authority stepped up to the closest man and held a semiautomatic pistol to his head.

"Swim or die!" he yelled and without giving the frightened sailor time to consider the choice, the armed man pulled the trigger.

The sailor collapsed and the executioner stepped to the next man. It was the young seaman that had given Spurs directions as he vacuumed the officer's country carpet when she first came on board. Big Track was next in line behind him.

"Swim or die!" the terrorist yelled again. It seemed that the next second took minutes as the young man stood, apparently frozen in fear. He paused too long. The trigger was being pulled.

Big Track leaped from behind, grabbing the kid as the shot fired narrowly missing the young sailor's head. The two tumbled over the lifeline and into the water.

It signaled the rest of the crew, now building to over a hundred on the deck. None of them were willing to wait for the gunman's offer. They dove over the side like lemmings. As more of the crew streamed from the hatch and some from around the superstructure, they followed the lead of their peers and sprinted over the side. At least they had a chance in the water. The numbers of the fleeing crewmembers slowed to a trickle and a few of the tardy ones were shot before completing their goal.

Half a dozen of the terrorists leaned over the side and began firing into the water.

"I've seen enough," North said and ran for the ramp. Spurs slung the Arab's M-16 over her shoulder and followed him.

Once off of the helicopter, North fired several three to five round, automatic bursts into the group of gunmen, laying five down, two of which went over the side, riddled with bullets. One remaining terrorist ran for cover and returned fire.

Chapter 59

THE *BIG E*

LIEUTENANT JG VICTOR Bowser watched as the helicopters came into view from the island superstructure outside the bridge. Doug was still out in his F-18 and Vic couldn't sleep whenever Doug flew. He was always there to see him take off and land.

He looked at the surface fog they were heading into, then into the bridge.

"Damn this shit," Admiral Pierce said standing by the port side windows inside. "Never fails when *I* go through *the Strait*, there's always fog. I haven't seen the Rock of Gibraltar once in the last seventeen years. Who else you got out, Richy?" he asked the ship's captain, viewing through binoculars.

"Besides the two incoming heloes, just two F-18s, Smith and Stedman," Captain Richard Fulk said. "They're not due back for about an hour. We'll be through this soup by then." He turned to the Admiral. "Probably better launch a flight of 14s for close support. We've got four warming up on the flight deck, ready to launch."

"Don't bother," the Admiral said. "Save their energy

for this Mauritania thing. They need to be fresh. They'll be doing flyovers this afternoon. Keep the 18s within fifty miles."

"Yes sir," the captain said, seeming irritated that the Admiral was running his ship.

"Let's hurry and get those heloes down," the Admiral said: "This crap's thick."

"Aye-aye, Admiral," the captain said

Vic looked back to the approaching heloes. Their ramps were already down even though they were a hundred yards out. Three aqua colored objects fell off of the leading helo and landed in the water. The large aqua balls bobbed in the sea.

"What the hell did they lose?" the Admiral asked, picking up his binoculars. "Some kind of buoys?"

Captain Fulk pulled down a microphone from an overhead console. "What's going on with those heloes, Bud?" he asked the air boss. "Those SEALs playing some kind of games?"

The reply crackled back over the microphone. "Not to my knowledge, sir."

"Well, tell them they lost something out the back."

All on the bridge watched curiously as the first helicopter landed.

It touched down on the circled area just forward of the Island and the men deplaned quickly. They fanned out, some dropping to the deck as though they were setting up a defensive perimeter. The second chopper buzzed the command center and landed near the stern, it's men deplaning and fanning out as the first had.

"The hell if they *aren't* playing games," the Admiral said. "You'd better get those assholes off your flight deck. They know better than to do that kind of shit!"

Two of the men from the helicopters carried large containers. Both moved toward opposite ends of the big flattop. They threw their loads out simultaneously and the deck lit up in two flaming explosions.

Gunfire came from below. Several bullets ricocheted past the bridge. The ship's security gunner, manning an M-60 machine gun, was only able to get off a half dozen shots from his emplacement on the island just below them before he was taken out by a terrorist sniper.

Three of the four two-man F-14 Tomcat crews on the flight deck, realizing they would not be able to launch, deplaned quickly and ran for cover. They were cut down along with a handful of the deck hands. The remaining pilot and weapons officer in the last F-14 lowered their bulletproof canopy, but the explosion from a satchel charge tossed under their fuselage lifted the bird straight up twenty feet as if it were a VTOL Harrier. It fell back to the deck like a huge, snapping rattrap and broke into sections, scattering flaming pieces across the flattop.

Vic ran for the ladder down to the flight deck as the Admiral and the Captain took cover.

Chapter 60

PASSAGEWAY OF HELL

USS Atchison

THE *ENTERPRISE* LIT up in several fiery explosions as both ships were swallowed by a thick wall of surface fog.

"What are we going to do?" Spurs asked as she and North hid behind the large cube holding four Tomahawk cruise missiles.

"Three things," he said, "Contact Admiral Pierce to tell him what these bastards are up to, then disable the Tomahawks to make sure they can't do it."

"What's the third?"

"Actually, it's the first. We get rid of the chopper. If they know they have no quick escape, it might take the wind out of their sails."

North leaned his rifle against the missile station. "Stay here." He looked toward the predawn Moroccan shoreline. A mile and a half out, the *Enterprise* was silhouetted in front of the rocky hills. North took off, ducking as he ran back into the helicopter. Spurs saw movement in the cockpit. The engines, already idling, revved loud.

Back at the superstructure, Chardoff stopped on the port bridge ladder. He frowned at the chopper.

The helo lifted quickly, but instead of going straight up, it tipped back and came up perpendicular to the deck. At first, it looked like North was going to fly it away, but certainly not like this, with its nose pointed to the sky.

The thing seemed to hover there and Spurs could see glimpses of North through the helo's side ports as he scampered like a rodent down the inside of the body of the aircraft. At ten feet above the landing pad, North dropped from the open back ramp just as the big back rotor beat the deck. The rotor blades splintered. Large pieces of it whistled across the ship, like a dozen deadly machetes. They slapped the superstructure, one flying past Chardoff's head, causing him to duck.

North rolled away, the cropped rotor chasing him, as the helo did a somersault and finally flipped onto its back into the lightly rolling sea, smoking as it slipped under.

Chardoff raised his weapon and fired a dozen semi-automatic shots as North scrambled back toward Spurs. She leaned out from the missile station. With her 16 on full auto, she put the fear of a short life in the Marine with eighteen ricocheting bullets along the bridge ladder forcing Chardoff to dive into the Conn hatchway.

North ran up and slammed his back against the protective steel box as several of *Allah's Gihad* opened up on them. Spurs ducked in.

"Where'd you learn to fly?" Spurs asked.

"Same place you learned to shoot," North said.

"What now, *Kemosabe?*"

North peeked around the edge of the missiles. A volley of shots convinced him not to take a long gander.

"There's no way we can get to the bridge or the message center to radio the Admiral," he said.

"Is there another radio we can get to?"

North's eyes brightened. "Jabrowski was working on a radio telephone in the CPO berthing area. I say we make our way to the aft hatch and go below for the *RT*. We can bring it back topside and see if we can get a hold of the *Enterprise*."

"Ready when you are," Spurs said, holding the rifle up.

"Might as well leave that here."

"Why?"

"You're out of ammo," he said.

He popped the taped-together, banana magazines out of his rifle, flipped them around and jammed the full side back in.

Spurs turned her M-16 to its side and saw the open, empty chamber. Hers had only a standard, short magazine. She tossed it to the deck and pulled the Beretta out from under her belt. She'd have to be conservative now.

"Let's go," she said and nodded to North.

They bolted from the right side of the missile station, North leading. He gave several three-round automatic bursts as they zigzagged across the deck to the hatch, amid flying steel-jacketed rounds. Spurs ducked through the open hatchway and North backed through, squeezing the trigger twice more before setting the weapon on semi-automatic.

North and Spurs raced down two companionways toward CPO country, North leading. On the second deck down, they ran forward through several compartments.

Five times startled gunmen turned to see the two flying toward them and five times North's M-16 sent them to meet Allah.

Finally North stopped at a side compartment and

went in. On the lower bunk of one of the two triple racks, sat the portable *RT*.

"We're in luck!" he said and ran to it.

He laid the rifle on the bunk and Spurs stuffed her pistol behind her belt.

While she helped him slip his arms through its straps to carry it on his back, Sergeant Krebs, Chardoff's number one henchman looked through the doorway.

Spurs pulled her Beretta from her belt as North went for his rifle but not fast enough to prevent the sergeant's first shot. She fired her two remaining rounds, one hitting the gunman's M-16 on the barrel guard, the other striking the hatchway. It was enough to make him duck for cover, but her pistol was empty.

North sat hard on the deck grimacing as he pointed his assault rifle to the hatchway and nailed Krebs in the center of his chest when the traitor Marine took another try.

And a red pool grew on the floor under North.

Chapter 61

RADIO FLYER

SPURS DROPPED TO her knees beside North, found the bullet hole mid-way up the inside of his right thigh and covered it with her right hand. With the fingertips of her left hand, she pressed hard above the wound to stop the gushing blood.

"Hold your hand there!" she told him.

As he did, she took off her field jacket, then yanked several times on the left sleeve of her fatigues until it tore off. She wrapped the strip around his thigh, and then grabbed a screwdriver that had been lying next to the RT and twisted the sleeve fabric tight. It seemed to do the job.

North held the screwdriver in place as Spurs helped him to his feet and grabbed the M-16.

"It's empty, too," he said. He motioned to the dead sergeant. "We can rob his magazines."

They made their way out the door of the stateroom and over the Marine's body.

Spurs leaned North against the wall and took the dead man's ammo, and they were off and limping.

"After we alert the *Enterprise*, we'll have to jump overboard," North said. "They'll have to sink us to stop them from firing the Tomahawks. There's nothing we can do."

"Can't we knock 'em out?"

"With what? They've got the fire controls. The missiles are in a bomb proof, steel box. We don't have any explosives."

"What about the control cables from the fire controls to the missile station?"

"They snaked it through, under the deck," he said, then his eyes became wide. "There is an access panel under the weapons station."

"Where?"

"One deck up and about four compartments back."

They hustled up the companionway and through the compartments, finally coming to the access panel without incident.

Four slotted screws held the small steel door in place, four feet up on the wall.

"We need a screw driver," Spurs said.

"It just so happens, I've got one," North said sitting down and pulling it out of his tourniquet.

"You fool!"

"Just hurry."

He held pressure against his leg and handed her the screwdriver.

She passed him the rifle and he kept watch while she took the four screws out, letting them fall.

She caught the last screw in her hand, but the panel door came loose, slipped and clattered on the floor.

They both cringed. Inside were dozens of cables.

"Which one?"

"It should be the big green cable. Under its sheathing are eight leads wrapped together. Probably on top since it was the most recently installed."

"Yeah, I see it." Spurs reached in and tried to yank it loose. It wouldn't budge. "What do I do with it?"

"You got your fingernail file?"

She remembered losing it when she and Sabre were escaping from the boiler tank. "Sorry. In all the excitement, I left my purse."

A motor whined above them. The Tomahawks were being positioned.

"Hurry," North said. "If we have to, we can shoot them."

Spurs began stabbing the cable with the screwdriver. The first couple of jabs glanced off of the thick rubber insulation, but the next few gouged deep. The motorized whine stopped, but she didn't know if she had stopped it or it had completed positioning.

Suddenly, bullets struck around the panel. She dropped the screwdriver inside the panel and heard it fall to the floor.

She turned to North.

"Damn it, let me get out of the way first!"

North seemed stunned as he let his rifle fall to the deck.

"It jammed," he said and pointed toward the hatchway, ten feet away.

One of *Allah's Gihad's* finest stood motioning with his M-16 for Spurs to move away from the panel.

She stepped back and the man moved between them and took North's rifle.

He backed away smiling.

"You think he understands English?" She asked.

"Let's find out. Hey towel head, how many humps does your sister have?"

The man rattled off several Arabic syllables, but didn't seem to understand as he motioned for North to move over to Spurs.

"My leg," North said pointing at his thigh, "I can't."

The terrorist spewed more Arabic, insistently.

"Okay, okay," North said, holding up his hand. He quickly tied the tourniquet tight and began to scoot over.

"I'll distract him with the screw," Spurs said, rushing her words, "you hit him with the panel door."

"What?"

Spurs flipped the screw through the hatch on the other side of the gunman with her thumb as he watched North.

The screw clicked behind the terrorist and as he turned to look, North got the idea. He picked up the steel access panel door and flung it like a Frisbee.

It caught the gunman in the chest and he fell against the wall, firing his weapon.

Spurs bolted to the terrorist as North struggled to stand. The gunman's rifle squirted out bullets on full automatic, but the shots weren't aimed. Spurs grabbed the muzzle of the blazing weapon, directing it away and snapped her foot up in a high kick to the man's chin. She brought her leg down, did a short hop and kicked again, catching him in the throat. Again, with a third kick, her toes broke teeth as the gunman fell back, unconscious.

North seemed amazed as he hobbled to her.

She turned. "I was a cheerleader in high school."

"Tough school."

More bullets struck around them and Spurs took the gunman's rifle and North's arm and they ducked through the hatch toward the companionway topside. At least three of the terrorists were shooting at them. Outnumbered and outgunned, they had no choice but to run and hope the wires Spurs had tore loose were the important ones.

On the main deck level they rushed through the still open aft hatch, North grabbing a life vest hanging on the bulkhead nearby as they passed. They staggered back to their position behind the now aimed cruise missile station. It would be the safest place on the ship to hold their enemy off, since they would be cautious not to hit the big steel box with more than small arms.

"Put this on," North said handing the vest to her, then he slipped out of the RT's shoulder straps. Spurs fired several rounds, answering a volley of snapping bullets around them, then put her head through the vest.

"Hope it works," North said, turning the unit on.

"What was wrong with it?"

"Had a short. Could only get it to work about half the time."

North keyed the mike several times and frowned. He tapped the unit with the handset. Keyed it again.

"Damn it!"

"Let me try," Spurs said, squeezing off several more rounds.

Handing North the rifle, she took the radio.

She rapped it several more times and keyed the mike.

North fired two more rounds.

"Shit," he said. "No more bullets!"

Spurs struck the radio with her palm. She picked the RT up and slammed it into the side of the missile station twice, screaming in a frustrated fit.

The two lights on the radio lit and the thing began to squeal, increasing into a loud static.

She looked to North surprised.

"I know, I know," he said, "you were a cheerleader in high school."

Spurs keyed the mike.

"Mayday, Mayday, Mayday! Ship in distress. Can anyone read me, over?" She tried again. "*Enterprise*, this is the *Atchison*. We are under siege and preparing to fire on you. Defend yourself, over."

Chapter 62

ON DEAF EARS

USS Enterprise

"GET SECURITY UP here, Richy!" Admiral Pierce yelled, as several explosions shook the huge ship.

"General Quarters," Commander Richard Fulk called over the ship's loud speakers. "Battle stations. Security, repel borders!"

The *Big E*'s engines slowed to a stop.

Fulk turned to the radioman. "Brown, get the air boss to order our fighters back. Carson, get damage control on those fires. I want a distress call to our fleet. Get the *Atchison* to come alongside and run blocker in case of a sea borne attack and order the *Los Angeles* to be prepared to surface and assist."

"Aye-aye, sir."

More explosions. Captain Fulk looked down to see a man in black fatigues aiming a hand-held rocket at the bridge.

"Get down, Admiral!" he said, shoving the older man to the deck. A tremendous explosion came from overhead as the missile struck ten feet above its target and the Conn shook violently.

"Everyone in the secondary Conn," the Captain said. "We can run this ship from there."

As they turned to go through a nearby hatch leading only a few feet to the huge, vault-door-like hatch into the secondary Conn, the radioman yelled out from his station, "Sir, no response from any of our radio messages. All we got on both radar and sonar is static bleeps."

"It's those damn buoys the helo dropped," Fulk said. "They're jamming everything."

The radioman rose to follow them into the secondary Conn. He paused at the windows. "And, sir, the *Atchison*'s changed her course. She's two thousand yards out and heading straight for us."

The admiral stepped back into the main Conn and peered toward the *Atchison*.

"Must have received our message and they're going to come alongside," Admiral Pierce said.

"I don't think so, sir," the young man said. "I'm sure they didn't receive us."

Captain Fulk came back through the hatch from the secondary Conn having to respectfully, but firmly push the Admiral out of the way.

"Jesus, Admiral," the captain said gaping at the encroaching frigate. "She's bearing down on us. She's going to ram us."

"My God," Admiral Pierce said, "What have I done? What have I done?"

Fulk gaped back at Admiral Pierce. He understood what he was talking about. Pierce had made sure that rusty bucket, the *Atchison*, was manned by the largest bunch of misfits ever assembled in the US Navy. All done to foul up the SecNav's retrofitting experiment on old ships slated for retirement—mothballs or scrapping.

Pierce wanted new warships. The *Atchison* was an embarrassment. In a moment, the *Atchison* would be his Waterloo.

Chapter 63

CARDS ON THE TABLE

SPURS FELT THE ship begin a hard turn to port. "What are they doing now?"

North looked up. The *Enterprise* was directly in front of the bow a little more than a mile out.

North said, "The bastards can't fire the missiles so they're going to ram her!"

A faint response to Spurs' continuous pleas for help came over the radio speaker, as the *Enterprise* began shooting one of its 20mm Phalanx guns, and the Atchison received the popping and zipping rounds.

Static " . . . Dog. We read you." *Static* " . . . is . . ." *Static* " . . . position?"

Spurs remembered the general location of the Strait of Gibraltar from a problem in her Basic Nav class in Officer's Candidate School. She keyed the mike and gave an urgent request. "This is the *USS Atchison*, bearing one eight zero, approximate latitude 30 degrees, 15 minutes 20 seconds, longitude 5 degrees 4 minutes 30 seconds. We are under siege. Sink us, I repeat, sink this ship!"

"What the Hell?" came Doug's voice. "Spurs, is that you?"

"Terrorists have taken over the ship, Doug." Spurs held her eyes closed tight. "They are attempting to sink the *Enterprise*. Destroy this ship. Do this right, Doug. Deep six us!"

"Good God!"

North tugged on Spurs' sleeve and pointed west. She saw a small dot emerge from the low clouds bearing down, perpendicular to their course.

"What in the hell have you gotten yourself into, Spurs," his voice came clearer as the dot enlarged and a second dot became visible trailing it.

"Espionage, sabotage, mutiny, murder, treason," she said. "Do it, sink us now!"

"I can't!"

The *Atchison*'s twin antiaircraft guns had turned toward the new airborne target and began firing its three-inch rounds. It seemed to make a convincing argument for Spurs' side.

"Jesus, you're firing at us!"

"Now, Doug!" she pleaded.

"Armed!" was the reply.

The ship's gun spat high explosive rounds. Spurs wished she could stop it, but there was no way to do so in time. The gunner was at a fire control console in the CIC, too far away. She could only watch and pray.

"Locked." Accompanying the voice was a pulsing tone indicating he had missiles locked on target.

He was hesitating. Too long. The guns were sure to knock him down.

"Damn it, fire!" Spurs screamed.

"Fox One!"

Nothing happened. The F-18 raced at them.

The fierce rat-a-tat-tats from the throats of the shipboard guns were the only sounds. Nothing came from the Hornet.

"My God, a misfire!" Spurs said, staring at the approaching fighter plane.

She remembered overhearing Doug and Cards in Barcelona joking about their stuck pickle buttons and loose cannon plugs.

The ship's three-inch projectiles hit their mark. The cockpit of the jet exploded, canopy shattering. Its right wing dipped as it approached, dead on.

Chapter 64

THE LAST STAND

"CARDS, GET OUT, damn it!" came the static shouts over the radio. "Eject!"

Cards? It wasn't Bird Dog's plane that had been tagged by the *Atchison*'s cannon? Those shouts were Doug's. He was still alive.

It was too late for the *Card Shark* Robert Stedman. There was no bailing out to do. The canopy and cockpit of his F-18 had been taken out by the three-inch Mk 33 antiaircraft guns as he finished his run, perpendicular to the ship. The entire top of the fuselage flamed. The plane nosed up sharply, turned right angle from its original path and made a slow arc, streaming smoke and flames. It passed parallel to, and within fifty yards of the *Atchison*'s starboard side, doing a lazy, dead roll.

Spurs and North watched horrified, helpless. The jet exposed its belly showing off the huge Harpoon missiles hung underneath each wing that it had armed and prepared to fire to end the melee. The ones that would have put under quickly and violently the very deck where Spurs now stood, if they hadn't misfired.

Over a thousand yards out, the jet fighter's right wing touched the white caps, then broke loose and disappeared as it knifed into the sea. The remainder of the plane stayed intact but cartwheeled briefly across the top of the water. It finally fell to within two hundred feet of the *Enterprise*, splashing onto its top, and lay like a dead carp on the foggy, rolling sea.

Spurs was surprised that the only thing the *Big E* had thrown at them were the 20mm rounds from but one of her Phalanx anti-missile guns. The sharp, ball-bearings-poured-down-a-steel-chute din from the triple barreled, Gatling-style weapon followed the faster-than-sound, riddling projectiles a full two seconds. Its large depleted-uranium bullets continued to rain down around them, tearing into the vessel's steel deck and aluminum superstructure, gouging out large chunks. It was a terrible, rapid-fire drumbeat that ripped through the frigate, but as of yet, it had not caused enough damage to halt the ship's forward progress.

She could see the *Big E* clearly through the haze. Her flight deck burned. It was not engulfed, but there were still several small fires that would prevent any aircraft from taking off or landing. Smoke rose from numerous places, and Spurs figured *Allah's Gihad* had destroyed its remaining guns.

The *Enterprise*'s single phalanx onslaught did take out the twin mounted deck guns that had just knocked down Cards. A screaming blast jolted Spurs and North to the deck as the antiaircraft gun turret spat a dozen serpentine smoke trails that arced through the sky. It laid open the deck, leaving a huge, jagged-metal wound belching a thick, black cloud.

The second F-18 broke through the low clouds off the stern. Spurs and North gazed at the small dark fleck that was to be their doom as Doug bore down on them.

"You bastard!" Bird Dog's voice pierced the radio speaker. "You're mine, you're mine!"

What could Doug do to stop the *Atchison*'s suicidal attack? A Harpoon fired at the ship's fantail would be a risky shot with the nearly disarmed *Enterprise* waiting to catch it if it missed.

Glancing back to Bird Dog's Hornet, expecting to see a puff of smoke, Spurs helped North to his feet. Doug had yet to fire as she had anticipated. He was probably concerned, as she had been, about a miss. He wouldn't want to take even the slightest chance of missing the *Atchison* and at his angle, hit and sink the world's most renowned ship instead.

"Damn it!" Doug growled sounding frustrated. It was apparent he wasn't going to fire.

A steady stream of 20mm cannon rounds erupted from the plane.

Time to go. If this ship had ever been a safe place to be, it sure as hell wasn't now. Steel shredding bullets struck the deck from both ends. They could possibly survive if they made it over the side, now. Spurs was glad North had shoved the life vest to her earlier as they came out of the hatch. She dropped the radio handset as North grabbed her by the forearm. Taking his left arm on her shoulders, she helped him up from the deck and toward the side, attempting to dodge the angry *Enterprise*'s continuous single gun volley, and Doug's cannon fire from the other direction.

Suddenly, one of the previously disabled Tomahawk cruise missiles came to life from the bow. It roared away in a violent eruption of flame and smoke.

The terrorists had been given too much time to repair the damage North and Spurs had caused. She hoped it would be the only one. One was a plenty, maybe not enough to sink the mighty ship though, even carrying nearly five hundred pounds of high explosives plus fuel. The *Enterprise* was a labyrinth of compartments and passageways, most with watertight hatches. She was at general quarters, so those hatches would be made secure. A second cruise missile would definitely threaten her integrity.

A second Tomahawk launched.

The other two remained silent; evidently enough damage had been done to keep them from flight.

Bird Dog's F-18 screamed past overhead in pursuit of the missiles.

Chapter 65

THE HORNET'S STING
Lieutenant Doug Smith's F-18 Hornet

TOO FAR BEHIND to stop the first missile, Bird Dog pulled up and chased the second Tomahawk. It was a more immediate threat than the *Atchison*. The *Enterprise* had turned her phalanx on the first missile that rocketed toward the huge ship's island.

But, suddenly, the *Enterprise's* lone gun puffed smoke and silenced. The terrorists had gotten to it, also. In the same instant an F-14 sitting alone on the flight deck began to turn. It stopped with its nose directed toward the first missile. It began to fire its 20mm cannon. If the parked jet could knock the first Tomahawk down and avoid the destruction of the most vital part of the ship, Doug might be able to take out the second one that headed directly toward the stern, the same part of the ship that the defending fighter plane was on.

He wondered what kind of bravery it took for the man at the controls of the F-14 to know a Tomahawk cruise missile had him dead in its sights, and yet to continue to fire at a different target. The man firing the gun must know that the first missile would be of little danger to him but that his courageous action wouldn't leave him time to destroy the one that would surely be his end.

Doug's F-18 Hornet streaked about five-hundred yards behind the second missile's flame. Twenty-millimeter rounds splashed the sea around his target as they approached the flattop.

"Come on, come on, damn it!" Doug said, his thumb aching from the pressure he applied to the pickle button.

He had to take it out. It must be stopped. He thought of turning his attention to the first missile that would do the most severe damage, but that target was so far ahead, he'd have little chance of success. Besides, it was the F-14's target. That gunner had to do his share. Doug hoped the man was a good shot. He wondered if it could possibly be Vic. Lieutenant JG Victor Bowser could do it. He hoped it was.

But then, as the second missile approached the F-14's position, and Bird Dog's own 20mm rounds followed, walking in fountain-like splashes toward the parked jet on the ship, he hoped it wasn't Vic in the cockpit.

His cannon fire should take the damn thing out. He was all over it, yet it still streaked toward disaster.

Doug saw that his own bullets were now striking the *Enterprise*, climbing its tall hull soon to come in line with the F-14 Tomcat and the brave man firing at the other cruise missile.

Chapter 66

ABOVE AND BEYOND

F-14 Tomcat aboard *USS Enterprise*

 LIEUTENANT JG VICTOR Bowser had seen the *Atchison* turn toward them. He understood only one thing about what was happening. They were about to be rammed—incredible as it seemed. He'd found a dead Marine's M-16 near the side of a warming up F-14 Tomcat jet fighter and popped a terrorist as the man wound up to throw a satchel charge into one of the Phalanx gun emplacements. He was too late to save the gun emplacement. The terrorist had tossed the charge as Vic's bullets struck him. While Vic climbed the ladder to the cockpit of the fighter plane the charge exploded taking out the phalanx.

 That was when he saw the first Tomahawk rip from the *Atchison*'s deck. He identified his new target and zeroed in on it by turning the aircraft in its direction, selecting the 20mm cannon and getting a tone from the weapons system as he locked on. The second one launched a moment later and he tried to observe it from the corners of his eyes as he depressed the pickle button and fired at the closest danger.

Vic could see that the first threat would strike the ship's island, where the Commander in Chief, Fleet, Navy Europe, Admiral Wayne Pierce stood. It was also where the majority of the sensitive and vital instruments and equipment lay. Not far below and aft of that position were the *Big E's* eight nuclear reactors. He must continue to attempt to down that target, even though he now realized, after another glance and a double take, that the second missile advanced dead on his position.

The 14's cannon roared at the first Tomahawk, torching flames. The missile flew at a slightly subsonic rate, only six hundred yards out. The explosion was imminent.

In his peripheral vision, Bowser saw the splashes from the F-18's cannon as it closed. He hoped it was Doug. If it was not his best friend, his lover had been killed in the first plane. He heard the clatter as the bullets climbed the side of the ship. He prayed they would stop short of him, but above all else, he hoped they would not stop until the missile was destroyed.

The first Tomahawk closed, one hundred yards out.

The approaching F-18's 20mm cannon rounds walked toward Vic across the flight deck and suddenly struck the F-14, starting at its landing gear, blowing out the tires and then the entire plane came alive with shredding metal.

A din of ricochets. The canopy shattered. Debris caught Vic in the eyes, but he kept pressure on the firing button and prayed.

Seventy-five yards out from the starboard side of the *Enterprise*'s island, the first Tomahawk exploded, shaking the ship.

Bowser grinned but then felt fire in his shoulder as a

20mm bullet grazed by.

He had no time to home in on the second missile.

His instincts told him to push himself out of the now smoking cockpit and he did, for what little good it might do.

Chapter 67

TARGET LOCKED

Lieutenant Doug Smith's F-18 Hornet

WHEN THE SECOND Tomahawk flashed only twenty yards from the ship, Bird Dog hoped he hadn't killed anyone—yet.

He flew through the cloud of debris caused by the 500 pounds of high explosive and pulled back on the stick, lifting the jet fighter vertically from the *Enterprise*. As he climbed, he jerked his head over both shoulders, attempting unsuccessfully to see what damage had been caused. The G forces that pinned him momentarily were taken instinctively, his mind undeterred from his concern for Vic and the *Enterprise*.

As he throttled down, shoved the stick hard left and jammed the left rudder peddle to the floor, the plane obeyed and slipped an about face that headed it in a dive toward the stalled aircraft carrier's deck.

Dropping from fifteen hundred feet, he could see that the F-14 that had been firing at the first Tomahawk had been demolished. The fierce explosion was so close to it that the intense pressure created by the weapon's detonation had caused it to explode, also. The rest of the ship seemed to have suffered only surface damage. But there was no sign of life.

Now was not the time to worry about one man, even though it could be Vic.

At five hundred feet, Bird Dog pulled back on his stick to begin his attack on the Atchison as his on board audio warning sounded, "Altitude! Altitude! Altitude!" He passed over the *Big E's* deck and noticed a tiny figure wave with both arms while emerging from the smoking wreckage of the F-14. Doug smiled, threw his stick hard to the right and did a victory roll while leveling out.

"Yes!" he said and punched the air like a schoolboy celebrating a sandlot victory.

That childish maneuver cost him a hundredth of a second and he realized it when he passed over Cards' belly-up fighter plane.

He tried to get down to business. He had no time to think of Spurs on the *Atchison*, that his next action would probably kill her. He had no time to think about that, but he did. At the end of his tour, two months from now, he'd be going home to tell his father and mother that he had killed the woman he had once been engaged to and was now in love with a man that he'd nearly killed, also. His world had really gotten screwed up.

The attacking frigate was now less than fifteen hundred yards out.

He slowed to give himself enough time to line up on the ship's bow. Armed the Harpoon missiles. Locked onto the target before him. Fired. Fired again. Doug watched, wide-eyed as the two Harpoons dropped to within a few yards of the sea's surface, then straddled the *Atchison*'s hull. He'd fired them too close to their target. The first missile did bump the frigate's stern and exploded, but most of the force was deflected. Now, seeing the escaping ship preparing to ram the carrier, he had no other choice.

Chapter 68

CHARDOFF'S STING

USS Atchison

AS THE SMALL ship jerked and yawed from the Harpoon's detonation, North tripped, his toes striking an M-14 rifle lying next to a brave, dead sailor. It was Ingrassias. Spurs came down on top of both of them. They lay in a pile only a yard from the side of the ship.

They had watched as the two Harpoon missiles shot from Doug's F-18 fighter and parted to each flank of the frigate. A deluge of exploding sea splashed down on them. It slapped hard against the back of Spurs' head and shoulders, driving her face into North's midsection. But the damage done by the glancing blow from only one of the weapons was nowhere near a George Foreman knockout punch.

As Spurs pushed off of North, she saw that the tourniquet had come loose and his thigh now gushed deep, red blood.

Doug's F-18 had turned quickly, and, from long distance resumed firing. The 20mm projectiles snapped over their heads. They zipped by, some clanking, punching holes through the steel and aluminum. Some ricocheted. Hand-sized pieces of metal splintered and tore loose from the frigate's skin, then rattled on the hard deck.

Spurs could make it over the side now and live, but looking at the life leaking from North's thigh, she realized he would bleed to death in the water. She yanked the rag tourniquet tight. Her hand slipped. North looked to her, helpless, weak, eyes wide begging for life. She grabbed the shirtsleeve tourniquet again. Tugged hard. The flow of red stopped. She tied the knot.

Now what? Overboard. They couldn't stop the imminent collision between the two ships. They could possibly save themselves—if the resulting explosion didn't trigger the huge aircraft carrier's high explosive ordinance or cause a disastrous radioactive leak from its nuclear reactors.

In the mist, five hundred yards away, the *Enterprise* waited for destiny. The *Atchison* was closing fast. Spurs wished that time could stop, allow her to devise a plan to save the proud, gray lady. But the clock ticked on.

Someone swung the starboard bridge hatch open and it hammered against the bulkhead. Chardoff emerged, a stinger antiaircraft missile hefted to his shoulder. He looked toward Bird Dog's plane and pointed the deadly little heat-seeker.

"No!" Spurs screamed.

Chardoff glared at her as steel-penetrating depleted-uranium bullets popped around him. He smiled, open-mouthed, ignoring the danger. Turned and put his eye to the sight. Aimed.

Spurs reached to the deck. She released the bolt of the heavy M-14 that lay beside Ingrassias as she raised the rifle. She hoped it had chambered a round and not just empty air from a spent magazine. The weapon was much heavier and more awkward than the M-16 she'd shot earlier and trained with in OCS. Nothing like the little .22 rifle her uncle Paul had taught her to use to plink cans on his ranch in Oklahoma.

Her target stood twenty-five yards away. *He's going to murder Doug.* She aimed. *I've got to stop him.* Over the span of no more than three seconds, her thoughts raced. *I have to shoot him.* The barrel wavered, sights circling Chardoff's torso. *He's trying to sink the Enterprise, over six-thousand sailors and Marines aboard.* She had never shot a man. *They depend on me.* She did not want to shoot even Chardoff. *This is the break we need.* She took a deep breath. *Get past Chardoff, we can turn the ship.* Held it. *This son-of-a-bitch is a traitor, the bastard of all time.* Her hands trembled. *He'd put Benedict Arnold to shame.* The heavy rifle bobbed. *Hurry, before it's too late.* The front sight rotated around Chardoff's head. *My aim must be good.*

She squeezed the trigger.

The weapon's kick stunned Spurs. It forced her thumb to punch her cheekbone. The results of her shot stunned her more.

She would get a black eye—but Chardoff?

His head jerked back, exploding. Half of his skull and brains decorated the bridge's outer bulkhead.

The M-14 could not have fallen to the deck faster if it'd leaped from her arms on its own, and nausea churned her stomach immediately.

But, the twitch of the dead man's finger dispatched the heat-chasing weapon.

Spurs' eyes trailed the missile to the rapidly closing jet fighter. It seemed in slow motion. Surreal.

The F-18, now only a hundred yards out, received the stinger missile just in front of the inlet nozzle of its left engine. It flashed, shredding the vertical stabilizer above it like confetti.

Bird Dog's plane spiraled from the sky, but it seemed

a somewhat controlled fall. He didn't attempt to eject. His intentions were obvious.

Hands. North's hands twisted Spurs' body toward the side, but her head did not follow. She froze, gripping the lifeline along the side of the ship.

"Eject Baby," she whined in a whisper, her jaw catching with emotion as she witnessed the horrific event.

Doug would die before her eyes. This was the man she had thought she would marry just four short months ago. She would have had his children, grown old with him. Her heart felt as though a pitchfork had been driven through and was being twisted inside. Unbelieving shock hypnotized her and she could not turn away.

"In our next lives, Spurs!" came "Bird Dog" Doug Smith's last words from the abandoned radio speaker, next to the missile station.

Just as Doug's war bird slammed into the *Atchison*'s fantail, causing a monstrous eruption of flames, Spurs felt North's hands on her back once again. The explosion was deafening.

Suddenly, she found herself shoved overboard and tumbled the twenty feet to the churning sea.

The intense heat baked her back as the ensuing fireball overtook and surrounded her. Fragmented pieces of ship and plane zipped past, peppering the sea.

Chapter 69

OCEANS OF FUN

THE WATER CAME quickly, but, upon submerging, Spurs found it was not the murky sea she expected. The underworld glowed, illuminated by the inferno erupting on the surface. The combined explosive power of Doug's F-18 and the two, dormant cruise missiles had done a big job.

Shock waves tremored through her lungs and eardrums painfully. Coming toward the surface, she hunted for a spot free of flames. The water had become engulfed. She swam underwater away from the ship, desperately looking for a clear and safe area. Her lungs ached, seeming to have less capacity than they should. She hadn't taken in enough air to stay below long and her life vest wanted her topside. Grabbing the water frantically, she searched for safety.

Finally, she found it, madly pulled at the water and at last burst into the air gasping. The warm Mediterranean waters tasted saturated with salt and oil, and what she could not cough out was involuntarily swallowed. She threw her collar length blonde hair back from her eyes and felt the globs of black bilge in its matted, water-tangled strands.

The entire ship's weather deck now fried, crackling in steel-melting conflagration, as Spurs watched bobbing on the huge swells of *Mother Ocean*. The smell of burning fuel oil and melting metals hung pungent in the thick sea air.

The frigate still drifted forward, but slower. Yet the speed would be sufficient to do terrible damage to the *Big E*.

Slower. Slower. Now only a hundred and fifty yards away.

Slower. The rough seas helped. A hundred yards.

Slower. Closing. Slower. Fifty.

It nudged the *Enterprise* with an echoing steel thud that reverberated through the water. Terrific screeching complaints came from the grating metal. The *Atchison* pushed back, leaving only a dent in the giant aircraft carrier's hull amidships the size of a Volkswagen, but no hole. No unrepairable damage.

More explosions shook the sea and rocked the *Atchison* as it listed to its starboard side. In seconds, its stern took on water and bow raised from the surface.

Again, shuddering explosions ripped through the metal.

Huge pieces of mangled steel blasted away from the blistering ship's deck and hurled through the air. They pummeled the sea's surface, some close enough to send cascades of water deluging Spurs.

Smoke billowed.

In the next sixty seconds, the gutted *Atchison* slid slowly, almost gracefully, stern first into the deep.

Spurs watched in awe of the sight. It had happened so quickly. Violently.

But now, there were other concerns. The raging sea

pushed the burning fuel on its surface, shifting the flames randomly around her. She had to remain vigilant for her own safety.

And where was North? He had pushed her overboard but had he made it?

As she struggled in the water and searched for her fellow agent, Cards' belly-up F-18 Hornet came into view. Miraculously, still floating with its nose pointing away from the aircraft carrier, the flames seemed to be avoiding it. She swam to the plane pushing away floating debris, life jackets and cushions. She found a life preserver on a line and hooked her arm through it for extra buoyancy in the rolling waves.

Spurs made her way to the remaining left wing of the jet and hung on to help stabilize her position in the water. The F-18 lay with its tail slightly submerged, angled about five degrees up to its nose, the wing still clutching one of the huge Harpoon missiles. She noticed the cannon plug connecting the control wiring harness to the missile. The ends were together but slightly angled from each other as if not lined up and fully connected. Cards' Harpoon missile had misfired. She remembered again Doug telling of the several misfires Cards had because of a loose cannon plug. He had been having trouble with the damn cannon plugs. This one was definitely loose. If it wasn't for that bad connection, she might have been killed by the missile—had it been launched when intended. They wouldn't have had time to make it over the side from where they had been on the ship.

Now a body appeared, floating with the ship's American flag over its face. A Navy officer's body.

Could it be North? Whoever it was seemed lifeless—dead. She swam the ten yards to the body to find out who it might be.

Chapter 70

THREE'S A CROWD

REACHING THE BODY, Spurs took hold of the flag covering its face.

She hesitated.

Took a deep breath.

Pulled the flag back.

Commander Nick Reeves. Hair singed. Parts of his face charred.

"Reeves!" she said and shook his shoulder.

She splashed water on his face, but there was no reaction.

"Reeves," she said again, "for God's sake, wake up!"

No apparent respiration. If he was alive, she couldn't tell it. For now, she could do nothing for him, even if a spark did still exist.

Where had he been? What had happened to him? She was unable to put those pieces of the puzzle together. The last time she'd seen him, he was standing in the dark on the flight deck as she left in the chopper with the recon team. He had waved. She had not waved back.

He must have been held hostage by the terrorists.

She hoped he had not been tortured, that his death had come mercifully.

Spurs could not leave Reeves' body to the sharks. When help came, maybe they could revive him. But help would have to come very soon.

She placed the life preserver over his head. Struggling, she finally brought his arms through, then pulled the attached line around his shoulders and tied it to prevent him from slipping out.

With Commander Reeves in tow, she swam back to the tail of the F-18. After a thought of securing the hundred-foot line to the plane, she quickly discarded the idea and tied the end of it around her waist. The plane would soon sink.

The *Enterprise* was only eight hundred yards away. Rescue parties would be sent. It wouldn't be long. Soon, she would be safe.

Poor North. She could have fallen in love with a guy like that. He was not the man that everyone thought. He was not the man that even he portrayed. Under his gentle, boyish exterior, he was tough as hardtack. She remembered how her body melted in his arms without her wanting it to in Algeria. He was the type of man she had searched for and dreamed of loving—not Doug, not Nick Reeves.

A bitter taste came to her mouth and a shiver tingled her spine. Her eyes burned.

She remembered that for a short time, she had been somewhat attracted to Reeves.

Now they were all gone.

Something brushed her left calf as she slowly scissored her legs.

Shark!

Spurs drew her feet up, hoping whatever it was would

go for a larger meal like Chardoff's body, if there was any of it left.

It didn't.

Something took her right ankle. Now knee. Now thigh.

Spurs screamed.

The water erupted in front of her.

She cringed.

It was North.

He gasped, lungs frantically raking in air.

She pulled him to her.

"My God, Dare! Are you all right?"

He still gasped.

"Darren, are you okay?"

He gasped.

"Darren!"

"Shut up," he said. "Give me—a chance."

She smiled and embraced him, her eyes clamped shut.

It was over. All over and they were safe.

They pulled back from each other and gazed with smiles. Nervous laughter erupted spontaneously from both.

Spurs thought of the body, and said, "I found Commander Reeves." Her smile wearing away, she said, "By the plane. I think he's dead."

North didn't look. His face became somber.

"There's something I didn't have an opportunity to tell you," he said, holding her by the shoulders as they kicked and treaded water.

Spurs frowned back, waiting.

"I found out who the Chameleon. . . ."

Suddenly, North sucked air. This time he gasped as violently as the very first time when he came up to breathe. His body stiffened. His face filled with pain and surprise. Then just as suddenly, he became limp.

Spurs released him, shocked, not understanding, and his body seemed to be shoved toward the downed aircraft.

Commander Reeves had come back from the dead and was before her glaring. His right hand held a huge knife, the end driven deep into North's back. Reeves wrenched it out and North's pain-weakened body floated against the Hornet's wing. Still conscious, his hand reached feebly for the gouged wound in his back.

Chapter 71

CHAMELEON OR JUST A SNAKE

SHOCK TOOK OVER and Spurs pushed away from Reeves. It was a Marine's K-bar knife with seven notches shining from its blackened and now bloody blade. He must have gotten the knife from Chardoff. He must have been on the bridge in control of the ship when Chardoff came out with the stinger. *He* was the Chameleon. He was the leader. The traitor. He was a turncoat to his country; had forsaken everything for money.

"Take it easy," Reeves pleaded. "North's the bastard we were after. North was behind all this. Don't you see?"

Reeves' words were just more bullshit. But this time she wouldn't believe his lies.

"No," she said, "I won't listen to your crap. Get away from me!"

Spurs swam around the wing of the sinking plane. Reeves came for her, the preserver still around him, as she struggled toward the jet's nose. The hundred-foot line that tethered the two together floated behind them, looping back to the tail. Her only hope was to keep the plane between her and Reeves until help came.

"Come on Spurs, don't you get it?"

He was on her, suddenly, grabbing, the huge knife still in his grip.

She reached for the nose of the jet to pull herself away. No use. Nothing to hold on to and he was too strong.

He grabbed the line that linked them together. He took part of it and quickly wrapped it around her neck.

"You little bitch," he spat. "You know, don't you?"

His face distorted maniacally as he twisted the line tight around her throat with his right hand that was already full of the big knife handle.

He pulled her close. His wild expression faded. He loosened the line.

"We could make it. Together. You and I."

What was he saying? She didn't understand. Had he already given up on his little lie?

"You're the only one left alive that knows about me." He took the line away from her neck and smiled. "I won't hurt you. I promise. It could be like it never happened."

He was crazy. Completely and certifiably insane. Spurs looked for an escape. Anything. A way out.

North's eyes blinked. Still alive. Dying. Too far away on the other side of the wing to help. Too weak.

"Come on. We were so close to having a good thing together," Reeves said.

She was sure he was toying with her.

He wiped water from his face and she saw his Annapolis ring. She remembered what North had said about the man that had thrown her overboard. That the man had been wearing an Annapolis ring.

He pulled her to him again, both arms wrapping around her, his left hand pressing the back of her head. He forced his lips to hers.

She fought to push away, but couldn't.

His right arm released her, but his left hand still pushed against her head.

What was he doing? That knife. He still had that knife. He was going to kill her as they kissed, she was sure of it. Any second, she would feel the huge, cold blade stab into her belly. He'd twist it to make sure. It was all clear, now. She knew everything about this man. His clever ways. His seemingly sympathetic and understanding behavior. He could turn his emotions on in a snap. Be what he wanted in order to get what he wanted. He truly was a "Chameleon." And now, what he wanted was to get her to submit and then die in his arms, the sick son-of-a-bitch.

Spurs jerked her mouth away from his lips.

She saw North raise his head weakly.

To Reeves she said, "You're a traitor."

He clenched his teeth.

His pause gave her just enough time.

Spurs brought her knee up to his groin forcefully and shoved away.

He released the knife, in favor of the more cherished but now painfully damaged possession.

She turned, looking frantically for an escape, swimming away, perpendicular from the plane. But there was nowhere to hide, and only a few feet in front of her the water flamed. She was cornered, exhausted. When Reeves came for her again, he would not be playing. He would surely kill her.

Spurs glanced back at North, behind the Harpoon. Her sight fixed on the cannon plug connector just behind the pylon that the missile was attached to. She didn't know why at first. Her subconscious seemed to be telling her that this was the way to stop Reeves. She remembered Doug had teased Cards, calling him, *Ol' No Shot* because his *pickle* button had been sticking. The button that fired the weapons. It'd been sticking, not allowing the weapon to be fired. If Cards had selected and armed the missile and then pushed the sticking pickle button—and it did stick in the "fire" position—maybe properly connecting the cannon plug would fire the missile. That is, if that troublesome button had stayed depressed even after the crash.

Reeves had recovered. He came for her again.

Chapter 72

SADDLE UP

SPURS GRABBED AT the water to get far enough away from Lieutenant Commander Reeves to attempt her plan. Her limbs ached, weakened from the physical exertion she'd endured. She finally stopped, drained of nearly all energy and emotion, and turned toward Reeves.

Taking the line closest to his end, she pulled the slack from between them as he swam methodically toward her. He took his time, taking slow wide strokes, obviously confident that he had her.

Spurs looped the line, making a quick lasso. She couldn't make a conventional one, with both ends of the line tied off to each of their bodies, and she didn't have time to untie it from around her waist. She raised her nylon lariat, waving it above her head and hoped when thrown, it would cinch down well enough to be effective. Hitched to the wing twenty feet away, her finned, white bronco waited.

"We'd already be dead if it wasn't for a loose cannon plug," she said, loud enough for North to hear.

Reeves smiled at her, apparently not caring to understand.

She looked behind and to the left of Reeves and her eyes met North's. He looked back hopelessly, his face pale, head limp to one side, mouth gaping. His was the face of a man with not long to live. He'd lost so much blood before from the gunshot wound—now a knife in the back.

She continued to swing the line in circles above her, glaring back at Reeves.

He came closer, gazing comically at her.

Could it possibly work? What would happen if it did? Even if North did understand, would he be strong enough to make the connection? And if he did, could she lasso the missile in one try, before it launched and not too soon to give Reeves enough time to pull free? She'd never thrown a lasso while being held up to her armpits by an undulating sea. Using shoulders, upper torso and even hips were essential in the accurate roping of livestock.

"Yep, just a loose cannon plug," she said, again looking to North, then to the loose connector.

North finally traced her sight and looked to the tail of the missile. He eyed the pylon. The cannon plug. He glanced back at Spurs and she gave him a nod. He reached slowly, touched the connection with one hand, grabbed with the other.

Not seeming to understand what she was doing, Reeves let up and treaded water, only eight feet away.

"Come on, Spurs," he said. "Go along with me. You and me."

"All right," she said mildly, smiling back. "I'll go along with you." She then gritted her teeth. "But it's going to be a quick and explosive trip. Hit the trail, Asshole!" she ordered, glaring into his face.

Reeves scowled at Spurs, then looked back to North.

He saw the loose connection, looked to Spurs again. His eyes lifted to the nylon line being slung above her head, looked back to her face.

Spurs slung her lasso at the nose of the missile, following through, extending her weakened arms. It sailed as they all watched.

A perfect shot. It caught the Harpoon with a slap and slid over the first set of fins.

Reeves gawked at the line wrapped around the death's messenger before him, as North shoved the connecting plug together.

Spurs fumbled with the knot on the line around her waist. She must get free. If the Harpoon fired, she might have just committed suicide.

The tail of the missile sparked. Commander Reeves gaped at Spurs, then jerked frantically on the line to free himself and, at the same time, tried to slip out of the life preserver.

Spurs pulled and yanked at the nylon rope attaching her to the missile and Reeves. She had secured it too well. She had killed herself.

The Harpoon's turbojet engine ignited. Flames torched from the back. Smoke plumed. It launched.

With only fifteen feet of slack line between it and Reeves, he left quickly. The horrified expression on his face was almost worth suicide.

The surface-skimming missile yanked him from the water as it streaked away. It dragged him backwards, his arms reaching limply, rag doll-like. His heels kicked up salt-water rooster tails as his body skipped across the rolls of sea.

Spurs was tied to that line, also. No use, too tight. Not enough time. She would be dragged away also. Her body became rigid, but as soon as it did, she reasoned that the rope was only one hundred feet long and it had been shortened considerably. If she'd been leaving on the Harpoon Missile Express with Reeves, she would have been gone long ago.

The turbo jet assisted bomb disappeared through the smoke and rolling flames. Within five seconds, it blasted thunderously, prematurely dragged down by Reeves' added weight.

Why had she not been taken along? And what of North? Had he been fried from the turbo jet's flame?

Spurs looked to the other side of the F-18. The missile's ignition had left a steamy fog. Through the steam she could only see North's blackened arm protruding from the water. In his hand was the smoking, burnt end of the line. His head popped from the water as waves from the explosion rocked them like buoys. A faint smile came over his face, but then he grimaced with pain as the low drone of a boat motor approached. A rescue launch from the *Enterprise* neared, four of its six occupants showing the business ends of their M-16s.

She saw something small bobbing in the water. The Tupperware container filled with Nader's letters was pushed toward her from the boat's wake. She smiled at the men in the boat.

There would be one hell of a lot of explaining to do.

Chapter 73

DEAD RECKONING

May 16, 1300
USS Enterprise, anchored fifty miles west of Rota, Spain

THE TERM *DEAD reckoning* took on a whole new meaning in the days that followed the turmoil aboard the *USS Atchison.* The answers to a multitude of questions seemed as fragmented as the bodies of the dead.

Taps played.

The afternoon sky shown bright and cloudless over an iridescent, royal blue sea.

A casket, weighted with brass casings, but empty of human remains, slid from under its red, white and blue drape and fell overboard splashing into the ocean. A small contribution to Davy Jones' locker—a symbol for the many dead US Navy and Marine heroes of days past.

More that five thousand sailors and Marines saluted in silent respect atop the gigantic aircraft carrier's deck. They stood in reverence, many teary eyed. Along with them were the survivors of the *Atchison's* crew, including Doc Jolly, Sanders, Botts, Hwa and Big Track. Numbness still gripped every soul.

The last note came from the bugler's horn and the ship's lieutenant called out, "To!"

All saluting arms snapped to their sides.

"Detail, dismissed!"

Most of those topside reverently drifted away. It was a quiet crowd of five thousand.

Three, however, would not be dismissed so quickly. Special Agent Janelle B. Sperling, still dressed in her Navy ensign uniform, stood to the left of Lieutenant Darren North's wheelchair. In one hand, she held the plastic container full of Nader's letters to his loved ones. North still wore his Navy uniform to keep his cover, even though Spurs found out Lieutenant Darren North was actually CIA Senior Special Agent Darren Hunter. Lieutenant, JG Victor Bowser was on her other side, left arm in a sling.

Deputy Assistant Director Paul Royse had surprised Spurs and Hunter by flying in from the states for the ceremony. He came by as the deck cleared and patted them on the backs.

"Thanks for coming, Uncle Paul," Spurs said.

Royse nodded solemnly and walked away.

The brief but emotional ceremony had honored all those who lost their lives in the terrorists' *Operation Dead Reckoning*. The names of United States Marines Lieutenants Douglas A. Smith and Robert E. Stedman were singled out during the memorial for serving their country honorably and making the ultimate sacrifice.

There would be another ceremony within the next week to award medals for heroism and valor. Many honors would also be bestowed on the three now gazing out at the horizon.

Sixth Fleet Admiral Wayne Pierce would not be present to bestow the awards, nor was he attending, now. A good part of the debacle had been his doing, indirectly. He'd hand picked the crew of the *Atchison*. Every misfit he could find in the fleet—in the Navy—he put aboard her. A strong advocate for new and modern warships he'd wanted desperately to prove the unworthiness of Captain Naugle's idea to retrofit old ships with new weapons, guidance and propulsion. He'd done his best to derail the plan, but at the same time he'd created the catalyst for the deaths of dozens of Americans. The Navy's Judge Advocate General had flown him back to Washington, DC to face criminal charges. They included more than two dozen counts of manslaughter and 6,000 counts of criminal endangerment for the unwitting part he'd played in the terrorist plot. His misplaced passion had left the door wide open for what could have been the worst disaster in US Navy history, dwarfing even the Japanese attack on Pearl Harbor.

Spurs shook her head and sighed, thinking of it.

"He loved you, you know—right up to the end," Vic Bowser said out of the side of his mouth while staring out to sea. "He was so confused."

His words broke her spell. She felt Hunter's bandaged hands clasp around her right hand. She turned to him, a tear escaping down her cheek.

He smiled up with one of those, nothing-to-smile-about-but-its-better-than-crying-everything's-going-to-be-all-right smiles. And his *eyes* still smiled, too. It made her lips curl up just enough to acknowledge him. She softly squeezed his hands then looked back at Vic Bowser.

"But he loved you more," she said.

"No, just differently. Ours was a forbidden love," he said, "destined to fail." He looked to his shoes.

Spurs felt his sorrow now, not only her own. She felt his loss.

"He was a good man," Vic said. "His confusion was my fault."

"Nobody's fault," she said, almost not believing the words came from her. "You were right to want what came natural to you—to Doug. The hell with everyone else who couldn't understand or accept it. If it was anyone's fault, it was God's, and God doesn't make mistakes. He just *tests* people to see if they're good enough for something better."

Hunter had been noticeably silent since the melee. Now he spoke, "Your friend Doug passed with honors."

Chapter 74

SOMEDAY

June 30, 1500
NCIS Headquarters, Navy Shipyards,
Washington, DC

SIX WEEKS PASSED. Special Agent Janelle Sperling had become bored of the paperwork piled high on her desk. She was eager for her first thirty-day leave, starting tomorrow. When she returned, perhaps another undercover assignment would await her.

That didn't matter now. Darren Hunter did. She stared at the fabric wall of her cubicle. They'd stayed in constant touch by phone since May, him from his hospital room in Rota, Spain, she from her office in Washington, DC. He was to be released today, then fly over, where she would meet him at Baltimore Washington International airport tomorrow morning at 0800. From there, they would see the sights from Baltimore to New York for the next month. It would be a wonderful time, and yes, she was sure they would be lovers.

The last time they had talked, the day before yesterday, everything was going according to plan.

Spurs smiled. She missed that jerk. She loved that jerk.

A soft knock came from around the corner of her cubicle.

It was the Director's secretary, requesting that she report to Burgess' office immediately.

With a curious smirk, she followed the woman to his office, fifty feet down the hall.

In his office, Director Burgess told her in an unusually grave tone to have a seat to the left of his desk. Her uncle, Paul Royse, sat to the right. Royse did not smile at her as was his usual custom. Neither did Burgess.

It would be about Hunter—she could sense it like a cloud of doom over her head. He'd been killed in an airplane crash, or maybe a car wreck on the way to the airport in Spain.

She gaped alternately at the two men, waiting for the inevitable. They said nothing, their faces solemn, seeming to study her. Why wouldn't they just come out and tell her? She could wait no longer.

"What?" she asked. "It's Hunter, isn't it?"

Royse answered. "Yes, Spurs, it's Hunter."

She hung her head trying to hold her tears. Unsuccessful, she tried to cry silently.

"How?"

Burgess said, "What we want to know is why."

Spurs wiped her eyes with her hands.

"What do you mean, sir?"

Royse stood from his chair and took two steps toward her, holding out a Western Union Mailgram envelope. She accepted it, noticing it was addressed to her—and that it had been opened. The return address read Darren Hunter, nothing more.

"What is this, Uncle Paul?" she asked, looking up as

he sat back in his seat. "Why is my personal mail being opened?"

"We had suspicions," Royse answered.

"Open it," Burgess said. "I think then you'll understand."

She spread open the envelope and pulled out the single sheet of paper, not big enough to need folding for it to fit inside.

She read it out loud.

"Dearest Spurs, You'll never know how much this hurts. Things have happened, and I won't be going with you to New York. I can't explain. I know you won't understand, but I love you more than anyone I've ever met. And, although seeing each other again someday could be deadly for both of us, I do hope we will."

There was more on the back, but Spurs looked up before reading it.

They watched her sternly.

Royse explained. "We've pieced together what we think actually happened. We believe Hunter had been contacted by *Allah's Gihad* during his last case, a theft bust on the *Syracuse*. Over the past five years, he's been the CIA's top investigator in the Med and he's made a lot of contacts and has a number of informants. When he found out what they were offering for the operation from one of his informant connections, he couldn't pass it up. He was sly, though. Neither the terrorists nor even his fellow traitors knew for sure that he was the Chameleon."

"What about Reeves?"

"He wasn't in on it."

Spurs' jaw dropped. She'd sent an innocent man on a rocket ride to hell.

Royce continued, "We think Reeves was trying to make retribution for his poor record. The speculation that he'd murdered his wife was never proven or on his record, but it still followed him around. He found out about *Allah's Gihad* and thought it was a big drug deal—right down to the end. He was clinically schizophrenic—illusions of grandeur. Goodman and Chardoff probably gave him some disinformation. *Allah's Gihad* used the fictitious drug *Jap Rap* to cover up their *Dead Reckoning* operation. But they wanted their Islamic terrorist organization named, to be sure that when their mission was accomplished, the world would know to whom to give the credit.

"Reeves apparently was hoping he could, nearly single handedly, uncover the traitors and turn them in. He probably thought it'd look good on his record and maybe he'd get his choice of duty stations, give him a chance at captaining his own ship."

"The *Enterprise*," Spurs said, shaking her head.

"I think, from what you told me," Royse said, "he might have felt that he was in over his head and a little overwhelmed."

"My God!" Spurs said, her hand attempting to shield her eyes from the truth.

"Don't feel too sorry for him," Burgess said. "All our evidence is circumstantial so far, but we've also linked him to as many as seven prostitute murders in Mediterranean ports. We just didn't have enough on him yet to bring him in."

Spurs thought of the list of women's names she'd found in Reeves' stateroom the night of the storm. "How were they killed?"

"Interpol says strangled," Royse said. "A couple of them had been drugged with roofies—Rohypnol. You know, that *date rape* drug. Probably dropped in their drinks."

She closed her eyes and sighed still not able to take it all in. She remembered the evening at the *Parador del*

Barcelona when Reeves tried to choke her—she'd suspected that she'd been drugged.

"Who was in the bridge—steering the ship—when they tried to ram the *Enterprise*?"

"Probably Goodman," Royse said.

"Why did Darren help me stop them?"

"Had a change of heart," Royse said. "You might have helped in that area. When you were separated that night in Tunisia, he probably told them that he didn't want to go through with it, so they snatched him. We think Chardoff found out that Hunter was either working undercover for us or that he was the Chameleon. If Hunter was with us, he'd be in the way. If he was the Chameleon, Chardoff figured he could cut out the middleman and get more money. After you helped him escape, Hunter found out he might be able to help save the day and to get the money, also."

"That silver case," Spurs said. "When he scuttled the chopper, it was inside."

"It had over five million US dollars in it," Royse said. "We think he went back with a friend or two and SCUBAed down to get it. He must have had help. His right lung was too damaged from the knife wound for him to go very deep."

"He got away with it?"

"He's slick," Royse said. "Wouldn't want to be him, though. Not only is the US Government after him, but also some really pissed off *Allah's Gihads*."

Spurs found herself shaking her head in disbelief and staring at the picture of Burgess and Hunter with the swordfish.

"Sir," she said, "the name of your boat. . . ."

Burgess glanced at the framed photo on his desk and gave a sideways grin. He nodded. "*Chameleon*."

Royse looked at the letter in her hand. "What's he

mean—the last part?"

Spurs finished the letter.

"I've got to run. It's time again to change colors. You've got to admit, as lizards go, I ain't so bad.

Love, Dare

P. S., Mommy says hi! He's almost completely recovered from a bad kitchen accident and says to tell you that he's keeping a sharp Saber."

Chapter 75

TRUE NORTH

July 4, 2300
Tunisian Beach

OF TWO THINGS, Darren Hunter was certain: he would never love another woman as much as he loved Spurs, and he would not live long enough to see her again.

The night was still. The sea peacefully washed the glowing sand, and no one was within sight.

Hunter sat back leaning on his elbows near the water's edge on the white moonlit beach of northern Tunisia. One of Ma'hami's steeds, a beautiful black Arabian, snacked patiently on a patch of desert grass thirty feet behind him. The full-faced lunar reflection shimmered on the sea giving him thoughts of a similarly beautiful night he'd witnessed a few short weeks ago. He'd shared—fallen in love with Spurs that night. It seemed like years ago.

But he had a score to settle, now, and the only way to do so was to alienate himself from his love and his country. He combed his fingers through his thick, brown hair wondering who the traitorous bastard was that had sold out his own country and how he could find and rid the world of him.

A dark figure racing along the beach five hundred yards away interrupted his thoughts. Although unarmed, Hunter didn't feel threatened. No one knew where he was except Ma'hami, and he was like a brother. Ma'hami had proven his allegiance before, and it had nearly cost his Arab sibling his life.

Still, the figure speeding along the shore made him curious. He watched as it came closer. Soon he realized it was a horse, a rider on its back hunkering low to gain the most speed. Wet sand shot from behind the horse like a cat covering up. The rider encouraged the animal fervently with rhythmic nudges from his heels. He seemed in a big hurry and an expert horseman. Judging by the long, loose fitting, striped jubbah he wore, he was probably a local Tunisian. But why was he pushing his ride so hard?

A hundred yards away, horse and rider galloped through a small, shallow cove, the beating hooves splashing water around them explosively. Once through, they angled away. Their present course would bring them past only ten yards behind Hunter, toward a sand berm lined with palms. He figured they must be heading for the road on the other side leading to Tripoli.

The horse, now only thirty yards out, frothed from its mouth and showed its exertion with thick lather flying back.

As he was about to pass, the Arab suddenly yanked the reins right. Ma'hami's Arabian horse bolted and the Arab's horse lunged toward Hunter.

He only had time to sit up from his elbows and turn before the rider drew a huge saber and leaped. The impact sprawled Hunter flat on his back. But as he fell, he pushed the attacker up and over with one foot and then dove on top.

Just as he was about to gain control, the sword's handle struck his temple and lightning shot through his skull. Darkness came momentarily. He recovered, sparkling lights before his eyes, and realized he was on his back again. As they wrestled, the Muslim glared down, only his eyes showing from the yashmak Arabic headdress. In the bright moonlight, the assassin's orbs were intense—and blue, clearly blue.

Hunter gaped as the fair-eyed Arab leaned back and raised the sword.

He grabbed his assailant's wrist, then realized that the saber had been held back purposely from doing its deed.

Their eyes locked and Hunter felt suddenly mesmerized like a sparrow by a cobra. The veil fell loose from the side of the stranger's face, revealing a beautiful woman's smooth cheeks and sensuous full lips.

"Spurs!" Hunter gasped.

The sword tumbled from her hand and their burning lips met as her body fell onto his, submitting like melting butter on a hot skillet. The warm Mediterranean water lapped at their feet, and the beach's radiating heat added to their passion as the tide began to come in.

Their hungry mouths played, tongues teasing, moistening the kiss. She bit at his lips, chin, cheeks, then returned to his mouth with a sensuous, probing tongue. The fever from her firm body penetrated the heavy wool garment and with massaging, groping hands, he soon realized she wore nothing underneath. She began rubbing her middle against his and he joined her knowing that she could feel his excitement growing.

As he pulled the jubbah up from her slender, toned legs, she broke away from his kiss. She yanked the yashmak from her head and tossed it to the side, revealing her soft, strawberry-blonde hair. It seemed to glow like the sand in the bright lunar light. By the time he'd brought the robe up past her smooth hips, she'd begun to unbutton his shirt. Then, with nostrils flaring, she ripped it open, popping off the buttons like an anxious child tearing open a birthday gift.

The advancing sea washed underneath Hunter's back as he helped Spurs off with the jubbah and then rolled her over while stripping off his own shirt. She had his pants unbuttoned, unzipped and down to his ankles before he had time to think about it and he only had to pull his bare feet out of them to be free of clothing.

He settled onto her and she welcomed him with legs parted eagerly. The musty smell of the warm salt water around them heightened his arousal adding to the clean but hot, naturally sweet scent of her body. Kissing her madly, he entered her moistness and she gasped and then gazed wantonly into his eyes. For a moment they took in each other's passion, faces close, drawing in the love they had each longed for, but until now, had been denied. They were finally together. Nothing else mattered. The rest of the world could go to hell. For now they would make love and that moment alone would be worth a thousand lifetimes.

They met with open mouths and she embraced him with her legs, arms and body. She moaned with his movements, and made soft, loving sighs as she nibbled on his ears and face, and then his neck.

They writhed, bodies moving in perfect rhythm, but soon their feverish lovemaking was out of control like a reactor reaching critical mass, and the encroaching, tepid waves lapped over their bodies. He drove deep, her encouraging limbs pulling him into her beyond limits, and they finally climaxed together in wild, ecstatic surges until their strength was drained, sapped away in the undulating tide. He smiled down at her and then collapsed on top, kissing her tenderly on the mouth, cheek and neck.

Spurs' lips spread in a fulfilled smile and she eased him over gently onto the soaked jubbah and rolled on top. Still coupled, she leaned back and looked down dreamily into his eyes, gently plowing through his thick chest hair with her fingers. He felt of her firm body; hips, waist and breasts, and she ran her hands over his. Still grinning, she leaned back, bending him to the point of discomfort, pushing him into her deeper yet. Her fingers glided along his inner thighs behind her, then cupped them over him and caressed softly, causing ticklish shivers to run through his body.

He gazed at her, the reality still soaking in, that he was with the beautiful, sassy, intelligent woman that he loved. It was like a dream. But no, it couldn't be some sort of delusion. This was better than a dream.

He wanted to go again, but first he had to tell her. "I love you, Spurs." His eyes searched hers for reciprocation.

She brought her hands to his sides and pulled at the jubbah as if she were tucking him into her love nest. Then, bending down she kissed him with puckered lips and squirmed, her breasts against his chest.

Pulling back slightly, she said in a soft, low voice, "And *I* love you." But her face suddenly grew somber.

Something sharp poked into his chest and he looked at his left side to see a fingernail file set to shove between his ribs.

She continued, "Now, tell me why I shouldn't kill you."

Chapter 76

ROYSE ROLLS

Paul Royse Residence
Silver Springs, MD
July 6, 1700

PAUL ROYSE STEPPED out of his fifteen-year-old dark green Mercedes and checked both ways. Seeming satisfied no one was watching, he went to his trunk and pulled out a black briefcase. Once again he scanned the area, then headed across the neatly trimmed lawn of his fine English Tudor home, unlocked the dead bolt and opened the door. Darren Hunter greeted him from the other side with an icy stare.

Royse appeared shocked. He paused briefly before turning back toward the car. Janelle Sperling stepped out from a blue spruce tree along the drive and blocked Royse's path.

Hunter walked around from behind him and set a silver case on the hood of Royse's car and opened it. Packed inside were fifty thousand, American, hundred dollar bills—five million dollars.

"I believe you expected this to be yours," Hunter said.

Spurs remembered the first question Royse and Burgess had asked her before sending her on her last mission to kill Hunter. "Why?" Royse had asked, "Why would Hunter do such a thing?" She wasn't able to answer that question. But they sent her to assassinate him because she "knew him better than anyone else and would be the only one he would allow close enough to kill him."

"Why?" she now asked Royse *his own* question, already knowing at least part of the answer.

Two nights earlier, on a beach in Tunisia, it had taken Spurs and Hunter only a few minutes to finally put all of the pieces to the *Operation Dead Reckoning* puzzle together. After Hunter recovered from his injuries and found the money on a shallow shelf in the Strait of Gibraltar, he'd posed as the Chameleon in order to trap the real lizard. His idea hadn't gone exactly according to plan, but at least they sent Spurs to track him down. And, with the clues he'd given her in his letter, Hunter had been easy to find. She was the only one that could help him piece the mess together.

The love that Spurs felt for Darren Hunter made her believe him long enough to hear his explanation and when he'd finished, it was obvious to her that he was not the Chameleon.

The puzzle finally meshed when they realized that Royse was the most likely candidate. He had the connections in the intelligence community. He had the ability to coordinate such a devious plan all from a cushy office in DC. He had the financial need.

The operation that her uncle Paul required for his wife to make her whole again would be expensive. The vacation trip to the holy land that the Royses made had seemed odd to her. Now it made sense. He'd made contact with *Allah's Gihad* during some point in their recent travels, probably to finalize the deal. The *Atchison* was chosen for his plan for obvious reasons—the new tomahawks, the drunken captain, the schizo XO, the misfit crew. Conniving with Admiral Pierce to ensure that the *Atchison's* retrofit program would fail, he'd helped Pierce handpick Chardoff, Krebs and Goodman from their well tarnished personnel records, and had them transferred to the *Atchison*. He then won them over to the plot through an outside contact who also informed them that Hunter—North—was CIA. Most likely Royse had been wrongfully assured that the big Marine would take care of Hunter handily and complete the mission.

It all jelled when Royse left his busy assignment and flew to Europe for the memorial ceremony. In actuality, when the *Atchison* sank, he'd most likely been waiting on a southern Spanish beach for Chardoff's helicopter to return with the money. There, *Allah's Gihad* would turn over the balance of the ten million and Royse would give Chardoff and his men half of the loot and the necessary visas and passports for safe passage to the countries of their choice and then vamoose with what was left.

They'd pieced all of that together on their own from speculation and the info they'd had. Their shaky theory had solidified after speaking with Spurs' aunt Katherine, Paul Royse's wife, twenty minutes before Royse pulled into the driveway.

* * *

The young nurse smiled when she greeted Janelle Sperling and Darren Hunter at the front door.

"I'm sorry," she said, "Mr. Royse isn't home yet."

"That's okay," Spurs said, "we're not here to see Uncle Paul. We're here to see Aunt Katherine."

The young woman looked surprised and defensive until a voice came from another room. "It's all right, Mary."

The nurse stepped aside and Spurs stepped in to see her aunt lying in a hospital-type bed, watching from the doorway of the atrium.

"That's my niece," the frail woman said. "You'll have to forgive Mary, Janelle. She's my new nurse. Please come in. I see Darren Hunter is with you. This isn't social, though, is it? I think I know why you're here."

Spurs and Hunter entered the large plant-filled room.

"That will be all, Mary," Katherine Royse said and the nurse left them to talk.

"Good afternoon, Aunt Katherine," Spurs said. She tried to smile.

"Hello, Mrs. Royse," Hunter said nodding.

She grinned at him. "Always so formal, so respectful, my dear Darren." To Spurs, she said, "It's been so long since you've visited, Janelle—months. And every time I see you, you look more and more like your mother." She seemed to leave them for a second, bemusing into the past. "She was so beautiful." She soon drifted back to the present. "Paul is very proud of you, young lady," she said grinning wide. "And, if I would have been able to have children, I would have wanted a daughter just like you. You know, you worried us sick when you were undercover?"

Spurs blushed. Aunt Katherine had been like a mother to her ever since Spurs' mother died. And, with her father seldom present, she'd sensed a mutual sort of daughter/father love with Royse. He'd always been the one to look out for her. And, he certainly hadn't wanted her to be mixed up in the Chameleon investigation. Before all of this, there'd been many times she'd wished

Paul Royse was her father. Now she felt betrayed, but somehow guilty for feeling that way.

"Mrs. Royse, I'm sorry, but we're here speak with you about . . . ," Hunter began.

"Please, Darren," she said, still smiling at Spurs. "Let's not play games. You're here to arrest my husband and me for treason. Isn't that right?"

Hunter drew a deep breath.

"Why would we arrest you?" Spurs asked. She frowned at her sympathetically.

"It was Paul's little surprise for me. But I knew what he was doing all along. I could have stopped him." Her eyes looked up to the ceiling as if seeing an epiphany and her voice raised in excitement. "But I wanted to walk again. I wanted to go out and dance again—to enjoy evening strolls and hold my husband in my arms again. I could have stopped him. I'm just as guilty as he is. Hell, I'm even guiltier—he was doing it for me." Now, she looked wide-eyed at Spurs. "The government health insurance wouldn't pay to fuse my spinal chord back together. 'The operation is experimental,' they said. There were certainly no guarantees that it would work, anyway. Only a twenty-five percent chance."

"What happened to Paul, Mrs. Royse?" Hunter asked.

She stared out into the flowers and vines.

"Last fall, I guess about nine months ago, the NCIS had been working with the FBI to uncover a terrorist plot to recruit US Navy personnel for some sort of drug thing. Well, they'd caught a guy but had to let him go for lack of evidence. His name was Tijani-Hewidi—something like that. Anyway, they'd found out the terrorists were willing to pay ten million dollars for whatever they were up to. Half was more than enough for my operation. Paul agonized over it for a long time. You see, he felt responsible for my accident."

"Responsible?" Spurs asked.

"Yes, I'd driven off furious when I saw him with her. You know—the affair."

Spurs flinched. It was as if someone had just slapped her on the back of the head. *Affair? Uncle Paul?* Somehow being unfaithful to Aunt Katherine was even more shocking than him being unfaithful to his country.

Katherine continued, "He never forgave himself. He promised me that, no matter what, he would make it up to me and somehow find a way to make me walk again. He meant it, too. We tried them all—the experts, the surgeons and scientists, all the big hospitals. None of them offered any hope. Then, we heard about this experimental surgery they were doing in Germany on people with severed spinal chords. They were having *some* success, but the price tag was so high. Coincidentally, this Chameleon thing came up and the money was right. Paul contacted this Hewidi guy through a third party and made the deal with him. With Paul's connections in the intelligence community, he didn't have to reveal his name or even show his face. He told him to call him the Chameleon—because that was what Paul felt like—he'd changed his red, white and blue colors to black, Paul told me later—a black field with a skull and crossbones in the middle."

"But how did he figure to get away with it?" Spurs asked.

"He didn't. Not really. Oh, we made plans. A man in his position has ways of changing identities. We talked about a small ranch in Brazil or a cabin in the Alps. It was just a dream, it all hinged on my surgery—and this terrorist operation. I think he just hoped he could get me through the surgery before the FBI found out he was spending millions of dollars that he couldn't have possibly obtained legally. I'm sure he was going to try to leave me out of any wrongdoing and take the blame himself. He finally told me about it on our trip to the Middle East. He insisted we go—I couldn't understand why it was so important." She frowned. "I've never been much for faith healing. It didn't matter to Paul what happened to him, just that I could walk again. He's always been such a sweet man."

Sweet, Spurs thought. He was responsible for so many deaths—it could have been thousands. And, he'd cheated on Aunt Katherine.

"You said affair, Aunt Katherine," Spurs said. "Do you mind me asking, what affair?"

"Janelle, you really *don't* remember, do you? We've wondered all along about that. You never did say anything. It was as if you'd blocked it out."

"Aunt Katherine, what are you talking about?"

"Janelle, you were the one who told *me* about it. You were twelve. You and your mother were staying with us on the ranch in Oklahoma while your father was away with the Pacific Fleet. Paul had his FBI job in Oklahoma City at the time. I'd just pulled in our long driveway and saw you racing up on Rocket. You stopped me halfway to the house, crying like your best friend had died. Said something about some rabbit you'd killed and that your mama and Paul were acting funny and making noises like they were sick. That's when I looked up to the house and saw Paul at the window of the guest room—your mother's room."

"My God," Spurs said.

* * *

It all flashed back. Crying. Riding Rocket. Wanting to tell her mother. Have her comfort her for the terrible thing she'd just done—killing the poor bunny. Running into the house. Looking for her. Hearing the groans—agonizing, pain-filled moans, she'd thought. Without pausing, she burst into her mother's bedroom. "Mama," she'd said, breathless, her eyes still blinded from the rest of the world by the horrible image of the dead rabbit at her feet. "I didn't mean to—I didn't want to hurt him—the poor little bunny. . . ."

But her sight returned, and big eyes stared back at her—her mother's. Uncle Paul on top of her mother—naked, squirming, kissing. Then, Uncle Paul had twisted around to see her. She couldn't help but stand and stare, dumbfounded at their entwined arms and legs, their glistening naked bodies. She'd pulled the door shut hard, as if that would make it stop.

She ran down the hall, the steps, out the front door and leapt on Rocket. She wanted to get away. She wanted to sort it all out. Make it go away. She saw Aunt Katherine turn in the driveway and rode wildly to her. All the while, it soaked in deeper, deeper. What had she seen? She knew a little about the birds and the bees. She'd seen the farm animals mate—horses, cattle, sheep, even dogs. That's what they were doing—her Uncle Paul and her mother were mating. Not her father and her mother—that would have been shocking enough for her twelve-year-old eyes. Not her Uncle Paul and Aunt Katherine. No, it was her uncle and her mother.

When Uncle Paul appeared in that window, it was the last blow. She turned Rocket toward the hills and rode and rode and rode. It was the look that did it. His face when he gaped down at them, broken, scared, guiltily. She loved the man so much. She'd wished he was her father. He was so kind and gentle, not like his stepbrother the Admiral—her *real* father. Uncle Paul was always so understanding and protective. And she'd broken that. She'd broken that thin glass case that encapsulated everything so neatly. She'd broken everything inside that neat little glass box. She'd broken the man who she'd trusted—loved like a father. She had done that, and she wanted to take it all back. For, after that day, she knew her life, Uncle Paul's life, Aunt Katherine's life and her *mother's* life would never be the same.

* * *

It was because of her. Her mother's death, Aunt Katherine's paralysis, Uncle Paul turning traitor, the Dead Reckoning tragedy.

Katherine was still talking when Spurs thoughts slammed back to the present. "... Paul tried to stop me, but I was mad as hell. I drove off, tears in my eyes, damned near choking, I was crying so hard. I was driving way too fast for those old hilly dirt roads. Lost control. Went in the ditch. Hit a tree. Never walked again.

"When I woke up three days later in the hospital, Paul was right there by my bedside. The room was full of flowers. His eyes were red as peeled tomatoes when he told me your mother had drowned. She'd packed up and took you to Hawaii to be closer to Oliver the day after the accident. She hadn't even told your father the two of you had come out. She'd rented a car and the two of you went straight from the airport to a beach. No one saw her alive again.

* * *

In front of the Royses' house, Spurs grabbed her uncle Paul by the shoulder and spun him to face her.

"I asked you a question, why?" Spurs said, "or better, *how*—how could you?"

Chapter 77

SINS OF THE FATHER

"*HOW?*"

The question covered more than just the terrorist plot. The affair. This was the man who had not only betrayed his country but also his own stepbrother and his wife. It was because of him that her mother had died and her father was so distant to her.

"I never intended for you to get hurt, Spurs."

"What about the other six thousand Americans?"

"They were just names on paper. You were different. Spurs, you can't begin to imagine how much I care for you," he said looking pleadingly into her eyes. "I tried to stop it once I found out you were on the *Atchison*. It was too late. The wheels had already been set into motion. They wouldn't listen to me."

Spurs had to turn away.

"Just names on paper," Hunter repeated.

Royse said, "I'm sorry Darren."

Hunter shook his head.

"You betrayed your country—everybody," Spurs said,

the anger and pain swelling up in her chest. "Over a hundred people died because of you!"

Royse laid his briefcase on the hood and opened it.

"It's all here. Documented times, places, notes. Names of the terrorists, contacts, their leader. The countries and world leaders who contributed money and weapons. It's all here. I knew you'd be coming to see me sometime soon." He glanced back at Spurs. "I didn't think you'd be able to kill Darren."

"You can't undo what you've done," Spurs said. "There's no kind of surgery that will undo what you've done to Katherine. And you really had me fooled. I thought you were the most honest, wonderful man I knew. Up until today, if I'd had my choice, I would rather have had you for a father."

Royse seemed unable to do anything but stare back at her.

Spurs thought of Royse's code name, Chameleon, and said, "But life's not about what you've done—what you are on the outside. It's what's in your heart. And, Uncle Paul, it's there, deep down inside you that scares me. That's the ugliest part of this whole thing."

"Always so bright, Spurs," Royse said. "You deserved a better hand than you were dealt."

"Me? How's that?" *Ironic*, she thought. Before, she'd wished he was her real father, now she was glad they weren't blood relatives.

"I guess it's time—for the truth. I owe you that much—the truth." He smiled at her, but that smile that used to exude warmth gave her a prickly chill. "You look so much like your mother—except for that beautiful strawberry blonde hair, of course. That's why Oliver could never tell you. He saw your mother in those beautiful eyes of yours. Poor man, at the same time, he saw your mother's unfaithfulness, my deceit, adultery."

"What are you talking about?"

"The afternoon your mother committed suicide was the worst day of all of our lives."

Spurs lost her breath. Her head swam and she felt dizzy. She leaned against Royse's car to steady herself. *Committed suicide?* "She drowned!"

"Yes, she drowned. She couldn't live with it anymore. The guilt was driving her insane."

"The guilt for the affair?"

"You."

"Me?"

"Still, you were the brightest spot in her life—don't forget that, Spurs. Not only did we have an affair, your mother and I, it went on for nearly thirteen years."

Spurs felt her eyes bugging. She took short gasping breaths.

"You're my daughter, Spurs." Royce reached out and touched her hair. "You have your grandmother's hair."

She took a step back so that he couldn't touch her.

He said to Hunter, "You knew Oliver Sperling—the Admiral—was my stepbrother."

Hunter nodded.

"His mother died when he was born. Spurs' Grandpa Sperling—my step dad—married my mother seven years later when I was six. Oliver and I were close, though, me just a year his junior."

Royse turned back to Spurs. "*You* knew all that. But, did you know my hair was just like *my* mothers? And *your* hair just like mine—except mine's mighty gray, now. The Admiral knew. That's why he stayed out to sea so much. He couldn't bear it. But he also couldn't shirk what he considered his responsibility. And he loved your mother so much. He got to the point he didn't care what went on, just as long as your mother was happy. He just buried his heart in the Navy. I know it sounds incredible—but love is different things for different people.

"And Katherine—she's a saint. She turned her head and chose not to see what was going on underneath her very nose. But when she and you saw me in your mother's window—well, that iced it. She drove off, sure that she was through with me. Then, after the accident—and your mother died—well, we became dependent on each other to cope with the whole mess—and to raise you. I know that sounds strange, and you probably can't understand it, but we still loved each other. And we loved you."

Royse gazed off dreamily and continued. "But your mother and I—God, Spurs—we were so *much* in love, like nothing else either had ever felt. We couldn't help it, Spurs."

The pressure built in Spurs' head, her eyes widened. "I don't believe you."

"I can't blame you. Everyone knew it but you. Somehow, we thought the truth would be wrong. It was better to live a lie. Seems like that lie turned everyone's world upside down. Be patient with the Admiral. He's a good man. He's done his best. He gave you everything he could because of the love he had for your mother."

"Except, his love—to me." Spurs looked to her feet and shook her head. "Now it makes sense. Poor Aunt Katherine."

"Of course, she's known it since she saw your pretty hair too, on the day you were born. Most kids are born with dark hair—but not you. It was like you were going to show the world who you really were that first day. Katherine hated me for a long time, but she never said anything. I think she tried to fool herself—tell herself that it was some sort of coincidence. And, your mother—it gnawed on your mother whenever she looked at me—hell, whenever she looked at you. Your mother was a good woman, though. It was just too much for her—your father being away all that time."

Nothing was said for a long moment. It seemed there was nothing more for any of them to say.

Spurs didn't look forward to the next step, taking her uncle Paul—her biological father—to jail, but, as they stood there, a car with three suits parked at the curb. Hunter pulled out a pair of handcuffs and began to place them on Royse's wrists.

"Please, Darren," Royse said. "Please let me see Katherine one more time—without the cuffs—once more—just me and her."

Spurs thought for a moment, then nodded to Hunter. "What could it hurt?"

They led him into the house and into the large atrium where Katherine waited in her bed.

Katherine smiled at them all, nearly glowing.

Hunter searched Royse for any kind of weapon and found none. He and Spurs glanced around the large windows and walls of the room. There was only one door that a person could escape through.

They left the Royses to have privacy, closed the door and turned to confront the officers who had just stepped onto the front steps.

As Spurs and Hunter walked down the hall toward them, it occurred to her that they should have checked under Katherine's mattress.

Two shots rang out.

Epilogue

DAYS OF SAND AND HORSES

AFTER THE *ATCHISON* sank, Spurs had been unwilling to check on her little hero Saber—thinking he'd most likely been run over by Chardoff and his thugs. She couldn't bear to find out that he'd been killed, preferred instead to imagine that, somehow, the wily little guy had evaded death's grip, again.

He had—and Ma'hami had been very fortunate as a result. Struck down by the terrorists' car, Saber had fallen into a cluster of trash barrels in the alley. He was able to conceal the pain from his severely twisted right leg, and, seeing that he wasn't moving and his leg was broken in two places, the thugs left him for dead. After they'd driven away, Saber was able to drag himself a mile and a half to Ma'hami's café—just in time to save the critically injured restaurateur's life. Unconscious from a blow to the head and his throat slit, Ma'hami was slowly bleeding to death. Luckily, Chardoff's knife had only nicked Ma'hami's carotid artery. Ma'hami's wife nursed him and Saber back to health after their short stay in the hospital. The doctor was sure Saber would be walking normal again in a few months, and the six inch scar on the right side of Ma'hami's throat was *his* only remnant of Chardoff's attack.

Three months later, a single cruise missile wiped out the terrorist leader Ma'amoun Al-Tayib and his followers at their hideout in Libya. On that day, Janelle Sperling and Darren Hunter heard the news and rejoiced while making wedding preparations for the following month. They would exchange vows in an Annapolis chapel and Oliver Sperling would give away the bride. Spurs had hopes that, even though her and the Admiral weren't blood bound, they could start a relationship in which a healing process could begin for the both of them—a relationship neither had found, but each had always longed for.

Harley Burgess was to be Hunter's best man. For the past three months, he hadn't been able to apologize enough for putting Spurs so deep into harms way. She had assured him that he'd done the right thing. He'd risked one life to save thousands. He'd had no other option.

Three days after the wedding in the states, the newlyweds would fly to Tunisia and restate their vows. In their second ceremony, Saber, most likely with a cast on his right leg, would give Spurs away, and Ma'hami would stand up for the groom.

For the next three weeks they'd honeymoon on the white sandy beaches of North Africa, riding Ma'hami's Arabian horses and making love under the moonlight.

Another thriller by Gordon A. Kessler

JEZEBEL
Sleep lightly tonight . . . Jezebel is on the loose!

And, coming soon

BRAINSTORM
You might not be who you think you are.

Your thoughts and comments are welcome.
You may contact the author from his website at
www.gordonkessler.com or by mail at P.O. Box 1101,
Newton, Kansas. 67114

Thanks for your valuable time.
I hope you found this story entertaining.
Gordon A. Kessler